THE BUCCANEERS · 1

LINDA CHAIKIN

MOODY PRESS

CHICAGO

ISBN: 0-8024-1071-5

5 7 9 10 8 6 4

Printed in the United States of America

To James S. Bell, Jr.,
with special gratitude for his patience,
sincerity, and enthusiasm for a subject
we both heartily enjoy—buccaneers
1 Corinthians 15:58

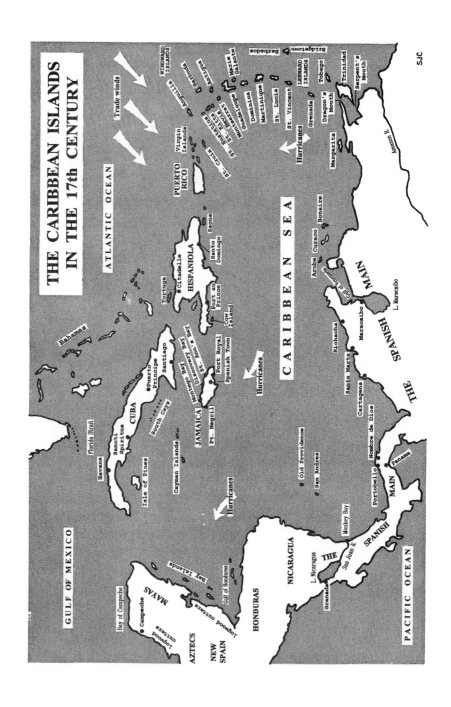

THE CARIBBEAN ISLANDS
IN THE 17th CENTURY

CONTENTS

1

PORT ROYAL, 1663

A ruby twilight thick with youthful promise bled into the paler sky above the miles of sugar cane stretching toward the lush Blue Mountain range of Jamaica. Emerald Harwick, sixteen, stood tensely in the narrow wagon road, staring ahead.

The tropical sun had saturated the brown earth of the Foxemoore sugar estate with the heat of the breathless day, and now the trade wind came as it did each evening, bringing sweet relief.

She heard the wind rushing through the stalks, saw their green leafy heads bend as though doing homage to the king of all the universe, and her eyes moistened as her heart joined the reverence, and she pleaded, "Please, Jesus, grant me the courage to face Mr. Pitt."

As she peered ahead, her young face was spirited and displayed a winning loveliness, yet its lines of tenderness and candor reflected a far deeper beauty than mere outward appearance. She lifted a hand to shade her eyes, listening above the sighing green waves for the dread sound of Mr. Pitt's horse trotting down the dirt road.

The tropical breeze was heady with the smell of the Caribbean and brushed her skin like cooling fingers. Today, however, she could find no pleasure in the familiar sights and smells surrounding her on this estate to which she'd been brought as a small child from the notorious pirate stronghold of Tortuga.

For Emerald, a storm was blowing across her soul, and its cruel blasts threatened to destroy those dearest to her.

Her thick dark tresses tossed in the gusts rippling against her, and she tied the faded calico ribbon on her hat beneath her chin to keep it from being carried away across the field. She turned from the road then and glanced toward an upper window in the tall, box-shaped wooden house where she lived with her fifteen-year-old half-French and half-African cousin, Minette.

Minette was staring through the window, her finely featured face—the color of amber honey—pressed against the pane. Her reflection faded into the evening shadows that fell ominously across the glass, obscuring her tear-stained cheeks.

Then Emerald sped down the road to meet Foxemoore's vile overseer, Mr. Pitt. The evening shadows grew long and began to speckle the miles of acreage. She rushed on toward the cutoff at the end of the narrow road, which brought her to the main carriageway, lined with fringed palm trees.

The wind lifted the hem of her full black cotton skirt, which was looped upward over a blue petticoat, reaching to just above her bare ankles and black slippers. Her blouse was white, full-sleeved to the elbow, and she wore, according to fashion, a tight-laced black stomacher around her slim waist.

Catching her breath, she stepped out onto the carriageway and gazed up to the planter's Great House. It stood a quarter mile ahead with white walls and red tile roof, looking serenely down upon her with the superiority of aristocracy. As always, its magnificence awed her and shut her out.

Foxemoore belonged to the Harwicks and the Buckingtons, who had intermarried since before the days of Oliver Cromwell. During England's Civil War, the Harwicks fled to the West Indies, where they built a sugar estate. The titled Buckingtons followed the exiled King Charles into France and then returned with him to reclaim the Buckington earldom. The family lived now in London under the dominion of Earl Nigel Buckington, who was often called to dine with King Charles at Whitechapel.

Emerald, however, was considered the illegitimate offspring of a daughter of a French pirate on Tortuga and was rejected by both wings of the family.

The vermilion twilight lingered long across the sky as she stood to the side of the carriageway, waiting, her eyes riveted ahead. Not far away a crow cackled at her and then flew from a wooden post, becoming a dark illusive shadow that swept low over the cane field.

The crow seemed to mock her with its freedom to escape while she could not, and words from the Psalms winged their way across her heart: "How say ye to my soul, Flee as a bird to your mountain? For, lo, the wicked bend their bow, they make ready their arrow."

Her eyes, the color of warm cinnamon, narrowed, and her clammy hands formed fists at the sides of her skirt. The sound of horse hooves!

Mr. Pitt emerged from the cane field astride his gray gelding and turned down the carriageway toward her. She saw the rust-colored dust rise beneath its hooves. She waited.

A minute later he rode up, reining in his horse a few feet ahead of her.

Emerald looked up at him, heart racing.

Pitt was a vicious man, and she loathed his cruelty toward the slaves, although she usually had no concern for her own safety. This indentured servant who served the Harwick family wouldn't dare accost *her*, not the daughter of Sir Karlton Harwick, even if she was rejected by the family and her father was in danger of losing his share in Foxemoore due to his mounting debts.

Mr. Pitt would fear to antagonize Sir Karlton. Her father, a big man, was known on the reckless streets of Port Royal to duel for the sake of honor, and he would call Mr. Pitt out by pistol or sword.

She trembled slightly though, trying to mask her apprehension, for her father was not presently in Port Royal. He had been at sea as a privateer for months now, and though she was expecting his return any day, those days came and went. And while his absence grew longer, her uncertainties mounted with the burdens and troubles that came hurling against her like a hurricane.

Mr. Pitt did not dismount but sat astride his Spanish leather saddle. His wide panama hat was soiled with dust and drawn low over a leathery brow that was dotted with sweat. His grizzled red hair hung limp to his wide shoulders, and his canvas shirt was torn, showing his huge muscled arms and bare chest.

The man's prominent pale eyes stared down at her without the deference he offered her spoiled young cousin Lav-

9

ender Thaxton, who lived in the Great House. His wide mouth spread into a grin. He flicked his prized whip absently against a bronzed hand with squat fingers.

Emerald raised her chin, and her eyes refused to waver.

"Evenin', missy," came the syrupy voice.

She would not favor him as though she were on his level, for he was dangerous. Safety came in aloofness, as though she did not notice that he scanned her. She remained polite but distant.

"I received your message. Why did you ask to see me?" she asked with a dignity that surpassed her youth. She wanted to choke on the next words, dreading the answer. "Have you news about Ty?"

He leered. "Aye."

She noted the evil gleam that sprang like fire.

"Yes?"

"I've found the runaway all right. Ain't an African who can flee me and my hounds. I brought him back in chains."

He must have seen her pale, for his lips turned and he appraised her again. "He needs a good lesson taught him, and I'm the man to do it. Aye, I aim to scourge the lad to an inch of his life, even if the half-breed is your cousin."

Mr. Pitt took delight in his whip, and Emerald loathed him for it.

She held her head high, refusing to acknowledge his intended slur. Both Ty and Minette had been born to her French uncle, a notorious pirate on Tortuga. The African slave who had been their mother was dead, but they had a grandfather on Foxemoore, the elderly cook—Jonah—from the boiling house.

Ty, who was nineteen, had made plans from childhood to run away and become a pirate, hoping his father's French relatives on Tortuga would take him in. And even though Emerald had warned him to wait until the day she could buy his freedom, his discontent had been too great. He took pride in his ancestry, and that was one of the reasons Mr. Pitt hated him. Pitt enjoyed making the slaves cringe and beg for his mercies, and Ty would not.

And now Ty had been caught.

Despite her inner struggle not to crumble before him, tears stung her eyes. "Touch Ty with your vicious whip, and you'll answer to my father when he returns," she whispered. "I promise you that!"

He didn't believe her, of course. His confidence remained. He slowly swung his hefty frame down from the saddle.

Emerald took a step backward in the dusty road. "And touch me, and my father will kill you."

He smirked, wiping his sweating brow on the back of his sleeve.

"Maybe your father's dead, drowned at sea. Maybe I have word he's been taken a slave by Spain. The Inquisitors will soon have him tied to a post and burned as a heretic."

No, she thought, trying to steady her nerves.

"He attacked a galleon like the pirate he is, though he denies it. And he lost to a Spanish don."

Her heart thundered in her ears. It wasn't true. Pitt was trying to frighten her, to make her cower before him. She would not beg of anyone except her heavenly Father.

"He's alive," she countered. "You'll see. And he'll soon be docking at Port Royal. And if you do anything foolish toward me or Ty, you'll live to regret it, Mr. Pitt."

"You can be glad it ain't your high and mighty ways that I'm wanting. No—" and his eyes narrowed "—I have me bigger plans, but I need you to aid me in getting them accomplished. And," he warned quietly, "aid me you will. If not, I'll see your cousin a quivering mass of bloody flesh under my whip."

Emerald wondered if the man were human. "Help you?" she breathed. "Never!"

"You're forgetting something, miss. It isn't your father who's managing Foxemoore anymore. It's me. And I have the run of the slaves. Lady Sophie trusts me—"

"And I mourn for my great-aunt's folly in ever trusting a beast like you!"

"Say what you will, it won't change things, and it won't stop my plans. Someday I aim to have land of my own. And I'll get the money and make myself a gallant gentleman. I may even have me a wife like your cousin Lavender."

"You dream. You're an indentured servant, and you always will be. And even if I could get you the treasure you lust for, I won't do it."

"No? You'll do it all right if you want to save your half-breed cousin from being flogged till his back is bloody. Think about it, Miss Emerald. You've seen such sights before. Remember how the sand flies come to cover the torn flesh in the blazing sun till the runaway slave is driven mad? You want that to happen to Ty?"

She winced and covered her ears. "You're worse than a beast—you're a fiend! If only I could convince the Harwicks of that."

"But you won't. You've no influence with your grandmother. And none with the others in the Great House. Oh, you might be called there to please the whims of your cousin Lavender, but has Lady Sophie received you as her niece?"

He read her expression. "Aye, nor will she. You're not deemed parlor fancy enough for 'em. If you're croaking-smart, girl, you'd cooperate with me. I'm the one who can spare Ty."

Unfortunately it was true, and she remained silent.

He smiled. "That's better, Miss Emerald. We can be friends. All I need is payment in them French and Spanish jewels that your wench mother left you before she died."

"I don't have them. They were stolen when I was a child. I've already told you that. You're mad, Mr. Pitt. Even if I did own them, do you think I'd turn them over to you to buy land with? I'd have paid my father's debts to the Harwicks long ago. My French cousin stole them from me before my father ever brought me to Foxemoore. If you want the jewels, then ask Captain Rafael Levasseur for them, if you dare! He has them!"

"Aye, I know as much. But he ain't likely to listen to *me*. And he's vicious with his rapier. He's as cold-blooded a pirate as any in Port Royal. No, you'll go to him, all right. You'll get them. I've heard from Jamie that Captain Levasseur asked your father if he could marry you."

At the mention of Jamie, she grew uneasy. James Bradford worked under Mr. Pitt as boss man in the sweltering boiling house that turned the cane into sugar. But Jamie's indentured service would end in months. He would be free, and they had made secret plans to marry and sail to the Massachusetts colony to establish a farm of their own.

"I won't go to Captain Levasseur!"

"You will if you want to save Ty. I've the authority to do with him as I fancy."

"The damnable result of slavery. It is a curse and a plague among men."

"The twitter of your preacher uncle. You want Ty in one piece? Then you'll get those jewels for me."

"Oh, don't you see? What you ask of me is impossible! I haven't seen Rafael Levasseur in a year, and I wish to keep it that way."

"I've news the buccaneers are arriving from the raid on Gran Granada. Old Captain Henry Morgan and Mansfield be leading his pirates into Port Royal in a few days. Your French cousin is with him, and he'll have booty enough and to spare. How you talk him into generosity is your problem, Miss Emerald. Just see you do. And don't be foolish enough to tell him about me, or why you want it. Remember, I'll have Ty— and Jamie Bradford—at my mercy."

Her heart lurched. "What does Jamie have to do with this?"

Mr. Pitt stood looking at her with a satisfied smile, like a fox who has trapped the hens.

"Jamie was fool enough to try to help Ty run away. For that, Miss Emerald, I can hang him if it pleases me. It's the law. You want your Jamie to hang in the public square?"

Devastation swept through her. Hopelessly she let out a cry, lunging at him, beating her small fists against his chest.

He laughed and seized her wrists. "A little minx, eh? Runs in that blood of yours from Tortuga, maybe? Well, you just go to your cousin Levasseur for the jewels. Jamie and Ty are both being held in Bridewell Jail."

He released her, and she stepped back, eyes stinging with tears.

"Pull yourself together, Miss Emerald. It ain't the end, if you do as I say." He tipped his floppy hat with its turkey feather and mounted his horse to ride back to his bungalow near the slave huts.

He looked down at her, his brown face unsmiling now. "You got two days."

"Two days isn't enough time!"

"It's time enough. I hear the buccaneers are bringing their ships into Port Royal now. You best go there, Miss Emerald. In two days I'll have the magistrate put Ty and Jamie in the town pillory to be flogged. Then I'll have 'em branded on the forehead—Jamie as a political enemy of His Majesty and Ty as a runaway."

"Oh, no, Mr. Pitt. Don't, please!"

"Then you get the jewels. After their branding—if you don't come up with them—I'll go so far as to see em' hanged."

Speechless and shaken, she watched until he had ridden down the carriageway and taken the cutoff into the fields.

Two days.

2

ON THE SPANISH MAIN

The deck of the *Santiago* smoldered. Spanish soldiers lay dying among the smashed bulkheads and broken mizzen-mast. Sagging sail burst into flame. A ten pounder crashed through the overhead rigging, and the Spanish flag toppled to the deck below. Another projectile ripped the blue waters of the Caribbean and brought it splashing over the stern. The proud galleon from Madrid creaked and listed heavily.

From the quarterdeck, Captain Valdez shouted orders to his lieutenant, who raced down the companion steps into the waist.

Soldiers waited there in steel breastplates, gripping their fine Toledo blades. Their black eyes looked gravely toward the sea where their nemesis, the twenty-gun pirate ship under the command of the ruthless English Captain Foxworth, came steadily on, her Union Jack billowing arrogantly at her mainmast head.

The soldiers knew the battle would end in hand-to-hand fighting, for few of the pirates from Port Royal and Tortuga were known to give quarter to their enemy. The Spaniards told themselves they were not afraid. The priest was walking up and down with the crucifix and rosary, blessing each brave soldier who fought to destroy the heretics. What chance could these English buccaneers have against them, brave and bull-headed though they be? And who could undo a Spanish swordsman trained in Madrid?

The English captain had kept beyond the range of the *Santiago*'s cannons, while bombarding them with longer guns. But now the *Regale* drew closer. The soldiers could see her billowing white sails through the gun ports below deck where they waited. They would defeat the *boucaniers*.

Captain Valdez watched with nervous satisfaction as the privateer approached, and his cannons spit fire upon her. But the *Regale* was now too close to repel, and little damage was inflicted on her low main deck. He swore into his neatly trimmed black beard as the English vessel audaciously bore down upon him, discharging her cannon into the galleon's waist.

The *Santiago* shuddered, flames leaping up. Confusion and panic reigned. *Capitan* Valdez knew his ship was a loss, and he cursed the pirates who plagued the Spanish Main, consigning them to the devil's inferno.

It was clear that the English would board.

His intense black eyes smoldered. "Come, then, *Señor* Foxworth," he breathed. "I shall impale you upon my blade as a pig for the flames."

The *Regale*'s captain was known on the Main as an English dog who ridiculed grandiose Spain, and the Spanish captain who took the English pirate as a prisoner to Cadiz would win a great name for himself. Foxworth would be a fit prize for the Inquisitors!

On signal the Spanish soldiers poured from the waist and forecastle, shouting glorious words to the rule of Madrid.

The *Regale* slipped through the haze of smoke, coming closer. The English buccaneers were poised and ready to board, with grappling ax in one hand and cutlass in the other.

He heard the English captain shouting, "Take her, lads! She's all yours! First man to find and free Lucca has my share of the pieces of eight!"

The Spanish captain glared and whipped his blade from its scabbard.

Wild shouts filled the noon air as the buccaneers' grappling hooks snared the Spanish galleon. A legion overran the ship's sides, using their axes to form scaling ladders. From the spritsail yard they swung down upon the deck of the *Santiago*, swarming like locusts, swords in hand and long-barreled pistols exploding with acrid smoke. They pushed forward, bold and unafraid, sword smashing sword, hurling deadly daggers.

A ring of steel and the moans and shouts of dying men encircled the Spanish captain. He stood at the head of the companion, sword at the ready, wearing breastplate and tasses of fluted steel. His black eyes narrowed, intently searching the mob of cutthroats below for Captain Foxworth. He expected a man with snarled black curls and wild eyes.

He cursed the man's secret whereabouts and was surprised when an answer came from behind him—in Spanish.

"The despicable English dog you seek is here, *Capitan!*"

Captain Valdez spun about to confront the ironic gaze of a young man of handsome and formidable figure in white billowing shirt, sleek black trousers, and calf-length boots. The faint smile on the chiseled tanned face was sardonic. The breeze touched his dark hair, drawn back by a leather thong. He mimicked a bow.

"At your service, *Capitan!*"

And he came at him, his blade ringing against the Spaniard's. The steel blades mingled, withdrew, parried, caressed. In a fraction of a minute, Valdez knew that he had met his match.

Sweating profusely, he could but hold him off as he was forced to retreat across the deck, fighting for survival every inch of the way.

Infuriated by the calm smile of his attacker, Valdez lunged.

The English dog deflected his blade with a swift parry, stepping aside as Valdez came in.

A single thrust might have run him through. Instead, the buccaneer struck the flat of his blade to the side of the Spaniard's head with a ringing blow.

The captain of the *Santiago* sank to his knees, stunned, as his sword clattered to the deck.

Captain Baret Foxworth turned as the Spanish lieutenant rushed in, but English buccaneers were now on the quarterdeck beside their captain and halted the man.

"Stay your sword, *Señor!*" said Captain Foxworth. "Yield. I hold the life of your captain at my disposal."

"Foul English dog! Pirate!"

"Softly, lad, softly." Then, "Yorke, Thaddeus, Chalmers. Form a guard about the captain," and he gestured to Valdez. Baret stooped, snatched up the captain's sword, tried it for balance, then went down the quarterdeck steps into the waist of the ship.

The sun was yet high in the sky when Baret Buckington Foxworth stood on deck of the *Santiago*, hands on hips, glancing about as his buccaneers scoured the captured vessel under his orders.

Few of the pirates on the Caribbean Main knew that the able Captain Foxworth of the *Regale* was a Buckington, a grandson of the powerful earl who was in court service to His Majesty King Charles II. The young Englishman was believed to be a rogue at best, with a growing reputation as one of the finest swordsmen on the Main and a reckless sea rover who preyed mercilessly upon Spain's treasure fleets.

Baret looked about on the laughing tanned faces surrounding him, enjoying the spectacle. As he did, he met the gaze of Sir Cecil Chaderton, scholar and divine from Cambridge. Sir Cecil wore a familiar wide-brimmed black hat, and the wind whipped his shoulder-length gray hair away from his lean face. He had a short pointed beard that curled a little.

The staunch Puritan was a respected scholar and a devoted friend.

As well as a timely goad, Baret thought, seeing the slight turn of the old man's lips and his look of disapproval. Baret swept off his hat and bowed toward his old Greek and Latin tutor. He knew that, hidden beneath that grim exterior, the old Puritan scholar might secretly rejoice at another blow to Spain in the West Indies.

Baret's decision to attack and board the *Santiago* had been a matter of concern to Cecil, but the occasion had proven to be a gladsome spectacle to Baret. The sight and sound of the *Regale*'s smoking guns and the crash of a mast carrying the Spanish flag had his heart thudding.

Sir Cecil walked toward Baret, stepping over the debris.

The captain of the *Santiago* interrupted with a shout, veins protruding in anger from his thick neck. "I am *Capitan*

Espinosa don Diego de Valdez! His Excellency the King of Spain will have you for this, you murderous English dog!"

Baret mocked a deep bow, sword in hand. "Permit me to introduce myself, *Capitan.* I am Captain Baret Foxworth, heretic." He smiled faintly, his dark eyes glinting as he gestured airily to members of his gloating crew. "Gentlemen, hang him for the misfortune of being born a Spaniard in service to Madrid."

The captain's eyes widened. *"Señor!"* he gasped, hand going to his heart. "You—you are not serious?"

"Si, Señor, very serious."

"Ai-yi, Captain Foxworth! I beg! I beg of you!"

"Do you indeed, my *capitan?"* he asked, maliciously amused. "Proceed."

The surrounding crew laughed and forcefully aided the captain down to one knee.

Just then, Baret met Sir Cecil's narrowing silver-gray eyes. Baret smiled. "Ah, you've arrived just in time to meet the illustrious *capitan* of the *Santiago.* Welcome, Sir Cecil, my esteemed scholar."

"And *counselor,"* retorted Cecil. "What is this fellow doing on his knees?"

Baret portrayed innocence. "Begging. He's about to be hanged. Perhaps you wish to counsel him in his prayers aforehand." But the expression on Sir Cecil's face affected in Baret a change of heart. "Perhaps, gentlemen, we should not hang our prisoner."

There followed a disappointed groan. "Aye, Cap'n Foxworth! But he'd make such a pretty thing twistin' in the Caribbean breeze!"

"Aye, indeed, but we have a more noble future for our illustrious *Capitan* Espinosa don Diego de Valdez," said Baret. "Chain him to the galley," he ordered two of his men. "And if he wishes to reach Maracaibo, he must donate some of his belly to the oars."

A shout of glee reverberated on the deck of the *Santiago.* Captain Valdez struggled to free himself from crew members who, with great fanfare, hauled him below to the oars.

Then cheering crewmen carried five ornately carved chests containing pieces of eight from the captain's cabin and deposited them with a heavy thud where Baret and Sir Cecil stood.

"Aye, Cap'n Foxworth, feast your eyes upon this."

Baret became strangely serious and looked at Sir Cecil, who mopped his brow with a white handkerchief.

"Baret, you scamp, this could ruin my reputation at Cambridge."

"Is that all you're worried about?"

Baret dipped his hand into a chest, spilling pieces of eight through his fingers. "It's the wealth of the Main loaded into the bellies of Spanish galleons that feeds, clothes, and pays the Inquisition army of His Most Christian Majesty. This is booty the king won't count in Madrid."

"Need I remind you," said Sir Cecil, "of the reason you captured this ship?"

Baret stood, his face grave. He had taken the *Santiago* believing the news from a paid spy that Lucca, a gracious old scholar and friend of his father, was on board. Baret believed that Lucca possessed secret information as to his father's whereabouts.

"Lucca is not here," said Baret soberly. "I've already searched, and the captain swore he'd never heard of him. I think he's telling the truth."

"Your grandfather the earl will hear of this. Yet it is His Majesty that arouses my worry. Remember, you must one day appear before him with a report of your father's whereabouts. What will he say if Spain's ambassador is also waiting at Court to accuse you of piracy! And *this*—" he gestured toward the deck's shambles "—after participating in Henry Morgan's attack on Gran Granada."

Baret smoothly changed the subject. "Morgan is on his way with the other captains to Port Royal." He threw an arm around the elderly man's shoulders as they walked across the ruined deck to reboard the *Regale*.

"I have promised to join him there. It is said the governor of Jamaica will authorize an attack on Porto Bello. Come! A pleasant visit to Foxemoore will soothe your glower. While you sip Lady Sophie's tea and snore on a featherbed, I will meet with the buccaneers from Tortuga. It may be that Charlie Maynerd has news of Lucca."

3
ARRIVAL OF
THE BUCCANEERS

Cannon thundered. Acrid gray smoke curled and drifted. The buccaneer king, Captain Henry Morgan, was entering Port Royal Bay with his fleet of freebooters and pirates.

In welcoming answer, the big guns at Fort Charles on the sea wall set off a volley that boomed like a cheer, splitting the blue waters as the projectiles splashed harmlessly.

Port Royal would soon burst open like a ripe melon and onto riotous debauchery onto its cobbled streets.

Emerald sat in her open buggy, watching the spectacle with mixed feelings. On one of the returning ships would be her cousin Captain Rafael Levasseur. White sails billowed in the wind as the ships, which sailed under articles granted by the governor of Jamaica, entered the bay. Brigantines followed and smaller pirate sloops—notorious for slipping into sheltered coves to avoid capture.

Morgan's flags were flying in the Caribbean breeze, and loud drums beat out the exhilarating news to the town that another triumphal raid on the Main was completed. This time they had made an epic journey three hundred miles to Nicaragua and attacked a city known to the buccaneers only as Gran Granada, about which they had heard stories of great wealth.

From her father, Emerald had learned about the manner of the adventurers that captained their own vessels. They were men from the society called the "Brethren of the Coast" —the infamous and formidable alliance of notorious pirates and the more gallant buccaneers. Their feared and respected commander, Captain Henry Morgan, was considered to be a mere gentleman admiral by some and a ruthless scoundrel by his enemies.

Morgan was a Welsh swashbuckler, who swore that he was not a pirate but rather a naval commander, sailing with a letter of marque from His Majesty King Charles. He was to harry Spain's shipping to Madrid and guard Port Royal from Spanish attacks. His second-in-command was Mansfield, who was from Holland, a land suffering under Spanish atrocities.

Emerald scanned the throng waiting on the dock, cheering and waving at the thought of gold, jewels, and other treasures—pieces of eight, silver ducats, silver and gold pesos, and more.

Her father had informed her that the Brethren were an assembly of variant men. Some were religious, mainly Protestants who had been driven out of France and Holland and who rallied on Tortuga. Others were political outcasts from France and England. Still others were notorious cutthroats and thieves.

Among the Brethren were men of high education and honor, with courage unquestioned and gallantry displayed. Their code of conduct consisted of articles they had drawn up themselves and which they adhered to at all costs. Should a sea rover break faith with the signed articles, he was marooned, a fate looked upon as worse than death, or he was hanged by his captain.

But they all shared one burning passion—hatred for Spain and memories of the Inquisition. The majority left their own alone and also refrained from pirating Protestant ships from Holland and England. But any Spanish ship was ripe to be plundered and scuttled, with no quarter given the crew.

If men of such varied background could band together under the term *Brethren* and live in reasonable peace among themselves, it was in order to raid New Spain and the Main and plunder the annual treasure fleet from Porto Bello on its route to Madrid. In return, Spain continued to torture and burn her prisoners while demanding that King Charles arrest the pirates.

Emerald had little doubt but that their ships were swollen with great treasure. She watched as the men left their vessels anchored out in the bay and rowed to the wharf in longboats. Port Royal would soon be ablaze with rum, and there would be duels before morning—for the Brethren were also known to have minor disagreements among themselves.

After the decade that Emerald had spent in Jamaica as a rejected member of the combined families of the Buckingtons and Harwicks, she wondered that she could yet feel pain from her mother's sordid reputation as the daughter of the French pirate Marcel Levasseur.

In the twilight she sat on the front seat of the buggy on a wide cobbled court by the Caribbean. The carriage's leather and fringe were a trifle frayed from weather and years of use and would hardly be recognized as belonging to a blood kin of Earl Nigel Buckington.

Beside her sat Zeddie, her English driver and bodyguard, who was to her more a friend than a freed indentured servant working for her father. Zeddie held the horse's reins, his one good eye fixed upon Emerald, a black patch over the other. He straightened his golden periwig.

"Sure, now, missy, this is a mistake. What if that rascally mouthed cousin of yours refuses to do you justice? Dare you draw wits like a cutlass with Captain Rafael Levasseur? And if he finds out what you plan aboard his ship, what then? Sink me, lass! And your father, Sir Karlton, what will I be telling him when he returns, should the daring risk you take go awry?"

She moved uneasily on the hard seat, thinking of her beloved father. That robust privateer had grand schemes of his own to marry her off to a man of nobility in England. *As if he ever could,* she thought ruefully. And not that she now cared for such thoughts. It was Jamie Bradford she wished to marry.

She cast Zeddie a side glance. "Nothing will go wrong. Levasseur's ship will be empty by midnight. He and his vile crew will soon be so raucous in their behavior that a Spaniard could capture his ship and he wouldn't know it till daybreak."

Zeddie gave a snort. "I fear, me lass, it ain't as breezy as all that, but I'm understandin' you plainly enough. You intend to see this through for Jamie."

Emerald shaded her eyes to peer ahead, watching the longboats being rowed across the jade green waters to the docks. The men came ashore like petty kings to claim their thrones, and soon her buggy was caught in the throng.

High Street was swarming with sea rovers. Shopkeepers left their little two-story structures on the narrow street to converge on the buccaneers, cheering the homecoming of their private navy.

Port Royal's citizenry was as diverse in class and character as were the pirates themselves, but even the most distinguished among them had an equal passion for red and green jewels, white pearls, creamy silk, and aromatic spices. What the pirates plundered, they spent in Port Royal, and the citizens' homes were decorated with looted treasures bought from the shops and stalls. A pair of silver candlesticks might easily have come from a bishop's table, silver dinner plates from some Spanish don.

She watched, embarrassed, as doxies from the bawdy houses hung out like flies on the wharf, waving to the buccaneers. The men carrying rapiers and baldrics with long-handled pistols were laying claim to familiar women with gloating painted faces, all snatching the gifts that the pirates dangled before their eyes like fish bait.

She saw the "land pirates"—men who were either too old or too maimed to go a-buccaneering—being tossed Spanish doubloons.

She watched barefoot whites, half-castes, Africans, and Caribs alike pour from the taverns at their owners' orders, rolling the familiar rum barrels into the street.

Emerald winced at the loud, impatient whack of hatchets cracking into wood, followed by gleeful shouts as the fiery liquid spilled and flowed into cups, soon to light fires of unholy passion in bellies.

Although accustomed to such sights, her upbringing by her great-uncle Mathias Harwick, a nonconformist minister, had instilled within her a loathing of the culture, a pity for its prisoners, and a desire to better her reputation by escaping Port Royal with Jamie.

Her only regret was to leave Great-uncle Mathias and the Singing School on Foxemoore, where she aided him in

24

his calling of translating the language of the African slaves into Christian music. She would also miss the few children who were allowed by the family to attend the school, the mulatto twin boys Timothy and Titus, and eight-year-old Lord Jette Buckington, who "owned" them.

She cautiously scanned the buccaneers, searching the throng for a glimpse of Captain Levasseur. Her cousin was not yet in sight as the other pirates cast pieces of eight into the street. Although it was money that she so desperately needed, she would not scrabble in the dust for an unwanted favor of a pirate. What was rightfully hers, stolen by her French cousin, waited aboard his ship. She must, in spite of the risk and her uneasy conscience, masquerade herself as a common cabin boy and board that pirate vessel secretly to retrieve it.

"Zeddie, we shall never see him in this madness! We shall seek him on the wharf."

"Wooden idols be tossed to the fire, m'gal, and your father would hang me on the yardarm should I allow you to go a-walking!"

"Oh, Zeddie, I've little choice. And anyway—" she said with determination "—most of them know I'm Captain Karlton Harwick's daughter."

"Aye, but remember the kill-devil rum pouring freely into the mugs, m'gal. It will soon make a rogue unfearful of ten men with the temperament of either your father or Levasseur."

"I haven't forgotten," she said uneasily.

She was soon down from the carriage, though, and pushing her way through the throngs of merchants and adventurers toward the wharf where other longboats were still arriving.

A northeasterly breeze was tempering the tropical heat of the day's blazing sun, yet her unease goaded her into rapidly swishing her fan of vivid blue-and-yellow parrot feathers. In the center of the fan a small mirror flashed like silver as it caught the sunlight.

Zeddie hobbled beside her, hard put to keep up with her rush, carrying his indigo-dyed shoulder sling with ornate pistol. In his younger days, he had been a decorated soldier in the army of Charles I. Zeddie had fought for a time in

England's Civil War, where he had lost an eye and had been sent to Barbados as a political prisoner in the days of Cromwell. Her father, who had known Zeddie in London before the war, had bought him from his indentured service.

Zeddie was the one person Emerald could rely on for protection in the absence of her father. And so for what ventures ill or good she might undertake in Port Royal, Zeddie was a staunch ally and never far behind.

Emerald stopped on the wharf and scanned the ships. They were various sizes; some had twenty guns, or ten, or as few as six. There were a few schooners and sloops—for pirates often preferred the smaller ships in order to maneuver shallow waters and harbor in secret coves.

She stood feeling the moist breeze, uncertain which vessel belonged to Captain Levasseur. He had, like the others, participated in the raid on Gran Granada. Zeddie had heard from the old turtle man, Hob, at Chocolota Hole that her cousin's vessel had been sorely struck in the battle and that he had limped home in danger of being overtaken by the Spaniards until he reached his allies among the French buccaneers at St. Croix. There his vessel had been repaired.

Her eyes scanned the names of the ships, all scarred from recent battle. Uneasiness crept over her, for most bore the names of merciless pirates, even though the flags bearing the skull and crossbones or other equally vile insignia had been taken down and stashed away for future ventures. In place of the pirate flag there flew the Union Jack, the French fleur-de-lis, or the Dutch tricolor.

She noted *The Black Dragon, The Kill-Devil, The Dutch Revenge,* and a host of other names humorously mocking the royalty of England or the dons of despised Spain. She saw an ill-drawn picture of the king of Spain skewered with arrows burning with pitch.

"Is the turtle man certain Levasseur returned from Saint Croix?" she inquired.

Zeddie lifted his prized periwig—which a pirate had tossed to him on a previous run, calling in jest, "From the king of France"—and scratched his head. He lowered the wig again, squinting his one good eye like a bird as he scanned the vessels anchored offshore. It was a terrible yet beautiful sight against Jamaica's setting sun, which had turned the sky into the semblance of a purple amethyst.

"M'gal, surely it is that fine one yonder. For the wretched rogue's come back with his sea chest bulging at the seams."

In the twilight Emerald followed his gesture to a handsome ship without a flag. It was anchored a distance away from the others, as though its captain preferred solitude.

She drew closer to the edge of the wharf to watch a late-arriving longboat. She did not see from which ship it had disembarked.

"Looks to come from the *Black Dragon*," was Zeddie's guess.

But Emerald was uncertain and wondered, Was her cousin in this longboat? Or could he still be aboard the *Regale?*

She stood with Zeddie watching until the longboat came near the stone steps below the sea wall. She glimpsed a half-naked brown Carib kneel in the prow and grab a rope to steady it against the dock.

Straining for a look, she saw not Levasseur but another buccaneer stand to leave the boat. She stared at the man. Wearing a white shirt with billowing sleeves laced tightly at the wrist, he was a handsome and virile figure whose features were shadowed beneath a wide-brimmed velvet hat and a cocky plume. His woolen hose were also black, worn over muscled legs with calf-length Cordovan boots sporting silver buckles.

He stepped out onto the worn sea steps and looked upward to where Emerald gazed down. He paused, and for a moment their gaze locked. Then he said something in jest to the man behind him, who laughed.

Why, he must think I'm a doxy, she thought, horrified.

Swiftly she jerked her head away in the direction of her buggy. "Come, Zeddie, Captain Levasseur must not have arrived ashore yet. We'll wait in Father's lookout house until it's dark."

Zeddie was scowling but not at the new arrivals coming up the wharf steps. She cautiously followed his stare across the street toward the gambling house, where a group of buccaneers was gathered, talking and laughing.

Emerald noticed a vaguely familiar man wearing maroon and black taffeta trimmed with Spanish lace. His short black beard was meticulously curled below an arrogant face, and his black periwig was of shoulder-length King James style curls dusting his broad shoulders. "Sir Jasper!"

She heartily disliked the conceited man, a widower—or so it was said—somewhere in his thirties. Beside operating a lucrative business as a slaver, owning two vessels that he sent to West Africa, he was a large landowner. Her father insisted that he had cheated his brother out of the family inheritance. No one in the West Indies had seen Sir Jasper's brother in several years. She put nothing past him.

Despite Sir Jasper's irrefutable reputation, there were prestigious families in Jamaica who would easily have given their daughters to him in marriage. The planter who gained him as son-in-law would end up with one of the largest sugar estates on the island. Because of the benefits from such a union there were those parents who were willing to overlook the man's character and receive him as a guest in their parlors and at their fine dinner tables.

Sir Jasper seemed to go out of his way to provoke Emerald when her father was away, for unlike most of the other women, who were flattered by his attention, she would have nothing to do with the rake, nor did her father approve of him.

"The knave's not only after my daughter, but he thinks to buy out my shares in Foxemoore. I'll duel the rogue first!" he had said.

It appeared to Emerald that Sir Jasper delighted to annoy her. He mocked her dedication to Christianity and spoke against her helping Great-uncle Mathias at the Singing School. Jasper had hinted that he might bring the work of her uncle before the Jamaican Council for teaching Christianity to the slaves. Doing so was forbidden by island law, but he had also intimated that if her father permitted him to call upon her, he might reconsider.

She took his interest lightly, for she was not the only girl in Port Royal that he sought to flatter. He was even more attentive to her cousin Lavender. But Lavender with her golden hair and blue eyes had already informed Emerald that she was in love with another man. Sir Jasper, she said, frightened her, for he was on her mother's list of eligible men, although he was not considered to be nearly the prize that Baret Buckington was, whom Lavender expected to marry. Viscount Buckington was the grandson of the earl in London and was heir to all that belonged to his deceased father.

Nevertheless Cousin Lavender was alarmed, for she had told Emerald that Sir Jasper was gaining political importance in Jamaica and was expected to receive a ruling seat on the governor-general's Council.

The news brought concern to Emerald as well. Her father said Sir Jasper was an associate of an uncle soon to arrive from London—an uncle who was close to His Majesty and having secret Spanish sympathies because of the lucrative business of clandestine slave trade on the Main.

"A merry countenance!" stated Emerald in a low voice of dismay behind her parrot fan. "It's just our luck to run into Sir Jasper now! Quick, Zeddie, before he sees us."

"Aye, lass, it's the bloke, and notice whose comp'ny he seeks? Pirates! But no less one than himself, if you ask me."

A chill prickled her skin.

Zeddie frowned and took hold of her arm to escort her across Fisher's Row toward the buggy. "This ain't a fair place to be hobnobbing, m'gal."

Emerald turned to march across the street, her slippers clicking on the cobbles, and Zeddie's gangling frame following closely behind.

"Sink me! Here the fop comes now!" he said. "Won't be just Jamie Boy thrown into Brideswell if I draw pistol."

To her discomfiture, Sir Jasper made a pretty movement, overtaking them and bracing himself in the middle of the street directly ahead of her. He doffed his wide hat and bowed low at the waist.

"Doth the lady rush away to join mongrels? Come, darlin', and shoo away this noisome plague who imagines himself a bodyguard. You are, madam, I humbly assure you, quite safe in my presence. We have much to discuss."

Masking her alarm at this fox, she stood her ground.

Sir Jasper walked toward her with a bold smile on his arrogant bronzed face, his hat held under his arm. With the other hand he reached to take hers.

"Ah, Miss Emerald, how fortunate to come upon you like this. I beg your company at supper." He gestured across the street to the gaming house. "It is a place noted for the finest turtles in all Jamaica. Miss Hattie will see we have all our wants met."

"Nay, Sir Jasper. If you have ought to speak to me, you can say it here and now in the presence of Zeddie."

His eyes flickered coolly. "Your company, madam, is preferred."

Zeddie stood behind her, and Emerald heard something of a growl in his throat.

"Come, m'gal," said Zeddie, taking her arm.

But Sir Jasper would have none of it. He blocked her way, and his eyes fixed on Zeddie with malevolence. "Off with you, before I lose my gallant patience before the lady."

Emerald felt Zeddie's arm tense, and she thought him to be in contemplation of a move for his pistol—a sure mistake, seeing that Sir Jasper could exercise his power against him if he chose.

She was deciding her next move, a whispered prayer on her tongue, when Sir Jasper smiled and she felt his strong fingers on her arm, drawing her away from Zeddie to propel her across the street.

Zeddie drew his pistol. One of Sir Jasper's men struck a blow to the back of his head.

Emerald let out a cry as he crumpled forward to the street. "Zeddie!" she gasped as she beheld the old man on hands and knees.

Sir Jasper said easily, "No alarm needed, my dear. He'll live—not that it's any great loss if he did not. See now! It's only your sweet face across the table of my supper I wish for. There are at least ten women with titles who would be pleased to dine with me."

A voice interrupted from a short distance behind her, a resonant voice that reeked calm yet cool challenge: "Your presence, Sir Jasper, is about as safe as a fox in the hen coop—and judging from the girl's desire to depart, nearly as bothersome. She's but a hatchling to be sent home. Let her go. As you say, ten titled women would be pleased to join you. I suggest you go find them."

Emerald forgot Sir Jasper and Zeddie and turned to the man who had pronounced her a hatchling.

Sir Jasper also turned toward that easy yet commanding voice, as though he recognized it and felt no pleasure.

"Ah! It is you, Baret. I see you've eluded the Spanish don. How fortunate for the cause."

His tone convinced Emerald that he had hoped otherwise, and she saw the buccaneer named Baret gesture with an airy wave of his hand.

"No matter. A simple device."

Sir Jasper gave a short laugh. "I wish I had your arrogance, Captain Foxworth, and your luck. You live a charmed life."

Emerald now realized that the buccaneer named Baret Foxworth was the man that she had glimpsed earlier in the longboat. He was smiling aloofly at Sir Jasper, and she could see that there was a barrier between them. Sir Jasper did not appear anxious to test the strength of that barrier, and Emerald swiftly sized up the buccaneer.

He was obviously an adventurer like the others who had sailed with Henry Morgan and raided Gran Granada. Yet she detected something more in his manner, a disciplined character that suggested uncompromising values.

His lively dark eyes bore a hint of sardonic humor. His hair, too, was as dark as ebony, and though absent the fashionable periwig, it was worn in the length of the king's Cavaliers who had followed King Charles into France during the days of Cromwell and the Civil War. Also like the Stuart king, he wore a thin mustache. About his mouth hovered a faintly mocking expression.

He was armed with a hearty supply of wicked things—a long rapier and a pair of pistols. He wore these, as all buccaneers did, at the ends of a leather sling studded with silver.

"Your dinner awaits at the Red Goose," he informed Sir Jasper. And with that same sardonic smile, more as a host than a challenger, he gestured toward the gaming house. As he did, the silver lace at his wrists gleamed in the light of the rising moon, now hanging like a shimmering orange in the black sky above Port Royal's quay.

If Sir Jasper wished to confront him over the matter, he was soon placated. With a smile equally as debonair as his opponent's, he bowed deeply to Emerald and completely ignored Zeddie, who was blindly reaching for his golden periwig lying in the street.

"Another time, madam," he said and added as he smiled at Baret, "Perhaps you have plans of your own, Captain Foxworth?"

"Perhaps, Sir Jasper . . . but I hardly find robbing nurseries a pleasant pastime. Adieu."

Sir Jasper took leave with his men and crossed the street into the gaming house.

Emerald turned toward the man, who now gestured to his half-caste serving man to see how Zeddie was progressing.

By now Zeddie had his periwig on, albeit crookedly. The serving man whom Baret had called "Charlie" retrieved the pistol Zeddie dropped and calmly returned it to him.

Emerald was about to express her gratitude to Captain Foxworth but found that he already appeared to have dismissed her. His manner was preoccupied as he spoke in a low voice to another of his buccaneers, who then followed Sir Jasper into the Red Goose.

When Captain Foxworth saw that she was still there, aloofness showed in his smile. He bowed. "Your servant, madam. You may go." The remark was spoken with the same casual tone of dismissal that the court of King Charles reserved for lesser servants.

Bewildered, Emerald wondered, *Who is this buccaneer with the airs of nobility?* She felt a small flame of embarrassment and rebuked herself for standing there as though her feet were planted in the street like the cobbles. She disliked her plain calico dress even more. And her lack of status. She painfully remembered Cousin Lavender, who had everything she did not—including a noble reputation.

Baret gestured toward Zeddie, who was now on his feet, though wobbly. "I think your bodyguard is now able to escort you to your destination."

She could think of nothing profound to say and hoped her behavior equaled that of a lady who may have come from a fashionable school in London. "My thanks for your gallantry, sir."

He smiled faintly and offered another bow, briefly appraising her. "It's getting late. Your carriage waits."

Quickly she tore her eyes from his and walked away as though wearing rustling satin.

Zeddie trailed behind, his hand holding onto the lopsided periwig sitting on his bruised head.

She and Zeddie had not gone far when she heard Baret say something to his buccaneers.

"Never saw her before, Captain," answered one. "Doesn't look like a doxy."

She cautiously glanced over her shoulder and saw Captain Baret Foxworth watching her. She turned her head and hurried on.

She was frowning as she and Zeddie crossed the street toward her waiting buggy. "Did you ever hear of Captain Baret Foxworth?" she asked casually.

"Aye, m'gal. A name growing as one of Morgan's men. Foxworth's a blackguard pirate to be sure, but a gentleman tonight, I'm thinkin', and grateful I am."

Emerald silently agreed and climbed into the buggy, not waiting for Zeddie to help her. She wondered that she was faintly disappointed that Baret Foxworth was one of Morgan's captains.

He came up after her to take the reins. The night was loud with music and voices.

As Zeddie turned the horse toward home, her offended emotions over Sir Jasper's odious behavior began to cool, and her reason was restored. She had come here for one purpose, which thus far was not accomplished.

"Oh, Zeddie, we can't go home. I've got to board Levasseur's ship, or Jamie and Ty will both be left to Pitt's cruelties. I must try!"

"Sure now, your cousin will be a rich man after the raid on Granada. But will the daw cock restore what he stole from you so many years ago?"

33

She knew he would not likely do so. She also knew there would be plenty in his cabin aboard ship from which to compensate for the dowry he had unjustly taken from her—which would suit Mr. Pitt just fine.

"I must risk Levasseur's ship tonight. Can you find us a longboat?"

He groaned, holding his head. "Aye, m'gal. But to be sure, you take a greater risk than coming upon Sir Jasper. And I'm in no good health to aid you none. Nor are we likely to come across Captain Foxworth again."

"What choice have I? Think of Ty! And Jamie! Do you think Mr. Pitt will show a morsel of mercy to them? Nay! The infamous dog will have his bribe, and it seems I've no choice but to see him satisfied."

4

PIRATES AND CUDGELS

It was nearing midnight, and the wharf was nearly deserted, for most of the pirates were in the bawdy houses and gambling dens or roaming the streets of Port Royal, where the noise of revelry saturated the night.

Emerald hid behind a stack of barrels on the dock, shivering despite the tropical warmth. She heard the lulling of the water against the pilings and the rhythmic creak of the wooden quay beneath her feet.

In the distance men were talking, and the sound of boot steps stumbled across the wharf. A woman's cackling laughter echoed, then the voices filtered away in the rising wind, and silence hugged her.

In haste Emerald donned calico drawers and cotton shirt, vestments that a common crewman aboard a pirate vessel would wear, grimacing as she slipped into them.

Ugh, she thought. *Ah, cruel, leering hand of circumstance!* As if to taunt her prayers to become a lady of noble cause, the image of her young cousin Lavender, dressed in ivory-colored silk, strolled across her mind.

Emerald felt the ugly cloth of the drawers, the roughness of the shirt. *Tsk!* Her eyes narrowed. What would it be like to be nobility? To have men of title and lands bowing over your hand?

And yet, she thought, it took more than dressing in silk and possessing a title to make a Christian woman of excellent spirit. God looked upon her heart, and it too must be clothed with fairness.

She frowned as she contemplated her actions, driven by desperation. Was she wise in secretly seeking Cousin Levasseur's ship?

But what if Jamie and Ty were branded? What if they were hanged!

She shut her eyes tightly, her small hand forming a fist. "Please, omnipotent God of my Uncle Mathias, do aid me in saving Jamie from such a dark fate."

A tiny flame pulsated within her soul, seeming to ask, *Is He the mighty God of your uncle only? Is He not your God also, even your heavenly Father through His Son?*

She hesitated, musing. Then as the urgency of the moment pressed in upon her, she swiftly concealed her hair beneath a blue pirate scarf and tied it behind her head. She placed her slippers inside her cotton frock and folded the awkward bundle.

A moment later, leaving hidden the rolled-up clothing, she crawled out from behind a dray of wooden barrels on the loading barge and, seeing that she was alone, stood to her bare feet, cautiously glancing about for rats and detestable crawling things.

A quiver raced up her back. What if she stepped on a cockroach and felt it squish against the sole of her foot? *I'll scream.* She placed cold fingers over her mouth and walked gingerly toward the quay steps, leading down to the water and Zeddie's waiting cockboat.

Her heart thudded, but she thankfully felt nothing but the rough, damp wood pressing against her feet. Zeddie had been careful not to light the boat lantern, and she called for him in a whisper, pausing on the landing steps and squinting ahead for a glimpse of him.

"Watch your step, m'gal. It's slippery with moss."

As she came down the steps she saw that he sat with the oars ready, his bruised head bound with a cloth, his prized French periwig sitting on his knees, reminding Emerald of a dozing lapdog.

Her conscience smote her. "You're sure you'll be all right?" She stepped into the boat, feeling guilty that she had involved him in the night's fiasco with Sir Jasper.

"As fit as the governor's milkmaid, I'm thinking. Sure now, no need to worry. That rascally-mouth cousin of yours ain't likely to seek an honest night's sleep in his cabin, but you must take no chances."

"Your head causes you no undue suffering?"

He sniffed with disdain, dismissing the notion that the injury troubled him. "His lordship's man might've been a plaguey kitten for all the damage he did me. I've taken worse in ol' Charlie's army," he boasted of the king. "Anyhows, I've daubed the cut with Hob's turtle rum." His good eye twinkled in the moonlight. "Nary an Indies vermin could live in that vile brew."

Emerald settled herself on a low seat in the cockboat, glancing over her shoulder toward the wharf to make certain they were not being followed. No one was in sight.

The oars dipped and sliced through the water as they slid smoothly out past anchored sloops and schooners with tattered sails and tacking toward Captain Rafael Levasseur's vessel some quarter mile out in the smooth waters of the bay.

As Zeddie rowed, Emerald gazed at the sleeping ship casting its tall silhouette against the lighter horizon, where the moon appeared a shining orb enthroned in the velvet sky. The trade wind pressed against her face, filling her nostrils with the aromatic scent of spicy nutmeg. The moonlight sent shimmers weaving across the water like schools of bright fish skimming in a dance.

A short time later the vessel loomed large and forbidding before her eyes. It was clean and swift, and, though she knew little of such things, it appeared to have twenty guns and sat strong in the water, a sure sign that it had recently been careened and freed of barnacles, seaweed, and worms, which in the warm Caribbean waters gnawed and devoured the underbellies of ships.

As they came alongside, Zeddie stilled the oars, and Emerald caught the mild groaning of the hull and the anchor chain taut in the water. All else was silent.

He brought the boat to the foot of the ship's ladder and quietly seized a rope to steady them.

Emerald blinked up past the side of the ship to where the tall masts reflected the moonlight. In a moment of dread she half expected to be met by a swarthy crewman leaning over the rail with a long-barreled dueling pistol.

But nothing moved. Naught stirred in the late night but the warm breeze moving through the tacking. She watched the long-legged Zeddie steady himself on the ladder and climb up awkwardly, and for a moment she feared a dizzy spell had seized him, but soon he disappeared over the side.

She waited. Her anxiety grew when he did not reappear. *Oh, no . . .*

But then he came to the rail and signaled for her to proceed.

She cautiously set her bare foot onto the rough rung of the ladder and began the steep climb up the ship's side, congratulating herself that the indifference with which she'd been treated by the family while growing up gave her benefits that Cousin Lavender did not have—Emerald could board a ship without fear of heights and could swim the Caribbean like a fish bred in its waters.

She forced herself to a spirit of calmness as she inched her way up, taking in slow breaths to quiet her heart. In another minute she slipped over the side as silently as the wings of a moth.

On deck Emerald crouched in the shadows, pressing against a bulkhead so as not to be seen, holding her breath, listening for the sound of footsteps, and feeling the wooden deck beneath her sweating palms.

Don't fear. Even if I'm caught, what can they do to me? Is not Captain Levasseur my cousin? He would rant and rave at my being here, but he would not harm me, nor would he allow any of his nasty crewmen to touch me.

What Mr. Pitt had said to her in their meeting on the wagon road was unfortunately true—Captain Rafael Levasseur *had* asked her father to marry her. Father, of course, had refused, and for that she was grateful.

She breathed easier. After all, she could say she had simply come to see a member of her mother's family from Tortuga. Or she could say she had come as a *periagua,* offering to sell Levasseur fruits and vegetables.

But the words of Great-uncle Mathias, taken from Scripture, warned against the sin of lying. The conflict waging within only added to her tension. Was she like Jacob in the Old Testament, using her wiles to secure her future rather than trusting God to guide her steps? One thing was always certain, God did not bless actions that contradicted His Word.

Oh, rather to be like the biblical Esther—to do what was right and to trust the outcome to His faithful providence. *"The Lord has His way in the whirlwind and the storm."*

She shivered in the moonlight. Was it a scepter of grace that awaited her appearance in his cabin or a pirate's cutlass?

As planned, she waited until Zeddie signaled again that the way was clear, and then he took up the position of watchman.

The urgency goading her into action silenced her fears. She crossed the deck as softly as though her feet were kittens' paws and went up the steps to the quarterdeck.

With eyes shining like round pools, she approached the Great Cabin to find a lantern glowing in the window.

Confusion rushed in, and her fingers closed tightly around the empty satchel she carried. Was it possible that he had not left the ship? But no, Zeddie had followed him to the gaming house—the Spanish Galleon—and had watched him go inside.

Escape, before it's too late, her emotions clamored.

She tensed, whirling toward the steps from where she had come. The dreaded sound of boot steps and low voices!

There was no chance of retracing her path now. And what of Zeddie? Had he gone undetected?

Wildly she looked around her for a place to hide. Dare she slip through the cabin door? No. If someone were inside . . .

The voices and footsteps approached. Soon she would be overtaken. She darted behind a barrel, drawing her knees into her chest and clasping her arms about them.

She heard two men come up the companionway and pause near the Great Cabin. Her breath stopped. Then she glimpsed a man holding a deck lantern, a dignified man with the look of a scholar. He stood facing another, whom she could not see except for his black boot with its glinting silver buckle. Emerald stiffened against the cabin wall.

They conversed quietly in a foreign language, and their words were lost on her. They walked on.

She waited until the sound of their steps vanished. Whatever schemes certain crew members might have aboard Levasseur's ship were of no concern to her. She had her own quest, and she must succeed now—or fail.

When she again heard nothing but the water lapping against the hull, her courage revived, and she crawled from behind the barrel.

Still on her knees, Emerald took hold of the knob on the heavy oak door and opened it just a crack. Silence beckoned. When certain the Great Cabin was empty, she entered, shutting the door softly.

In the glow of the oil lantern she was confronted by heavy dark beams and shadows. There was a large captain's desk of what looked to be fine mahogany, its contents neatly in order—a rather strange sight, considering her fiery and reckless young cousin.

Her eyes swiftly raked the bed in the corner. Again, it was neatly made and to her surprise, covered not with looted Spanish tapestry or French cloth of gold but with what she recognized as fine Holland tapestry.

Holland? Had Levasseur also pirated a Dutch merchant ship from Curaçao? Yet it was not like the buccaneers to harry men of their own faith, and they had no cause to be at odds with Dutch merchants. It was Spain that both the French and the English scorned.

The pieces of furniture were also of exceptional quality, as though their owner relished a taste for nobility. She frowned and paused to take a closer look at where she was.

The lighting did not do justice to the texture and color of the furnishings or the carpet. Nevertheless she knew from her father's privateering ventures in the East Indies and Europe that these goods were of high value. Her eyes feasted on items of beaten gold, of silver mined by slaves and Protestant prisoners in Peru, of pearls from the island of Margarita, where Spain misused Carib slaves to cultivate oyster beds.

Then she began her quiet search for a certain silver box she was well acquainted with from the past. She quietly opened bureau drawers and rummaged through fine Holland shirts and others made of expensive cambric with ruffles. She lifted one that felt smooth to the touch and sniffed the pleasant scent of spice. She frowned again. Her cousin had changed for the better. No more heavy French perfume for his sleek black locks?

A teakwood trunk stood open, and she stooped, looking through vests and doublets embroidered with silver, Cavalier suits of black and sage green velvet, taffetas, as well as under-drawers of linen.

Again she paused uneasily, considering. She stood and went to the large desk, but the top drawer was locked. It was too narrow, in any case, to hold the box she sought.

It was then she noticed something that commanded her attention. On the desk lay a half-finished sketch, which sug-gested a mind that found release in creativity. Again she was learning personal things about Captain Levasseur that she had not suspected. Did she know him at all?

The sketch was of a woman—well done and suggesting nobility.

I didn't know he had anything so fine within his unrepentant heart, she thought grudgingly. *His ways are usually left to swords!*

She left the sketch and opened the bottom drawer, drop-ping to her knees to search. At last! A treasure box of fili-greed silver.

But it was not as she remembered. She had been a child when she last saw the box in her mother's possession—before Levasseur had stolen it—but the box she remembered had been engraved with the fleur-de-lis of France.

She studied the coat of arms but did not recognize it. It was not English, certainly not Spanish. From Holland? Where had Levasseur gotten it?

"Stolen, without doubt," she murmured to herself indig-nantly and opened the latch. Perhaps it might still hold the heirlooms she searched for.

She stood then, turned up the wick on the oil lamp, and emptied the contents on the desk. To her disappointment the silver box contained no rich bounty—only a simple silver chain with one large pearl that looked to be of another gener-ation. She picked up a miniature portraying a young woman of winning loveliness, with fair hair and intelligent eyes that looked to be blue. Connected to the silver frame was a small cross, an unusual one woven of golden hair.

Emotionally stirred, she studied the portrait and the cross, wondering. She did not know how, but she knew with-out being told that whoever owned these items before Levasseur stole them had a deep affection for the woman. The Christian faith was also held in reverence, for who would trouble to weave a cross from her hair—and who would keep it as a treasure?

She was still holding the miniature when her eyes strayed across the cabin to a teakwood dresser. Startled, she stared at the undeniable portrait of her cousin *Lavender!*

So! Levasseur was also infatuated with her. She nearly laughed. As if the family would allow anything between a pirate and an heiress to title and wealth!

How had Levasseur even gotten hold of the portrait? she wondered. Certainly Lavender hadn't given it to him. She was a bluestocking, a league above them both in status. It wasn't likely that Lavender would give a framed portrait of herself to a known pirate that London hoped to hang at Execution Dock!

Emerald's mind stumbled over her own conclusions. Then how . . .

She caught her breath as reality rushed in. She whirled and looked about at the cabin that was so foreign to the nature of Rafael Levasseur. The clothing, the furniture, the neatness, the sketch on the desk, the silver box with hints that it came from Holland . . .

Vapors! This was not her cousin's ship!

With a smothered gasp, Emerald rushed for the door. How could Zeddie have been so wrong?

Footsteps sounded from without. She halted. *Trapped.* The door opened. Stricken, silencing her alarm, she stepped back, confronted by the buccaneer that she had met at sunset on Fisher's Row, the smooth and arrogant man that Sir Jasper had addressed as Captain Baret Foxworth.

He stopped short upon seeing her standing in his cabin, but whether he recognized her as she was now dressed was not clear. He stood blocking the doorway.

His eyes took in the faded calico drawers and cotton shirt, the blue scarf tied about her head, then came to rest on the object clutched in her hand. His expression hardened. Temper glinted in the darkness of his narrowing gaze.

Emerald looked at what she held so tightly, and when she saw what it was, her heart sank to her bare feet. In her haste to escape, she had held onto the silver chain and pearl —the heirloom of endearment, undoubtedly worth more in memory to him than a bounty of silver ingots stashed in the hold of a Spanish treasure ship.

She glanced helplessly at his rummaged desk and silver box. "I . . . uh . . . I didn't mean to take *this*. I was looking for . . ."

Her voice trailed off as her eyes rushed to his and she could see her doom approaching. He thought her a wench without morals who had crept aboard his ship to steal whatever she might find. And what could she do but deny his verdict? And her abominable clothing only reinforced his conclusions.

Under his level gaze glinting with cool anger and something like malicious amusement, she blushed to her hairline, believing she was reaping the just chastisement of God for taking matters into her own hands.

In an exaggerated move of weariness at finding her in his cabin, he removed his maroon cloak and dropped it onto the nearby chair. Wearing a white shirt with full sleeves, dark trousers, and calf-length boots, he leaned in the doorway, unhurried, arms folded.

He studied Emerald, gesturing toward her with casual indifference, his hand flashing with gems. "And who is this wench, looking like a cross between a mouse and a cabin boy, who has dared board the *Regale* to rummage through my cabin?"

Shall I faint? she wondered, dazed. It would be so easy— and a sweet relief. Or she might scream or burst into a shield of tears.

The directness of his glance was extremely disconcerting.

"They hang pirates," he announced smoothly, a faint sardonic expression around his mouth. "Are you any better?"

5

THE BUCCANEER

Emerald threw the cherished pendant across the cabin to distract him. When his attention was taken to where it landed and he straightened from the doorway in annoyance over its treatment, Emerald darted under his arm.

His fingers briefly caught the back of her hair before she slipped away from his grip, leaving the blue scarf in his hand. She raced like a fleeing hind with wolves at her heels across the quarterdeck and down the stairs.

Zeddie! Where was Zeddie!

Emerald glanced back to see Captain Foxworth coming down the steps after her. He did not call out, though surely he could have had a dozen men quickly at his command.

In horror, she straddled the ship's rail, giving one last glance in his direction. "Please! Stay away!" she gasped.

He stopped at the foot of the companionway and seemed to contemplate her hair, streaming in the trade wind.

"Well, now," he said. "At least you're not a cabin boy."

"I've a dagger," she suggested in a warning tone.

He folded his arms, and she saw his smile in the moonlight. "I tremble. What is your name? Do you have parents?" He gave a laugh. "A doxy for a mother, no doubt. I suppose you both make your living preying on poor pirates with honest hearts?"

She ignored the goading humor. She hesitated, trembling, uncertain about him, looking away to the dark shimmering waters below. A quarter mile to shore!

He walked slowly toward her.

Emerald leaned toward the sea. "Stay away."

"You're to be congratulated," he said. "There aren't many who manage to secretly sneak aboard. Your skills must surely inspire songs in the bawdy houses."

Tears stung her eyes. "Stay away, or I'll jump."

He folded his arms. "Go ahead," he challenged with a smile.

"I will!"

He bowed and gestured to the sea. "But if you get lost out there, don't say I didn't warn you. And don't think I'll take pity and bother to send a longboat. If you do drown like a sodden mouse, Port Royal will be less one thief. You'd surely grow into one of the worst wenches that could plague a man."

Stung, she cried, "I am not a thief! I'm a lady!"

He threw back his head and laughed.

"You blackguard! You're no better than Rafael Levasseur!"

At the name of Levasseur his manner swiftly changed. "What do you know of *him*?"

Emerald swallowed and remained silent. Did he know her cousin well?

His eyes narrowed. "Down from the rail with you, you sniffy little brat. With what other of my cherished goods did you think to run off with?"

As he came toward her, Emerald slipped over the rail and dove straight into the Caribbean, hardly making a splash. She began swimming toward the distant shore.

He leaned over the rail. "Go on with you then! And if I find so much as a thread missing from my cabin I'll come looking for you, if I have to invade every bawdy house in Port Royal. Enjoy your midnight swim," he challenged. "By the time you get to shore maybe you'll have learned a thing or two! And if I ever catch you or any other thieving doxy sneaking into my cabin, I'll dangle all of you from the yardarm!"

"Fly your skull and crossbones, Captain Foxworth!" she cried breathlessly. "You'll surely hang at Execution Dock!"

She heard him laughing.

Oh! she thought furiously, already shivering. She continued to swim toward shore. Several times she paused to catch her breath and, glancing back, was certain that he watched her progress with a spyglass. Whether it was to see if she could make shore or in malicious satisfaction of witnessing her struggle, she was not sure.

45

Mustering all the remaining determination in her body, she swam on toward Port Royal.

But Zeddie. Where was poor Zeddie? *Dear God, what have I done?*

Hiding behind the barrels on the wharf, still wet and shivering from her long swim, Emerald waited to hear the welcome sound of Zeddie's returning with the cockboat. Several hours crept by before she resigned herself to the worrisome fact that he would not be coming.

He was caught! He had to be! He would've been here by now! *Oh, Lord, please take care of him. This is all my wrongdoing. Please help us.*

Disillusionment assailed her. Where was the hope to continue believing that she could succeed? Yet how could she give up and return to Foxemoore and leave Jamie and Ty to the injustice of the magistrate? There must be something she could do! But what?

The sky became heavy with rain clouds as an unexpected frontal assault of wind brought in the warm humidity of the sea. The threat of a tropical squall did nothing to sober the sea rovers, however. A brawl broke out somewhere, and pistol shots rang from the direction of the Spanish Galleon gambling den.

Winking back tears of weariness and frustration, Emerald was faced with little choice, in the absence of Zeddie, but to return to Foxemoore. *I must get home.*

Beneath the big guns of Fort Charles, recently renamed in recognition of the king's return to the throne, Emerald ran along Fishers Row close to the sea, darting here and there to take cover when she heard rum-sodden voices.

This narrow old street could have told tales of Spanish treasure looted from Cartagena, from Hispaniola, from Porto Bello. Many of the town's inhabitants were rich with pieces of eight, silver plate, gold, emeralds, and pearls. Pirated treasure circulated freely, exchanging hands in the taverns, much of it ending up in the hands of the planters themselves.

Her feet sped over the cobblestones. These had been brought as ballast on the ships, like the bricks that had been used to build the wealthier houses and shops cramming Port Royal. Nearly everything in Jamaica, except sugar and turtles, had to be imported.

"'Tis the glaring Achilles heel of Jamaica in time of war," her father had once remarked, scowling. "King Charles is making a mistake calling home Commodore Myngs to fight the Dutch. Who can guard Jamaica now but the buccaneers from Tortuga?"

She was intent on reaching the western end of Fisher's Row at High Street and emerged near the square where Zeddie had parked the buggy. But on arriving, to her alarm she saw a pirate sprawled on the buggy seat with a jug of rum, looking as though he intended to spend the wee hours there to sleep off his stupor.

Her head jerked at a loud challenge: "The devil take you, you jackanapes!"

"Sink me if'n you think you can best *me!*"

Not more than ten feet from where she crouched in the shadows she saw two more pirates with drawn blades. Although dueling was strictly forbidden, the buccaneers obeyed no law but their own.

One made a murderous lunge. The other parried in a flash that dazed her.

How pirates inflamed on kill-devil rum managed their wits enough to stay alive she could never guess, but Uncle Mathias said they drank it instead of water and were accustomed to the venom of poisonous serpents.

The familiar ring and clash of metal filled her ears. She winced.

But what caused her heart to thud brought a cheer from the pirate sprawled in her carriage. He flung his hat down. *"Esprit de corps,"* he shouted, as though a friendly contest were underway to entertain him.

The clouds gathering overhead sent a sudden squall of rain, but the men were oblivious.

Emerald huddled in the darkness, squinting against the downpour pelting her face. In dismay she wondered what to do. If the ill circumstances that had plagued her footsteps all night continued for the remainder of the late hours, the

47

pirate who had comfortably claimed her carriage would surely fall asleep there!

Again tears filled her eyes. *Lord, help me.*

She looked up as, from somewhere ahead, the echo of
running feet clattered over the cobbles in her direction. Her
spirits brightened. *A patrol of militiamen?* she wondered hopefully, teeth chattering.

The militia, weak as it was, tried to serve the governor-
general in an attempt to keep the peace. The buccaneers had
the run of the town, and few attempts were made by the authorities to control them, for both Council and merchants
feared that the pirates might take their stronghold back to
Tortuga and leave Jamaica vulnerable to an attack by Spain.

The church-attending citizens complained to the governor-general of the violence and debauchery. "Will you bring
the judgment of Sodom and Gomorrah upon us?" But it was
to no avail. What was a disturbance of the peace compared to
the profits earned by the merchants and the protection they
received against Spanish invasion?

But as Emerald huddled there, her hopes were dashed.
It was not the militia who came running but more pirates to
choose sides in the duel.

A privateer pushed his way through the group, and she
recognized the Dutchman Roche. A former planter in Brazil,
he had been expelled and came to Port Royal to launch a new
career as a pirate. It was said that Roche feared nothing and
had proven his claim by capturing a Spanish galleon right
under the guns of Fort Havana.

Roche was captain of a large following, including an
elite band of black pirates who had escaped slavery on the
West Indies plantations. Bearing cutlass instead of hoe, they
were welcomed among the crews of the buccaneers as brothers.
They had signed the "Articles"—the law of the buccaneers—
and had sworn that they would never be taken alive to return
to slavery.

As Emerald watched from her hiding place, one of the
black pirates walked up to the Dutchman, lugging a barrel of
rum on his shoulder. He was tall, with a shaven head, and big
gold earrings flashed in the torchlight.

At the Dutchman's order he smashed open the keg with his cutlass. The Dutchman stepped forward and drew a long-barreled gilt-edged pistol. He leered at the two men who had now ceased their duel.

"You'll drink with your captain, both of you! And if you don't, I'll cut the liver out of the first hog who don't honor me!"

With the pistol pointed at them and scorn written on his pocked face, he stood by the barrel and gestured for his crew to bring mugs.

Emerald held her arms, teeth chattering. *Please, God, don't let them see me.*

How often did Uncle Mathias and the other ministers warn Port Royal's inhabitants that their violence, injustice, and immorality would bring a day of reckoning with a holy God?

She closed her eyes and covered her face. For a desperate moment she went so far as to wish to see the arrogant and handsome buccaneer she had just escaped aboard the *Regale*.

O God, I don't know what to do! If only You would bring my father home from the sea!

Praying about her father brought a sudden thought: What of his lookout house near the guns of Fort Charles?

Yes, of course! She'd been so upset that she'd forgotten. *Thank You, Lord.* She could find her way there easily and wait until morning to take the carriage back to Foxemoore. The lookout would be a welcome refuge from the rainy night, and perhaps there would even be dry clothing available. By morning light her hopes might be renewed. Why, Zeddie might even somehow manage to escape.

The lookout appeared deserted as the rain beat against its tall, narrow structure. Houses and shops, crammed together in what looked to be a solid mass along the town's edge, were built upon the unstable foundation of the sandy cay reaching out far into the harbor waters. It was here, extending into the bay, that her father's lookout house was located.

Emerald always had an uncomfortable feeling as she made her way past these houses built on pilings driven into the sand. She couldn't help but remember the Lord's parable about the two builders. When the storm came, the house on the sand collapsed. "And great was the fall of it," He had said.

Am I truly building my life and its future on the words and will of the Lord? she wondered. Just what purpose did God have for her?

She approached the lookout, and the head wind from the sea chilled her wet clothing as she climbed the steep wooden steps toward its oval door. She paused.

High above in the lighthouse-style window a feeble lantern glowed. Had her father returned sooner than expected? Oh, if it were only so! She yearned to feel his strong arms around her, granting security once again.

Exhausted, wet, cold, wishing for hot tea or coffee, she placed her hand on the latch and squared her shoulders.

This was one night when she would not be turned out of her father's beloved abode to sleep amid barrels and barnacles! She would sleep in his old seabed and cover herself with comfortable blankets.

To her surprise the door was unlocked, and she stepped inside.

All at once she entered a different world, where dry surroundings and a promise of safety brought relief. Her gaze swept the steep flight of steps that led up to her father's room.

Standing on the stairs and holding, presumably, the lantern she had seen in the upper window, was a stoop-shouldered African with white hair, tall and thin beneath a dark woolen sea coat that reached to his knees.

"Jonah!" she cried.

The grandfather of Ty and Minette started. "Miss Emerald! Is you hurt? Where's Zeddie?" He took in her disheveled array with alarm. Then he shuffled down the steps, holding the lantern before him.

Almost immediately he was joined on the stairs by Minette. She clambered down after her grandfather, her form lost within an ankle-length tunic.

Minette was unusually pretty. She had amber eyes and a unique shade of wavy hair the color of honey, which framed her poignant face. Her mother had been a chieftain's lovely daughter from Guinea. With education and proper dress, Emerald believed, Minette would do well in getting a worthy husband. She had already considered the possibility of bringing the girl with her and Jamie to New England but had not yet broached the idea to Jonah.

"Did you get your mother's dowry?" Minette cried.

Emerald saw the light shining in their eyes. They looked on her as their one human hope that would save grandson and brother from whipping and branding. She had no heart left to tell them she had failed, that both Ty and Jamie would be left to the injustice of tomorrow's hearing at the courthouse.

Jonah must have taken notice of her paleness, for the light went from his eyes and his thin shoulders sagged as though he guessed the plan had not worked. Yet he showed nothing to his granddaughter and gently scolded her.

"Where's your high-flung manners, child? And after all the schoolin' Miss Emerald's given you with her books and Bible and such. Let her catch her breath!" He rested a gnarled, overworked hand on her shoulder. "Run get that coffee in the cook house."

When Minette reluctantly left, looking back, Emerald nearly collapsed.

Jonah caught her. "You going straight to bed. I'll send Minette to see you outer them wet clothes."

"I can't deceive you. I've failed," she whispered.

His eyes brimmed with tears. "I knows, Emerald. You needn't say nothing more. But Mr. Mathias says the Holy One who makes wind to blow and rain come down has His ways in the whirlwind and the storm."

"I won't give up," she said wearily, holding his arm as they walked to the steps. "I'll be doing what I can tomorrow."

"Yes, you bound to keep trying. And maybe Sir Karlton be home tomorrow."

But they both knew he would not, and she looked away from his careworn face.

Later that night, Emerald fell into her father's bed, exhausted, yet sleep eluded her. She lay there hearing the wooden building creak in the wind and the rain pound the window, rattling the pane that faced seaward. She could never get used to the structure. Seawater sucked at the pilings and seemed to intimidate the foundation. She supposed her father loved the lookout house because it reminded him of a ship at sea.

Her anxious thoughts turned inevitably back to Mr. Pitt and his demand for jewels. The possibility remained that she might still get what she needed from her cousin. The *Regale* had not been his ship, and she had made a fool of herself before its arrogant captain, but there was no mistaking that her cousin was in Port Royal.

She might make good on her first plan to board his ship if she knew where it was anchored. But even the thought of repeating the trauma she had faced tonight turned her squeamish. Besides, she no longer had Zeddie to aid her, nor did it seem the Lord was blessing her plans with success.

Zeddie! What if that buccaneer decided to try him for thievery? But perhaps Zeddie would evade him after all and make it safely to shore.

She might send a message to Captain Levasseur that she wished to see him. She could lower her dignity and plead with him to lend her the amount demanded by Mr. Pitt. But she knew her cousin too well to believe he would have sympathy for her cause in saving Jamie, especially if he discovered her plan to leave Jamaica and marry him.

Restlessly she tossed the cover aside and went to the window, peering out through the rain to where the ships were anchored. Somewhere out there were two ships she had particular interest in: her cousin's and the *Regale*. She still blushed with shame, remembering the agony of being caught by the buccaneer who claimed her to be a wench and a thief. She shuddered. "Abstain from all appearance of evil," the Scriptures said.

Oh, the gossip that would stain her already sullied reputation if the news got out that she had sneaked aboard Captain Foxworth's ship in the dead of night dressed in calico drawers and a pirate's scarf!

"I knew she was just like her mother all along," she imagined Cousin Lavender saying to her gossipy friends, all daughters of rich planters and members of the governor-general's Jamaican Council. And that vile Sir Jasper, just what would he say if he learned about it? He would think the worst, of course. No doubt he'd become even more offensive.

And her father! What would the stalwart privateer say as he scowled and insisted she explain every detail. What of dear and godly Great-uncle Mathias?

During the years between her thirteenth and sixteenth birthdays, she had the good fortune of having Mathias come to Jamaica from England, where he had taught theology at Cambridge. He had come to live at the Manor with her father, and she'd been taught the Scriptures and the love and acceptance of her heavenly Father.

But Mathias was nearing his seventieth birthday and was not strong, for he hadn't fully recovered from last year's attack of island fever, which often racked his body, bringing weeks of sweating and delirium. He was up and about now and carrying on his work in the Singing School, but he certainly had no money to lend her to pay Mr. Pitt.

Nor did he approve of Jamie, questioning his Christian faith. "His is a restless spirit."

She thought of Cousin Lavender.

Emerald had lived in the Great House until she turned twelve, though her bedchamber had been small and plain compared to Lavender's. During the season of childhood they had been friendly, sharing the same governess and tutor, although her great-aunt disapproved. Lavender too never let Emerald forget that she was lacking as a Harwick and that their Great-aunt Sophie and Lady Geneva Harwick would never leave her a dowry nor plan for her marriage to a man of title. She was at the Great House out of charity because—after all—despite her shameful birth on Tortuga, she was the offspring of Great-aunt Sophie's wayward nephew, Karlton.

But once the truth that Ty and Minette were related to Emerald by marriage became known, Emerald did not even have the good fortune of living in the Great House. She'd been sent away to live in the Manor when Great-uncle Mathias arrived.

During the last two years the relationship between Emerald and Lavender had taken a change. It began when

53

Lavender became deathly ill with the same island fever that plagued Mathias. Lavender, the darling of the family, became bored in her long months of convalescence and, lacking someone her own age to talk with, insisted that Emerald be called up from the Manor to keep her company.

Although the family at first balked at the request, it was clear that Lavender would not take no for an answer. Illness and beauty had resulted in her being pampered, and both Great-aunt Sophie and Lady Geneva doted on her. There was little she didn't receive when she put up a fuss, and Emerald had been sent for.

In those early days Emerald arrived by way of the kitchen door and was ushered up the grand staircase by the mute governess, who heartily disapproved. Once in Lavender's bedchamber, Emerald would spend the afternoon hours in her cousin's company.

At first they had not been happy hours for Emerald, but as her confidence in the Christian faith grew because of Mathias, she found that she could even begin to feel sympathy for her cousin, which was odd in itself, since Lavender had everything in the world that a young girl with a future title could wish for, and Emerald herself possessed so little.

Thinking of all this now as she stood weary and hopeless before the window in the lookout house, she did believe that Lavender had a mild affection for her. If she turned to Lavender, would *she* help her? There was a glimmer of hope that she might, and Emerald decided to visit Foxemoore first thing in the morning.

With her mind made up to try every possible door of escape, she felt some relief. Then she thought of that nasty buccaneer Captain Foxworth.

A small shiver touched her skin. Suppose he unmasked her visit aboard his ship to the Harwicks? *Impossible,* she soothed herself. Captain Foxworth would have no opportunity to bring the matter before them. His reputation as a pirate forbade his being known or received by such a family. And anyway, he didn't know who she was or where to find her.

"Perhaps," she murmured dourly, "there's some good in his thinking I'm a wench after all. Foxemoore will be the last place he'd ever seek me. He probably thinks my father is the owner of a tavern." She winced at the thought.

Then new fears rushed in like a gale. *Unless*, she decided nervously, *Zeddie's tongue is loosened through torture.*

Who knew what manner of man this buccaneer was? True, he had seemed gallant, even a man of the nobility, when he had rescued her from the unwanted advances of that loathsome Sir Jasper. Had he recognized her in his cabin as the same girl? She didn't think so, for he would have mentioned it and accused her of following him to his ship.

No, she'd been disguised as a cabin boy. There was small chance she would ever see him again or had any need to worry about his accusing her to the family.

She shut her eyes, leaning her head against the pane. Her ability to think was growing dull through lack of sleep. Then suddenly an image flashed across her mind as clearly as though she were standing in his cabin again. *The portrait of Lavender on his desk!*

She drew in a breath. Could Lavender possibly know this pirate? No! But what if . . .

Her hand clenched the drapery. She had laughed when finding that unlikely portrait, believing the ship to belong to Levasseur. Now the find was no longer amusing.

What was the name of the earl's grandson whom Lavender was to marry in England?

"Baret," she breathed aloud. "Baret Buckington."

But Sir Jasper had called him Captain Foxworth. He couldn't be the earl's grandson, she told herself desperately. Could he?

She thought back to Lavender's bedchamber. Lavender had a number of paintings of the family from London. Surely she would have one of the earl's grandson, whom she would marry one day. Yet Emerald could not recall having seen such displayed on her bureau.

Now there was a second reason to seek a visit with Lavender. She must know if there was any connection between this mysterious Captain Foxworth and Lord Baret Buckington.

6

VISCOUNT BARET BUCKINGTON

The Jamaican moon appeared from behind the racing clouds and scattered a wake of shimmering jewels across the bay of Port Royal. The captain of the *Regale* left the quarterdeck, his boots ringing on the steps up to the high aftmost deck. He stood at the taffrail, the curved walk over the stern, looking every inch a roguish buccaneer in a white Holland shirt partially opened against his bronzed, muscled chest. He was oblivious to the strong tropical wind blowing his dark hair, shaking the billowing sleeves. He stood as still as a statue with his gaze fixed upon the big guns of Fort Charles looming ominously over the seawall. His dark eyes beneath even blacker lashes narrowed, but it was not the guns that he saw in his memory.

The captain of the *Regale*—heir to the title of viscount—was Lord Baret Buckington, recently known among the Brethren of the Coast as Captain Baret Foxworth.

Gripped in his hand, which wore the family ring of his grandfather Nigel Buckington, earl in London, was the small silver cameo and a cross woven of delicate golden hair. His mouth hardened, his dark eyes becoming warm with righteous anger. The knuckles on his hand turned white.

He gazed now at the intricately carved frame that held the portrait of the woman, rubbing his thumb over the silver. He had deliberately placed her portrait in that despised silver frame.

Baret had hired artisans to design the frame from a silver ingot taken from a Spanish treasure ship. *So I'll not forget what arms and feeds the Inquisition army of King Philip of Spain,* he thought.

56

The silver had been mined in Peru by religious prisoners, men who died from exhaustion and disease. The whips of the Spanish captains serving the powerful family dons were not lax for long. The quota of silver bars brought by the yearly mule train on its long overland route to the treasure fleet at Porto Bello would not wait for the recovery of the depleted health of a slave. When a man died he was merely abandoned and replaced by a new prisoner: European, African, or Carib.

The Europeans were usually heretics—Protestants from Holland and France. King Philip's Inquisition army raged in the Netherlands, and many of its prisoners were sold to the colonies on the Main.

Again Baret touched the silver with its ruthless heritage. The silver was as much the cause behind his leaving Cambridge Divinity School to take to a life of buccaneering as was his present search for his father's whereabouts. As he stood with the wind blowing against him, he saw himself as a small boy hiding on the wide stairway at Buckington House in London. His grandfather and his father, Viscount Royce Buckington, were in a hot argument that set his boyish heart pounding.

The earl, wearing a green satin dressing gown embroidered with gold thread, paced the red carpet in the drawing room. A painting of King Charles I was framed in gold above the hearth. Handsome portraits of the Buckington family, all lords, viscounts, and earls, surrounded the king like a royal entourage.

"I forbid this lunacy of yours, Royce. What of your reputation as viscount? You're to inherit the earldom after me. What of His Majesty! Civil war tears England asunder! Cromwell's Roundheads number in the thousands! If His Majesty's brother must flee, the Buckington family is sworn to go with him into France and to draw sword to protect him abroad as king in exile! I for one will go with him, and so must you."

Royce's rugged voice sounded with impatience. "Your ways slay me, Father. You bid me die for Charles—to fight my own brothers in England for a cause I question—but it is *Spain* who is the enemy of England and the Netherlands. Shall I not rather stop the stench of Spain's Inquisition army?

Every Spanish treasure ship I sink will be a fortune lost to King Philip which he would otherwise use to feed his army in the Netherlands."

"You'll not bring Caroline back by throwing away your life to become a common pirate!"

"Pirate?" his father had repeated scornfully. "Is that what Felix says? Let my brother call me as he will. I vow my ship to become a dread and a terror to the Spanish dons. This is my answer!"

"Put your sword away."

"I shall sink every treasure ship of King Philip that I find in the Caribbean Sea!"

"Felix is right," came the earl's bitter voice. "Before this madness of yours is over you'll have stained the Buckington name! Look on the wall—what of them?"

Royce gave a laugh. "Family portraits? There isn't a saint among the ancestry of scoundrels, my father. As for Felix, I've begun to think he's spying for Spain."

"You speak thus of your brother!"

"Half brother. A foe, just as sure as I stand here!"

"And my son, even as you! And what of your own son? If you'll not think of yourself or the Buckington name, what of Baret? You owe him more than a blackened reputation."

"I have fair plans for Baret. When he's of age he'll be sent to Cambridge as Caroline wished. He's not to know what happened to her yet. He's too young."

Crouching on the stairway, Baret had listened thoughtfully. Cambridge! Divinity training! While his father took to sea to sink Spanish ships? His small hand formed a fist. Where *was* his mother?

His father and grandfather were arguing again. He strained to hear above his pounding heart.

"One day Baret will know that I loved his mother more dearly than a man may love a woman. That I love her still. He's to know I have honor, a cause to serve far nobler than civil war in England. I'll return from the West Indies to see him. I'll find no shame in my new life as a buccaneer, and I don't think he will either. When he's older, he'll understand the cause."

"And if we must flee England with Charles into France?"

"Then I'll find you in Paris. I'll see him again. And when it is safe to be Protestant in France, train him in the words of John Calvin. I've also asked Sir Cecil Chaderton to be his tutor. He's agreed to stay with the boy until it's safe to return to England."

"Royce! How can you throw away your title for a memory?"

"A memory? Do you call Caroline naught more than a memory? God have mercy! In Holland the Inquisitor questioned her faith until she fainted, but they revived her again on the rack. Oh, yes! They used all their devilish weapons to break her faith—the thumbscrews, the Iron Maiden—do you know what that is?"

"I have no desire to hear tales of horror—"

"You *will* hear! It's a form-fitting coffin studded with five-inch iron spikes! They slowly crushed her ribs, all the while the Inquisitor kept asking in his soft voice from hades, 'Where are the other heretics hiding? Where? Speak, child, speak.'"

"You'll go mad! Do you think all Spain is a beast? That all the men who carry the cross and wear hooded cowls are Inquisitors?"

Royce banged his fist against something hard. "Do you think I can ever forget? Then they buried her alive!"

On the stairway Baret sat white and shaking, clutching his stomach. Dread, dark as a pit, sucked him into its hopelessness. He understood the hellish face of the terror his father had explained. Bending down his dark head on the stair, young Baret convulsed with silent sobs, hot tears splashing over the fist pressed against his mouth.

Mama, they buried you alive. After they did all those horrible things, they still hated you and covered you with dirt. He could imagine his gentle mother with golden hair, screaming, clawing for air—his mother, who had prayed with him beside his bed, who had comforted him in his fears, who had cared for him when no one else was there.

Baret suddenly saw the face of the only Spaniard he had ever seen—the ambassador to the court of Whitehall. A man named Bernardo, wearing rich black velvet with a high white ruff around his neck. He envisioned Bernardo, with his V-shaped beard, his cool dark eyes—the friend of Uncle Felix Buckington—staring down at his mother while shovelfuls of dirt buried her alive.

Bernardo's once kindly face was forever changed into that of an enemy.

His mother's voice echoed in his memory: *"Jesus said to forgive your enemies, to pray for those who persecute you."*

"I can't," wept Baret on the stairs amid the shouting of his father and grandfather in the drawing room. "I can't."

The new face of Spain was branded on his heart. His father! Oh, how he loved his brave father!

"Destroy them, Father," he choked, clenching his fist. "Destroy Spain!"

On the *Regale*, Baret stood gazing at the portrait of his mother while holding the cross woven from her hair. "Destroy Spain," he murmured to himself.

"Like your father, you'll not forget," came a familiar voice.

He turned from the taffrail toward Sir Cecil Chaderton. Baret had been friends with the Cambridge scholar since childhood, when Chaderton had reluctantly journeyed with the earl, his family, and other members of England's nobility into France with the exiled king.

Although a secret supporter of Cromwell's Roundheads, and a loyal scholar with a seat at his beloved Corpus Christi College at Cambridge, Chaderton had left England because of his affection for Baret and his father. The man had been Baret's tutor in New Testament and Greek but also a personal counselor during the years of exile. All that Baret knew of staunch Calvin theology was due to the brilliant scholarship of "Sir Cecil," as Baret affectionately called him.

Chaderton claimed a bloodline to that noble Puritan Laurence Chaderton, who, along with Lancelot Andrewes and other Greek and Hebrew scholars had been commissioned by King James I to translate the Authorized Version of the Bible.

"It does not deserve to be forgotten," Baret answered him. "Nor will I forget my father."

Sir Cecil made no immediate reply, and Baret left him on deck and returned to the Great Cabin, where he placed the small cameo and cross inside the silver box along with other items of intimate value. This time he locked the box and the desk drawer into which he placed it. He doubted that the girl had swum away with anything that would unmask his identity.

Remembering the incident that had failed to locate Lucca aboard the *Santiago,* he was reasonably assured that his secret goal as a buccaneer with Henry Morgan remained guarded and that his true identity was unknown. There were few sea rovers he could trust. Nor could he trust members of the family, least of all his father's half brother, Felix.

Felix, a member of the High Admiralty Court in London, had secretly been involved in the verdict handed down three years earlier against Baret's father, declaring Royce a West Indies pirate. With that black mark upon his father's reputation as Cromwell's privateer had come the added news of the sinking of his ship off Havana. Felix had brought this dark news to the earl at Buckington House. He produced a legal paper written in the hand of the governor-general of Jamaica witnessing to the fact of his father's escape and arrival at Port Royal. Later, his father had been killed.

"Killed in a duel on the street of Port Royal."

By whom? As yet, Baret had not been able to discover the pirate's name. He had reason to doubt Felix's story.

Now that his father was declared to be dead, Baret had first right to the title of viscount, but the earl was furious with him for having taken to sea as a buccaneer and thought nothing of holding the title in abeyance. Baret's inheritance of his father's lands and jewels in England and his shares in the vast Foxemoore sugar plantation in Jamaica were also denied him in the hope that he would return to England chastened and willing to take his position in the family as his grandfather wished.

He would return. But not yet.

Baret stood now, hands on hips, and glanced about his ransacked cabin. His eyes narrowed. He thought of the little wench who had sneaked aboard. It would serve her well if he returned to Port Royal and found her—if only to make her correct the disarray in which she had left his cabin!

Impatiently he snatched up a linen shirt and black trousers that she had pulled from his teakwood trunk. He replaced them.

He glanced up then, aware of Sir Cecil's presence in the open door.

Few of his peers would now recognize the staunch old Puritan who had taught at Cambridge before embarking with Baret in the dangerous pursuit of buccaneering on the Spanish Main. Absent his scholar's cloak with fur collar and his flat velvet hat, Sir Cecil was now garbed in an elegant Spanish suit of black taffeta trimmed with silver lace designed in Madrid for some wealthy don. Baret had retrieved the suit and matching broad-brimmed hat from the *Santiago* and with straight face had awarded the outfit to his Cambridge tutor, never believing that the dignified Puritan would wear it.

Baret's memory flashed back to a certain wooden desk in France where as a boy he had watched Sir Cecil bent over a sheaf of papers, his pen scratching, occasionally pausing to dip the quill into the inkwell. The man now standing at his cabin door seemed a stranger. His jaw-length gray hair remained neatly paged against a lean hawklike face, once pasty from London's fog but now toughened and browned by long exposure to the tropical sun. The short, pointed Sir Walter Raleigh beard remained, now lightly oiled.

He entered and stood, and Baret glanced at the serving tray in his hands. He lifted a brow and looked at his tutor for an explanation, for it wasn't Sir Cecil's typical manner to wait on him.

Sir Cecil gave him a dry glance. "I bring you a worthy 'gift,' rowed out from Chocolata Hole by a musky old sea urchin who looks ripe for treachery." He gestured dubiously at the wet and sandy canvas bag sitting on the tray.

At the mention of Chocolata Hole, Baret came alert. He thought he knew who the "sea urchin" was.

"Where is he now?"

"He insisted he couldn't stay. He's rowing back in his cockboat."

Sir Cecil sniffed the bag with a show of disdain, but he held the tray with the deference due the crown jewels. "Smells odiously of something dead. Would you have me open the bag?"

Baret folded his arms and leaned back against his desk. "I wait with fond anticipation."

Sir Cecil's deft fingers opened the canvas sack and delicately removed a hard, dark green object. He placed it gingerly upon the desk.

They watched. A moment later a small head with round eyes and a long wrinkled neck emerged from the shell and appeared to size up its new habitat.

"From Hob," said Baret simply. He lifted the Jamaican green turtle, a staple food for pirates, and inspected it carefully under the overhanging lantern. As suspected, he discovered a rolled bit of damp paper under its shell, smoothed it with his thumb, and read the scribbled message that was partially spelled out in stick drawings.

"I've other news concerning the thief who broke into your cabin earlier this night," said Sir Cecil meanwhile. "We've found the man who brought her aboard. A miserable looking fellow with a bump on his head. He's awake now, but seems a bit dazed in the cranium to me. Says his name is Zeddie. He's quite adamant in defending their innocence of all intent of thievery. They boarded the . . . er . . . wrong ship, is what he's saying. Says they thought the captain was a French pirate."

At the words "French pirate," Baret showed interest for the first time.

"An antagonist of yours," explained Sir Cecil. "His name is Captain Levasseur."

"Ah!"

"The girl was his . . . er . . . cousin, so the fellow Zeddie insists."

Baret didn't trust Levasseur, who suspected his allegiance to the Brotherhood at Tortuga. Had he sent an unlikely wench to search his cabin, looking for evidence to use against him? He scowled. Perhaps he had not taken her presence as seriously as he should have. Maybe she hadn't boarded on her own to search for loot but had a more sophisticated purpose.

"Do you wish to see the man Zeddie for interrogation?

He's putting up quite a fuss, demanding to know where his ward is being kept."

"You can tell him that he best not squawk too loudly. He's blessed the captain of the *Regale* is a generous man. I could dangle him at the end of a rope."

"Shall I release him then?"

"No. Shackle him in the hold. Let him worry a little. See to him at your leisure. And when I return I'll see him also. Other matters are of import now."

"You're going to Chocolata Hole?" asked Sir Cecil dubiously.

"A necessity." He walked to where his weapons hung on a hook, ignoring Sir Cecil's frown.

"You would trust the wily old pirate again? Was he not quite wrong about Lucca being aboard the *Santiago?*"

"The information he hints of now is worth the risk."

Baret passed his leather baldric—the weapons' sheath worn diagonally from shoulder to hip, holding rapier and pistols—over his head as Sir Cecil handed him his cloak and hat.

"I would caution you. You may yet inherit more from your father than his title and lands. You also have his enemies to reckon with. Nor must you forget the Admiralty Court has little patience with privateers turning pirates."

"Your concern is well taken. I've not forgotten." Baret handed him the turtle with a slight smile. "I prefer English pie."

Sir Cecil reluctantly received the creature.

Baret smiled and went to the door, then glanced back. "I won't return until after the wedding. I hope to talk some sense into Geneva. You'll be attending?"

"Unfortunately, yes." He looked worriedly at Baret. "Felix has arrived."

Baret already knew that his uncle was in Jamaica, and he showed no expression. "I'll see you at Foxemoore on Sunday. I've another call to make first."

When the cabin door shut behind him, Sir Cecil stood staring at it, troubled. He knew where Baret intended to go, of course, and he felt uneasy. He hoped Sir Karlton Harwick could oblige the young viscount on the whereabouts of his father's journal and map. If not, Baret would confront Lord Felix, who was in Jamaica to marry Geneva Harwick.

There was also the matter of Jette, Baret's eight-year-old brother. The very thought of Jette's being turned over to Felix was a hideous thought to Baret and to Cecil as well. Sir Cecil worried about the child's health and about his Christian training. He had written Lady Geneva asking permission to become his tutor in England when she returned with Felix, even as he had served the family in tutoring Baret.

There was only one drawback, he thought. Returning to England to instruct Jette would mean leaving Baret alone in his pursuit to find his father. Was his father alive as he thought? Sir Cecil could only wonder. There were times when he believed that the youth's suspicions were fed by anguish rather than fact. Recently he had taken to worrying as much about the young viscount as he did about the boy Jette.

Cecil frowned. He believed that the lives of both heirs to the Buckington estate were at risk. He was also concerned for the condition of Baret's faith. How long would he continue to neglect his upbringing and training?

He glanced across the Great Cabin to the portrait of Lady Lavender, a young woman of both charm and title, whom Baret intended to one day make his wife. She'd been quite ill with island fever for the past year and a half and had written Baret, asking to see him. The marriage between Lord Felix Buckington and Lady Geneva Harwick at Foxemoore afforded that opportunity.

Unfortunately it also gave Baret the responsibility of meeting with Felix.

Sir Cecil looked down at the turtle, anxious to turn it loose. Later, as he did so, watching it swim away, he vaguely wondered what the scholars at Cambridge would think of turtle soup.

7

CHOCOLATA HOLE

The year 1663 gave to Mother England two prized ports on the Spanish Main: Port Royal in Jamaica and English Harbor in Antigua. Even so, there was no presence of the Royal Navy, and the sugar planters and governor-general relied on the buccaneers for protection against Spain.

Unfortunately, the ships serving Charles II in the West Indies were not the stalwart protection that planters wished for. The rumblings of a second war with the Dutch troubled England, for Charles believed France would join Holland against him.

As the possibility of war with two old enemies gathered like clouds, the West India Sugar Interest in England's parliament feared losing their vast plantations on Jamaica to a sneak attack by Spain and, dismayed, insisted that His Majesty permanently station squadrons of warships at Port Royal.

However, King Charles lacked the finances for such a navy and often permitted Governor-general Thomas Modyford to authorize privateering under the protective flag of England. It was ironical that the buccaneer serving His Majesty today could tomorrow be hanged at Execution Dock as a rascally pirate.

It was dawn when Baret paused on the waterfront to watch the sun rise from the Caribbean, turning the waters gray-blue in the dusky light. The rain had ceased, but fat clouds tinged with dark edges continued to assemble on the horizon. Hurricane season was not many weeks away.

Baret knew by experience what hurricane-force winds could do to a vessel caught in their onslaught. He had watched the carcass of a ship fade into darkness, her masts shattered, the sullen seas washing her deserted decks.

66

The upcoming storm season was of benefit to his private quest, however. Usually His Majesty's ships, now scarce in the Caribbean, underwent repairs at this time of year, while some of them were secretly sent off cruising for prizes as they covertly turned to buccaneering in the southern Caribbean out of storm's way.

Baret would take a risk of another sort—perhaps more dangerous than a hurricane. He must risk his favor with his grandfather the earl and His Majesty the king by joining Henry Morgan's buccaneer fleet in its upcoming attack on an undisclosed location on the Main.

There was the danger that he too could be hanged at Execution Dock. But he had reason to believe that his father might yet be alive, held by Spain as a prisoner, and Baret had gained passage on a small vessel for Chocolata Hole to meet secretly with his old friend and informer, Hob.

The ship was a squat, ill-painted schooner that had preyed on fishing boats close to the Main. Baret was anxious to disembark the leaky craft and had no confidence in its captain, a fat, barrel-chested man who sprawled near the rail, one knee drawn up, the other foot propped against a rum barrel.

Baret saw the captain hungrily eye the leather baldric he wore, stiff with Spanish silver bullion and housing sword and ornate silver-handled pistols.

The foul-smelling pirate took another guzzle of his kill-devil rum and wiped his wet mustache on the back of a dirty, cotton sleeve of faded red. He belched loudly. Whether his coarse satisfaction came from his rum or from speculation that he might end up owning the bullion that glinted in the morning light, Baret couldn't ascertain.

From beneath a scarf tied at the back of his head, the pirate's lank hair whipped in the breeze like the skinny tail of a nervous rat. He cast Baret a furtive glance, as did several members of his crew.

Baret watched them as he leaned against the rail, his polished Cordovan boots crossed negligently at the ankles, his arms folded.

The captain popped the plug back into his jug and leered, though he may have intended an affable smile.

"We's nigh Chocolata Hole, Cap'n Foxworth."

Baret was already familiar with the environs of Port Royal. The main harbor was on the north side, where the water was six fathoms and ships could come alongside the wharves to load and unload cargo. Most of the wharves and warehouses, including the King's Warehouse, were located there.

Here on the western side the waters were shallower. Larger ships had to anchor some several hundred yards out and use lighters to haul their cargo to shore. Chocolata Hole was a large secluded cove where some one hundred different small sloops and schooners belonging to smugglers, privateers, fishers, and turtlers were anchored.

As the captain mentioned Chocolata Hole, Baret looked ahead toward the cove, his hand on the rail, rings gleaming, knowing their sparkle was not lost on the bulging eyes of captain or crew.

"Sure now, Cap'n Foxworth, it's the cove your heart's desirin'?"

"Quite certain." He casually turned his head to look at him, his dark eyes glinting. "Captain, I pray you are not a stupid fellow."

The pirate looked at him, dumbfounded. "Huh?"

"There'll be no treachery from you or your crew," said Baret too calmly. "If you think to try, I fear I must deliver your head to a watery grave."

The pirate recovered from his surprise, and his brow went dark. He stood as though sorely tempted to unsheathe his blade and slurred something that came out less than intelligible. But when Baret's grim smile remained, and it became obvious that he did not take alarm, the pirate captain appeared to reconsider his rashness.

He glowered. "The plague take you, Cap'n Foxworth! None such as you will e'er deliver my head. Sink me if'n you think otherwise!"

One of his crew, a man with a long golden mane, turned toward Baret as though waiting for a word from his captain.

Baret added smoothly, "You best keep to your steerage, Dutchman. Your captain would be loath to see his noble craft run aground on a sand bar with a squall brewing. There'll be naught left of it come morning."

The man shot a second glance toward his captain as if waiting for orders. But the pirate only glared at Baret and restrained himself. He turned away, opting instead to humor his ill temper by shouting at a slave who had the double misfortune of being owned by an evil man. "Get to work, you shallow swine, lest I corpse you."

Baret was anxious to disembark, and as the vessel set anchor he picked up his leather satchel from the deck, paid the sullen captain his due, and stepped onto the quay.

As he walked the shore, pirates were everywhere. Then a familiar voice sounded at his elbow.

"Har, me lordship, 'tis you. And d'you ever blink upon a sweeter lookin' turtle for the soup pot? 'Tis all tender, it is."

Baret turned and looked down into the creased leathery face of wily old Hob, who held up a sandy turtle for inspection. Hob wore an unlikely visage for a spy, but one that had proven its worth in the past.

Hob had first come from the seafarers' haunts of Bristol, where homeless and hungry waifs provided rich prospects for future pirates. It was on the street of Bristol that Hob vowed he had first met the arch-buccaneer of them all, Henry Morgan. But some who knew Morgan insisted he had been the son of an indentured servant on Jamaica, and still others insisted he had come from the wild coasts of Wales.

Hob had lived in Port Royal for years, where he owned a weather-beaten boat that was permanently anchored in Chocolata Hole. Here he lived and harvested turtles to sell to the buccaneers, becoming a valuable source of paid information.

Hob held a bucket of the hard-shelled creatures, his floppy hat pulled low over shaggy white hair, his baggy trousers wet and sandy.

Baret smiled into the shrewd blue eyes that were alert with mischief. "It warms my heart to see you again, old pirate. I'm surprised the governor-general hasn't hanged you by now," he said lightly. "His Majesty is firm in eliminating even past culprits from the Caribbean waters."

"Aye, me lord, I be wonderin' 'bout that meself." And he pushed his hat back to scratch his locks. "You received me gift? 'Twas a youngun, it was."

"And fully appreciated, Hob," he said with grave affectation. "You're a gentleman pirate to be sure. What news do you have for me, old spy?"

Hob's wrinkled face grew sober. He spoke in a low voice. "There be a new pirate who says he knows where Lucca is."

Baret's heart quickened. "Who is he?"

"He ain't be givin' his name so eagerly. But I brought his contact turtles only a day ago, and he says he'll contact me again. I'll be telling you an earful more for a bit o' coin." He grinned. "Aye, just a wee amount in exchange for a sweet turtle. You knows how the belly doth sorrow for the little green things cooked all hot-like in soup."

Baret couldn't help but smile. He could trust the scoundrel, even if Hob's loyalty did turn thin at times when faced with what he called "better pickin's."

"A gold piece for your services, Hob—but if your information proves false, I shall find you again, if only to mince your hide for the kettle."

"Aye, me lordship—har, I means Captain Foxworth!—a bargain, yes, a bargain it is. You won't be finding yourself a better spy than the likes o' me. No, and not a more loyal servant neither." He gave a toothless grin.

Baret smiled again and saw the man's shrewd gaze take in his fine suit of black velvet.

"A goldie be more'n enough for telling tales. But a few pieces of eight be a mite kinder."

Baret folded his arms and lifted a dark brow, affecting wounded dignity. "And where would the grandson of the Earl of Buckington get Spanish pieces of eight? Do you take me for a pirate, Hob? I am gravely offended!"

Hob was quick to catch the tone of mockery and joined in with a chortle. "Oh, nay, me lordship! Nay, me great defender of the English Admiralty Court! Har." He laughed, "Just a slip, me lord, just a flapping tongue. Aye, a fair and noble English goldie be pleasant enough. Sure of it! Stab me if I be lyin'."

"Morgan is gathering the buccaneers for a campaign," Baret told him. "We'll be meeting at the Spanish Galleon to sign the Articles. Tell this contact of yours to be there."

Hob gave a crafty glance about the cay. "There's more. I've heard 'tis your friend Erik Farrow you be wishin' to see in Port Royal now. I've a bit o' news that won't prove pleasing, seein' how Erik's loyalty and sword doth now work for your uncle."

Baret stared at him, taking the shocking news in stunned silence. Then, "Working for Felix?"

Erik knew about the strained relationship that he had with his uncle, who was a member of the esteemed Admiralty Court that had brought in the guilty verdict of piracy against his father. Erik also knew of Baret's secret plans to search for his father in the Caribbean. If Erik was in the pay of his uncle, would he not be obligated to share with Felix whatever information he had?

"When did Erik become a hired man of Felix?"

"A month ago, I'm thinkin'. Maybe a mite longer. And it be not to your good nor to your father's, if he be alive, you can be sure of that. That Erik be in it for himself. Got himself knighted by your uncle. Be Sir Erik now," said Hob with a leer. "Erik was always a cool one, says I. Erik got no more warmth in his blood than a barracuda."

Baret was tempted to agree, and he was disturbed. Their friendship had always kept him guessing as to whether or not he could fully trust Erik. In one breath Erik would risk a sword fight to aid him; in the next he might stand aloof.

"You are certain? Who told you Erik works for my uncle?"

"Be knowing better than to ask me that," said Hob, as though to question his role of spy was to accuse him of disloyalty. He lifted a turtle from the bucket and tapped its hard shell. "Sink me sails! Ain't be a pirate nor a buccaneer in Port Royal who don't buy from old Hob. Ain't a freebooter who don't trust me. Me ears grow keener with age 'stead of growin' deaf. Me picks up many a tale as I makes me rounds. Sure now, why, I has me buyers even among the respectable. Even the Harwicks buys me turtles. And that daughter of Sir Karlton by the name of Miss Emerald, she be known to turtle-hunt once or twice herself in me company. A pretty thing, she."

Hob leaned closer to him and whispered. "Be talk among the pirates that Erik's been paid plenty by your uncle to keep you under his spyglass."

So, thought Baret. Then he was right. Felix did suspect him of looking for his father. What had Erik disclosed to him?

"It's evil news for you and your father, me lordship. That Erik be a hard man, and you know it." Hob rubbed his chin thoughtfully, looking at Baret's scabbard. "Be your match with the blade maybe."

Baret *knew* that Erik was his match—it was Erik who had polished his fencing skills. Erik had been his mentor in England during the beginning of their friendship. Baret had still been a student at Cambridge then, and Erik was in London convalescing from a serious wound taken in the first war with the Dutch. "Ain't be easy for you now, having Erik on the side of your uncle."

Baret bridled his anger and said, again too calmly, "And just where is the newly knighted Sir Erik?"

"At the Red Goose, gamblin'."

Baret removed a piece of eight from his drawstring pouch and gave it to Hob with a faint smile.

The turtler chuckled and, holding it up between thumb and forefinger, kissed it. "Har!" He laughed. He blew on it, then rubbed it on the front of his soiled tunic. "Spanish king ain't be missing it, says I. And you be of a kinder heart to pass it on." Hob offered the turtle. "Sure you won't take the little green thing for soup?"

"Another time, old pirate. A storm's rising, and I've business with another."

Hob squinted out to the Caribbean where the water shone with silvery ripples. "A gale, says I, a real blow. Hard, from the feels of it. I'll be in touch with you, me lordship, just as soon as I learn a thing or two."

With his anger toward Erik subdued beneath his calm demeanor, Baret left Hob at Chocolata Hole, troubled over his relationship with Erik Farrow. Erik had been the one buccaneer he counted as a friend.

He frowned. Perhaps it was wiser for the present to allow Erik to go on believing that he trusted him. He would even suggest that Erik ride with him to Foxemoore to pay the needed visit to Sir Karlton Harwick. Even though Erik was sure to report everything he did to Felix, he must take that chance.

Erik—friend or foe? He wondered.

8
JAMAICAN JUSTICE

It seemed to Emerald that she had hardly closed her eyes in her father's bed at the lookout house when Minette came with a lantern.

Minette shook her, tears in her eyes as she knelt beside the bed. She was wet with rain, appearing to have just returned from somewhere.

"Wake up, oh, wake up!"

Emerald's head throbbed from lack of sleep. She raised herself on an elbow, and one look at her cousin's face convinced her of dark news. She sat up. "What is it?"

"Jamie and Ty's been sent to the magistrate early!"

"What! But Mr. Pitt gave me until Friday!" Emerald threw aside the blanket and was on her feet. "My clothes, quick! What happened to my petticoat?"

"It wasn't with your other things. You must've dropped it when you ran here from the buggy."

In frustration Emerald looked about. She'd certainly not find a petticoat in her father's room.

"Wait!" Minette sped to a high cedar trunk in one corner. "There's all kinds of frocks here." Her eyes shone. "I'm not supposed to know about it, but this was sent here yesterday morning. A half-caste brought it to store here. It belongs to one of the captains who sailed with Morgan. The half-caste told me the frocks had been on their way to the viceroy's daughter at Porto Bello. Imagine! The trunk was taken from a Spanish ship near Panama."

Emerald studied the trunk uneasily. "Why would it be stored here in my father's lookout?"

Minette shrugged. "He said the captain knew Uncle Karlton and that he wouldn't mind. Said he would come for it in a week."

73

Emerald grew uncertain. As a privateer, Sir Karlton was involved in selling contraband to the colonies—she knew that much. On several occasions she had watched his large merchantman arrive in Port Royal laden with goods from Europe. She had once heard him secretly discussing transferring the goods from his ship to smaller, swifter vessels that could enter coves and trade for treasure undetected by the Spanish officials.

Her father, however, wasn't the only privateer trading with the Spanish colonies. Spain claimed, but could not enforce, an exclusive monopoly on trade with its colonies on the Main. Even so, her ships were unable to satisfy the colonists' desire for European goods, and after the destruction of their two treasure fleets in 1656 and '57, Spain's commerce with her colonies had almost come to a halt.

"I looked at the frocks," said Minette, her eyes glowing as did Emerald's at the thought. Minette knelt and opened the heavy top. "Vapors, they're as fine as anything Lavender wears."

Emerald knelt beside her and gazed. "There look to be at least three with fancy petticoats." She ran her palm across the yards of lace and shiny cloth. She lifted out first one gown and then another, judging their size, amid Minette's moans and sighs.

"Oh, Emerald, wouldn't it be grand to own a gown like this one? And to be invited to Geneva's wedding? The both of us, I mean." Her face fell. "But that isn't possible, is it," she stated. "Even . . . even if you could go, I couldn't, 'cause my mother was African."

Emerald avoided her eyes. They had discussed this on many occasions. It was far kinder not to give Minette false expectations. "No," she said quietly. "It isn't possible. Not for either of us." Then she shrugged. "But I don't want to go anyway, and you should forget such dreams. It's enough that our futures belong in the hand of God. Surely He has good plans for us both."

Minette nodded and quickly changed the subject, but whether she accepted the verdict was another matter.

"Look, Emerald—they call this 'velvet'—and pearls it has," she breathed. "You'd look mighty fine in it."

Emerald gave her a smile. "So would you. Here, let me see it."

If she'd not been in such a dire state of mind over the magistrate's hearing, she would have sighed in admiration as did Minette. Now there was no time for that, she told herself and was swiftly to her feet. She held the dress up against her. "It's too big for me. Look."

"I can pin it on you—and see!—ribbons to cinch in the waist—and a hat! Oh! That evil Mr. Pitt won't be knowing who you are when you arrive to stop him."

"*He's* at the courthouse?" cried Emerald.

"Yes, I saw him. He asked if you'd seen Levasseur, and I said you couldn't get the dowry."

"So that's why he's aiming to see Jamie and Ty whipped. I must stop him. There's still a chance. Oh, Minette, you shouldn't have told him."

"He frightens me, the way he stares at me." The girl shivered. "And before I knew what I'd done, it was too late."

"Well, it doesn't matter now." Emerald ran to the tall bureau. "Swiftly then. Help me into it, and let's hope I can walk in it as fine as Lavender prances about. We haven't a moment to lose. If I accomplish little else at the hearing, at least Mr. Pitt will be sure to think I've gotten what he wanted from Levasseur's ship after all—and a few prizes of my own."

During the night there had been a brief alarm. A small ship had dropped anchor at the eastern end of the channel to await daylight. As Emerald and Minette made their way on foot toward the town square, the commander at Fort Charles was sending a longboat out to identify the vessel's captain.

The fishermen too had been busy during the night, despite the rain. June was the month when thousands of turtles crawled ashore on the cays and beaches to lay their eggs and were easily captured.

On the beach, as she and Minette walked past the fish markets, appreciative heads turned toward Emerald. For the first time she felt like some wealthy planter's daughter, and she held her hat in place, making certain that it covered her hair. Her tresses had been hopelessly unmanageable after her swim, and there'd been no time to rinse out the salt. She

75

had it pinned up out of sight beneath the wide-brimmed hat with its pretty escalloped edging of lace.

She glimpsed several fenced areas known as turtle crawls near the water's edge. A bent old fisherman was transferring turtles from his small craft to the crawls, where they would be kept alive until needed at the market. She recognized the friendly character as Hob, who sometimes sold turtles to Uncle Mathias.

Hob stared at her, unbelieving, lifted his hat to scratch his tangled white locks, then replaced it.

"Sure now . . . is that you, Miss Emerald?"

"It is," she called, holding onto her hat and smiling. "And I've some Buckington blood in me too."

"Har!" He laughed. "Ain't one to argue with a fine lady." He hitched a thumb over his shoulder toward the anchored ships. "I be meetin' with his lordship soon."

She wasn't certain what he meant and was anxious to find the magistrate.

"You be wantin' a turtle?" he called.

She shook her head and hurried on.

Other small boats, belonging to the water men, were coming in from their night's work between Port Royal and the mouth of the Rio Cobre on the northwest corner of the harbor. Because there was no fresh water in Port Royal, all water was brought from the river in large wooden casks. The pirates used the water to dilute their hellish kill-devil rum, which was the main liquid sold in the taverns. Emerald had heard that newcomers, upon drinking it, would develop a high fever that often took their lives.

Unlike the water men and fishers, there was no early start for those who had spent the night in the taverns and gambling dens. Emerald steered clear of the dazed sea rovers who, with empty pockets and bleary eyes, were frowning at a new day. She saw patrols of militiamen hauling men off to the lockup, a small jail near Fort Charles. Other prisoners were being escorted at pistol point to the magistrate for hearings before being ushered off to be deposited at Brideswell. Those judged for public punishment were herded to the town square, where hangings, water dunking, whippings, and brandings were carried out as a public spectacle.

Ahead she could see that a crowd had already gathered. Surely Jamie and Ty were not there yet. *Please, God,* she prayed, picking up her skirts and beginning to run toward the square. *Save Jamie and Ty!*

Minette had run ahead and now came rushing back, her face contorted. "Hurry," she screamed. "They have Ty!"

Emerald raced breathlessly into the courtyard, revolted by the sight of the gathered townsfolk. It seemed a bitter thing to her that the inhumane punishments were always well attended and enjoyed by the spectators, many of them gleeful that they themselves had escaped arrest during the night. Depending on the nature of the crime, the prisoners might be kept bound in the stocks the entire day and pelted by garbage and rocks.

Mr. Pitt was nowhere in the crowd, and the magistrate had already left, presumably anxious to go home to his comforts and breakfast. Evidently this morning he had been in a particularly disgruntled mood, for as she looked anxiously about for Jamie, she gasped. Two runaway slaves had already been hanged!

She stepped back, her fist going to her mouth to silence a horrified cry.

The men's owner was shouting angrily. "Foulness from the pit, that's what it was! You all saw! I begged the magistrate to let 'em go. Do you think I wanted this loss? The punishment was too strict. Now I'm out two slaves, and the magistrate goes home to fill his belly!"

"Best keep your silence, Tom, or you'll be dunked for insurrection," advised one of the crowd.

A fire was crackling near the pillory, and Minette grabbed her arm, pointing. "There's Ty. They have my brother."

Emerald was sickened by the sight and clenched her fists. "The animals."

Ty was held fast in the pillory frame that would hold his head and wrists still for the branding. The magistrate's man thrust the branding iron into the flames.

"Stop!" cried Emerald, rushing forward. "He's my slave! You turn him loose this moment. If you don't, I'll have the governor-general throw you into Brideswell yourself!"

The man stopped and looked at her, and a buzzing broke out from the crowd.

A captain of the magistrate walked up then, his sweating face perturbed. He scanned her attire and lifted his hat. "You be related to Mr. Pitt from Foxemoore, miss?"

"Mr. Pitt," she said heatedly, "is a fiend. But I am a Harwick. My father is Sir Karlton. Release this slave at once."

"I canna do that, miss. The slave's a runaway. He's been brought before the magistrate early this mornin' and condemned to brandin', and there's no stoppin' it. Now, miss," he said more kindly, "this be no place for a lady. You best have your driver take you home. There'll be a shipload of new slaves arrivin' on the fifteenth, and you can get yourself another boy."

Emerald's horror and rage mounted as he gestured to the man to proceed.

"Go home, Emerald," came Ty's cracked voice. "You tell my grandfather I'm all right. I'm takin' it like a man."

"Ty! I've tried—"

"I know. You go. Don't watch. Jamie escaped!" he said victoriously. "He's out to find a ship, and he will too. He'll send word—"

Emerald cried out as the branding man came between them. "No, please!"

She tried to break past, but the captain took hold of her arm. "Now, miss, he's right. There's nothin' you can do for him now. You go home."

Emerald caught a horrifying glimpse of the man with the branding iron thrusting it firmly onto Ty's forehead. A faint moan came from the boy, and she heard a sickening hiss.

Ty did not cry out, but Minette fell to her knees, covering her face with her hands.

Ty fainted, and, unless she could do something to stop it, he would remain in the pillory throughout the heat of the day to be tormented by flies. "Lord," she whispered, and her helplessness stung her eyes with tears. She stood there overwhelmed, the sight emblazoned on her soul.

"Calhoun!" the captain called. "See the lady and her serving girl to their carriage."

"Don't touch me," she cried, jerking free of Calhoun's hand. "Your cruelty will come back on your own heads, you'll see."

"Yes, miss, I be understandin' your feelin'. But lest you become the governor-general hisself, or maybe his daughter, you ain't goin' to be the one to stop the laws of Jamaica and Barbados."

He limped away. Emerald stood, desolate.

Minette was still kneeling, weeping, and Emerald knelt and drew her near. She remembered her decision to appeal to her cousin at Foxemoore. "We won't give up yet."

As she led Minette from the square, she saw Jonah standing on the outskirts, wiping his eyes on his sleeve.

The throng parted for her to walk through, but from the expressions on some of those standing there, mainly the riffraff of the town, she believed that if she had not been dressed as some fine lady she might have been rudely accosted. Since no one was quite certain who she was, all held back, afraid to offend some father who might prove to be related to the governor-general.

Jonah was waiting for them and placed his arm around his granddaughter. Emerald could see how deep was his misery.

And yet, before Minette he sought to conceal his despair. His words cut through Emerald. "Why, brandin' ain't everything, Minette child," he murmured.

"Oh, Grandfather, it is! It is!"

Despite himself, tears welled up in Jonah's eyes and rolled between the creases in his cheeks. "They might've hung him," he mumbled.

Emerald was touched deeply by his courage to seek for something to be thankful for, something to comfort Minette.

The thought that Jamie might elude capture kindled hope. But what if he were caught? What dreadful sentence would be heaped upon him? Mr. Pitt had threatened to have him hanged.

Somehow she must convince Lavender to intervene. Rousing her cousin to take action that might cost her something in the eyes of the family appeared an impossible feat. *Still,* Emerald told herself, *I must try.*

She left Jonah loitering on the edge of the public square, hoping to alleviate some of Ty's suffering as the heat of the day grew by bringing him water and seeking to anoint the burning wound with salve. It dawned on her as she left that he had not truly believed she would succeed. He had brought salve, knowing he would need it.

With Minette, she arrived at the waiting buggy, gratefully discovering that the pirate who had lingered the night before was gone.

How swiftly life's plans were altered, thought Emerald wearily as she drove back to Foxemoore. Ty was forever marked as a runaway, a seal of doom that would follow his running feet down any path he might flee seeking refuge.

Refuge. Where was it for a slave who was robbed of his manhood, his creation in the image of God? Ty believed in the Lord Jesus and in the promise in Scripture of being a child of God through the righteousness of Christ. But he had not been spared the shameful agony of being branded and dehumanized.

Tears welled in her eyes as she drove the buggy down the road, and she blinked hard in order to see ahead. For the rest of his days, however long they were, whether in chains or as an escaped slave, Ty's mark, like Cain's, would bring him under the suspicious eye of others. And what would the future hold? Even if light came to her own darkness, what of Ty, Minette, and Jonah? What hope did they have for relief? What of the thousands of slaves and political prisoners who were brought as mere animals to Jamaica and the other colonies on the Main?

A new sobriety settled over her soul as she contemplated what was to come.

African slaves made up a high percentage of the population in Jamaica and across the West Indies. Most of them were bought by Spain's colonists to work the treacherous silver mines in Peru. Others were sold in Havana to the tobacco plantations. The French colonists on Martinique, Guadalupe, Marie Galante, and Hispaniola were always willing to buy from the French, who came yearly from the Gold Coast, having taken their spoils in the grotesque bounty of human cargo.

If a slave was both strong and loyal, the European planter on Jamaica made him into a bodyguard, for an uprising among the slaves was always a fearsome possibility. Some slaves became unrelenting overseers to their own, who cut the cane and worked in the sugar mills producing molasses and rum. Slaves who became boss men fared better than their unfortunate fellows and had to prove their willingness to use the whip on rebellious workers.

"The fallen world is full of cruelty and injustice," she told Minette. "But it will take more than one man with a sword to change it. It will take many men. And it will take more than swords to bring justice and mercy. It will take righteous laws and changed hearts born anew by God's Spirit."

Emerald thought of Great-uncle Mathias's work. She had always believed it to be important, a well of water beside the long, hot, dusty road to those who cared enough to sit and drink. Now she believed that work could also become a great voice, declaring truth that would spiritually unshackle the prisoners.

She envisioned a rainbow hovering over his small Singing School, built of little more than palm branches and containing rattan furniture. She saw Great-uncle Mathias—a Cambridge scholar—willing to turn the cultural chants of the Africans into a message of deliverance in their own language. A deliverance that transcended iron chains.

The Singing School. Here, at least, was a candle in the darkness, she told herself. But the flame must burn brighter, must grow, must expand. *And I want to be a part of its light,* she thought.

"Oh, Father, may Your light shine through me."

9

INSIDE THE PLANTER'S GREAT HOUSE

In a lavish bedroom decorated in pink and gold in the upper story of the Great House, Emerald stood tensely in the flickering afternoon shadows that fell upon the giant four-poster bed.

There were no portraits of Baret Buckington in the room. If Lavender had one somewhere, she did not display it. With relief Emerald realized that her fears had proved unfounded. Captain Foxworth was a blackguard pirate, nothing more.

The meeting with her cousin over Ty and Jamie had not gone well, although Lavender had been more sympathetic to her dilemma than she had expected. In quiet despair, Emerald released her grip on the carved mahogany bedpost. As she turned from the bed with its silk coverlet embroidered with seed pearls, she was again reminded of the hypocrisy woven into the British society living in and ruling Port Royal.

The coverlet had been brought by adventurous buccaneers from a raid on the Spanish Main. While the nobility scorned the buccaneers and ejected them from participation in social affairs among the better families, those same families who owned plantations, or were merchants, or sat in seats of authority on the governor-general's Jamaica Parliament depended on them for island protection and the delivery of wealth and rich material goods.

It was ironical that while Lavender's featherbed was covered with the prize of some buccaneer, Emerald was disowned by the family for having been related to the French pirate Marcel Levasseur.

Wistfully she thought how pleasant life would be if she were like Lavender, whose mother, Lady Beatrice, had made grand plans for her future marriage. Beatrice, a cousin of Emerald's father, kept a secret list of suitors for her daughter in a gilded box with a key. The names, listed in order of importance, belonged to the eligible men whom she considered worthy of marriage to her peerless daughter.

Lavender was in her early twenties, certainly older than most unmarried young women of the day. Her health had postponed her marriage to the Earl of Buckington's grandson, Baret, but from what Emerald had been able to ascertain, Lavender would soon be voyaging to London where the wedding was to take place within the following year.

Lavender was sitting on a daybed of cane and carved oak when Emerald secretly arrived. She couldn't help noticing that Lavender's skin, unlike her own, was untouched by the tropical sun and was a translucent white. She often thought that Lavender was the embodiment of the British view of beauty—fair complexion, golden hair arranged in lustrous waves and coquettish curls, and graced with an outward poise that made Emerald feel awkward. Strong-willed men became pliable tools in her hands.

She admired Lavender's cool self-confidence, for her own self-image had been marred by the scandal surrounding her birth.

Lavender had no such feelings. Whatever she did, she usually did well, whether riding horses, reading poetry, or entertaining a roomful of admiring guests with her charm. She took pleasure in showing Emerald how proficient she was. She liked to parade her sophistication, and as long as Emerald accepted her superiority, their relationship went smoothly.

It hadn't taken Emerald long to understand that Lavender could become a rebel, though few others in the family had seen that side of her. With Emerald, Lavender held nothing back.

Emerald, Lavender told her, was "plain," and Emerald believed her. She would naturally be the expert on such matters. Lavender often adorned her own flaxen hair with pearls, for her hair was magnificent and the adornments called attention to it. "You should try harder with yours," she often lectured. "It's so common to wear it in a coiled braid, and actually the color is rather nice."

A compliment coming from Lavender always bolstered Emerald's poise. But she continued to wear her hair in a braid only because she didn't want Lavender to completely rule her, which she desired to do with those she considered her own.

Somehow Lavender's self-assurance saw her through her difficulties with her health. "I know what I want in life, and I'm going to have it," she had told Emerald.

Emerald knew better than anyone else in the family what Lavender wanted: Baret Buckington. And from what she had heard about the earl's grandson, the feeling was mutual. Lavender's family, however, was beginning to have second thoughts. The viscount had turned adventurous, it was said, rebellious to the earl and politically embarrassing.

As Emerald introduced her concerns about Jamie and Ty, Lavender frowned. "I can understand your worry about Ty since you're scandalously related to him. But if I were you, I would want to forget that! As for that indentured servant—what did you say his name was? Jamie?—there're men out searching for him now. They're bound to catch him. And if the family discovers you want him to escape, you'll have much to explain."

Emerald had not told Lavender of her plans to marry Jamie, knowing how she would look down on the idea. Instead she only pleaded for her intervention to her great-aunt to withhold punishment should Jamie be caught.

"The overseer insists that Jamie Bradford is dangerous to Foxemoore. You know how much Great-aunt Sophie relies on Mr. Pitt," Lavender said.

"A mistake. He's an evil man, can't you see?"

"Of course I see, but convincing her is a horrendous task. You know how opinionated she is. And she's still mad at your father, blaming him for the trouble. Said he was too lenient with the slaves. 'Give an inch, and they take a mile,' she says."

"That's not true of my father. The family was wrong to remove him from managing Foxemoore." Emerald still smarted over Lavender's indifference to her pain. "If he were still in charge, this wouldn't have happened."

Lavender shrugged. "Maybe. I've no strong opinion about Sir Karlton," she said casually. "But honestly, Emerald, there's little I can do about the matter of the indentured servant. Once I marry the viscount, perhaps things will change. I'll be in authority then, since Baret's share of Foxemoore is nearly as large as Cousin Geneva's. But I've my hands full already convincing my mother that Baret is the right man for me. She's considering Sir Jasper. Imagine! As if I'd marry *that* fop!"

Emerald was not interested in her marriage trials at the moment and pled impatiently, "But she'll listen to you. Great-aunt is convinced you can do no wrong."

Lavender's clear laughter was part of her outward charm. "Thank goodness she does. What will I do if she doesn't leave me her portion of the Harwick fortune?"

There was no doubt in Emerald's mind but that Sophie would leave Lavender a hefty portion of the Harwick wealth in Jamaica.

"Emerald, I'll be truthful with you. If I involve myself now in something as unpopular with the family as slave reform, it will put me in a most uncomfortable position. I can't afford to disturb matters as they are, not with Felix arriving to marry Geneva. There are already nasty political problems in the family over Baret."

Lord Felix was the son of the earl by his second marriage to one of the Harwick women. As such, Felix was only distantly related to Geneva. There was controversy over the marriage, for Geneva, a woman in her early forties, had never married, and her portion of Foxemoore was double that of either her younger sister, Beatrice, or her cousin Karlton.

"They'll find Jamie Bradford," said Lavender. "They always do find the prisoners who try to escape. And if I help you by coming to his defense, I'll confront the displeasure of Felix. He'll be here tomorrow."

Emerald had heard much about Felix from her father, and little of what he had said was good.

"But you can go to Great-aunt Sophie," argued Emerald. "And if they do find Jamie, ask for leniency. He only has six months until his indentured service is fulfilled. It's unjust to arrest him now."

But Lavender showed no interest in being talked into anything and sipped her glass of limeade. "Mr. Pitt's convinced her that this Jamie fellow was involved in stirring up a rebellion among the slaves. You know the concerns about the possibility of an uprising. The planters don't talk about such matters, but it remains their worst fear."

The planters' as well as the family's inability to act fairly in this matter provoked Emerald's temper. "How absurd! Did Mr. Pitt tell Lady Sophie they were planning a rebellion?"

"He advised her that Jamie Bradford must be caught and . . . hanged."

Emerald paled. The beast! No words were terrible enough for what she thought of Pitt.

"Jamie did nothing more than anoint the bloody back of a slave who was whipped unmercifully. For that deed of kindness should he be hanged?"

Lavender grimaced, showing her boredom, for she often appeared impatient when Emerald reminded her of the horrors of slavery. "I don't want to hear about such cruelties. Truly, Emerald, there's little I can do. As for hanging, I'm told that any indentured servant can be hanged if deemed necessary for the safety of the plantations. And it's true that the slave was a runaway. That's against the law."

"It's an unjust law, and the more I see what happens, the more I realize just how wicked slavery is. Men made the laws of Jamaica, men who care for little except making money from their plantations. Not even a runaway animal deserves to be whipped—much less a man!"

"They don't consider slaves to have the rights of men," said Lavender wearily, picking up her parrot fan and swishing it.

Emerald walked toward her. "They wouldn't, of course. If there were laws acknowledging them to be men, slavery would soon be outlawed, and the sugar plantations would have to hire workers. That's why the Jamaican Council has outlawed teaching the slaves Christianity. If we worship God with them, we surely cannot keep them as slaves. But whether the law says they are men or not doesn't matter. God says they are made in His image!"

Lavender tossed aside her fan and stood. "Vapors! I didn't make the law, did I? Must you burden me with evils I'm not guilty of?" She paced. "I shall be glad to leave Port Royal for Buckington House. There's been nothing but tension over the workers since Uncle Mathias arrived and began that Singing School."

"Be fair. It isn't so. Uncle Mathias has nothing to do with the tension among the workers. It's Mr. Pitt. The ill-treatment of the slaves has grown worse since my father was removed as manager."

Before Lavender could reply, they were interrupted by a sound coming through the windows that faced the sugar cane fields.

A breeze filtered through the cane shade, bringing with it the melancholy fragrance of the rich warm earth and the Caribbean Sea. In the distant fields the wind set the miles of cane rustling, and the sound came to Emerald's ears like a chorus of the restless sea.

Then somewhere on the plantation the African slaves began to chant. She tensed. If the family heard, they would send Mr. Pitt to stop them. It was also against Jamaican law for slaves to meet together to sing. The big planters feared that would lead to a unity of purpose resulting in a rebellion.

The distant chanting arrested her concentration as surely as though hands had taken hold of her shoulders and given her a shake, bidding her to pay heed. The singing was not engaged in for happy purposes. Wearied souls moaned their sorrows in chants, their longings speaking in universal language within the echo of African drums, their hopelessness in the shaking of rattles. The haunting African music moved through her soul like the trade wind coming through the veranda. Again she felt a restless discontent that she could not fully understand, a beckoning that urged her forward down a long straight road to—where?

She turned to gaze into the afternoon shadows. The rhythm of the chant, the drums, the rattles, the cry of the soul went on to fill the velvet afternoon and wrap about her like a mantle, as the folk song from West Africa filled her ears.

> "The lightning and the flashing,
> The lightning and the flashing
> The lightning and the flashing,
> Who set this poor man free?

> "We run to the mountain,
> We run to the mountain,
> We run to the mountain,
> But the soldier he follow me.

> "The lightning and the flashing,
> The lightning and the flashing,
> The lightning and the flashing,
> There be no hope for me."

Emerald felt her skin prickle. The rattle of drums intruded into the satin-adorned bedroom, bringing a tension of its own.

As they stood listening, Lavender's own eyes showed her unease, and her gaze clung to Emerald's. Then from one of the upstairs chambers an insistent bell clamored.

Emerald looked toward the bedroom door. From downstairs hurrying feet mounted the stairway in answer to the summons.

But before the house servant reached the upper hall, a door opened above, and Lavender's mother, Lady Beatrice, demanded, "Henry! Tell Mr. Pitt to stop that dreadful noise! They'll soon go on a rampage!"

"The overseer done took a horse already, Miss Beatrice."

"Must the overseer be told every night to silence them?"

"It's because Sir Karlton done used to let them sing—"

"I don't care what my cousin once allowed. He is no longer in charge of Foxemoore. The noise is dreadful and speaks of trouble. Sounds like devil worship. Voodoo, they call it."

"Yes, madam."

Lady Beatrice's door shut firmly, and the serving man Henry made his way back down the stairs.

Emerald stood staring toward the open veranda, where she could see the rising trade wind rustle the jasmine vine and the late afternoon sky flame the horizon. As if coming out of a trance, she tried to recall what had concerned her before the singing began.

Emerald turned and faced Lavender. It was plain to see that her cousin was not going to use her favored position with Great-aunt Sophie to intervene. Emerald realized she had been foolish to think she would. Once again her expectations had come crashing down. Lavender had her own plans, and no one would be allowed to do anything, or expect anything from her, that might keep them from coming to fruition.

Lavender appeared to read her thoughts. She walked up, troubled, and took Emerald's arm. For a moment they looked at each other, then Emerald pulled away and walked to the door.

"I must get home. It's getting late," she murmured.

"Do be careful. Don't let Mr. Pitt see you on his way back from the slave huts."

"If I do, I shall tell him what I think of him."

Lavender looked at her ruefully. "If I were in your position, I would be more cautious about confronting authority."

Her suggestion was meant as a slight affront, but Emerald behaved as though she hadn't noticed. "I know exactly what I would do if I were blessed to be in your favored position," she told Lavender. "First, I'd work to get Mr. Pitt dismissed. Then I'd convince the family to end slavery."

"You'd never accomplish such a thing."

"Then I'd at least make certain their situation was bettered. And I wouldn't give up easily."

Lavender studied her briefly. "So there lies the difference between us, dear. I wish for nothing more than to leave Jamaica and return to England. I have one purpose—to marry Baret and sup with the king." She opened the door and looked into the hall to make certain it was empty.

"Run now," said Lavender, "before the family catches you here. They won't like it, you know. And Emerald—" her voice changed "—where did you get such a grand dress? Perhaps I should wear it to the ball."

Emerald leaned toward her. "You're impossible, Lavender. Your wardrobe is overflowing with French ball gowns, and yet you must wear *my* one pretty dress? No. What do you think of that?"

Lavender turned pink, but she managed a smile. "I think you are selfish," she said and shut her door softly.

Emerald tiptoed down the hall, her steps making no sound on the highly polished wood floor with its bright rag rugs. She neared Lady Geneva's room and was about to sneak past. But the doorway stood partway open, and she heard voices arguing.

Oh, no, now what?

She paused, precariously, glancing back toward Lavender's room. Perhaps she would need to somehow shinny down the vine from her veranda.

Great-aunt Sophie's voice sounded clearly in the hall. "Karlton is home. He arrived last night."

Father was home! Oh, joy! But the angry tone of Geneva's voice and the alarm in Great-aunt Sophie's halted her thoughts. Something was dreadfully wrong.

"If you'll not pay heed to me, Geneva, I shall need to go to him with this letter."

"It's *my* marriage. Karlton has nothing to do with it. Whether he approves of Felix or not won't alter our plans for the wedding."

Emerald knew how much Foxemoore meant to Lady Geneva. She was a bright woman, who had expended her energies into making Foxemoore into one of the largest sugar-producing plantations on Jamaica or Barbados. At least two rich planters had wanted to marry her, but Geneva was wed to Foxemoore and determined to make the Harwick name as respected as the Buckington nobility in England.

"If I ever marry," she was reported to have told the family, "it will be to a man whose position strengthens Foxemoore."

Emerald had heard that Geneva's marriage to Felix would give them control of Foxemoore. And if Felix inherited the earldom, Geneva would become a countess.

Great-aunt Sophie's voice shook. "You are making a mistake ignoring this letter. There is Jette to think of."

"And I wish to adopt Jette. Felix agrees."

"You're forgetting what Baret might think. After all, Jette is his half brother. They had the same father."

"And their father is dead."

"Jette will never take to Felix. You can't destroy childish memories of his father."

"The child dreams too much."

"Let him dream if he wishes. It is the way of small boys. His father was a great seaman."

"Seaman!" There was a tinge of bitterness in her voice. "A buccaneer! I told him not to go to sea that last time. I begged—"

Geneva's voice stopped abruptly, and when she spoke again the old calm that Emerald remembered was back. The strength of will sounded in her dignified voice. "Come, Sophie, must we speak of all this on the eve of Felix's arrival? He's an important man in London, a counselor of His Majesty. He's quite confident once we've married and brought Jette to Buckington House that the earl will agree we should adopt him as our own."

"No one can replace the image the child has of his real father. It's a mistake to try. So you think me foolish and meddling, do you?"

"Never mind Jette for now. It is Felix we are discussing. That letter!" came the scornful tone. "It's from an old busybody in London. It's absolute nonsense."

"Doubtless you wish to think so. Lady Thelma is a decent woman. So do you intend to ignore it?"

"Can I do anything else? It's quite absurd. It's purely Shakespearean."

"Shakespeare knew the vices of human nature quite well. I suspect he would look into Felix's heart as though it were transparent. You ought to read him more often."

Geneva gave a taut laugh. "I suppose you recommend *Macbeth* in this instance?"

"It will do quite well where Felix is concerned."

"Poor Felix. He doesn't know what he's coming up against in this family. He's not only inheriting an eight-year-old child who has already decided to dislike him but now a great-aunt who chooses to believe foolish gossip from one of London's worst dowagers."

"I am certain Felix feels quite a match for the Harwicks as well as the gossip in London. His confidence is quite offensive."

"Do shut the door, for goodness' sake! In a moment you'll arouse everyone."

"Is this the gratitude I receive in my senior years? And after I've invested my entire life in you, giving up my own plans for remarriage and a life of my own?"

"Sophie, that's unfair. You know I adore you, only—"

"If anything happens to you in London—"

Geneva's laugh cut in. "Some people will believe anything if it's whispered. That includes you, dear, if you believe the hysteria of a nasty letter. Burn it, tear it up—do anything with it you like, but don't come to me on the eve of my wedding with gossip. I won't listen. It's gone too far."

"To back out? Far better to admit you were wrong than ruin little Jette's life. And your own. You're still young, Geneva. And his first wife did die, you know."

"Of course she died. Felix said she was ill for many years. We can be pleased the poor woman is now removed from affliction. He said she suffered so."

"Did she now? The letter says she died quite suddenly. And without a physician."

Geneva gave a laugh. "You always imagine the worst. Just like Beatrice, always suggesting a slave uprising on Foxemoore. Sophie, I fear your imagination has gone too far this time. Do you actually expect me to believe Felix would deliberately refuse to call a physician?"

"Tsk! Did I say that?"

"You hinted—"

"I didn't hint. I said he may have deliberately eliminated his wife in order to marry you."

A gasp came from Geneva, followed by a moment of silence.

Outside in the hall, Emerald's fist went to her mouth.

"I've never heard anything so wild and ridiculous. Give me that letter, Sophie. I shall burn it myself."

"No—"

There followed a small thud, as though a chair had tipped over in someone's haste to stand.

"There!" came Geneva's breathless voice a moment later. "It's reduced to ashes. Have you mentioned this to anyone else?"

"No," came Great-aunt's weak voice.

"This is my concern. I'll hear no more of this nonsense."

"I think you're making a dreadful mistake. Felix doesn't love you."

There was a startled gasp, then something fell and shattered.

Geneva's voice shook. "That will be quite enough. You may go now."

"I was already leaving," came the crisp reply.

Emerald quickly stepped back, but there was no place to hide. She cast a glance over her shoulder, too late.

"Emerald!"

Emerald turned swiftly and faced her father's cousin, standing in the chamber doorway. She desperately hoped that her expression was hid in the shadowy hall.

Unlike that of her golden-haired sister, Beatrice, Geneva's hair was a light auburn. Her skin was so pale that tiny veins showed in her temples. It was whispered that as a young woman she had lost the one man in London she had loved and that she had never loved again until meeting Felix. By the time Geneva had returned to Foxemoore she had been betrothed.

Emerald had always considered Geneva to be a more gracious woman than Aunt Beatrice, but perhaps that was only because Geneva treated her with a trifle more kindness.

Emerald felt the pale blue eyes rivet upon her as though trying to detect whether or not she had overheard. Her heart pounded. She must not know.

"I . . . um . . . was just leaving Miss Lavender's room," she said, her voice oddly calm.

Geneva made no reply and watched her in the shadows.

Emerald added, "I . . . also wished to inquire about Jette."

Although Emerald looked upon Jette as a nephew, he was far removed from her bloodline. She got on well with him and knew that he was not looking forward to the marriage. Geneva had raised Jette from the time he was three years old, and brought him to Foxemoore soon after the death of his father, Royce Buckington. The child's mother was unknown.

Jette had told Emerald that he did not want to journey with Geneva and Felix to London. Geneva knew this as well, and her expression showed tension over the matter of Jette's response to Felix.

"As a matter of fact, Emerald, I'm pleased you're here. Jette has learned your father is home from sea and wishes to spend the night at the Manor. I've granted him permission, hoping to appease him. You know how upset he is about the wedding on Saturday."

Emerald felt embarrassed. "Yes, he is rather nervous about getting a new father."

"Make certain Minette brings him back to the house early in the morning. He'll breakfast here and then remain with his new governess until Lord Felix arrives."

"Yes, I'll see to it at once."

Geneva turned to walk to her room, then paused. She looked back at Emerald with a softer expression. "You look lovely in your new dress. Did Karlton bring it to you from his voyage?"

Emerald felt her face warm. What could she say? "It's not mine. It's borrowed. It—it belongs to a friend of my father."

"I see. It does wonders for you. I never realized how pretty you are."

Emerald stared at her, taken aback. It was painful to discover that a mere casual compliment coming from Lady Geneva could please her so much. Realizing she hungered so deeply made her vulnerable.

Geneva too seemed a little uneasy and hesitant. "You may go now, Emerald."

"Yes . . . yes, of course. Good night."

"Good night," came the cursory reply.

Emerald walked past her, careful not to cast a curious glance into the bedroom. Great-aunt Sophie had chosen not to let her presence be known.

Then they didn't suspect I overheard, she thought.

"And Emerald—" interrupted Geneva.

She turned, managing a studied calm. "Yes?"

"Mr. Pitt has informed me that we have some escaped convicts. A Jamie Bradford, for one. He said you knew him well. Is this true?"

Emerald's heart thundered as she wondered how she could answer. "Jamie is a friend of Ty," she stated. "I know him well, yes. He's no convict though and would never plot with Ty to create an uprising among the slaves. Mr. Pitt is a cruel man, and I would go so far as to say he's lying about him."

"Mr. Pitt is a good overseer. He's doing his duty to the family in hunting down the runaways."

It was on the tip of Emerald's tongue to protest, but she said nothing and felt the perspiration break out on her forehead.

"If Jamie Bradford was a friend of yours, I am sorry, but he's a wanted man," said Geneva. "If he contacts you, it's your duty and obligation to send word at once. Ty will be coming back tomorrow from Brideswell with Jonah."

"He was branded," came Emerald's tight voice, and her eyes met Geneva's evenly.

Geneva let out a breath, as though the entire incident, as well as Emerald's relation to it, was a trial.

"An unfortunate situation. Mr. Pitt said he ran away and, when located, put up a struggle. He tried to kill our overseer and was taken to Brideswell with Bradford. If the magistrate deemed a branding necessary, then there is little I can say about it."

"It was not necessary, Lady Geneva," Emerald found her shaking voice saying boldly. "It was inhumane. And I doubt that Ty tried to kill Mr. Pitt—I'm quite sure it was the other way around."

A sharp voice interrupted from the doorway of Geneva's bedchamber.

"That will be quite enough, Emerald. You may go now. Karlton is waiting for you at the Manor. He came home last night."

The voice belonged to Lady Sophie, her father's aunt. She was an elegant woman in her seventies with immaculate white hair and bristling pale eyebrows. Dressed in dark satin with pristine white lace at the throat and wrists, she overwhelmed Emerald. She had never spoken more than a dozen sentences to Emerald at one time in her entire sixteen years.

For a moment Emerald had the notion that she should curtsy, as though to a countess. She held back the lump in her throat. Something within her was deeply hurt, and she believed that the wound would never heal.

Keeping her head high, she turned and walked down the hallway. She reached the grand staircase, polished and gleaming, and came to the wide hall below and the large mahogany front door. The serving man Henry appeared but, seeing she was not a family member, went on about his business instead of opening the door.

Emerald planned to depart by way of the servants' entry at the back. She passed through the cook room on the way.

Grand preparations for the wedding were already under way. An outdoor supper was to be held on the front lawn. She saw a dozen fowl plucked and ready for the smoking pit, and sweet cakes and breads were baking in the stone ovens, sending off a mixture of aromatic smells. But she had no appetite and went out the door to be greeted by the late afternoon wind.

I must get home to Father, she told herself.

She quickened her steps and hurried across the backyard and around the side of the large house to where Minette waited with the buggy.

Her brooding amber eyes fixed on Emerald. "Is Lavender going to help us?"

"No," said Emerald dully, her weariness showing.

Minette scowled and glanced over her shoulder at the big white house.

Emerald climbed onto the buggy seat. "We'll take the main road home even if it's longer."

"It's going to rain," said Minette, looking up at the gray sky.

"I don't care. Anything to avoid Mr. Pitt coming from the slave huts." She picked up the reins.

"Aye, I saw him riding that way," said Minette coldly. "To stop the singing, no doubt." She looked at Emerald with flashing eyes. "He's dared to tell Mathias the Singing School should be shut down. Said that Lord Felix would do it when he came."

"Mathias will never close the school," said Emerald, staring ahead and giving the reins a flip. The horse trotted down the road as the dried fronds on the tall palms rustled in the wind.

Minette frowned but said nothing and drew her worn cane hat lower over her head. Her long hair fluttered like ripened wheat.

Emerald too was frowning. She knew an uneasy moment. What would her father say when she returned to Foxemoore after being away? She would need to do some explaining for spending the night at the lookout house. He would not be pleased over her making a spectacle of herself trying to stop the public condemnation of Ty. Worse yet, he would hold no sympathy for her wish to marry Jamie. But now that Lavender had failed her, she must try to convince her father to intervene in his plight.

10

STRANGER ON THE ROAD

The dirt road was hedged with palm trees, and pools of shade dotted the path of Emerald's buggy. Last night's rain had only added to today's sultriness, and the breezes rattling the palm branches did little to cool her. The air reeked of wet earth and tropical flowering vines. Nettlesome insects were thick, and she was grateful for the thin veil on her wide-brimmed hat that helped protect her face.

Her troubled thoughts left her own plight to mull again over the conversation she had overheard between her great-aunt and Geneva.

Impossible. Geneva is right—it can't be true about Lord Felix, she thought. *After all, Sophie was a brilliant woman in her younger years, but she must be nearing her seventy-fifth birthday. Perhaps she's begun to imagine things.*

But had she imagined the letter from London? Then again, whoever this woman was who had sent it, she too could be aged and, as Geneva insisted, a "gossip." And yet . . .

Emerald remembered that her father had disapproved of his cousin Felix. The man was overbearing and managed to manipulate others by pretending a false interest in family concerns.

What if it were true? What if Felix had forced the matter of his ailing wife in order to marry Geneva?

Like a harbinger of ill to come, sullen clouds threatening a sudden tropical storm were blowing in over the sea, black racing clouds that erased the sun and darkened the late afternoon sky.

She gave a light flick of her whip, and the horse quickened its trot down the road. The tall cane rippled in the wind like green waves.

A drop of rain wet her hand.

She had heard that Lady Geneva could be stubborn. If a decision was deemed to be the right one, there was little room for compromise. Emerald had always secretly admired Geneva's strength, even when she would not accept Emerald into the family. And she had never admired her more than when she had lost the man she loved. Geneva had gone on with life, head unbowed by discouragement. And yet, although her spirit of determination could be a strength, if pursued with a wrong motive it could also become a flaw.

"Just why would Geneva marry Felix?" she murmured thoughtfully to Minette at her side.

Minette appeared in no pleasant mood. She gave her a dry look. "Because she's misguided enough to love him. I can't say I blame her, though. I'd marry too, if a man could make me respectable."

Emerald gave her a look that rebuked her, but Minette met her gaze evenly. "I'm going to marry a Frenchman. You'll see. No slaves for me, even if my mother was African. And I'm going to have me a whole trunkful of silks and lace frocks, and a dozen pert hats, and silk stockings—"

"Will you hush, Minette? We've more to worry about now. I overheard something dreadful back at the house."

"It's no great wonder to me. The house is full of mean folk."

Shall I tell her? wondered Emerald and scanned her face. She decided against it. Minette was in no mood to hear. She would need to keep the dreadful words she had overheard to herself until she knew what to do about them.

Her father was home. Surely she could tell him.

Emerald believed that Geneva would go through with the wedding, despite Great-aunt Sophie's warning. And Lord Felix sounded like the kind of man who knew exactly what he wanted.

Blinking against the raindrops, she glanced up at the rolling clouds, then lowered her veil again. "If it rains, it will ruin the wedding supper on the lawn."

For a moment she was inclined to earnestly pray that a hurricane would come and sweep everything away—including Geneva's marriage.

Emerald drove the carriage past the breadfruit trees planted years earlier by the Spaniards to feed their slaves. Parrots squawked peacefully in the branches.

Suddenly, pounding hoofbeats from behind cut through the lazy somnolence like bold intruders determined to change events. Startled, her thoughts were diverted as the horses thundered closer.

Minette turned to look over her shoulder. "Vapors, they're about to run us over!"

Swiftly Emerald reined her horse toward the side of the road, coming to a slow trot into some low creeping brush under the palms. She stopped, her dark lashes narrowing as she stared behind her. No planters would be riding from that direction.

She found herself frowning. Change indeed rode the wind, and she was not certain she wished it so. A moment later, two men came into view.

They saw her buggy by the side of the road and brought their muscled horses to a nervous, prancing halt. One of the men rode up beside her as she sat clutching the reins.

"Is your buggy stuck, madam?"

Emerald was vaguely aware that because of her elaborate fashion he mistook her for some wealthy planter's daughter. She straightened her hat and made no immediate reply, pleased over the deferential treatment.

The man was perhaps in his late twenties. He had fair shoulder-length hair, drawn back under a flat cap that was stylishly tilted to the left. His features were somber, decidedly rugged in character, and his manner and way of dress gave her the impression that he might be some sort of guard. She caught a glimpse of light mesh under his black velvet tunic. He showed no emotion as he looked at her with gray eyes as cool as melting snow.

Another pirate, she thought.

He looked at Minette on the seat beside Emerald and scrutinized her.

Emerald said loftily, "I beg pardon, sir, but you are traveling recklessly. Why, you might have run me down—and would have, had I not been quick to turn my buggy."

He looked back to Emerald. Her accusation was met with a straight face and a lifted golden brow. Slowly he turned in the saddle and spoke to the second man, who had ridden up.

"My Lord Viscount, you do stand rebuked by the young lady."

An exchanged glance between them suggested that they shared something amusing.

Her thoughts took a hard tumble. *Viscount!* She tensed, her fingers tightening on her reins.

Viscount? The title repeated itself ominously in her mind. Confusion set in. Then, her alarmed gaze darted to the second man, who sat astride a fine-blooded horse, watching her with interest.

Her breath stopped. For a horrified moment she couldn't move. His dark eyes glinted with a touch of humor, and he wore a faintly sardonic smile—one that had become all too familiar since last night.

It can't be, but it is, she thought, staring at him. The "viscount" was Captain Foxworth, the roguish captain of the *Regale.*

Her worst fears had come true. Zeddie must have talked, and now he had come to Foxemoore to find her!

For a long moment he looked at her, then his gaze casually studied her gown. She sat motionless. *Does he recognize me?*

"Sir Erik Farrow is quick to remind me of my faults," the viscount told her smoothly. "I plead your pardon, Miss . . ."

He was inquiring for her name. She remained mute. *Oh, scads of horror . . . what can I say?*

When she said nothing, he allowed her silence to pass politely, as though he hadn't noticed.

"Henceforth, I shall ride at a more leisurely gait." And in a gesture smoothly perfected and befitting a position of high nobility, he removed his wide hat with its cocky plume and bowed his dark head. "Your servant, madam!"

She sat nervously waiting for his courtly manner to alter into one of malicious recognition.

"Madam, I'm in a hurry," he said, replacing his hat under the trickle of raindrops and giving her a disarming smile.

"It's been a time since I was here last—not since I was a small boy. Foxemoore sugar estate—would you know how far it is?"

Her confusion grew as he simply looked at her with a faint smile. Suddenly it dawned on her. *Of course, he doesn't recognize me dressed like this.* Her hand reached to touch the veil that descended from her hat and concealed her face, making certain it remained in place. She swallowed with relief, thinking that she must keep her tone of voice as elegant as her costume. Would he wonder why she didn't have a serving man for a driver?

But before she could speak, Minette did. "Oh, it's not far, monsieur." And she pointed ahead. "We're on our way there now. Emerald and I can show you—*ouch!*—you pinched me—" Minette stopped abruptly, as if she caught her mistake. Her amber eyes gleamed, and she turned her head away, toying with the fringe on the buggy.

Minette just gave my name away. Did he recognize it? She glanced cautiously at the viscount and saw that he was studying her with subdued curiosity. *Then he didn't notice,* she thought.

"Foxemoore," he inquired again. "How far?"

I must stay calm. He doesn't know anything yet. She lifted a hand toward the cane fields on her left. "All this is Foxemoore, m'lord. I . . . um . . . assume you've come to see Lady Lavender Buckington?" she inquired warily.

He watched her from beneath his hat. "I seek Sir Karlton Harwick. Do you know him?"

He had avoided answering her directly about Lavender, she saw, and was watching her response to the name of Karlton.

"Well . . . actually, yes."

She noticed him take in the worn buggy, and that brought a moment of discomfort. *He must think I'm a friend of Lavender's who's come to call on her.* How long could she keep up this masquerade? Oh, if only Jamie Bradford would suddenly come riding up and whisk her away to a waiting ship!

"I am Baret Buckington," he said. "I've come to have audience with Sir Karlton. I've been told he waits for me in a private bungalow somewhere near here."

The news added to her confusion. How could he have received a message from her father since last night aboard the *Regale?* Could it be her good fortune that he had come for a reason other than to locate the wench who had ransacked his cabin?

Safe behind her veil she retained her dignity, telling herself that she might manage to avoid him at the house. Once he was gone, if he did say anything to her father about last night, she could explain the situation about Mr. Pitt's demands and perhaps win his understanding.

"I . . . um . . . shall bring you to the Manor," she said.

"I am obliged." He bridled his horse to follow her.

Without another word Emerald flipped the reins and set forth at a fast clip, leaving him to keep pace. He stayed just behind her carriage.

"Vapors," breathed Minette. "What are you going to do? He's bound to recognize you from the ship."

"I don't know . . . oh, this is the worst possible thing to happen now!"

"Did you notice the gentleman with him?" Minette whispered. "Did you ever see anyone more handsome?"

Emerald frowned. "What could the viscount possibly want with my father?"

"Maybe he's come about the debts Uncle Karlton owes to the family."

What if Minette were right? Had the dread hour of reckoning come? Only last year he'd returned from a voyage on the Main where he had lost a ship and most of his crew in a skirmish with the *guarda-costa* of the Spanish *Asientos.* The loss of his precious goods and ship had not only spiraled his indebtedness to the family but also to secret merchants who had quietly invested in the voyage. Her father, never a man to be content for long on land, was a privateer at heart, having been in command of the family merchant vessels, but his losses at sea had changed all that, resulting in a melancholy mood.

The wind blowing against her, although bringing light rain, felt refreshing, and the horse's swift trot helped relieve her tension. But then another possibility came to the forefront of her thoughts.

What if the arrival of Lord Felix complicated the growing problem of the snarling debt-hounds that threatened her father's claim to his portion of the sugar estate?

Far worse, what if Baret Buckington had come to join ranks with his Uncle Felix against her father?

The vast estate of Foxemoore had not changed in the years since Emerald had been brought here from Tortuga. The boundary walls of the Great House traversed for miles along the outer road, fringed with tall palms. Just how her father had come to control his share in the sugar estate was another matter of gossip.

The old earl—Great-grandfather Esmond Stuart Buckington—had gone out of his way on his deathbed to alter his will and leave a double portion of the sugar not to grandsons Royce and Felix but to Karlton Harwick, whom the earl had allegedly knighted before his death.

However, members of the family denied this. Any change in the will of Esmond had been manipulated by the unethical practice of Cousin Karlton's barrister, they said.

Her father denied any wrongdoing. "Any disagreement between the family and me is on account of Felix. He's a Spanish sympathizer, with aims to sell religious prisoners into the silver mines of Peru," he had said angrily. "Felix knows little of plantation management—and even less about decent treatment of slaves. Had I proof, I'd accuse the man of even more," he had told her. "I question his sorrow over his half brother's death."

Emerald had wondered why her father would say such a thing until she remembered that Felix was second in line to the inheritance.

"It is Royce's son, Baret, who is primary heir," her father had said gravely. "The young viscount had best be cautious of his uncle."

Thinking all this as she drove the buggy, Emerald remembered Geneva's marriage to Felix. Through Geneva, Felix would control a greater share of Foxemoore, at least until Baret married Lavender and combined their portions.

Emerald frowned. Was it Baret or Geneva who stood the greater risk by this marriage?

She felt a tiny shiver and tried to dismiss it. She had no proof for such dark suspicions—only the argument she had overheard between her great-aunt and Cousin Geneva at the house.

And yet the foreboding remained.

She found her mind straying into paths of darkness overgrown with thorns and thicket. There was also the eight-year-old child Jette Buckington—Baret's half brother. Jette would become the stepson of Felix if the adoption was permitted.

Speckled sunlight filtered now through the line of trees and dotted the road. Thinking of the strong men and women who stood to gain materially by the elimination of others in the sugar dynasty brought to mind her own situation. Aside from her father, no one on either side of the family would seriously consider any right she might have at Foxemoore. She was only the offspring of a pirate's daughter.

"If I do not legally own a large share of the sugar production, then why does Felix not take it to the court, I ask?" her father had once remarked. "He'll not take the matter to law because the man knows I hold a legal document. And not simply a lease either, but I hold it free—and will! Forever! It is signed by the deceased Earl Esmond Buckington himself."

A legal document. Did he truly possess one, or was the mysterious parchment that he kept locked in a box in his chamber merely a spurious invention?

One morning he had brought her to his chamber to unlock the treasure box and show the deed to her. Emerald had been twelve then, too young to understand the writing, yet the seal had impressed her with the sincerity of her father's claim. A good portion of the cane fields, as well as the Manor itself, belonged to her father and therefore to Emerald. For years she had comforted herself with the thought that regardless of family rejection, she would always have security in the Jamaica estate. But now, because of the debts owed by her father and Felix's marriage to Geneva, she no longer believed her father's assurances true.

At least I have Jamie, she thought.

Emerald turned from the main road to ride up the carriageway lined with fringed palms shaking in the wind. Ahead, the planter's Great House came into view.

The English planters on the colonial Sugar Islands of Jamaica, Barbados, and Antigua sought to build their Great Houses on knolls facing windward. Emerald now had a clear view of the white-pillared house with its red-tile roof and of Port Royal Bay. Because of the coral reefs, the water sometimes appeared different shades of blue, green, amber, and even red, while on her left lay a sweeping view of green cane fields as far as her eye could see. She slowed the carriage midway between the road and the Great House and turned down the smaller wagon road between the rustling cane. The Manor loomed some distance ahead.

The square white house was tall and narrow with flowering ramblers crawling up toward Emerald's window in a profusion of red roses. How many nights had she sat alone at that window, arms on its sill, dreaming of her father returning from one of his ventures at sea. He would come with treasures enough to sweep her away on his horse and ride her up to the front porch of the Great House, where the family would welcome her.

The dream, of course, had long ago withered in the harsh light of reality.

The truth was, her father's emotional strength was on the decline. Depressed over the ship he had lost to the guns of the Spanish galleon, he spoke of earlier days when as a privateer he had fought on the Main with a navy made up of buccaneers.

More often than not, her father lapsed into moods of morbid silence. He would rise early in the morning to saddle a horse and spend the day at the wharves of Port Royal among the privateers or brooding inside his lookout house on the cay.

She shaded her eyes and looked toward the fields. What if he were out riding now? He might not be home until dark! How could she possibly avoid disclosing who she was to the viscount if he were to wait at the Manor until her father returned?

In front of the porch steps, Emerald whispered to Minette, "Say nothing to the workers of what happened to Ty. Leave the matter for Jonah to explain. Anger runs deep. Instead, share the good news that Jamie escaped."

Minette nodded and climbed down, glancing cautiously toward the men. She leaned toward Emerald and whispered, "I'll see if anyone's heard from Jamie and bring you word later."

Emerald watched her hurry toward the boiling house, then climbed down from the buggy herself, refusing to look in the viscount's direction. She hurried up the steps to the door.

Drummond, the English steward who had accompanied her father during his privateering voyages, met her.

"We've a guest," she told him in a low voice, and her eyes warned her father's faithful steward that while the guest was important, his arrival might be troubling. "Viscount Baret Buckington."

Drummond's horselike brows quivered. "A merry development! Here, miss? *Now?* 'Tis the worst of luck. The master's in a dank mood. He's done nothing since we arrived last night but vow he'll take to sea again to search for and destroy that Spanish man-of-war."

"He's not threatening *that* again?" she whispered.

"He's been up in his chamber all afternoon. He's packing a trunk, no less. Nothing I could say would quiet him this time."

Emerald groaned. "But he just came home!"

"More's the pity, Miss Emerald."

Usually, between herself and Drummond, they could quiet her father for a time, but like some cankerous wound that would not heal, thoughts of revenge returned to plague his tormented mind.

"Where is he now?" she whispered anxiously.

"Still in his chamber, pacing the floor like a caged beast, I dare say! I should rather face a real lion than your father this day, but I shall call him if you wish."

Emerald twisted the handle of her whip, frowning as she looked ahead toward the stairs. "No, I best do it. I'll need to prepare him. I'm certain the viscount has brought us ill news."

"The debts again?" he asked in dismay.

Emerald glanced over her shoulder and saw that the viscount had dismounted. Her eyes narrowed. "I don't know.

Whatever it is, it means trouble. Keep his lordship occupied until I prepare Father for his arrival."

Drummond's long fingers moved about restlessly. "Yes, yes, I shall do my utmost."

As she hurried ahead, she heard the sound of boot steps on the hall floor behind her, and the formal voice of Drummond welcoming Baret Buckington to the Manor. She glanced back and saw that the steward was taking his hat and riding cloak.

I must prepare Father for the worst. Would he be strong enough to deal with Baret Buckington's demands? And how could she avoid being recognized?

Emerald hastened across the floor with its woven cane mats, hearing the others behind her.

"Ah . . . those wall tapestries are a wondrous sight. Where did Sir Karlton come by them?" came Baret's questioning voice.

There was a steep flight of stairs carpeted with indigo-dyed hemp, and she began the long climb, lifting her skirts and petticoats as she went.

The upper hall was quite narrow, but there was a tiny gallery, which her father humorously named the "crow's nest," after a ship's lookout platform, overlooking the room below. She paused there.

Baret Buckington had crossed the room and stood below the crow's nest, studying the wall-length tapestry. Although she could not see the design from the gallery, she knew which hanging had arrested his attention. Her father often stared at it while he stood lost in some moody reverie of the sea.

All of the tapestries in the collection were of ships, many of them at risk on turbulent seas. It was the portrayal of the defeat of the Spanish Armada in 1588 that Baret was admiring. Fire ships were floating toward the galleons, culverins exploded, and English and Spanish swordsmen were boarding while many others were falling overboard. A great wind —the "Providential Wind of God"—had arisen and hurled King Philip II's galleons out to sea, carrying many to destruction on the rocks.

As though he felt her gaze, Baret's head lifted, and he looked up toward the crow's nest. Her veil remained in place, but she swiftly stepped back and sped across the dimly lit hall to her father's favorite chamber. Her heart pounding, she knocked rapidly. "Father! Open the door! Quick, Father, 'tis me, Emerald."

A sullen voice retorted, "Not now, girl. Begone!"

Her heart lurched. Drummond was right. He is in a dark mood.

"Father! Viscount Baret Buckington is here. All is not well. I must talk to you!"

There was silence, then she heard heavy footsteps and a bolt sliding back. The door jerked open wide.

11

SECRETS AND SCHEMES

Startled, Emerald faced her father, looming in the doorway. She said nothing for a moment as she gazed at him. The attire of a well-dressed Jamaican planter had been exchanged for that of a man prepared to go to sea.

Her distraught gaze drifted over the sleeveless woolen tunic that reached to the thighs of his rugged leather breeches. A long cloak was thrown over his strong shoulders, and the lantern light fell on the silver cross that rested on his broad chest. The cross she had seen many times. "A gift from your mother," he had told her.

A big man, Sir Karlton Harwick was nevertheless light on his feet, and he stood blocking the doorway with the dignity of an earl. His short pointed beard, auburn in color, curled upward, but his wide brows were straight and slashed across a roughened bronzed face with piercing eyes that could look almost silver in hue.

Emerald stepped back, hands pressed against the sides of her satin skirts, and her eyes dropped to his leather boots. Beyond him she could see his familiar scarred sea trunk, apparently packed and ready to go, and she felt her throat cramp.

"Papa! Where are you going?"

His eyes softened as they gazed down on her, and he reached an arm to draw her to him, planting a kiss on top of her head.

"To sea again."

Her heart wrenched. "But you just came home—and you promised me you'd give up the ways of a privateer."

He looked a bit sheepish. "So I did, and it's a lesson to me never to make vows impossible to keep. God forgive my rash tongue. 'Tis necessary, little one. Hush now," he soothed.

110

"There's nothing to worry about. I'll not lose our sugar holdings to the rest of the family, not if there's a ship to sail or a sword to be had."

He smiled, patting her back. "I'll even bring you back a pretty. Maybe pearls from Margarita, if Morgan goes that way."

Her eyes widened. *"Morgan!* You're not sailing with that pirate?"

"Buccaneer," he corrected with gravity. "Nay forget the difference between the two. A most astounding difference, to be sure."

She wasn't so certain. Her frustration mounted. "It's Lord Felix, isn't it? He's the one to blame. He's goading you into taking this risk. I wish he wasn't marrying your cousin."

His eyes hardened. "Aye, Geneva's making a mistake. I told her so, but she's not one to listen."

"You saw her?" she asked quickly. "You talked to her?"

He looked troubled. "Aye, last night. I let her know what I think of Felix."

She wondered why Geneva had said nothing about the meeting to Great-aunt Sophie.

"As for what I must do, I'll see my debts paid and our future on Foxemoore secure. You don't need to worry about that."

"By turning to buccaneering?" she protested, her eyes pleading.

"Now, now, none of that, lass. Naught will befall me with Morgan that won't worsen if I stay and do nothing. Felix intends to control all Foxemoore through marriage to Geneva, but he won't get my portion of the estate! I'll soon pay the debts I owe the family."

"You know the English penalty for piracy," she whispered.

"Piracy, she says! 'Tis war, that's what—war to weaken Spain's ability to wage the Inquisition in Europe, and why shouldn't we sink her galleons, I ask you?"

"Call the trade what you will. On pain of hanging, His Majesty calls it piracy."

"Aye," he remarked as though memory brought him down a forbidden path. "And the noose also swings at Port

Royal. Pirates have been hanged recently." His eyes hardened. "And we can thank the Spanish sympathizers in the Jamaican Council for that—especially Felix."

Emerald shuddered. Her father had known many of the more respectable pirates, whom he had insisted were not pirates at all "but excellent captains, navigators, explorers, and maritime seamen. All having fought valiantly against Spain." She looked up into his rugged face and saw that his silvery eyes gleamed, and she guessed that he was not thinking of the Jamaican Council but of his love for the sea, of the waiting treasures of spices, silver ingots, pearls, and gold.

He must have noted her concern, for he smiled tenderly. "Fear not, little one. Your father is not going off in a crazed fit, brandishing a cutlass. Despite Drummond's concerns for his moody master, I've been planning this voyage for a year, though I've kept it from the family. And for good reason," he said dourly. "Enough, now! Cease your fretting. I've not gone a bit daft, if that's what you be thinking."

His confident words did little to cheer her. Another long voyage on the Main only meant that her beloved father would be gone another year, perhaps much longer. His stalwart presence at Foxemoore so recently rejoiced in would be taken away. She thought of Jamie. If he could only escape Port Royal and she with him . . .

"I'm doing it for you, little one," he said quietly. "This house at least, and my share of the cane fields, will not revert to Felix. I'm determined to see you have a secure future should anything happen to me."

He stepped out and closed the door behind him. "But what is this you say? Baret is here at Foxemoore?"

Baret? Did her father call the viscount by his first name?

"Papa, I fear his presence brings trouble. He's come to side with his uncle against us."

He sobered. "If there's trouble he's come about, it's not over Foxemoore."

"He's the nephew of Lord Felix," she reminded him cautiously. "How can you be so confident?"

"I've my own reasons."

He walked down the hall, and she followed him.

"And he's a man of the sea, even as I, with a hatred for Spain." He scowled. "Nor does he have allegiance to Felix."

She did not share his confidence and wondered at it.

There was also the possibility that the viscount had learned who the "cabin boy" aboard his ship had been and had come to inform her father about her and Zeddie's excursion.

"He is in a great hurry," she protested, walking beside him down the hall. "I met him on the road. He and his men nearly ran me down," she said a little crossly.

He paused, cautious. "He's not alone then?"

She wondered at the change in his mood. "A man is with him, fair but somber. He's dressed all in black."

He gave a slight frown as if he guessed who it might be. "You know the viscount's friend?"

"Sounds like Erik Farrow. He's been knighted by Felix."

"Yes, I remember now—he called him 'Sir.'" She studied her father's profile and saw his displeasure. "You know him also?"

"I knew him when he was a lad aboard a slave ship."

At the mention of the slave trade, Emerald felt her stomach turn into knots. She would need to tell him about Ty and how Jamie had escaped, or did he already know? If he had met with Geneva last night, *she* would have told him—yet he showed no alarm.

"Farrow later took to privateering as though born in the water. Recently he's been too friendly with Felix. I wonder that Baret would have him at his side. 'Tis a curious thing. As for myself, I question if Farrow can be trusted."

He gave her a hard look. "And you, lass—the quicker I take you from here the better. After this night, London cannot come too soon."

She halted, thinking she had misunderstood him, and they stood facing each other. Surely he would not be thinking of sending her to London!

"London?" she said weakly. "Oh, but—"

"Aye, I've a distant cousin there. John Clark and his wife are humble farming folk in Berrymeade Village, but he will treat you well enough, and they've a daughter near your age. But even my cousin's farm isn't good enough for you. I vow! When the wretched debts are paid, I'll put you in a finishing school. You'll marry nobility if I die seein' to it."

Her eyes searched his with trepidation. "You know it's impossible, and I wish you'd not say such things, Papa. After the ugly things said about my mother? A pirate's daughter! That's what they think of me!"

"Enough!" He raised his big hand, his eyes like silvery ice. "I know what the sharp-beaked carrion say, be they family or strangers. The refuse they feed upon 'tis not worthy for your godly tongue to repeat. Your mother was a lady of the French aristocracy who fled France in the persecution of the Protestants. Later some of the family went to the French island of Tortuga, and that's where I met her when my ship docked. Your mother died of the fever soon after you were born." He looked at her. "That is all you need to know to hold your fair head high."

Yes, but no one else believes it, she wanted to say.

The look of sorrow on his face touched her heart. He had loved her mother. No matter what the family said, he must have loved her very much.

"Yes, Papa. I didn't believe their gossip," she hastened to say. "Not for a moment." Her gaze faltered.

He made a disagreeable sound as he strode on. "A pack of clods, the whole lot of 'em, my cousin Geneva included. Got no more sense than to go around hissing lies. But the wise won't listen to their adder tongues. Yes, your mother's father was a *boucanier* on Tortuga—and I'm proud of it, and so should you be. He was a gallant swordsman, and your mother a fair mademoiselle. If she could walk here again on Jamaica soil for a day, she'd put them all to shame with her beauty and her soul."

He glowered. "Mean and small they are, like croaking frogs in a stagnant pool. Aye, she was godly," he repeated, pausing to look down at her. "And fair to look upon."

He took her by the shoulders and gave her a slight, affectionate shake. "And that goes for you too. None of the young girls compare to you, and none of the men in Jamaica are good enough to marry you. And that goes for that indentured renegade Jamie Bradford! Ah yes—I know all about that, so don't look so stricken. The sooner they catch and hang the rascal the better. He's a pirate, and so is his brother! And you've been deceived by him. I'm ashamed of you, lass."

"A *pirate!* Jamie? Papa, it isn't true. Jamie is—"

"An indentured servant for the time he's been on Foxemoore, but I know his past. As for your wanting to marry him, I know all about that too. Do you think your father doesn't know what's going on? The rascally mouthed wolf in sheep's garb is a runaway looking for a ship to steal! A pirate, that's what he is, and I'll vow to it. And if he shows up in Port Royal looking for you, I'll duel him in the street!" He looked down at her with a scowl. "And win, I will."

"He's not a pirate! He unloosed Ty, who was chained mercilessly to the whipping pillar. For that, Mr. Pitt had them both put in stocks. Ty was branded in the square this morning, and Jamie escaped. I'm glad he ran away!"

"You won't see the lad again," he ordered. "I'll shoot him fair and square if he shows up on Foxemoore."

"Papa, you wouldn't!"

"Oh, wouldn't I? I'm going to see you marry nobility, either in London or in Jamaica. Preferably a Buckington."

A Buckington! The idea was so preposterous that she momentarily forgot the disagreement over Jamie. Emerald nearly laughed. "Since when would blooded nobility in England marry me?"

"You'll see." His mouth curved above his beard as if he nurtured some secret plan. "The viscount will do nicely."

Emerald drew in a breath. The horror of the previous night came rushing in.

His eyes twinkled mischievously as he smiled down at her.

"A handsome rogue that one. I suppose you noticed?"

"No. I think he is quite knavish—and arrogant."

"It's lying you are. Why are you blushing? Aye, you like him. Good, then."

"Papa, no. Please don't embarrass me before him—"

"Well, your shyness is to be expected. But I've good reasons for seeing you his wife. Baret has the blood and wit of a buccaneer, despite his father packing him off to Cambridge to study Latin and Greek. Aye, he's a man of character, and a fiery hatred for Spain is newly kindled in his bones. It pleases me to no end." He chuckled. "He knows the ways of the Brotherhood all right, and is smooth with a blade. If I didn't know better, I'd vow he's the one who's the offspring of a French pirate."

"Papa!"

He glanced at her with a twinkle. "But he's not French. He's a cold-blooded Englishman, that one. Nerves like steel. Just the man to protect my daughter from the hissing adders in her path."

Emerald felt her cheeks flaming, for she did not wish to entertain such thoughts about "Captain Foxworth." How could her father even suggest the possibility of marriage?

"Surely you've a tropical fever," she breathed. "The man's a viscount, the grandson of the earl himself!"

"That he is," he said calmly. "His bloodline goes back to the Earl of Essex. And since his father was the firstborn son of the Earl of Buckington, Baret is primary heir of the title and inheritance—plus a lordly portion of Foxemoore."

"You've forgotten Jette," she said shortly.

"Nay, and neither has Baret forgotten. Jette's his brother. And he'll take pride and pleasure in the little rogue."

"Even if such an unlikely thing could be, 'tis cousin Lavender he wishes to marry. He's in love with her."

"That bluestocking? Whisk! And what makes you think so?"

"Because I saw her photograph on his—" She faltered, her eyes swerving to his.

But he had missed the slip of tongue. He waved a careless hand. "Aye, no doubt she's sweet on him, and the family will try to pawn her off on him." He gave her a crafty glance. "But even the earl will agree you make the better match for the viscount when I return with a fortune fat enough to bring you to Buckington House in London."

Her nerves grew taut. Again she thought of Jamie. "I don't want to go to London, Papa. There's only one man I want—Jamie Bradford. Please understand."

"There'll be no Jamie," he said flatly. "And it won't be Lavender who'll have the most to offer the viscount in marriage. They'll want to keep my newly acquired fortune in jewels in the family—and that means that Baret must marry a Harwick."

Emerald fidgeted as she thought of the man downstairs. She could not imagine Baret as the sort who would permit himself to be manipulated into anything, least of all marriage. And a dowry heavy with Spanish treasure was not likely to win him. The thought that her father might try was embarrassing, considering her position, her mother's reputation, and that he had caught her breaking into his cabin. She must not see him. How could she?

"I don't want you to scheme on my behalf," she pleaded. "Uncle Mathias prayed with me to yield my life to whatever God may call me to do."

"Did he, now!"

"And Mathias speaks kindly of God's providential grace in leading us through this life, and surely Jamie—"

"And surely Jamie's not the scoundrel the Almighty has in mind for my lass. I've not left God out of my plans for your future. I confess I unwisely lived my better years without seeking Him. Ah! But you—you, little lass, have your entire life before you, and I have consistently pleaded for you since I have tasted His grace."

"And so you'll go with Henry Morgan!"

"'Tis war. Spain persecutes the Protestants, and she must be stopped." He added with a merry glint in his eyes, "'Tis enough argument now. I shall see you marry Baret Buckington."

She stopped, feeling exasperated. "I won't allow myself to be caught up in dreams—I don't want to be hurt anymore."

"Cease! In one breath you have confidence of God's ways, even urging your sinful father to lean hard on His grace. In the next you balk like a mule stiffening its legs. Nay speak a thing about the doings of the Almighty. He is sovereign and does what He may. And He is always right. Remember that. And most of our pains we cause ourselves or taste because others force their miserable dregs upon us."

Emerald wrapped her arms around his waist. "And you tell Mathias you don't understand theology," she said with a little smile.

117

He winked. "'Tis to keep a meddlesome uncle in his place. He'd make me a planter if he could."

She sighed. "Oh, Papa, I am going to miss you!"

He gave her a gentle pat, smiling down at her, his eyes shining. "Now you listen to me. When I return from Morgan's expedition I'll be a wealthy gentleman again. We'll go to London. You'll soon see how quickly the fiery tongues of the bluestockings are silenced when they know that Lady Emerald Harwick is very wealthy and soon to become the bride of the viscount."

Her smile faded. She took anxious hold of his woolen sleeve as they moved toward the staircase. "Please don't talk like that. He's downstairs now. If you say anything so blatant, I shall simply die. He'll laugh, and I'll feel a fool!"

He chuckled. "Don't worry. Your father is not that arrant. I won't need to be. Baret will have his own mind where a woman is concerned. I know him well enough. He is a handful even for the domineering likes of the earl." He appraised her with pleasure, throwing an arm about her. "You're a delight to the eyes, and—knowing him—he'll be agreeing."

She stiffened. "I—I can't meet him, Papa. I won't."

"What's this chatter?"

"Um—well, he hasn't come on a social call. I could tell by his manner. Something is wrong. Something troubling enough to bring him here unexpectedly."

"Then I'll find out what it is. Now go and freshen up a bit. You've got a smidgen of dust on your nose." He appraised her dress. "And where'd you get the frock? From Lavender?"

She wondered that he didn't remember the trunk at the lookout—unless he didn't know about it yet.

"No matter," he said. "Now go and prepare your hair, lass. Then come down. I'll be showing him what a fine young lady Sir Karlton's lass has grown to be."

She stood, her cheeks colored with anxiety. *I'll not go down*, she thought, her heart pounding. She avoided his gaze.

He lifted her chin, but Emerald's eyes dropped under his knowing search.

"Now you listen to me, lass. I'll not have you hiding yourself in your room like some frightened kitten, too afraid to show her face to important people. I expect my daughter to conduct herself with pride. You'll come down. And you'll hold your head high."

She couldn't tell him her worst fear. Suppose Baret Buckington accused her and Zeddie in front of her father?

They reached the gallery, and Sir Karlton paused. "It's settled. It's high time I introduced you to your distant cousin the viscount."

The viscount was not her blood cousin, but evidently her father insisted on pretending they were related.

"Yes, Papa. I'll do as you say."

He smiled again. "You've a will of your own, to be sure, and it makes me proud, but trust me, little one. If I didn't know the manner of man the viscount was, I'd not force you into the lion's den."

Yes, she thought. *And Captain Baret Buckington Foxworth is one of the lions.*

"You can't blame a father now, can you?"

She watched him descend the steps, then forced herself to walk to her bedroom.

Inside the shadowed cloister of her chamber, Emerald knew a minute of emotional security and shut the door on the world of Port Royal. The silence shielded her from prying eyes and wagging tongues, but she knew she couldn't stay here long.

How trying that life demanded so much of her!

She paced. Her father was right. She did possess a strong will and a desire to run the course that God might have for her future. It was not in her plans to hide away from the challenges life brought. She must cultivate reliance on His Word that would support her in every circumstance. She must develop endurance, as Uncle Mathias told her. Who knew where her ongoing steps would bring her?

She wrung out a cloth in the water basin and freshened her complexion, then tried to brush the signs of saltwater from her long hair, yet a glimpse at her reflection in the mirror evoked an uncomfortable twinge.

The dress was becoming, and she indeed looked the lady he had mistaken her for on the road, but no change of garment would make up for last night. "A wench," he had called her on the ship. What would he say now? What would he do?

She knew a man as knowledgeable as Baret Buckington would have heard the tale about her mother, even if he had not visited Foxemoore sugar estate since a boy. At Buckington House the family of the earl knew all about Sir Karlton's offspring. He would know her history even as he knew the fine-blooded background of Cousin Lavender.

Her eyes narrowed as she stared at herself in the long glass with critical scrutiny. She reached a hand to her hair, drawing it tightly away from her face. Yes . . . that made her look a trifle more severe. Tonight Emerald Harwick must not resemble the daughter of a French beauty on Tortuga. She must look cold, even puritanical.

A thought came to her. She looked quickly toward her small wardrobe. A tiny smile formed on her mouth.

Breathing hard from exertion and rush, Emerald left her small room to go downstairs as her father had bidden. He would not approve of the colorless garment she had deliberately chosen. But he would not say anything in front of the viscount, she thought victoriously. The Puritan belief in sobriety provided her the right image that just might counter any memory Captain "Foxworth" had of a pirate in calico drawers.

Minutes later, she came to the steep flight of steps that led down to the parlor, her unrelieved black frock rustling stiffly over her pantaloons.

The plain bodice was tailored with a high ruffled neckline that scratched beneath her chin, and the puffed sleeves were plain, without a trace of lace or buttons. She had last worn the dress to the funeral of a town friend of Uncle Mathias. And she had brushed her hair away from her face into a chignon that turned out to be too heavy for her slender neck. Yet, even though pale, more from fright than anything else, the comely features that were all her own could not be hidden.

Emerald stopped on the bottom stairstep and stood stiffly as the door to her father's small office opened. She drew in a small breath and waited, heart fluttering.

Her father walked out with Baret Buckington.

12

SUMMONS TO THE GREAT HOUSE

They talked in low tones and did not glance in her direction. Her father's previous mood, she noted, had been wiped away as thoroughly as though hurricane winds had swept over him. She was certain that the last thing on his mind now was the impression his daughter would make on Baret Buckington.

Emerald took anxious note of the strain in her father's expression and saw the viscount place what looked to be some manner of document inside his doublet. Baret too appeared preoccupied. To her surprise, her father did not seem to notice her altered appearance. What had they discussed?

At some word from her father, the viscount's gaze briefly swept the hall and came to rest on her. She held her breath.

He stood without moving for a moment, simply looking at her. His expression was unreadable.

Her eyes searched his face for any sign of recognition, yet there was nothing in that remote gaze that said he knew her. Indeed, if she had wished to hide behind her ugly black frock and unbecoming hairstyle, she had succeeded—perhaps too well. The viscount seemed totally unimpressed by her and anxious to be off.

Emerald stood stiffly, her cold, clammy hand clutching the banister while Drummond brought the viscount his riding cloak and hat.

Then, appearing the essence of gallantry, Baret walked with her father to where she stood.

Emerald avoided his eyes and felt her knees weaken.

"May I present my daughter, Lady Emerald," her father was saying. "Emerald, your cousin Viscount Baret Buckington."

She did not have a title, nor was Baret a cousin. The fact that her father would claim so added to her discomfiture.

There followed a moment of acute silence. Her gaze swerved to Baret's to see that she had failed a social propriety. According to custom, he had reached for her hand to bend over it, but she had not extended it. Quickly she did so, but only after he had withdrawn his own and had straightened.

Her gaze met his, mortified.

A malicious glint showed in the depths of his dark eyes. *He recognizes me.*

Her curtsy came off awkwardly, her stiff skirts hardly moving. "My Lord Viscount," she said breathlessly, waiting like a condemned prisoner for the noose to slip about her neck.

He bowed. "Why, my dear Lady Harwick. Now this is a surprise—a most gratifying experience."

Oh, thought Emerald. Now it was coming.

Her father turned an inquiring look on her. "You two have met before?"

"Oh, no—" began Emerald with a rush.

But Baret said, "A most unforgettable occasion, Karlton." He turned to Emerald. "Surely you recall the vivid moment, Lady Harwick?"

Her eyes rushed to his, imploring his silence. "You must be mistaken, your lordship."

His gaze swept her austere hairstyle and frock. "I was certain I had met you returning from some nightly festivity. A masquerade ball perhaps?"

The rogue. "Oh, not at all. I'm sure of it. I—I've never been to London."

"How unfortunate."

"Nay, m'lord, I've no wish to travel so far," she said quickly.

"I'm sure you'd find passage aboard my ship comfortable indeed."

"Pardon, I'm quite certain I wouldn't. I have my work here to do, you see. Jamaica quite contents me."

"Does it so? Yes—I can see how certain aspects of life in Port Royal could be advantageous to a young lady."

She wanted to wince at his smooth tone of voice.

"I serve a Christian cause in aiding my uncle!"

"Ah? I see. Your uncle supports you in this work of yours?"

"Uncle Mathias is a godly man, m'lord!"

"A Puritan, no less."

"Yes! He's begun a Singing School for the slaves, and I've every intention of carrying on his work one day."

Obviously he didn't believe her. Her embarrassment rose higher when he turned with a faint sardonic smile to her father.

"May I encourage you, Karlton, to send my cousin to Buckington House? Her presence will prove a rewarding diversion to the earl and family. My grandfather will heartily approve of her."

Emerald's lips closed tightly. He was mocking her.

But Sir Karlton took his suggestion at face value and gave a wily smile of subdued pleasure. "Agreed, her education and introduction to society is a decision I've too long kept at bay. I feel certain we'll soon be changing all that."

"Nay, Papa, you know how I've vowed my dedication to the Singing School, and Uncle Mathias—"

"Mathias will soon get you into trouble with the Jamaican Council, lass. 'Tis against the law to educate the slaves, and teaching them Christianity is forbidden. He may risk his own neck if he wishes, but he won't bring my daughter with him." He turned to Baret and shook his head. "Pay her sprightliness no mind. She's inherited a stubborn will from me, but sound training in the ways of a fine lady will soon set her well in the eye of society."

Emerald's dismay grew when she heard Baret saying smoothly, "May I suggest you introduce your daughter at the wedding celebration?"

Her head turned swiftly toward him, but Baret was looking at her father. The "celebration" was the outdoor barbecue and evening ball following Cousin Geneva's wedding to Lord Felix Buckington.

I'd rather die than face them all, she thought with horror. And she suspected the silky-tongued Baret Buckington of having already guessed as much, and that was the reason he suggested her presence.

Before she could make a fitting excuse, he turned his attention back to her with a touch of smile. "Then it's agreed upon. I won't take no for an answer. I will look forward to your presence, Lady Harwick, at the ball. You too, Karlton. Now I must say good-bye. Business at Port Royal demands my full attention." With that, he took a step back from her, this time not bothering to see if her hand was extended, bowed, and left the room.

Emerald stared after him, her frustration restrained until the front door closed behind him and the sound of his horse faded into the twilight.

Slowly she sank to the bottom step.

"Now what's ailing you, lass? Too excited at the prospect of the fine ball? Ah! Did I not tell you he would think well of you?" He chuckled with the secret pleasure of his own thoughts. "Aye, 'tis going far better than I first thought it may."

"Papa, I won't go!"

His brows rushed together as he gazed down at her. "There'll be no sass from you, or I'll need to be turning you over my knee," he said testily, shooting her a scolding glance. "You'll go in the fine dress you were wearing earlier, and you'll hold your head high. And what was the notion of changing into funeral clothes, I ask?"

"Can't you see he was only mocking me?"

"Mocking you! Why, he behaved the perfect gentleman that he is. Have you no eyes in your head?"

"Gentleman indeed. Why, he may be the grandson of the earl, but he's nothing more than—" She stopped. If she accused Baret of being a pirate, her father would be alerted and demand to know how and why she would say such a thing. She suspected he already knew that Baret was also Captain Foxworth of the *Regale*, but he didn't know that *she* knew.

"Do you stand there, daughter, and tell your father a viscount's invitation to the family house is to be scorned? He has more say than either Sophie or Geneva, and that's saying a great deal when it comes to their insufferable ways. Baret is heir to half of Foxemoore! And who'll dare scorn you when he's asked you to show yourself?"

"Oh, Papa, please. You don't understand. It's his *reason* for insisting I show myself tomorrow that matters," she said obstinately. "He wouldn't look twice at me, and he's going to marry Lavender. He only wishes to—" She went silent under his narrowed gaze, for she feared she had already said too much. At least the captain of the *Regale* hadn't told her father that she'd been aboard his ship.

Sir Karlton gave her a close look. "And just what is his reason, or maybe I should be asking *your* reason for wanting to avoid the man? And if it has anything to do with your moonstruck feelings for that rascal Jamie Bradford, you had best dismiss the notion. Jamie's a runaway, and he'll stay far from Jamaica if he has an ounce of wisdom in that head of his."

"It's not Jamie—it's the family and their guests. Do you think I want Lavender's friends whispering about me and snickering behind their fans? I won't go." She rested her chin in her hand and gazed ahead.

His mood softened as it always did eventually, and he patted her head as though she were a child. "I'm proud you're determined you won't be treated lightly, and you won't be, lass. I'll be seeing to that when I return with Henry Morgan. There'll be no more hiding you out here in the overseer's bungalow, no more hobnobbing with men of the likes of Jamie Bradford. I'll be regaining my fortune soon. And you'll accept the viscount's invitation to visit Buckington House."

Emerald turned her head away. *Buckington House!*

"Now don't get flighty with me, Emerald. You'll go to London some day—and to my cousin Geneva's wedding reception as well. And stay for the ball like he asked you. You're as good as any brat who'll show her face, including Lavender. And you'll let them know it."

He doesn't understand, she thought dismally. *He actually believes all he has to do is push me forward and I'll end up a countess!*

Her father wearied of the discussion and walked back into his cluttered office with its collection of navigation books.

The minutes ticked by as she sat on the stair listening to the big clock in the gallery overhead, dazed.

Slowly she stood, resigned to having lost the battle. She listened to her father moving about, opening and shutting desk drawers and cupboards as if searching for some item he couldn't find.

She recalled the document that she had seen him hand to Baret and wondered what that might have been. Had the viscount confronted him about the debts they owed the family? She must find out. *Dear God, have mercy on us,* she prayed.

Emerald picked up her skirts and left the stairs, briskly crossing the floor to her father's office.

Entering quietly, she shut the door. "Papa?"

Sir Karlton sat bent over his desk studying a drawing of what appeared to be the Spanish Main. She could only guess the displeasure of Uncle Mathias when he learned that her father would take to sea again, joining Morgan and the other buccaneers in a raid. Mathias was adamantly against such practices and had often fallen out with her father over the difference between "pirates" and "buccaneers."

A buccaneer, or privateer, sailed under a letter of marque —authorization granted by the king through the governor-general. The king and the Duke of York—who was High Admiral—received their share of booty as well as the governor-general and members of his ruling body. But a pirate sailed without authorization and wished it so, not wanting to share his plunder.

She walked softly to the front of the desk, trying to quiet her awful skirts.

"Mathias believes I've talent to start a legal Singing School in Spanish Town," she said of Jamaica's capital. "I showed him a hymn tune I wrote. He likes it. My English students would pay, of course."

He looked up, bewildered. "Singing school?"

She tapped her foot. "Like the one Mathias has here on Foxemoore for the slaves, only mine would be much larger, with students from the colonial families who would pay me for my service. You've seen my hymn tunes. Mathias insists they're quite good."

"Oh." He looked sheepish. "Aye, the hymns. Yes. Now I remember."

She doubted that he did. "I'm certain I can get students."

He stared up at her blankly, then frowned. "Singing pupils? A pleasant diversion for you, to be sure, when it comes to Jette and the twins." He shook his head. "But there's no need to go to Spanish Town."

"To help pay our debts? I should gladly work."

His eyes came to rest on her face. "The debts to the family and the London merchants? What about them? Did I not tell you my plans?"

She was confused. "Did not the viscount come to see you about the debts?"

He sighed. "No."

She was not convinced. "You can tell me, Papa. What is it? Did he threaten you?"

"Threaten me? Great Scot, no! Hardly that!" He gave a whistle through his teeth, a familiar sound of dismissal, and a wave of his hand. Pushing back his chair, he stood. "Nay, nothing like that." He walked to the open window and stared out toward the cane fields.

Emerald's anxiety was growing as she came swiftly up beside him. She took hold of his muscled arm, looking up at the side of his face.

"It is Foxemoore, isn't it? You gave the viscount the document to our share of the sugar."

"The one from Earl Esmond? Nay, it is quite safe. I'll tend the wolves that prowl the gates—don't worry about that. This voyage will end matters. Nay," he repeated. "It was nothing like that."

He rolled the parchment and placed it inside his desk drawer, frowning thoughtfully. "'Tis Baret's own father he came about. He came to discuss a certain map and journal once belonging to his father."

This information she had not expected. A map and journal? The viscount was wise in the ways of the sea, and she suspected he had taken more than one Spanish galleon in his time. Yet this map and journal had been important enough to discuss with her father.

"Isn't Captain Buckington joining with Henry Morgan? Why does he need his father's map?"

127

He gave her a shrewd glance, as though to judge her motive for inquiring. "Aye, he is, but 'tis information he seeks on another matter concerning his father."

She came alert. "Oh? From a map and journal? But why would he come to you?"

He hesitated, as if wondering how much he should explain. "Baret has inherited more from his father's death than a title. He has his father's enemies. He has a notion that Royce was betrayed into the hand of the Spanish admiral. Say nothing to anyone in the family—not even to little Jette—but Baret has reason to believe their father may yet live."

"Viscount Royce Buckington?" she whispered. "But how? I thought—"

He interrupted, his expression troubled. "Baret believes that Royce was sold as a convict slave. By now there's no telling how he fares. He doesn't wish Jette to know yet. And least of all Lord Felix."

She could understand not wishing to disappoint Jette if the idea proved false, but why did he not wish Lord Felix to know? Surely the half brother to Royce would be pleased . . .

Her mind faltered.

No. Of course the man would not. The conversation she had overheard between Great-aunt Sophie and Geneva took on new significance.

Her father's eyes, never known to be dispassionate, turned fierce. "Baret vows to find his father. It is the reason that brings him to Port Royal, though the family believes 'tis the wedding. They suspect nothing. And they must not find out."

"I'll say nothing, of course." So Baret believed his father had been betrayed. "Betrayed by whom?" she whispered. "Someone in Port Royal, or in London?"

"Maybe both. The journal may offer some interesting facts, as well as prove the innocence of Royce when it comes to piracy."

She wondered. *Or,* she thought dubiously, *perhaps prove his guilt?* Maybe the deceased Royce Buckington and his son were both pirates, hiding behind titles, and the journal was an excuse for learning of prized Spanish targets. Baret would surely come to the same violent end as his father.

As she contemplated, Karlton warned again, "See you say nothing of this to anyone."

"What was the document you gave him?" she pressed. "I saw him place something in his tunic."

He hesitated. "A map from Jonah. Baret intends to journey inland to the Blue Mountains. A bit of prowling about among the Cameroons may uncover some information."

The Cameroons had been slaves who served Spain on Jamaica until Cromwell sent Commander Venerable and Sir William Penn to the West Indies. Although the British failed a larger conquest, they had driven out the small Spanish garrison on Jamaica and laid claim to that island in 1655. Her father said that Henry Morgan had fought with the indentured servants from Barbados to take the island.

The Spanish slaves there fought against the British, and when the island was colonized, many of them—the "Cameroons"—escaped into the Blue Mountains to an area called the "Cockpit" because of its caves and rugged terrain. Through the years, other runaway slaves joined them and intermarried with the Arawak Indians. Together they had continued to fight against the English planters until a peace treaty was drawn up with the governor-general, which gave the Cameroons the Cockpit for a sovereign territory of their own.

Ty had wanted to escape to the Cockpit and take Jamie there until they could acquire a ship. Had Jamie risked going alone? Though unfriendly to the planters, the Cameroons were known for taking in runaways.

Then there was still the possibility that he might gain passage on a ship and send for her!

"A fiercer lot cannot be found, but they know things others do not, and it's what the viscount is depending on. They may have some bit of information that could help him."

"But Lord Felix said his brother's ship went down in a hurricane."

His eyes hardened. "Baret's convinced Felix lied to him four years ago. 'Tis the reason he's been searching for information."

Emerald shuddered. And Lord Felix was about to marry Cousin Geneva!

"We must speak to Geneva."

"I have. And Baret too will speak to her tonight."

Emerald had no doubt about the harm that an insatiable appetite for power could do to a man's conscience if he lusted for it to the extent that Lord Felix appeared to.

"Felix is not a man to be thwarted easily," she said. "He'll surely not allow anything to come between him and this marriage."

"Aye, but when a man has a just cause, there is no turning aside from what must be done. If his father was betrayed, what choice is left to him?"

She recalled how Baret had stood looking at the sea tapestries. Now she understood the thoughts that must have raced through his mind as he studied the ships in peril and thought of his father and the death of so many. She could not blame him for wanting to know about how his father died, but it seemed to her a hopeless task, one fraught with danger.

"Knowing his father may yet live as a slave, shall he pursue a goodly life in London and pretend it is not so?"

It was not only his father who had suffered from this despicable deed, but Baret himself and Jette, she thought. Still, she couldn't blame Baret for confronting dangerous and impossible odds in the hope of finding his father.

Anxiety suddenly gripped her. What of her own father? He too would go to sea.

"It is not the viscount I worry about, Papa, but you. Oh, I wish you wouldn't take to sea with Captain Morgan," she pleaded. "You know what Uncle Mathias says. He insists it's little different than becoming a pirate."

He scowled, but she noted that his silver-gray eyes were not unpleasant as he thought of Mathias.

"Every ship sailing with Morgan flies the colors of His Majesty. I shall return a happier man for sailing, and so will you be happier."

She wished she might tell him she wanted nothing more than Jamie's freedom and a voyage to the New England colony, but his mind was set, and so was his determination to join Morgan's buccaneers.

Emerald went back up to her chamber. She had not been there long when she heard the door quietly open behind her. She turned quickly.

Eight-year-old Jette Buckington peeked in through the crack. "Emerald," he whispered.

"Jette!" She threw open the door, and the boy stepped inside, pulling the mulatto twins Timothy and Titus in behind him.

Two pairs of dark eyes and a pair of gray-green eyes stared up at her.

Jette whispered excitedly. "I overheard! My father's alive! And I'm going with my brother Baret to find him!"

Emerald felt her heart sink.

13

A CHILD-KEPT SECRET

"And I'm taking Timothy and Titus with me," whispered Jette. "You can come too, Emerald. My brother is the viscount. His ship is big enough for all of us."

She must move cautiously to discover his plans in order to alert her father. She could not bring herself to believe that Baret would allow Jette aboard his vessel in such a dangerous search. That being the case, what did Jette have in mind? To convince his brother to take him? But what gave him such confidence that Baret would do so?

Stooping to his eye level, she took hold of his small shoulders and drew him near, careful to appear calm and worthy of his secrets.

Now that she had met Baret, she was able to recognize in Jette the physical similarities—the dark hair, the handsome features. But the illness that had confined the boy to his nursery chamber for a year after his arrival on Foxemoore showed in a body that was small for his years.

"Did the viscount come to see you at the Great House and take you on his ship?" she asked warmly.

"No, it was old Peter in the kitchen who told us about the *Regale*. His son works at the harbor unloading ships from all over, and he saw Baret."

"And of course you want to go away with the viscount when he leaves again. But won't that make Geneva unhappy? She loves you very much. Remember how sick you were, and she looked after you day and night?"

His dark brows tucked together, and he nodded.

"After Cousin Geneva marries Felix, she'll want you to voyage with them and Lavender to London to Buckington House. Your brother will want you to stay there and attend school."

He gave her a swift look, and there was a glimmer in his eyes as if he understood the motive behind her words.

"How do you know? Did he tell you?"

"No, but if he's any kind of a brother, he'll insist on your education."

He squirmed. "He wouldn't do that, because he didn't like Cambridge. And I'm going to be just like him, so I'm not going to like it either."

So he had attended Cambridge. "How long did he attend?"

His eyes solemnly gazed at her, and, as though troubled, he whispered, "So long he was old when it was over. And then they made him go somewhere else and learn the king's laws too. But Baret was smart—this time he didn't stay a long time. He just left."

Her mouth turned. "He sounds hard to please."

"Oh, he is, Emerald. Very hard to please. So then he went to the best place of all."

Her brow lifted. "And where was that?"

His eyes glistened. "The Royal Naval Academy."

She covered her surprise. The Baret Buckington that Jette was describing was far from the "rogue" she had met on the *Regale*.

"He likes having his own ship and doing what he wants."

"Indeed. Well, we can't always do as we please. We must also think of others and what our Lord wills for our lives."

"Does that mean you too?"

"Of course—" She stopped, uncomfortable. In running away to marry Jamie, could she be following her own will?

"He's easy to get along with when he has his way," explained Jette proudly. "And he doesn't like to wear velvet and satin, he said. He likes boots and leather and swords. He has lots of 'em."

"He looks as if he might. I suppose he likes his rum too."

He shrugged. "I don't know. He never talks about that, but he talks a lot about all the land he saw in the American colonies. He said it was very green and handsome, with lots of lakes and trees and bears too. Have you ever seen a bear?"

"No. Did the viscount promise to show you the American colonies?"

"No, but I will see them, because I'm going with him," he said again. "You can come too. I don't think he'll care much. I love Cousin Geneva, and Great-aunt too, but I don't like Felix. I want my real father."

"But you haven't met Lord Felix yet," she said easily. "You may like him very much."

"But Baret has his own ship. He'll teach me to read maps. You too, maybe."

"Did he tell you he would teach you the ways of a ship?" she asked casually, still wondering if somehow he had already seen his brother.

"No, I haven't seen him yet. But he will. He's my brother," he said as though that in itself was all the answer either of them needed.

So he had not seen Baret yet, and his big dreams were all of his own making. She could not imagine Baret's taking the boy with him on a dangerous voyage, yet she must know how much he had overheard of her conversation with her father in the office.

She shuddered to think that he may have understood the meaning behind her father's words when he had cast doubt upon Lord Felix. Such knowledge could be risky for both Jette and the twins.

"I know you're very excited about what you heard my father and I discussing in the office. Suppose you tell me again what it was?"

His eyes narrowed into the guarded expression that she knew only too well. He nodded solemnly. "Baret's come to search for our father, because he thinks he's alive," he stated.

Then he smiled so happily that her heart twisted.

"But Jette, it's only a *hope*. He doesn't know for certain. Hopes do not always come true. Anything else?" she pressed gently. "My father and I talked for a long time."

He looked at her from beneath long silky lashes, then shrugged his tiny shoulders. "I didn't hear everything 'cause old Drummond caught us and sent us back up here to my room. Just that my father is not dead after all. Oh, Emerald! I was so happy I cried and cried, and old Drummond thought it was over him catching us downstairs."

She reached out a hand and cupped his chin. "Dear Jette, I wish you hadn't heard."

"Oh, no, Emerald! This is the best news I've had in my whole life! That, and that Baret's come back."

"Jette—I know you want with all your heart to believe it, but I want you to pay close attention to what I say. Will you do that?"

He tilted his head with a cautious expression. "Yes, but—"

"Good, because I don't want you to be disappointed," she whispered. "Things don't always work out the way we expect or want them too. Yet if we love Jesus, *whatever* happens to our hopes, we need not be disappointed."

He moved uneasily beneath her hands. "You're going to tell me what I heard isn't so."

"I can't say that, because I don't truly know. And that's just it—neither does anyone else, including the viscount. He is hoping his secret information is true, but he isn't certain."

"Yes, but—"

"It would hurt very much to hope for something that proves not to be true after all, wouldn't it?"

The desire in his eyes seemed to burn like small coals, and he stiffened a little. "Yes, but it's got to be true, Emerald. My brother wouldn't come if it wasn't so."

"But remember, he could be mistaken about the information. Or the man who gave him the information may have been mistaken. That is possible, isn't it?"

He frowned.

"And if you hope too hard—if you believe with all your heart something that isn't true—that won't make it happen, Jette. It isn't how much we believe something that makes it true. We can believe things that are wrong."

"But if I pray!"

Her heart ached as tears welled in his eyes and spilled over his cheeks.

"Oh, Jette . . ."

His mouth quivered. "You said Jesus answers my prayers!"

"Always. But not always in the *way* we ask them. Because He never makes a mistake, He will do only what is the very best for all of us who trust Him. As our Great Shepherd,

He will lead us in the right path for our feet. Perhaps He has your father with him and—"

"But Baret said our father is alive. And I've prayed. So he is."

"Yes, someday all those who die believing in God's Son will live again in new bodies, but you will need to wait until that day comes."

"But my father didn't truly die—I heard what Karlton said."

"Maybe. But if your brother's hopes prove false, your prayers will still be answered, though in another way. You will need to wait."

"But my brother wouldn't look for Father if he wasn't alive. Baret's too smart."

"Yes, I think you are right. He is quite smart. But he too can make mistakes. Only God's Son Jesus never makes a mistake. When Jesus tells us something, we can believe it with all our heart."

He stared at her and said nothing for a moment, then nodded yes.

"So you will be careful to understand that searching for your father is only a hope."

He nodded.

"And if Baret wishes the information to be kept a secret—you must tell no one. Understand?"

Again he nodded. "I'd never betray my brother."

"I'm sure you wouldn't." She smiled and brushed a dark strand of hair from his damp forehead. "You're sweating. Here, let's wipe your face with a cool wet cloth. Come, sit on the settee."

He did so, while the twins sprawled on the floor and watched her with round eyes, their spotted hound between them.

As Emerald wrung water from a clean cloth and wiped the boy's face and hands, Jette too watched her.

"Just think, Emerald, my brother captains his own ship —just like our father did." His eyes shone. "He's even fought pirates. And he knows how to use a sword. Wherever our father is—" he stopped and cast her a glance "—I mean if he's alive, Baret will find him. And I'm going to help."

136

He turned to the twins. "And so is Timothy and Titus."

"Not me, I ain't be liking the sea," said Timothy, his large dark eyes troubled. "Heard Minette say, when them waves climbs high over the sides of the ship, why, they's like fingers ready to drag sailors down, down to the sea monster."

"Only if there's a storm," said Jette gravely. "But the fingers won't snatch us away, because we'll hide in the hold. I know the perfect place to hide on a ship—on Baret's ship."

Emerald glanced at him, but Jette was smiling at the twins. "Know where?" he asked them excitedly.

Emerald pretended to be busy.

"Sure I do," said Timothy. "Ain't me no fool, not me. Just like you said—down in the hold. Right where the master keeps the ammunition locked."

"You only know 'cause old Peter told you, but I knew 'cause I know about ships from Baret."

Titus gave a firm shake of his head. "Uh-uh, no sir, not me. I'm not going neither. Like Timothy says, Minette says them waves roll too high.'"

Jette's eyes clouded. "You have to come with me, 'cause I don't want to go alone." He added more firmly, "And I own you both."

They jutted out their chins and stared at him in brooding silence.

Jette stared back and folded his arms.

"Then we'll go with Father and Baret to America. I'm going to preach to the Mohawks."

"Mohawk be worse than Arawaks," said Timothy.

"When I preach to them, both of you will guard me with your swords."

"We ain't got no swords," stated Timothy. "And it's the angels' job to keep you from bein' scalped, not me and Titus."

"Then you can sing while I teach the Mohawks," Jette argued gravely.

They shook their dark heads. "We don't like to sing—" They stopped abruptly and looked up at Emerald with guilty expressions. "We like to sing with Miss Emerald, though, don't we, Titus?" asked Timothy, elbowing his brother.

He nodded firmly. "And Mr. Mathias too."

Emerald smiled and looked at Jette.

He sat quite still now, small hands folded in his lap, his eyes searching her face. "I don't want to live with Cousin Geneva anymore. Felix will be with her." He gave her a brooding look. "Do you like Felix?"

She caught the faintest suggestion of anxiety in his voice and realized that Jette feared the man. She could not lie to the child, for she could find little about Lord Felix that appealed to her, but it was wrong to discuss the man's flaws. If she filled Jette's mind with suspicions now, there would be no undoing them later.

And yet she saw a dilemma. If she sided with Felix, she would risk losing Jette.

"I know little about him," she said truthfully. "Only what I've heard. And what we hear others say can many times be wrong. I've never met him. What I think of him doesn't truly matter, since it is Geneva who wishes to marry him."

He said nothing and watched her through guarded eyes.

"You must say nothing of what you heard tonight to anyone," she told him again. She looked firmly at the twins. "And that includes both of you."

They nodded, eyes wide. Timothy placed his small hand over the mouth of Titus, who did the same to Timothy. Jette jumped up and crawled over to the hound, placing his palm on his wet snout. He quoted:

> "'Our secret is bound,
> to death in the ground.'"

The hound's whiplike tail beat affectionately against the floor.

Jette hesitated as if he were going to say something else. Then instead, he stood, the twins and hound with him.

"Are you going to the wedding ball, Emerald?"

She smiled. "I fear I must. The viscount's orders."

"Then Baret will be there?"

"I suppose so," she said casually, trying not to think about that.

"Baret must think I'm at the Big House."

"You will be, first thing in the morning. Minette will bring you there for breakfast. Geneva's orders. I'm sure the viscount will come see you there tomorrow."

He nodded. He walked to the door and looked back, his eyes pleading.

"Emerald, will you come with me and Baret when we sail?"

So she had not convinced him. He was still determined to go with his brother. She decided that only Baret himself could persuade Jette and calm his excitement.

"We'll talk later," she said.

He nodded sagely, went out with the others, and shut the door gently behind him.

Emerald stood for a moment, then left her room and hurried to the stairs. She must tell her father that Jette had overheard their discussion. The viscount would need to be informed.

Drummond was clearing away some dishes from her father's desk as she entered. He looked up, a disconsolate expression on his angular face

"A wicked day for the Harwicks if you ask me, miss. With Lady Geneva's wedding to take place, and now the master up and gone for his ship at Port Royal. I fear we shall not be seeing a merry moment more."

"He's *left* then?" she asked, a dullness settling over her heart.

"Said he had important matters to attend to about Ty. He'll be back before setting sail though. The day appointed for departure by Captain Morgan hasn't been decided yet. There's to be a meeting in Port Royal in a few days, so I'm told."

Weariness assailed her. "Has Minette returned?"

"No, not yet, but if it's the whereabouts of Jamie that's troubling you, miss, I've heard they're still searching for him. Mr. Pitt is out with a crew of ten men. The word is he'll hang. I'm sorry, miss. About Ty too."

She nodded and said nothing. Wearily she went past him up the steps, turning to look back. "And Drummond— Jette and the twins must be brought to Lady Geneva first thing in the morning. You'd better go with Minette to make certain they arrive on time. Geneva wants Jette there before his lordship arrives."

"As you wish, Miss Emerald."

14

EXECUTION DOCK

Baret knew that his uncle's arrival in Jamaica was motivated by more than his marriage to Lady Geneva Harwick.

Lord Felix Buckington had arrived from Barbados with two other of the king's courtiers, who for monetary gain were Spanish sympathizers. His mission was to convince Governor Thomas Modyford that King Charles frowned on the use of the buccaneers to defend Port Royal from the danger of an attack by Spain.

When in London, Felix had been a secret member of the controversial Peace Party, which was seeking to convince King Charles to make a treaty with Madrid as war with the Dutch appeared inevitable. Felix told the governor he was to put a swift and terrible end to the use of pirates by making an example of any privateering scoundrel held in Brideswell. The king's orders were indeed to deal harshly with pirates preying on Spain's treasure fleet, but Baret believed that Felix had reason to want a particular buccaneer hanged.

And he suspected that his uncle had his own reason for desiring peace with Spain. Her colonies in the West Indies bought slaves through the Royal African Company, and Felix, in league with others, was selling slaves all along the Main.

As to war, Baret's own sympathies were with Holland, but—being also of British blood—he felt his loyalties pulled in two directions.

For months he had been seeking to locate a man named Captain Maynerd. He learned on arrival in Port Royal that Maynerd had docked at Carlisle Bay in Barbados. But before Baret could contact him, his uncle arrived from Barbados bringing Maynerd in chains. The privateer was to stand trial for piracy on the high seas. And to convince Port Royal that the king meant business, the trial was already underway with Felix as His Majesty's representative.

Felix sat with the other judges on an elevated platform in the Bailey. The embossed thirty-three-inch silver oar that symbolized their jurisdiction in the name of England lay on a wide table in front of the black-robed and white-periwigged judges.

Baret, seated on a stone bench in the upper listening gallery, took his eyes from his uncle to look at Captain Maynerd, on trial for his life. The outcome of the piracy indictments was academic. What today was called piracy could tomorrow be legal, once authorization was issued to the buccaneers. They then magically turned from being bloodthirsty pirates to being the king's navy in the Caribbean.

Doubtless they would hang Maynerd—and not that he was worse than any others who this very night in Port Royal waited for Morgan to call the Brotherhood together. Unfortunately for Maynerd, his neck would be stretched because Felix wished it so.

As a boy, Baret had witnessed similar sights at Execution Dock at Tilbury Point in London several times. The condemned pirate, once hanged, would be taken from the gallows, dipped in tar, bound with chains, and encased in an iron framework. There the wretched scoundrel would hang in heat and cold, fog and rain, with chains creaking in the salt-laden wind blowing in from the estuary. The grisly object lesson welcomed many seamen home as their ships passed the Thames.

Whether Felix would bother to order Maynerd to be tarred and left creaking in the Jamaican trade wind for a few months was anyone's guess.

In times past, when Baret was studying at the Inns of Court in London, the trial of a pirate would have been only of academic interest for him. Such was not the case with Maynerd. Maynerd had been sailing with Captain Royce Buckington on board the *Revenge* when Baret's father had disappeared.

But the West Indian voyage that had brought his father and crew into the pirate-infested waters around the coast of

Tortuga had been secretly commissioned by Cromwell and several influential members of Parliament. Royce was to sail under his own flag and make contact with the *boucaniers* on Tortuga in the hope of assembling a privateer navy on the Spanish Main.

That navy of buccaneers not only helped take Jamaica from Spain but also established another English colony, Providence, made up of Puritans. Spain later retook Providence and massacred the Puritans before they could escape to their brethren in Massachusetts, but Jamaica, thanks to the buccaneers, remained in the control of England.

When Cromwell died and Charles returned to England as king, Royce and the crew of the *Revenge* were accused of piracy against Spain and of having unlawfully confiscated the *Prince Philip*, the *Isabella*, and three unnamed ships. The Admiralty Court also said a hefty cargo was missing. Where was the silver bullion from Porto Bello and the pearls, emeralds, silks, and wine that were unaccounted for?

Although some treasure from the *Prince Philip* was in London, it was said that even more remained missing, having been buried by his father, and that several trusted crew members also knew of its location.

When Baret set sail some three years ago to join the Brotherhood at Tortuga, he had not realized that three men yet lived from the sinking of the *Revenge*—Felix had claimed that all the crew perished. But Baret discovered otherwise on Tortuga. Two of the living crew members were Captain Maynerd and the man Lucca. The third remained a mystery.

For a year it had been reported that Viscount Royce Buckington had died not at sea but in a duel at Port Royal, but Baret was almost certain that Felix was involved in this false report. Only Felix benefited from the death and piracy charges against his father.

Now, amid the red velvet that draped the listening gallery, Baret watched the sham trial proceeding in the chamber below. His cool, dark gaze fixed on his uncle, who pretended to be unaware of his presence in the balcony. Baret knew Felix watched his every move through spies, especially the newly knighted Sir Farrow.

Baret smiled faintly. He had even allowed Erik to ride with him to Foxemoore, where he had met with Karlton Harwick in the Manor. As yet Erik was unaware Baret knew he was a friendly foe. How long their relationship would remain friendly depended on Erik's allegiance.

Baret lounged easily on the cushioned bench, his muscled legs, booted to the knee, crossed negligently at the ankles. He appeared as a man of nobility, for he had changed his rugged sea garb for the refinements of his position as a viscount.

He absently ran a bronzed hand across his black velvet cloak, collared and lined in silver fox. His satin doublet was a muted hunter green worn over a spotless white silk shirt with full sleeves. His periwig was missing, and a stylish Spanish hat was cocked to the side of his dark head—a careless affront to the Admiralty Court in session below, for he deemed the justice about to be meted out by Lord Felix little more than a mockery.

If Captain Maynerd was indeed a pirate, then so was his uncle, yet Felix managed to hide behind the silver Admiralty oar.

Shifting his position, Baret glanced down at the proceedings again. The judges were listening as the prosecution railed.

"Maynerd is an archpirate in the Caribbean, cruel, dreaded, and hated both on land and sea! No one in this day has done more evil or has occasioned greater mischief and debauchery, attendant with all the circumstances of pistol and sword."

Baret's mouth curved as his lazy gaze left the prosecutor to look at Maynerd, slouched in his chair, arms resting across the long table, staring at the judges in black.

Maynerd had no lawyer. He had to represent himself and do his own cross-examining. He had blundered badly in his defense, and Baret wanted to wince.

"Will you ask the witness any more questions?" asked the solicitor-general.

"Ye all be sworn to me death, sure it's plain to see. Ye scoundrels in robes! The devil take ye all!"

As the witness stepped down, slinking away, Maynerd shouted, "Jackanapes! You've been promised your own thievin' neck to take away mine!"

Baret was sure it was so. The jury of Jamaican planters and merchants deliberated for less than twenty minutes and found Maynerd guilty.

The court clerk leaned from his chair, his lean face gravely framed with his wig, the black robe making him appear grotesquely pale.

"What can you say for yourself that you should not die according to the laws of the English colony of Jamaica?"

"Aye, Felix, I've been lied against by devilish dogs," said Captain Maynerd. "And I'll see you in hades, I will."

"You have been tried by the laws of His Majesty," the clerk continued. "Naught now remains but that sentence be passed according to the Admiralty law. And the sentence of law is this: 'You shall be taken to the place of execution, and there be severally hanged by your neck until you be dead. And the Lord have mercy on your soul.'"

As Maynerd was removed from the building, Baret stood and gazed down upon his uncle. Felix did not look up into the gallery but gathered his judicial robe about him and walked from the court.

The chamber below began to empty. Baret was turning to leave when he saw the gallery drapes part slightly. He had only a moment—an inner instinct warned him of imminent danger.

He threw himself to one side as a dagger struck the carved wooden pillar with a sickening thud. Only a second ago he'd been standing in front of it.

Then he was on his feet, unsheathing his sword and moving cautiously toward the faintly moving drapes.

He struck his blade across the curtain, slashing it to one side, and stepped back, lifting his sword.

The hall was empty, but he heard fleeing steps hastening down the back stairway. Baret darted down the narrow, dim hall to the head of the chiseled steps in time to catch a glimpse of a cloak disappearing around the corner.

He pursued the man through the corridor toward an arched doorway with drawn drapes. He knew the environs well. The exit into the next chamber offered no escape at all, for it led to a balcony that overlooked the estuary.

He paused as he entered—the chamber was empty.

Then he saw a small trapdoor, which led down some steps to where a boat had evidently been tied, waiting.

He ran to the balcony rail and looked out at the water, but the boat was being rowed away, and he could not identify the man at the oars. A moment later it disappeared behind a ship at anchor in the bay. He watched, but the small craft did not reappear.

Someone wanted him as dead as Maynerd.

A crowd had already gathered outside Brideswell for the execution of Captain Maynerd. Baret heard their hoots and howls as he leaned over the railing to look below into the dungeon hall where a group of prisoners was being led. The filth and stench was nauseating, curses filled his ears, and he heard the crack of the gaoler's whip.

"C'mon, move, ye infamous curs! D'ye think the Admiralty has all day?"

"Where is Captain Maynerd!" Baret shouted down. "I demand to see him before he's hauled to the gallows. I've a letter authorizing an audience with him."

The burly gaoler looked up and, seeing Baret now donned in the common garb of a seafarer, spat to one side.

"And who might you be? One of his vermin crew?"

Another prisoner hooted at the gaoler. "Watch your sticky tongue. That there be Cap'n Foxworth himself. Go ahead, m'lordship, draw sword and cut off his stinking head!"

The gaoler struck savagely with his whip. A bell rang. Shouts echoed through the chamber. More guards came.

Baret looked on, and he turned as the chief prison captain approached him at the rail.

"The curs! 'Tis the second brawl in two days! I'll have them all flogged for this!"

"Where is Maynerd? I'm authorized to see him before his execution."

Baret shoved toward him the document bearing the seal of the Lord Chief Justice in London.

The chief captain frowned. "Aye, me lord, I fear you be too late. The Admiralty's deputy marshal already took him from the dungeon for the gallows. And Lord Felix Buckington with him."

Baret snatched the document from the officer and swiftly ran down the stone steps leading into the front courtyard.

His gaze swept the yard, taking in the grisly onlookers and hard-faced guards. Maynerd was already inside the black-draped cart that would transport him to the gallows. Baret's uncle was seated beside the deputy marshal in the open carriage that would lead the somber procession. Felix, dressed in black with a white wig, held the silver oar of the Admiralty on his shoulder.

Baret felt a dart of anger. Of all the ministers of the High Admiralty Court to represent the Crown's demand for an end to piracy in Port Royal! It was a cynical jest to permit his uncle to carry the oar.

The procession wound its way through the shabby hovels toward the tidal flats facing the bay. A small crowd followed on foot after the cart, shouting, "How now, Cap'n Maynerd! Toss your admirers some sweet pieces of eight!"

At the place of execution, Maynerd was hauled up a ladder to stand on a rickety platform with the backdrop of blue Caribbean sky and sea. Several buccaneers' ships were in view, their white sails billowing and snapping as they made for open ocean.

Watching from astride his horse, Baret felt the tropical wind on his face, and its fingers tugged relentlessly at his cloak and hat. His gaze left Maynerd to settle upon the minister, who climbed the steps after the pirate, firmly urging him to call upon God's mercy.

Baret recognized old and faithful Mathias Harwick, nearing his seventieth birthday and still showing pity on pirates.

"Aye, lad, though the chime is poised to strike midnight, the death angel tarries to claim his prey! A minute is left in time. Redemption is yet a gift from the One who died your death between two thieves on the hill of Golgotha. Repent of your crimes, lad! Accept His forgiveness, take the robe of righteousness, for though your sins be as scarlet they shall be as white as snow."

"I am innocent of piracy upon the high seas!" shouted Captain Maynerd.

"Get on with it, gov'nor!" shouted someone in the crowd. "If the cap'n begrudge us a bit of treasure, then stay the pretty words, I say! Hang the pirate!"

Baret watched the noose being placed around Maynerd's neck and thought of his father. If he was alive . . . if the authorities caught him before he could prove his innocence . . . he too would hang from a gibbet.

For that matter, so could I, he thought.

He felt a wave of anger toward Felix, who had manipulated Maynerd's death. What had his uncle feared from the pirate's remaining alive?

The black-masked hangman pushed Maynerd from the platform. A grizzled old woman screamed as the rope snapped, and he fell.

"God 'ave mercy!"

Mathias seized the extremity of the situation and scrambled to his side.

"See how an angel hath snapped the rope! You've been spared a minute more to cry for the mercy of Christ!"

Captain Maynerd choked forth words of sorrow, and Mathias knelt, praying with him.

Only God knew if Maynerd's repentance was a genuine act of faith in the redemptive work of Christ, thought Baret.

White-faced and shaking, Maynerd was again hauled up the ladder.

Baret's jaw tensed as he watched the man die who could swear to his father's innocence. His gaze again swerved to fix upon Felix. His uncle's expression was immobile as he looked on in silence, holding the Admiralty oar.

According to custom the body would remain fixed until the tides washed over it for three days.

"Take heed, you paltry reprobates," stated the king's gaunt-faced deputy marshal, newly arrived from England with Felix. The wind whipped his black judicial robe. "Hear well and gaze with trembling upon the just end of the wicked doer. Here the archpirate Captain Maynerd shall hang in sun and cold, wind and rain, as a deterrent to other buccaneers who partake in piracy on the Main! And let all seafarers who sail past Port Royal take note of his carcass. So shall His Majesty do to all who dare scorn the Admiralty laws."

The birdlike eye of the marshal briefly fixed upon Baret, who returned a measured look before turning his horse to ride from the wharf, its hooves echoing on the cobbles.

Those in the taverns were aware of the death of Maynerd, and most believed the hanging to be unjust. He had been no more guilty than Morgan and the buccaneers commissioned by the governor-general to secretly attack the Main.

A number of ditties were sung lustily within the noisy bawdy houses as Baret walked down the street toward the gaming house with its weathered sign barely readable: "Ye Black Knight."

The structure was built with pieces of abandoned ships, and he entered the common room with its dark overhead beams and low tables to be greeted by the unpleasant smell of frying fish and rum.

It took a moment for his eyes to adjust to the dimness. Some dirty lanterns glowed, hanging from hooks on blackened rope. Rough wooden tables were crowded with men gambling. Amid the raucous din a group of English pirates was bellowing:

> "King Charlie loves his piece of eight—
> He sighs for his bottle o' rum—
> So Morgan sails the pretty Main
> To take it all from Spain!"

Laughter and the sound of rum sloshing into mugs filled the tavern.

Erik Farrow was not at the gaming table, and Captain Levasseur and his crew of French pirates were also absent— strangely, for Ye Black Knight gaming house was the hangout for many of the sea rovers.

Hob came through a back door carrying a sandy bag of turtles to sell, and Baret suspected he had followed him here with news. Hob made his rounds of the tables and eventually came to Baret.

"I bring news you'll find worth your trouble, Cap'n Foxworth. Aye, a bit of a shocker 'tis." He leaned toward Baret, eyes glinting. "Your goodly grandfather, the earl himself, has set his fine feet on Port Royal."

"In *Port Royal?*" questioned Baret with disbelief.

"Now, ain't that be curious, Cap'n? Aye, he's at Foxemoore now. Word about town has it he's come for the marriage between the lady and Felix. But I be wagerin' a gold piece there be more on his mind—say a certain blackguard pirate with Buckington blood?" said Hob with a mischievous grin.

"Curious indeed, Hob. A matter I should look into, don't you agree?"

Hob grinned. "You best be careful, me lordship, seein' how I seen Sir Erik Farrow with him but ain't seen hide nor hair of Felix since Maynerd dangled."

The arrival of the earl complicated matters considerably, but there was also now an opportunity to convince him that his father may yet be alive. The confrontation might be worth the risk. He thought he knew what his grandfather wanted.

He pressed a piece of eight into Hob's hand.

"Aye, me lordship—I means Cap'n Foxworth—and will I be seein' you among the Brotherhood when the good Morgan sails, or be you returnin' to the noble life?"

Baret considered, straightening Hob's battered hat so that it tilted fashionably to one side.

"You'll be wantin' a good man to look after you. To fix your supper aboard the sweet *Regale*. What say, Cap'n?" he wheedled with a twinkle in his eye. "Will you be lettin' an old pirate feel the way of wind and sea for a last time?"

"Now, Hob, would you be giving up your turtles to brew my coffee?"

"I be thinkin' so—for a price, that is." He leaned toward him. "Say one share of all the booty taken on the next run with Morgan? Har! Word about town says he has a worthy Spanish port in mind."

"Of that I have little doubt."

"What say you, Cap'n?" he pleaded. "A sweet share for old Hob?"

The captain of a ship always received five to six times the share of an ordinary crewman. A master's mate received two shares, and other officers and carpenters in proportion, down to cabin boys, who received half a share.

"So you wish the risk of hanging in old age, do you? His Majesty is not keen on the governor handing out commissions to Morgan."

"I'll be risking it, seein' as how this be me last chance to buy a new fishin' boat with me loot."

Baret removed a dagger from inside his jacket. "Ever see this before?"

Hob squinted, studying the ivory handle inlaid with silver. "A handsome thing, says I."

"Someone was careless. He hurled it at me in the balcony after Maynerd's trial. Evidently he felt confident enough to believe he wouldn't be losing it for long."

Hob rubbed his chin. "A fancy weapon—and it don't look Spanish."

"You're right." Baret examined the ivory handle. "It's as English as Gin Lane."

Hob looked at him with gravity. "Or as English as a fine lord's chamber?"

"Maybe. But which lord's chamber?"

"Aye, that be the question. Best walk with caution, seein' as how titled gents pay well to do their odious work. You best keep an eye on Sir Erik Farrow."

Baret placed the dagger inside the sheath beneath his jacket. "Keep your ears open. I'm waiting for that message from your informer about Lucca—unless he decided the message should be a dagger instead."

Leaving Hob, Baret slipped away into the night and came to where he had secured his horse. He mounted and rode toward Foxemoore. With Felix in Port Royal, tonight would be the hour to speak to his grandfather in privacy.

His ironclad grandfather would not be an easy man to convince of anything. And now there was the matter of Baret's attack on the *Santiago*. Did he know about that?

His thoughts returned to Felix. Had he been involved in the attempt on his life at the Bailey? If so, he would be alert to the assassin's failure and perhaps concerned that Baret might report the incident to the king's magistrate. But Felix did not know the ways of Port Royal—the buccaneers handled matters for themselves.

Baret would not report the incident even if he wanted to do so. With Governor Modyford under pressure to deal harshly with the buccaneers, Baret might find himself called to answer for the *Santiago*.

He told himself that when the appropriate time came to confront Felix, he would do so on his own. The time was not yet. He must first locate Lucca. Only Lucca knew if his father lived and where he was held along the Main.

Thinking of Lucca reminded him again of the contact Hob had told him about at Chocolata Hole. Who was this man who insisted he knew where Lucca was?

Then Baret mused, *Does not Maynerd have a brother somewhere?* He could not remember his name, but the boy had been sold into Jamaica as an indentured servant.

His hand tightened on the reins. To which planter had he been sold?

He was nearly certain now that Maynerd's plan in coming to Port Royal had been to help his brother escape from slavery. Perhaps together they had formed plans to find Lucca and extract information from him on the reported treasure.

Was Maynerd's brother desperate enough to seek out "Captain Foxworth" and the *Regale* as his means of escape?

Baret believed that he wouldn't need to wait much longer for contact. He would let it be known among the Brotherhood that he intended to sail with Morgan. With the buccaneers anxious to sign articles, the upcoming gathering of all the privateers in Port Royal to hear Morgan lay out his plans would offer Maynerd's brother the security of a crowd.

Baret arrived at Foxemoore late. Tossing the reins to a boy to care for his horse in the stables, he emerged from the palm trees and walked across the stone carriageway toward the lower veranda that encircled the entire front of the Great House.

The residence was dark except for a lantern burning brightly in a lower chamber near the front door where the porter slept. The door opened to his insistent knocking, and the slave he remembered as Bristol carried a lamp and peered out at him.

"Welcome home, Mr. Baret. Miss Lavender be highly pleased that you've come. Heard Miss Geneva and Miss Beatrice saying you wouldn't."

Baret stepped past him into the hallway and glanced up the wide stairway where wall sconces shed amber light. All was silent.

"I understand my grandfather has arrived."

"His lordship arrived before dinner, but he chose to sup alone. Not at all what the family had expected." He whispered, "Miss Sophie, she were offended."

Baret gave a wry smile. Both his grandfather and the elderly Harwick great-aunt were of too strong personality to appreciate each other. Since his grandfather held the highest title by birth, however, he retained final control of both sides of the family—and of Foxemoore.

"Is he asleep?"

"He rang some minutes ago for tea, and Jitana brung it up, but he said it weren't East India tea. Said he's taken ill on his arrival from Barbados."

Bristol was struggling to shut the heavy door as Baret started up the steps of the wide, darkened stairway two at a time.

"Would you I ready a chamber, sir?" the servant called, nimbly climbing the stair after him.

"Yes, Bristol, while I speak with my grandfather. Has Miss Lavender retired for the night?"

"Miss Beatrice gave her something to sleep. Said she must be well for the wedding."

Baret was satisfied. He preferred not to see Lavender yet.

After pointing out the earl's chambers on the east wing, Bristol went to ready Baret's room.

What would his grandfather say when Baret told him his son was not dead? That Felix had lied?

15

THE EARL'S ULTIMATUM

Baret stepped inside the dimly lit room and shut the carved oak door behind him. Instinctively his gaze went to the canopied bed, where he expected to see his grandfather confined, his body feeble with illness. The bed was empty.

"I am not in the crypt yet," came a tart but familiar voice.

Baret turned toward a window with drapes drawn open. His grandfather was known for his love of the outdoors, and despite his illness the window was open with the tropic breeze winging its way in from the garden below.

He hadn't seen his indomitable grandfather in nearly four years and, having heard of his illness, was unsure what to expect. He felt a surge of affection, even sympathy, but perhaps far stronger was the determination to remain aloof, knowing that the earl had severed all ties when Baret left London against his wishes.

A shadow detached itself from the darkness and stepped forward from the window. Whatever Baret felt as he looked at him was washed away like rain beating clean the court below. His grandfather might be ill, but he was not an object of sympathy. Baret confronted the same man he remembered so well as a boy when they rode together at the family hunting lodge outside London.

Earl Nigel Buckington remained a handsome figure for his sixty years. His shoulders remained unbent beneath a sage green dressing gown, and his white hair was thick and drawn back from a lined but tanned face, making a striking contrast with the keen dark eyes. He stared at Baret from beneath strongly marked brows that were speckled with white.

"I suppose Sir Cecil was misguided enough to tell you I'd welcome you with open arms? 'Bring the best robe,'" his grandfather quoted, "and a Buckington ring—let us feast and celebrate your repentance."

Baret made no reply to his grandfather's allusion to the homecoming of the Prodigal Son. He might have suggested that the father spoken of in the Lord's parable was not a cantankerous earl but a God of grace, but that would hardly have gained the earl's acceptance.

Nor was he returning in repentance from a life of indulgence. If he was guilty of anything, it was in failing to live up to his grandfather's expectations.

"Cecil remained aboard the *Regale*," said Baret casually, trying to keep the tense moment from erupting further by a display of his own emotions. "If he had known you were at Foxemoore, he would have wished to see you again."

The earl's hard gaze took him in. "Royce would be proud if he were alive to see you now. You look more like a pirate than even he did. I am sure you'll have a long career of reckless ventures, if you can avoid getting yourself hanged."

Baret retained his easy demeanor through his grandfather's caustic remarks. "My father was not a pirate but a buccaneer, a fair difference. Though I admit my own reputation suggests otherwise."

"That you admit to any wrongdoing is a startling disclosure. You've not only troubled me, but your uncle. Felix is quite concerned with your reckless ventures here in the Caribbean."

"Is he indeed? An uncle's warm affection for a wayward nephew, no doubt. You'll forgive me, Grandfather, if I am not moved to sentiment. You err in listening to Felix. He has personal reasons for turning you against my father and now me."

The earl gave an airy wave of a hand sparkling with gems. "Felix hasn't the wit to persuade me of anything I'm not already convinced of. Was it also a plot of Felix to turn the High Admiralty against Royce? I suppose he schemed to falsify charges?"

"Evidence was withheld to give the impression my father fired first on the *Prince Philip*. Not so!" Baret insisted. "In taking the galleon, he did so in the name of England."

"And I suppose you also had a patriotic reason to board the *Santiago?* His Majesty's wrath is not lightly appeased."

So he knows, thought Baret. Felix had wasted no time.

He folded his arms and stated wryly, "Surely the king's outrage will soon be placated. A goodly portion of the booty will be shipped back to the shepherding care of the English Crown. For every galleon the buccaneers seize in the Caribbean, both Charles and the Duke of York receive a commensurate share. After all, once in His Majesty's coffers, it is no longer deemed the evil fruits of piracy, and they never rush ambassadors to Madrid to restore gold and silver ingots."

He risked his grandfather's ire in speaking bluntly, for others beside pirates were engaged in smuggling. Dukes and earls—including his grandfather—were made rich through their secret ties in the Caribbean.

"But then," said Baret, "if a pirate does not captain a vessel, he is free of transgression, is he not? It is the well-manicured hands that matter, the satin and velvet doublets worn at Court! The unsullied hand which lifts the Spanish goblet to toast His Majesty's health is a good deal safer when he sits in Parliament!"

The earl raised a hand as though to strike him. "Are you accusing me of piracy?"

"Would I be so bold, Grandfather!"

"You're audacious! I should have you tossed out in the rain without a Buckington shilling to your name."

Baret smiled. "I was under the impression you'd already disowned me."

"As of this moment you are!"

"If I have any inheritance, I should like to know where it is, other than being left to my cousin Grayford."

"Ha! I think the fear of losing your inheritance is the one agent to shepherd your reckless head. Had I been wiser I would have used it with your father before he was cut down in a duel." He sank wearily into the green velvet chair.

"There was no duel, Grandfather—and I will prove it by finding the man who is said to have killed him."

"And get yourself slain as well? Leave the ugly past alone, Baret."

"The words of Felix. Does he not bid me to leave the past buried for fear I shall unearth the unpleasant truth? And if I had been able to speak with Captain Maynerd before he was hanged, he would have sworn to my father's innocence. He may even have written a confession disowning him of blame. But if he did, it was destroyed."

"More of the intrigue of Felix! I suppose he burned the pirate's confession to retain hope of gaining right to title and inheritance? Nonsense. Felix is also my blood son."

"It is not the blood of nobility which concerns me—it is treachery of the basest sort. And heaped upon my father."

The earl sighed. "Heaven knows I could wish Royce were blameless. Yet for you to speak so of your uncle is treachery of another sort."

"Felix envied him to the point of hatred. As a child I overheard them in debate. Felix was bitter that you favored my father to inherit the title."

"You persist in trying to turn me against him, but what proof do you offer me of his intrigue?"

Proof of his uncle's treachery was the difficulty. Baret had none that would yet convince his grandfather.

He turned and walked to the open window, feeling the humid night air against his face. The wet courtyard below reflected the lantern light.

"So I thought," said the earl when the silence only grew. "You have no evidence. It is your dreams that are broken where your father is concerned." Hopelessness was in his voice. The earl sighed. "I'll hear no more. What ill your father did, he chose willingly. His love for vengeance against Spain lured him into a trap that took his life. Now Felix is the only son I have left."

Baret restrained his anger. "I can see that during my absence from England he's managed to win your trust at my expense."

"Then come home where you belong."

"I cannot. Not yet."

His grandfather paced. "The lion's share of the family inheritance would have gone to your father. Now the one grandson I had the highest hopes for has affronted the Admiralty with insolent privateering on the high seas! The threat of war with Holland and France thunders ominously on the horizon. And what country's ship do you attack? Peaceful Spain! Don't you realize you have given the Peace Party ammunition to call for your reprisal before the king?"

"It is Spain who is the foremost enemy of England and all Protestant Europe. The Buckington name you worry about being tainted with piracy may one day be on the list of heretics." Baret's eyes pled for understanding. "If Spain can be defeated as a world power, it will be here! In the West Indies! And not by the Royal English Navy but by buccaneers! It is the scorned privateers and pirates alike who keep treasure from arriving at Madrid to feed Spain's army."

His grandfather's eyes flashed. "You need not sail as a pirate to serve England's cause. You might have commanded a ship for the king. Now that honor has been given to your cousin Grayford."

Baret was surprised. Grayford was not the experienced seaman that he was. He tried to hide his disappointment, but his grandfather must have seen it.

"Losing the king's appointment was your own fault. I warned you not to take to privateering, yet like Royce you pursue your convictions with stubborn abandon. Is it any wonder Felix advised the king to give the command to Grayford?"

"None at all," said Baret flatly, thinking of his uncle's ambitions. "Grayford's his son, is he not?"

Yet his disappointment was acute. He had trained far longer in the Naval Academy and with more success than had Grayford. And his long and ofttimes dreary education at Cambridge had not been without pain. He had earned his degree with highest honors in order to hold a high position in the king's navy. Instead it had been given to his cousin.

"You may blame your father for the ruin of your plans, not Felix," said the earl wearily. "You were advised to distance yourself from Royce's reputation, but you would not listen."

Baret had known the risk of contesting the accusations heaped upon his father. It had been painful to hear the piracy charges read against him, which stripped Royce of his past naval honors under Cromwell. Now Baret too had his future forfeited.

"Whatever Grayford feels called to, let him pursue. I wish him only well. The sinking of an enemy ship knows the same result from my cannon as Grayford's—even if he wears the uniform and I the garb of a buccaneer."

"Then the fact I shall disinherit you is of no consequence?"

It was, of course, but Baret refused to be intimidated.

"My father's private journal may prove he was under the lawful commission of Cromwell, rather than acting alone in the Caribbean."

The earl was alert. "What journal?"

Baret hesitated, for if his grandfather was determined to see no wrong in Felix, accusing him of having the journal would make matters worse.

"Father always kept a journal," he said simply. "If I had it, the secrets surrounding his mission in the West Indies for Cromwell might be brought to light and validate his innocence." He met his grandfather's gaze. "I did not come tonight to plead for either my father's title or inheritance. If necessary I can live without both. But I do want the journal."

His grandfather looked at him sharply, yet curiously. "I have no such journal, nor does the Admiralty."

"What of Felix?"

His grandfather's expression hardened. "I doubt very much if there is a journal." He walked away. "As for your future, Baret, you know I am not a man to change my mind easily once I've decided to cut you off." He looked across the chamber at him, his face grave. "Unless you become what your birth and title demand of you, you will become a family outcast."

"I am aware of that."

"And you are willing to take that risk?"

"Where my father is concerned I have no choice."

"Unless you return to England, I shall disinherit you in favor of Grayford."

Baret turned in anger to leave the room, but his grandfather hurled his cane against the door. "You'll not leave until I give you permission. Walk out now, and I vow you will live to regret it!"

"Your son and my father is alive. And I will find him whatever the personal cost to me."

For a moment the silence was like thunder. The earl stared at him, a perceptible paleness about his mouth.

Baret said swiftly, more gently, walking toward him, "I made contact with two men who sailed aboard the *Revenge* with my father. There is only one man left alive now—Maynerd was hanged."

"What are you saying?" the earl breathed.

"The one remaining witness I seek is a man named Lucca. He served Father as the *Revenge*'s chaplain. Lucca can swear to his innocence and to the fact that he was not killed in a duel in Port Royal."

His grandfather's sharp eyes searched his, his hand grasping his shoulder. "Lucca? A chaplain you say? Do you know where this man is?"

Baret masked his despair. "I will find him."

The earl's hand dropped to his side, and a perceptible sag showed in his shoulders. Then he recovered and sank back into a chair.

"I cannot blame you for entertaining dreams, but I'll not allow my emotions to be caught in this web of self-destruction. You do yourself harm, Baret. Where will it all lead in the end?"

"I can prove otherwise, but I need time."

Baret came to the side of his chair and knelt on one knee, placing a strong hand on his grandfather's arm.

"I vow to serve His Majesty in the war with the Dutch, and if it's honor you want for the Buckington name, I shall fight for England! For King Charles! And in the process I shall prove my father was not a pirate but a God-fearing ambassador of England. And when I return to London I'll bring evidence of his innocence—and if God wills, I shall bring my father home as well."

His grandfather studied him with sober gaze. "Then proceed. For war will surely come. Win deeds of valor for His Majesty as a privateer. But to make certain you do not fail to keep your vow, I will turn to Grayford to carry on the family name."

What did he mean—"carry on the family name"? Baret wondered.

"Even though you are more at home at Port Royal with its buccaneers than you are in company of His Majesty—I shall go a step further and grant you a small inheritance."

Baret could read nothing but challenge in his eyes.

"I shall leave you a portion of Foxemoore," said the earl with a thin smile.

"Foxemoore!" Baret stood to his feet, almost impatiently. "I've no interest in sugar."

"Then develop a taste for it. To keep Felix and Geneva on their toes, I shall give you a double share. Any decisions on the estate will also need your cooperation to implement in the future."

Sugar!

But if his grandfather was impressed by his disinterest, he ignored it. He was smiling now with a hint of victory.

"Make something of your share in the estate, fight for King Charles in the war with the Dutch—and I may reconsider your position in my will. In the meantime I shall show favor to Grayford. He's here in Port Royal by the way, commanding the king's vessel."

He rose from the chair and walked to the window, then looked back at Baret. "I shall see which grandson is more fitted for the Buckington name and title."

Against his will, Baret smirked. "For all your condemnation of the reported 'duel,' what you do now in forcing Grayford and me to contend is little better."

"Perhaps using Grayford to goad you back on the right path will be effective."

"I see you are not above tactics that smell of bribery."

"Oh, come now, it is a matter of family survival. The Buckington name must be preserved in London, and if it means choosing between the two strongest heirs—then so be it."

"I am sure Uncle Felix will have something to say about the outcome. He would also have had something to do with Grayford's getting command of a king's vessel."

The earl's eyes glinted. "Ah, you are jealous of your cousin."

Baret stood, hands on hips, and his dark brows lifted. "Grayford may have a command in the Royal Navy if he so wishes. I shall be pleased enough with the *Regale*—and my freedom to come and go on the sea as I wish. But Felix will not be pleased. You may do as you will with me," he stated tonelessly. "Yet the child Jette should not be held accountable for our father's actions."

"Jette? Of course not! I'm bringing Jette to London where he belongs. No more Jamaica and no more of the Harwicks, even if Felix intends to marry Geneva. I want Jette with me. He's the last Buckington I have who might live up to his name."

The earl grew thoughtful and stared out the window. "It may be," he said unexpectedly, "that I'll not leave my inheritance to Felix but to Jette, regardless of the woman who bore him."

Baret gave him a measured look. "The child is my brother, regardless of his mother. I'll not turn him over to the wiles of Felix—especially if you've let it be known you're considering making him your heir."

He turned his head sharply. "What are you saying?"

"I think you know," said Baret quietly. "And if you take Jette to Buckington House, I wish to name his governess. I won't have Felix choosing for him."

"Sir Cecil has already written to me. He wishes to be Jette's tutor."

Baret was surprised Cecil had kept that from him, but he was not displeased. He could trust Jette to Cecil without concern.

He wondered what his grandfather would say if he told him he believed Felix was behind the attempt to kill him at the Bailey. He said nothing of that, knowing it would only give his grandfather more reason to doubt his convictions.

"I can think of only one reason why Felix suddenly wishes to marry Geneva," Baret said.

"There is no cause for wonder. After her two-year stay in Lyon, Geneva came to London for a year. They took to each other," said the earl, sounding pleased. "It's true she owns a large portion of the sugar. Since she was an only child, she inherits a double portion of the Jamaican estate. But are you not being cold-blooded to accuse him of marrying her for that reason alone?"

"Yes," said Baret dryly. "And if Geneva marries him, I will place Jette in Cambridge before Felix has jurisdiction."

"Don't you think I'll have anything to say about what Jette's future may hold? If anyone has that right, it is his grandfather. And," he said, scanning him, "I shall make certain he doesn't follow in the buccaneering steps of his older brother."

Baret smiled. "On that we agree."

His grandfather gazed out the window for a moment in silence. "There is something else. And you won't be pleased." He turned his head and looked at Baret, who came alert.

"I have said you and Grayford can each prove who is best fit to carry on the family name. What I haven't told you until this moment is that I intend to see Lavender marry your cousin. Unless of course," he said smoothly, "you change your mind and return with me and Jette to London. Lavender will voyage with us."

Baret stared at him, his expression unreadable, but his heart raced with anger.

"Lavender will not marry Grayford!"

"You best think on it. Good night, Baret."

Baret stood, refusing to show his dismay. It was like his grandfather to wait to the very end to unleash his strongest weapon!

The earl smiled slightly, and Baret's jaw set. He turned and went out, shutting the door firmly behind him.

Never. He would not lose Lavender to Grayford. She was in love with him and as determined to have him as he was to marry her. She would not be clay in his grandfather's hands. Lavender was spirited, and she knew what she wanted.

Between them, he decided, they could thwart the earl.

16

OMENS FOR A WEDDING

Emerald overslept and awoke to sunshine and the screech of parrots. She'd forgotten to lower the hemp shade over her window before retiring, and her room was already airless and hot. Apprehension over the day's events and the requirements placed upon her came flooding into her soul, bringing a queasy sensation to her stomach. Her pulse quickened as she thought of the socially important people she must mingle with.

I can't, she told herself. *What if the family openly shuns me? What if I'm left alone at the supper and ball? What if the important guests watch me, and the girls gather to whisper? Father God, I don't think I can endure more shame.*

As if in answer to the fear and insecurity she felt, Great-uncle Mathias came to mind. What had he told her so often? "You are a child of the heavenly King. You stand robed in the garments of royalty. If God is for you, who can be against you?"

Repeating these words for the courage they brought her, Emerald dressed hurriedly and went down the steps to the back of the house, where she expected to be greeted by the pleasant business of breakfast. Minette was not there, nor was Drummond, Jette, or the twin boys and hound.

The silence of the house seemed almost ominous as it closed in around her.

Sight of the as-yet-unwashed breakfast dishes stacked on the wood table eased her concerns. Of course, she told herself, she had overslept, and everyone had gone on about his business. She remembered her own orders to Drummond to make certain he take Minette and Jette up to the Great House, where Geneva would be expecting the child to meet Lord Felix on his arrival.

Thinking of the Buckingtons inevitably brought the viscount to mind. Her heart fluttered anxiously. Baret Buckington. The unwanted dilemma she was in now was all his fault!

Emerald poured lukewarm coffee into one of the china cups her father had brought home from a voyage years earlier and swallowed a mouthful. The brew tasted like bitter molasses and seemed to stick in her throat. She couldn't drink it and set down the cup with a clatter, opting instead for a dry roll and smearing it with breadfruit jam.

Her thoughts left the day's events to focus on Jamie Bradford. Had he managed to elude capture during the night? She had awakened on several occasions thinking she could hear the barking of the hounds sniffing out his fleeing trail.

The bread too stuck in her throat. Her eyes narrowed. Mr. Pitt. That callous man would enjoy hanging Jamie! The idea that one so vicious was in charge of Foxemoore in place of her father was more than she could comprehend.

How could a family such as the Harwicks, with nobility in their bloodline and a nominal reverence for God, turn the running of the slaves over to him? How was it that otherwise decent people such as Great-aunt Sophie could be so misguided as to trust him? Mr. Pitt was rough in manner and speech, and so obviously—at least to Emerald—ruthless.

The likely reason that the family had accepted him was not pleasant to contemplate. They were far removed from the ugly reality of the life of the slaves. Unlike the gracious I AM who told Moses that He heard the groaning of the Israelites in Egypt, the owners of the Africans did not wish to hear of their misery. Deliberately they removed their hearts from hearing, their eyes from seeing. Slaves were mere tools to accomplish the planters' goals, and they did not wish to think that the sin and brutality of their culture existed—not when that culture must be protected to produce large Jamaican plantations.

It was far easier to live removed from reality in the Great House and leave the wretched business of runaway slaves and misconduct of indentured servants to men such as Mr. Pitt.

Emerald recalled the words of Cousin Lavender: "So there lies the difference between us. I wish for nothing more than to leave Jamaica and return to England. I have one purpose. To marry Baret and sup with the king."

Emerald went up to her room to prepare herself for the lawn supper and ball. What would the viscount say to her about her misguided venture aboard his ship? Did he suppose she had stolen jewels? If only she could convince him that she was far from being the "feisty wench" he had met on the *Regale*. If only he would think of her as a girl of noble cause, a daughter of the King.

She paused in the midst of her outward adornment, however important it was. If the viscount were ever to see her as she wished to be, then much more was needed than finery and manners alone. Baret must see her faith in Christ. He must come to understand her commitment to the spiritual good of the downtrodden slaves and the growing hope she was placing in Mathias's Singing School.

It was not likely that Baret Buckington would ever truly see her in that wholesome light, Emerald thought wearily. She sighed. She would always be the brat granddaughter of a French pirate on Tortuga.

She struggled to reject a new flood of despair. *But my heavenly Father does not see me that way.*

"Lord, You are the Shepherd of my faltering feet. Guide me now and do not let me stray from Your purpose for me."

Lady Geneva's ostentatious wedding ring flashed with momentary luster in the noonday sun as Lord Felix Buckington handed his new bride down from the coach onto the carriageway. A long line of coaches followed closely behind, returning from the ceremony held at St. Paul's Church in Port Royal.

Outside the Great House, prominent officials from the Government House were met by serving attendants clothed in black satin livery. Wealthy planters, including Sir Jasper, arrived on horseback, showing off their fine-blooded animals and accompanied by personal slaves.

As grooms led the horses around to the back of the Great House, more guests continued to arrive. The wives and daughters of officials carried crimson-and-gold-fringed silk parasols as they strolled across the green lawn to the reception area, while their young African girl slaves followed behind, bringing large boxes containing even more elaborate gowns for the evening's ball.

Emerald left her buggy parked out of view farther back on the road, concealed by the tall cane, and walked alone up the carriageway. Lifting her hand to shade her eyes against the glitter, she paused and glanced toward Harwick House. She had deliberately arrived late, hoping to fade into the throng and thereby remain unnoticed.

She saw Geneva standing with Lord Felix in the receiving line and had to admit that her father's cousin appeared quite happy.

It was Lord Felix Buckington, however, who held Emerald's curious and cautious gaze, for this was the first time she'd seen him, and, after what she'd heard, she was curious indeed. He was nothing like the man she had expected to see. He was not large and physically powerful but tall and spare, as swarthy as a Spaniard, with eyes a startling blue. In their determined glance, Emerald detected a ruthlessness that agreed with the thin but strong mouth and hawklike nose.

His coat of black camlet had bone-colored lace at the wrists, and there were more ruffles at his cravat and a haughty glimmering sapphire.

Planters with their families from all across Jamaica thronged the wide lawn, partially encircled with palm trees. Picking up her burgundy velvet flounces looped with Spanish lace, Emerald walked hesitantly toward them. The palpable waft of smoking beef, pork, and turkey drifted to her.

As she approached the lawn area where guests were already enjoying plates of food and cool drinks, her courage failed. How could she possibly face them? Did the family know she was coming? What if the viscount had forgotten to inform Great-aunt Sophie that he had bidden her to come?

Glancing about, she didn't see him anywhere. Perhaps he had not come with the entourage bringing Felix back to the house from the wedding. But why would he? If what her father had told her last night were true, she wondered what Baret thought of Felix's marrying Geneva Harwick.

Noticing an arbor shading the outer path that led to the garden behind the house, she took momentary refuge beneath the vine, thick with white passionflowers.

I must be daft to have braved this moment, she told herself and looked toward the front porch where Lavender stood with her mother, Lady Beatrice, greeting some guests.

Emerald clenched her hands. *I haven't the courage to walk up there even if I am dressed as fine as Lavender.*

She took a closer look at Lavender's father, Lord Avery Thaxton. Frail and fine-boned, he was attired in blue taffetas with thick gold lace. His was a poet's face, narrow at the chin with sensuous lips. A shock of curly brown hair waved across a white forehead, and moody eyes gazed out upon a world with an expression of perpetual boredom.

Avery Thaxton had married Beatrice Harwick in London. Having lost their first two children soon after birth, they had overcompensated by indulging their only child, Lavender. They sailed to the West Indies when Avery was appointed by His Majesty to aid the governor-general as a strong voice for moderation in Jamaica's relationship with Spain. It was known that Avery had failed to curtail the raids of the buccaneers on the Main.

Not that it was Avery's fault—the governor-general was hard pressed to keep the buccaneers' headquarters in Port Royal without issuing them commissions, and without the buccaneers Jamaica had no naval defenses. But already there were rumblings that Lord Avery might be called back to London to answer to King Charles for failing to curb them.

She listened to the pleasant din of voices and laughter, the tinkle of glasses, the excited cries of children playing, and felt disappointment at her lack of courage.

And just where was the gallant Captain Foxworth?

She drew in a small breath. *Well, I won't stand here in the shadows like a turtle with its head pulled in,* she scolded herself.

She was stepping from the arbor when an anxious voice called, "Miss Emerald, has you seen Jette?"

Emerald turned to an older African woman, hurrying down the arbor path from the back. It was Jitana, the head housekeeper.

"He's not with his new governess?" She had been certain that Drummond had left the house with him and the twins early that morning.

"He's been gone since the family returned from the wedding."

Knowing of the child's displeasure over Geneva's marriage, Emerald assumed that he was hiding.

"He must be in the house somewhere. He has to be."

Jitana shook her head. "The governess says he was with Timothy and Titus, but they's missing too."

"I'll look for them. All three are probably somewhere amid the picnic guests."

"Lady Geneva's sprouting thistles over this. His lordship Felix being here and all, and they was supposed to dine together at the head table."

"I'll do what I can."

"Thankee, Miss Emerald—and you're sure looking pretty this afternoon." She turned and hurried back up the path in the direction of the house.

It was not like Jette to disappoint Geneva even if he did disapprove of her marriage. Geneva was as close to a mother as the child had. Although his blood mother was unknown and Viscount Royce Buckington declared legally dead, Jette had been entrusted to friends of the viscount in France. It was there, in a village close to Lyon, that Geneva had gone to find the small child and bring him to Foxemoore.

He's got to be somewhere nearby, thought Emerald.

As always, if she could locate the mulatto twins that he had "adopted" and named Timothy and Titus, Jette was likely to be with them. No doubt they would be on a hunt to capture bugs in a bottle, and Jette would be oblivious to the time.

The three boys had become nearly inseparable since Jette had grown up enough to hear of his father's disappearance. The close relationship among the three appeared to be part of a healing process that eased his emotional loss.

Concern for the boy rallied Emerald's courage, and her steps quickened in the direction of the front lawn, where she skirted the edge and scanned the numerous guests.

She recognized only a few important faces from Port Royal, most of them officials in Governor Modyford's parliament.

Jette was nowhere in sight. It was true that the boy had been upset about the marriage and going to London but not enough to deliberately run away. She recalled his desire to join his brother and search for their father! Would he have run away to find the ship?

I should have taken the buggy back to Port Royal last night to warn Father, she scolded herself, but her own dilemma over Jamie and Ty had divided her mind.

But surely Jette wouldn't run away. He had promised her.

No, he must be with the twins playing somewhere nearby. She knew for a fact that once they had their bugs in a bottle, they could sit for an hour, simply shaking it to keep the insects crawling and buzzing, and never realize the passage of time.

Emerald's own concerns for the child had developed slowly during the past two years. Frail and often ailing, Jette had responded to her warmth at the Singing School. His interest in spiritual matters had no doubt been cultivated by the loss of his parents, but Emerald believed he had a heart that was open to knowledge of the Lord.

Even though Geneva and most of the family were Anglican, not only had she allowed Great-uncle Mathias, a Puritan, to take command of Jette's training, but when Jette pleaded to be allowed to enroll in the Singing School, the family had surprisingly given permission.

Worshipful singing was a new concept, for congregational hymns were unheard of in England and the American colonies. The first singing schools had originated in Boston. God had mightily worked through the evangelistic preaching of certain Puritan leaders, and part of the spiritual movement included the careful teaching of both the Bible and the traditional chanting of the Psalms to children in a school setting.

In order to teach the Psalms with her uncle's first tunebooks, Mathias had introduced his own idea of a singing school for the slave children, patterned after the adult schools that trained singers in Psalm singing and hymn tunes deemed appropriate to teach to church congregations.

Although the traditional adult singing schools were held within the church, Mathias had strongly believed that God was leading him to begin an independent work for the slaves, translating their chants into a gospel message they would respond to favorably.

The idea was so foreign that neither of them had mentioned it to anyone on Foxemoore except Ty and Minette.

Emerald had been drawn to the idea from the start and had worked with him from the day he had built, near the slave huts, a structure made from palm branches and old sections of a boat that the turtle man Hob had told him about.

At one time—before she decided to marry Jamie and escape Foxemoore—Emerald had nourished her own unspoken dream for the school. She had wanted to write a children's hymnal: "Songs for Slave Children." Great-uncle Mathias had encouraged her in the project, but somehow the struggles of simply living each day in Port Royal had robbed her of the will to carry it out.

Now as she searched the area of the lawn and trees, she did not see Jette or the twins anywhere. She stopped to inquire of the servants, but no one recalled having seen the three boys.

The rising voices of planters discussing their anger over the French sugar trade with the American colonies drifted to her from a cluster of palms, where a group of men had gathered and stood drinking from tall glasses.

"How long will England tolerate the French islands dumping cheap sugar on the market? Our trade and land holdings are at risk. Does His Majesty intend to protect us or not?"

"Since when has the king protected Jamaica?" came a scornful voice. "Our safety depends on the buccaneers."

"But for how long? Lord Felix and the Peace Party are against them, but if they leave and return to Tortuga . . . Governor Modyford must issue new letters of commission to Morgan and his captains."

"Pirates! And with them preying on the Main, how do you expect to ever trade with Madrid? They all ought to be arrested and sent to Execution Dock."

"And where will the safety of Jamaica be without Morgan and his buccaneers? What stands between our plantations and either Spain or France but the rogues?"

Emerald was well aware of the politics of King Sugar. Anger over the exports from the French islands of Martinique and Guadalupe bought by American privateers was growing stronger by the day. Mention of the privateers from the colonies lit a spark in the already hot afternoon. Grumbling voices crackled in the air as others joined the debate.

Today, after the outdoor supper, Felix would be speaking to the planters about mounting difficulties with France over the sugar trade.

Emerald had heard her father say that Felix held a high position within the Society of West Indian Planters and Merchants in London. The lobby was an established political power in the court of His Majesty King Charles, and it used all available means, public and private, to stress the importance of maintaining an English sugar monopoly. Lord Felix worked tirelessly against the French sugar islands. The London lobby, her father said, "has organized one of the most rigid and vigorous parliamentary power blocks England has ever known. And many of them wish for peace with Spain."

What all this might mean for Jamaica and the family sugar estate, Emerald did not know.

Above them all, the arrogant voice of Sir Jasper called out, "But who can trust the buccaneers for long? Their loyalty is not to Jamaica but to their greed and hatred for Spain. While King Charles seeks a treaty with Madrid, the buccaneers embarrass him by attacking peaceful galleons in the Caribbean. Lord Felix has come to Governor Modyford from the king with orders to stop this piracy! He intends to hang any pirate or buccaneer who attacks a Spanish ship."

She turned her head away quickly, so that Jasper wouldn't recognize her, and crossed the lawn toward the carriageway. *Why, he has gall to speak so,* she thought indignantly. *He's naught but a pirate himself.*

Their voices faded into an argumentative din as she hurried on.

She paused, the breeze tugging at her hat, as several riders came through the white-pillared gateway from the outer road. As they cantered up the palm-lined roadway toward the house, she stepped back out of sight, believing she recognized the fair young swordsman named Sir Erik Farrow. Was the viscount with him?

Glancing back toward the Great House and seeing that the milling guests were too busy to notice her, she picked up her flounces and sped down the sloping lawn, keeping close to the shade trees that lined the road.

Emerald was intent on swift departure when a voice halted her flight.

"Fleeing the lion's den?"

17

FACING THE FOXES

Emerald's eyes narrowed. She clenched her hands and turned her head toward a cluster of palms.

The familiar fine-blooded horse that she had encountered the morning before on the road stood munching a grassy clump. She glanced about the trees but saw no one at first. Then Baret Buckington straightened from the shadowing palm where he'd been lounging, evidently waiting for someone.

He was resplendent in stylish hat and suit of fine velvet cloth with a broad white collar. The pale blue ostrich feather that curled on his broad-brimmed black hat fluttered. His high leather boots were polished, and their buckles gleamed. His dark eyes flickered with amusement.

"Or does my cousin make a hasty retreat from Sir Jasper? We can't have him win now, can we? Not when you're so handsomely dressed for the ball."

Emerald swallowed and made a little curtsy. And despite the warmth in her cheeks, her eyes courageously met his. "I've no appetite for the barbecue, your lordship. Nor do I care to mince about the floor to music like a goose. So begging your leave—"

"I'm certain Geneva will have some dainties to tempt your finicky appetite. And as for mincing about the floor to music—I've a notion any girl who can don calico drawers and swim a quarter mile to shore will have practiced a bit, even if only in secret."

She blushed, for she had indeed waltzed about the Manor many times with Minette, both pretending to be great ladies at a ball, and the idea that he already knew her well enough to guess that was unnerving. But it was the mention of her disguise that provoked her.

"Oh, please, won't you forget that?"

"My dear Lady Harwick! Forget that you dared my ship in the darkest midnight donned in the garb of a pirate? Madam! You request too great a sacrifice even for my esteemed gallantry!"

His eyes glinted, and a faint smile touched his mouth. He was being miserably mean and enjoying it.

Emerald retained her dignity. "Your gallantry is in want, m'lord."

"Is it? Well. We'll need discuss my manners at a more convenient time." He tilted his head, glancing toward the guests. "Lunch is being served. Shall we join them?"

"Oh, please, I . . . can't!"

"Not afraid, are you?"

She didn't want to admit her courage was lacking. "I can explain everything about mistakenly going aboard your ship. I vow I can!" She glanced nervously toward the barbecue.

A dark brow lifted. "You will indeed explain." He took hold of her forearm. "But later. Shall we go? The lions wait."

"I . . . can't . . . please." She tried to pull away.

His hand dropped. He appraised her as though bored, folding his arms. "I'm disappointed in you."

She had turned, bent on retreat to the security of her concealed carriage when his words stopped her.

"Disappointed?"

"You can risk what you believed to be a pirate's cabin, but when the moment comes to demonstrate pride in being the daughter of Sir Karlton you flit away like a nervous chickadee."

Had she heard him properly? She *was* proud! It was the gossip about her birth that she cringed to face in public, but he already knew.

Emerald looked at him as she held onto her hat. Her eyes searched his. Had it been a simple mistake when he called her the daughter of Sir Karlton? Did that imply he accepted her birth? Or was he only interested in keeping her there until she explained about the night before?

She saw her opportunity and changed the subject. "I must talk to you about little Jette."

Before he had time for a response, they both spotted Lavender walking toward them. Evidently he had been waiting for her.

Emerald froze as her cousin approached, but Lavender appeared not to see her. She turned her full attention on Baret, her blue eyes glowing, a shy smile on her lips. Emerald knew Lavender too well to believe the shyness to be genuine, and she wasn't as sweet-tempered as she now appeared, but on Lavender the affectation was flattering.

She wore a white satin frock with tiny red rosebuds and French eggshell lace. Her golden hair was elaborately done in a cluster of French-style curls.

Emerald stepped back, lost in her cousin's shadow, fingering the ribbon on her hat uncomfortably.

"Baret! You kept your promise. Mother thought you might not come."

"And intentionally miss seeing you? Hello, Lavender."

Lavender's eyes warmed as they looked up at him. "How pleasant of you to surprise me."

"I may need your good graces before your mother and father."

Lavender clasped her hands together in distress, pearl rings glimmering. "Oh, Baret! You didn't risk your reputation to attack another Spanish ship? You shall enrage your grandfather."

"I'm afraid I already have," he said ruefully. "I met with him last night."

"You were here last night and didn't see me?" she asked, pretending hurt feelings.

"You were asleep. As for the *Santiago,* I performed my duty admirably."

She appeared genuinely troubled, but Emerald, watching, remembered that Lavender had once told her she admired Baret's daring on the Caribbean.

"I've something I must discuss with you alone," Lavender murmured. "Will you come to the ball?" She took his arm. "Oh, you must! I shall be horribly saddened if you don't."

"I wouldn't want to disappoint you."

Lavender smiled up at him, then lowered her lashes and managed a faint pink blush.

Observing the feminine display, Emerald felt oddly irritated. Her gaze narrowed as she glanced at Baret to see how he was taking the flirtation. He had removed his hat and was reaching for Lavender's pale hand. He brought it to his lips. He had come to the ball to be with Lavender, willing to face criticism over the sinking of the Spanish galleon.

"But Great-aunt Sophie will be delighted to see you," Lavender was saying. "You know how she adores you. I shall call for her at once."

She looped her arm through his, smiling happily, her rich skirts rustling softly as he turned to walk with her toward the green.

Not a word for me, thought Emerald.

"Your health hasn't appeared to improve," he was saying. "You've always been frail. You need to leave the tropics for Buckington House."

Lavender gave a sweet laugh. "It shall not be too soon for me, and now that you'll be returning within the year, I know I shall be feeling much better."

Emerald noticed his sympathetic affection. It was true that Lavender often took to spells of illness that kept her confined to her chamber, but most of the time she was convinced that her cousin was exaggerating to win support for her plans.

But Baret's amused attitude had transformed to courtly chivalry as he focused his attention on Lavender. And that annoyed Emerald. *Nothing for me but barbed remarks and malicious amusement.*

Suddenly Baret must have remembered her, for he stopped and turned. "You know Karlton's daughter, of course," he said. "Emerald is our guest."

"Yes, I received your note that she was coming."

Emerald thought she would choke at the expression that crossed her cousin's face, but Lavender recovered with a poise more typical of her mother.

"A delightful surprise, Emerald. I was hoping you wouldn't turn down my invitation again." She turned to Baret with a smile. "It's such a trial to get the child to come out and meet people. She's so shy and . . . well . . . a trifle awkward."

She looked at Emerald. "Dear, you mustn't be ashamed of your background on Tortuga. It's not your fault about your mother . . . and how nice you look! I'm so pleased my dress fits you."

Emerald stared at her, confused and embarrassed all at once. She caught the unpleasant gleam in her cousin's eyes.

She was on the verge of insisting she must leave when the too-sweet smile on Lavender's face checked her. *That's just what she wants me to do. Slink away in shame and make a ninny of myself while she impresses Lord Buckington with her sweet spirit.* Could he not see through her false charity?

If Lavender wished to pretend that she had invited her, and that she accepted her as a cousin, then the others would most likely fall in line. *I won't run,* she told herself. *I'll stay and eat if I choke—and I'll attend the ball too.*

"Why, I just had to come, Cousin Lavender," she said truthfully and looked at Baret. Did he smile? "And you'll be leaving soon for Buckington House, Lavender. I may not see you again for years, if ever."

Lavender's eyes turned to shivers of blue ice. But she recovered and came back to loop her arm through Emerald's. "How thoughtful of you to care. Come, dear. The family will be happy to see you."

"Will they?" asked Emerald quietly.

Lavender looked away as though she hadn't caught the question.

Before they walked ahead, Emerald thought she noticed a look of subdued admiration in Baret's dark eyes. It surprised her and offered more courage. *He thinks I did well.*

She walked beside Lavender. *I'm a child of the King,* she repeated soundlessly to strengthen her growing resolve.

The babble of voices, the tinkle of glasses, and the excited shrieks of children filled the hot afternoon air. The outdoor supper was well under way on the rolling green lawn fringed with tall palms. Mulatto house slaves carried silver and chinaware vessels from the back kitchen of the planter's Great House to the dozens of tables that were shaded by woven cane and bright umbrellas. The male slaves had donned white

177

knee-length pants, and the women wore ankle-length dresses of bright yellow, with red bandannas tied about their heads.

Somehow Emerald had gotten through that heart-stopping moment when, in the company of Lavender and Baret, she'd found herself face-to-face with Great-aunt Sophie, standing with Governor Modyford.

Emerald could not recall what introduction was given. If it hadn't been for Baret's strong hand clasping her elbow, she might have remained speechless when Sophie turned to look at her.

At first, her great-aunt hadn't recognized her. Then in a flash, awareness showed in her frosty gray eyes. *What are you doing here?* they seemed to ask, but Sophie recovered swiftly. Without so much as a hesitation, she smoothly welcomed her nephew Karlton's "precious daughter" as though Emerald's presence at such affairs were customary.

Then Sophie turned to Baret, and, though she frowned, it was clear the silver-haired matron set great store by him.

She reached forth pale and thin hands with veins showing. "Baret, you naughty scamp. You've stayed away much too long. Come, give me a kiss. And how dare you bring scandal to the family by sinking that dreadful Spanish galleon?"

Baret took her hands and bent to brush his lips against her upturned cheek, his eyes showing amusement. "I didn't sink it, dear Sophie. I merely borrowed its treasure chest," he said glibly and lifted her hand, heavy with emeralds. "Ah . . . Madrid would be envious."

Sophie gave him a hard look but doubtless was not offended. "They came from Felix."

"A gift for your endorsement of his marriage to Geneva?"

Sophie's eyes hardened. "I did not endorse it." She lifted her hand, turning it so the gems shone. "Do you like them?"

"Rather gaudy. So Felix gave them to you. Ah. That accounts for everything."

"So it does. But he's likely to be offended if you suggest it to him. And the earl is here, did you know?"

"I've already spoken to Grandfather," he said, but Emerald noted that he didn't mention his Uncle Felix. Baret turned

178

to Governor Modyford. "I regret I couldn't bring Henry Morgan, but he is quite busy making plans for a pleasant voyage."

The governor-general's eyes sparked with subdued irony as he picked up the humor. "Hello, Baret. You best keep an eye on your uncle. Felix has arrived to put a pistol to my head in the name of the king. No more letters of marque to be issued against Spain."

"A tragedy. Felix is active in the king's Peace Party. I am sure, however, you'll have authority to exercise your concerns for the safety of Jamaica. There's news of a planned attack by Spain on Port Royal."

The governor-general affected surprise, but Emerald noted the twinkle in his eyes. "An attack against Jamaica, you say!"

"Yes. You might wisely consider sending Morgan and his captains on a mission to discover if the secret report is true," suggested Baret smoothly.

"An excellent suggestion. His Majesty can hardly call me back to London to answer for actions deemed necessary to safeguard his interests in Jamaica."

"My sentiment exactly, Governor. I am sure the report of Spain's gathering ships at Havana will prove accurate enough by the time all is known."

"Yes, and it does take months for news to reach His Majesty. You'll be joining Morgan again?"

"Not so," spoke up Lavender sweetly, taking Baret's arm and looking at the governor. "We'll both be returning to London soon."

Emerald had stood there trying to behave as though she belonged in the conversation but was grateful when at last the ordeal was over. When Lavender was briefly called away, Baret walked Emerald across the velvety lawn and deposited her on a cushioned settee. He picked up a palmetto fan some girl had left and handed it to her with a smile. "You look a trifle vexed."

She fanned herself briskly.

He leaned his shoulder against the tree. "Was it worth it?"

Her fan stopped in midair. She looked at him, startled. "Worth it! You know very well, sir, I didn't want to come! It was your malicious way of getting even with me for boarding your ship."

He smiled. "Ah, but you obviously did want to come. Karlton wanted it as much as you, perhaps more. I did you a favor by insisting." He folded his arms.

"Is that what you call the ordeal you've put me through? A favor?"

He laughed. "I'll wager that when you slipped into that pretty frock you took from the trunk and gazed at the change in the mirror, the first thought crossing your mind was how you'd enjoy showing the bluestockings on the hill what a fine lady you could be! I merely gave you the opportunity to fulfill your wish. What you do now where the family is concerned is up to you."

She glanced at him cautiously as she ran her palm across the soft velvet of her sleeve. "But Lavender said she loaned me the dress. How do you know I took it from my father's trunk?"

His dark eyes smiled. "Because, Lady Harwick, it wasn't your father's trunk. It belongs to that rogue Captain Foxworth. He took the trunk as booty from the *Santiago*—along with some other interesting prizes. I stored the trunk in Karlton's lookout house."

She stared up into his smile with her hands hidden in the folds of her skirt. *So that's why Minette said the trunk hadn't been there the day before.* She had once again broken into his things—and this time she had taken something. Her cheeks flamed.

"Aboard the Spanish vessel I opened the trunk to check its contents." He cocked his head and scanned the yards of burgundy velvet and lace flounces. "I rather liked it. In fact, it was to be a gift for Lavender."

If her earlier meeting with the family had proved an ordeal, then this moment was its equal. The dress was meant for *Lavender!*

"I confess the dress looks better on you than it would have on her."

She left the glass of lime refreshment on the lawn and stood to her feet swiftly.

"Then—then you recognized the dress on the road yesterday. You knew all along who I was, yet you let me go on pretending."

He smiled. "I did."

"You—you might have said so then."

"And ruin your disguise? It's not often I meet such a capable young lady who can don a pirate's drawers one night and the velvet gown of a Spanish viceroy's daughter the next." He pretended to be impressed. "But you did take me off guard when you appeared on the stairs donned in the black mourning clothes of a widow."

"And I suppose you'll give Lavender the added satisfaction of telling her I broke into your trunk."

"Which trunk?" he asked innocently. "There were two if I recall. The more important one being aboard the *Regale*. You do owe me an explanation of why you sneaked aboard my ship."

Her rage melted into alarm. What if he did tell Lavender? "Oh! Please, m'lord—you—you won't say anything?"

The malicious amusement in his eyes was maddening.

"Being a gallant gentleman, we shall keep the notorious secret between us."

She sighed, hand at heart. "How can I thank—"

"On one important condition."

Emerald stopped, seeing his eyes flicker with subdued temper. She moved uneasily. "On what condition?"

"That you tell me why Captain Levasseur paid you to break into my cabin."

The suggestion completely stunned her. "Paid me! Levasseur?"

"Yes, Levasseur," he repeated dryly. "Your cousin from Tortuga. That infamous blackguard you likened me to. I suppose you want to deny you're his cousin and that you were working with him. What was it you were expected to find, madam?"

"I vow he didn't pay me! He had nothing to do with it."

His brow went up. Obviously he didn't believe her.

"I can explain everything," she whispered desperately, glancing about, for it would be her luck to have someone overhear his odious charge. She saw Lavender coming from the house and walking toward them. It was one of the few times that Emerald was relieved to see her.

Baret noticed her too and straightened from the tree. "You will indeed explain," he said in a low voice. "Unfortunately this is not the moment to do so. Alas! I'm sure you're relieved. It will give you time to think up something. But I'll learn the truth eventually, so you might just as well confess. I may decide to show grace and allow you to escape the wrath that Levasseur will face."

"Baret?" called Lavender, stopping some distance away. "My father wishes to see you in the library."

He looked at Emerald and gestured to the white linen tables where a rich assortment of food waited. "And now—I'll leave you to your appetite. It may be you can find some dainties that meet your approval."

He offered a deliberate bow. "If you'll excuse me until tonight."

"Tonight?" she whispered anxiously as he turned to leave.

His mouth turned. "The ball, madam. You'll explain all then. So don't get any notion of slipping away to Levasseur's ship. I should hate to board and take you away by force. Duels are rather unpleasant."

It was on her tongue to say that it wasn't her cousin's ship that she hoped to board but Jamie Bradford's, but that would have been the worst mistake she could have made.

She watched him walk across the grass toward Lavender, and together they went up the wide steps into the house. Vaguely she wondered what his meeting with Lord Avery was about. Perhaps the upcoming marriage? The expression on Baret's face had not shown anticipation. Nevertheless she was certain that he did want to marry her.

Emerald thoughtfully approached one of the picnic tables where a roasted suckling pig with pudding in its belly was the centerpiece of an extravagant supper. There was so much food that it was impossible to taste it all.

She recognized some of the meats: mutton, beef, goat, turkey, duckling. She heard the uniformed slaves offering servings of foods she had never heard of, all exquisitely decorated and proffered in large silver platters or bowls: capons, loin of veal, sweet shoat, heaps of marrow bones, an assortment of minced pies made with tart fruits soaked in wild honey and suet. There were pickled oysters, Westphalian bacon, and an entire table of fresh tropical fruits: plantains, watermelons, custard apples, guavas.

Did nobility always eat like this? she wondered. Did Baret? What was it like at Buckington House? How did the earl dress, and what did he drink? Certainly not kill-devil rum!

Her curiosity over Baret grew. How had he lived before becoming a buccaneer? *He must think me terribly ill-bred,* she thought and winced. Outwardly Lavender was so poised and gracious.

Had Jette been telling the truth about Cambridge and the Royal Naval Academy?

Jette! Had Jette shown up yet? She must inform Baret that Jette knew about his plan to look for his father.

Emerald left the table to go in search of Jette again. Perhaps he was in the back garden.

Emerald had said nothing of her conversation with Jette to anyone at the Great House, knowing the importance of keeping the information about Royce Buckington secret.

As the afternoon wore on and the guests milled about the barbecue, she cast another quick glance toward the house. Lavender had come out again and was speaking with guests on the lawn. Other members of the family including Geneva and Felix were also with the guests. But Baret was not in sight.

Thinking he might yet be in the drawing room with Sir Avery, who also was nowhere about, Emerald drew in a breath and swiftly made her way across the yard and up the front steps into the hall, glancing behind her to see if the family noticed her. They had not, and she slipped into the house.

The hallway was empty, the house quiet, with most of the family and guests down at the barbecue. From the back of the residence, where the cook room was located, she could hear the muffled voices of servants busily keeping glasses washed and pitchers filled with refreshment.

The drawing room was to her left, and the door stood open. She walked in quietly and peered inside. The room appeared empty, but an unpleasant odor of pipe tobacco tainted the air. Then she heard someone rise from the leather sofa that faced the front windows.

She did not know whom she expected to see—perhaps Baret—but coming across Sir Jasper now was the last vexation she wanted. Her expression must have told him so, for his mouth turned down and his eyes boldly swept her with a glance.

"Tsk, tsk, m'dear. Not disappointed, surely!"

Emerald stood still. She could see that his mood was far bolder than usual, and she guessed it was because he knew that her father would soon take to sea again and be gone a year.

"Let me guess. Like the other girls, you were hoping to accidentally meet the viscount. But you've always been more mature than some of them, and I'm disappointed in you."

Emerald said in a cool, steady voice, "If you will excuse me, Sir Jasper, I've other business to attend."

She turned to leave, but as swift as a cat he came between her and the door. "There's plenty of time, Emerald."

It was the first time he had dared to use her first name. She pretended not to notice.

"I haven't had a chance to speak with you yet. You are always avoiding me, skirting the lawn a mile out of your way."

Emerald tried to appear casual. "I'm sure I don't know what you mean. I've spoken to you many times."

"But never alone."

She glanced toward the outer hall. The door was still open, and she could see past his shoulder. "I believe Lavender is calling me."

A dark brow arched, and there was a mocking glint in his eyes. "She's quite taken up with interests of her own, darlin'."

He scanned her dress. "Most becoming. You should have many more. And would if you'd—"

She tried to brush past him, but he caught her.

"No use pretending offense. We both know what you are. It's time, darlin', you discarded your virtuous airs."

Stung, Emerald slapped him. And no sooner had she done so than she saw her mistake.

His eyes narrowed, and he grabbed her. She struggled, turning her head away as he tried to kiss her.

Footsteps in the hall sobered him, and his grip loosened enough for Emerald to twist free. Not waiting to see who was coming, she rushed breathlessly through the door and into the hall—colliding with Baret.

He steadied her and studied her face. He looked toward the drawing room.

"I—I must talk to you," she said with a rush. "It's about Jette."

His expression was unrelenting. "Give me a few minutes. I've an appointment with Jasper. Wait for me outside."

"Yes—of course," she said with a breath of relief. Holding her hands against the sides of her skirt to quiet them, she turned to walk past him.

Jasper had come to the doorway, and he stopped when he confronted Baret in the hall.

A brief side glance at Sir Jasper as Emerald turned to leave showed his face still mottled with temper, but his countenance had swiftly altered at seeing Baret.

As she walked to the outer door to wait on the veranda, Baret shut the drawing room door.

She looked back, briefly wondering what interest had prompted him to meet with Sir Jasper. From the blunt inflection of his voice when mentioning him, Baret had not appeared too friendly.

Emerald looked at her palm, still stinging from the slap. She had surely made an enemy of Sir Jasper now!

Baret stood in the drawing room, arms folded, and raked Jasper Ridley with a cool look, his mouth turning, deliberately goading him by doing so.

"I wasn't expecting you yet, Baret."

"So it appeared. She must have walloped you pretty hard. The red mark mocks you, Jasper."

He hoped Ridley would become angry and make a mistake. If it was true that the man had information on the whereabouts of his father, he intended to get it from him—

one way or another. "Masquerading as a respectable planter does not fit you," Baret challenged.

Jasper's first reaction was a brief look of surprise, but he swiftly recouped his equilibrium, and his black eyes measured Baret as warily as one male tiger sizes up another.

"I do not know at what you hint, your lordship. I am exactly what I appear to be in Jamaica."

"A smuggler? A traitor to England? A spy for Madrid?"

Baret watched Jasper draw himself up to his full height. In a quelling manner used to put the pretentious in place, Jasper said, "What hideous charges you hurl against me!"

"Yes," came Baret's dry retort.

"Do you mean to question my honor?"

Baret smiled slowly. "What honor?"

A quick flush darkened Jasper's face, and his jaw tightened. "By the saints! If it is a duel you are begging for, you shall very well have it!"

Baret's smile continued to press him. He raised a hand in dismissal. "I do not duel mere commoners. It wastes my reputation." He flecked off a speck of lint from his exquisite black velvet jacket. "Have you forgotten I am earl after my father? I shall soon be the most powerful landowner in the West Indies, with political authority to eliminate my enemies. Not to mention the assets I possess in London."

Jasper stiffened with grudging wariness.

Having set him off guard by his haughty pretense, Baret added, "After all, I am heir after my father, and Royce is dead, is he not?"

Baret saw what he was searching for—Jasper's momentary flinch.

"It has been so said for several years."

"Yes. So said by Felix." Baret watched his unease grow.

"Your father's death was a most regrettable turn of fortune, your lordship. The viscount was an excellent seaman. It is a pity he set sail from Port Royal in the hurricane season."

"Most regrettable," said Baret, his gaze dwelling lazily on Jasper's right hand, which had begun to flex uneasily by his lacy cuff. He suspected that the man carried a blade within reach. He remembered the dagger thrown at him at the Bailey.

"You are right. My father was a skilled seaman. Far too seasoned to have recklessly taken his ship into heavy seas during the hurricane season."

"You know the facts as well as anyone."

"But not as well as you. I mean to have them."

"I? And what do I know except what the English authorities announced. Lord Buckington left alone. He attacked the *Prince Philip*. There were few survivors—and your father was later killed in a duel in Port Royal. I know nothing more and am most grieved you think I might. And I am a respectable landowner, with acreage second to none but Foxemoore."

Baret's eyes mocked him. "So I am told. Second to Foxemoore, yes, but respectably acquired? I beg to differ. I find myself interested in the means by which you attained the wealth to buy."

Jasper's false humility was shed as he snapped, "Viscount or not, I owe you no explanation. By marriage to Geneva Harwick, your uncle Lord Felix now has more authority on Jamaica than you. Your uncle is satisfied with the fact that I own my land."

"We won't quibble about that. My uncle has few scruples. In that he is like you—he knows an advantageous situation when he sees one. So he married Geneva Harwick. You, of course, have ready plans for my cousin, no doubt secretly agreed upon by Felix, but I must disappoint you again."

Jasper's mouth twisted. "Emerald is not your cousin. Perhaps it is you who have designs?"

"It was not Sir Karlton's daughter I had in mind but Lavender. But it is neither the wedding of Geneva nor concerns for Lavender I've come about. It is the illegal trade by which you acquired money to buy out two lesser planters. Now that, Jasper, interests me much."

"Have you come to me to harp about African slaves?" he scoffed. "How hypocritical, when Foxemoore has more than its share! If I'm involved in slave trading, what is that to you? Have you emerged from your religious studies at Cambridge to go on crusade? Hundreds of upstanding gentlemen in England are involved in slaving. Where do you think they got their money? Why worry yourself about my profit?"

187

"For the moment let us forget the African slaves. I have a particular concern on my mind. It is the white serving class I speak of—farmers, servants, tradesman—all of them illegally abducted by your pirate traders working out of Saint Vincent. These poor miserable men are then sold by you as convicts to Spanish planters. Then there are the silver mines in Peru. Suppose you tell me about those mines."

Jasper paled under his sun-darkened face. Even so, he was too seasoned in the art of deceit to be mastered for long, even when cornered by fear of discovery, and Baret knew it. Still, he hoped by open accusation to discover something.

"Lies," snapped Jasper. "I have nothing to do with crimes on the high sea."

Baret folded his arms and goaded him further.

"Where's the sword and pistol you bravely flaunt aboard your ship of convicts? Where do you sell those miserable wretches you've abducted? To Porto Bello? Havana?"

Jasper was now as wary as a stalking cat. "You have no proof."

"I could come up with enough evidence to see your neck in a noose where it belongs."

For a moment all the fight went out of him. "Felix will never permit you to go to the authorities."

"And I know why. So do you, Jasper. I want the truth."

Jasper looked worried now. "I've not engaged in the business for three years. I swear it's true! It is land I wanted, and I have it now. I've a chance for respectability, for marriage into the family dynasty. Why plague me? If it is fear of losing Lavender to me, you need not. Not even Felix could deliver her to me. There is talk she'll be given to your cousin Grayford Thaxton."

"It is *information* I want."

Jasper's black eyes fixed on him. "What information?"

"You've sold convicts to Spanish smugglers. To what island? To what Spanish don? I suggest my father was among those prisoners."

For the first time fear showed on the man's face. "Impossible. Such talk is madness. Sell the earl's son as a convict? I should as soon take a knife to my throat! Do you think I do not know that you—that others in the family—would hunt me down?"

"The others? Perhaps not. Not Felix. Shall I refresh your memory? Those smugglers you did business with sold their convict slaves to whoever would buy them in the West Indies. They found a ready market with the Spanish dons. I suggest some of those smugglers came across my father and some of his crew, still alive but trapped aboard his ship that was in the process of sinking. I suggest they took them prisoners, and you bought them and sold them as slaves to Spanish smugglers."

Sir Jasper stood still, nothing moving.

"I suggest you found out the mistake only after it was too late. In fear, you rushed to Lord Felix with the dark news, promising to try to get my father back if only he would say nothing to the governor-general. But to your surprise my uncle did not threaten you with the noose your neck deserves. Instead he made it easy for you to forget my father was sold into slavery. In fact, Felix paid you a handsome sum to remain silent. You took that sum and bought out several lesser planters on Jamaica."

"This is preposterous, your lordship! Would I knowingly sell the Earl of Buckington if I knew who he was?"

"No, you are a coward. Like a shark smelling blood, you only feed on those poor farmers and laborers who are too weak to defend themselves." Baret straightened from the doorway. "I believed my uncle for a time while I was a lad in Cambridge, Sir Jasper. I am no longer the trusting student. I have returned to refresh your memory. And you will tell me exactly to what colony in the West Indies my father was sold."

"I swear I do not know!"

"You lie."

"No. I can only tell you the slaves were sold to one of the Spanish colonies."

"Havana?"

"I don't know, I tell you. It might have been, or one of the others. The smugglers sell up and down the Main. I make it a practice not to know. I am not in that part of the business."

"The name of the man who ran your smuggling. What was it?"

Sir Jasper's lips went white. "Say nothing to Lord Felix of this?"

"I've no reason to at the moment. He would seek to hire assassins to kill my father."

"And me."

"The man's name. I want it!"

"Charlie Maynerd."

Baret stared at him for a long moment. Finally his breath released. "He's been hanged. You know that."

"Still, he was the man. He drifted away soon afterward. Went to Barbados and took up piracy."

Had that been another reason that his uncle had eliminated him?

"If you are lying, I will find out sooner or later. I will call you out, Jasper. And I will see you dead."

"I speak the truth that I know. There is no more to tell."

Baret faced him evenly, then reaching behind him to open the door, he went out, closing it.

He frowned. And scooping up his wide-brimmed hat from the hall table, he left the house, going down the porch steps.

In the distance on the green he saw that supper was well under way. He noticed Harwick's daughter sitting on an ottoman with her skirts spread about her, a plate on her lap, and he thought of the scene he had walked in on minutes earlier.

Obviously Lavender was not the woman Jasper wanted.

Although Baret appeared to be unperceiving when it came to Sir Karlton's desire to somehow involve him with his daughter, he was well aware of the man's hopes.

He saw her look in his direction and remembered she had mentioned Jette. As he left the steps to join her, she stood and, picking up her skirts, walked briskly toward him across the grass.

What must he think, my appearing so bold as to have sought him in the Great House? Emerald thought uneasily. Did he know that Sir Jasper had accosted her again? Had he heard the awful slap?

He was waiting when she came up. Emerald glanced about, looking over her shoulder. She was beginning to feel conspicuous, for she saw Cousin Lavender watching and no doubt wondering what business Emerald had with the viscount.

He walked along beside her, and for a minute they said nothing.

"You mentioned Jette," he said.

"He has the notion he's going with you aboard your ship. I know the risk in searching for your father and—"

She was startled to feel his hand close tightly about her arm. His eyes searched hers.

"Who told you about my father? Karlton?"

"Yes, but there's no cause for alarm."

"Have you mentioned it to anyone else?"

"I'm wiser than that. You're holding my arm too tightly."

"I'm sorry." He dropped his hand. "You must say nothing of this to anyone in the family."

"I am aware of the need for secrecy, sir, and I do not nurture the habit of gossip."

"Let us hope so. Most young girls find nothing more pleasurable than to engage in mindless chatter."

Of all the arrogance . . . "Your secret, Viscount, is quite safe with me. It is Jette I worry about."

"What about Jette?"

She wanted to cringe beneath his gaze. She had just told him secret information was safe with her, yet she must now tell him about the biggest mistake of all—that of Jette's overhearing the conversation between herself and her father in his office.

"I'm afraid he overheard my father and me talking," she said lamely.

As he understood what she was saying, his eyes took on a hard glitter. She saw his jaw tense.

"I did everything I could to dissuade him," she said quickly. "I've told him your search is only a hope, that he must say nothing—"

"Where is he?"

"His governess says he's not been seen since the family returned from the wedding ceremony. I suspect he's playing

191

with the twins and hound. But he doesn't care for Lord Felix, and I wanted you to know about his dreams of sailing with you."

"I'm glad you told me. I think I know where I can find him."

She looked at him curiously, for she thought she knew Jette's hiding places far better than anyone else. "You've seen him then?"

"We had a good visit this morning before the wedding."

"He's not in the Great House," she suggested.

He smiled. "Don't worry. He's showed me his secret hideaway. He and the twins have a hideout in the cane field."

She smiled too, relieved. "I was afraid he might have tried to sneak away to the harbor and stow away on the *Regale*."

"He knows he's leaving for England with his grandfather. He's pleased about that. They've gotten along well. But I'll have a guard keep a lookout just the same."

"The Earl of Buckington! He's here on Foxemoore?" she asked, surprised, a little awed by the thought.

"Yes, you'll meet him tonight at the ball."

They turned as a serving man came up and handed Baret a small folded piece of paper.

Emerald saw a flicker of subdued impatience as he read it, then a glance toward Lavender, who watched them. Evidently the terse note had come from her.

Emerald felt embarrassed. She had the idea he was in the mood to insist she join him and Lavender, and she wished for not the slightest hint of gossip.

"If you'll excuse me," she breathed quickly, "I think I shall make up a plate of barbecue for Great-uncle Mathias and have one of the servants bring it to him. He's not been well recently."

Before he could reply, she hastened across the soft lawn in the direction of the tables.

She smiled wryly. *If Lavender knew what the viscount thinks of me, she wouldn't worry. Imagine! Lavender jealous of me!*

18

THE BALL

The ball was about to begin. Emerald glanced about, and her senses were beset on every side by the lavish display of thick scarlet velvet drapes arrayed over all doors opening into the drawing rooms, where the guests congregated about cool refreshments.

A staircase led up to guest chambers used to hold wraps and bags and for giving finishing touches to wigs that were sometimes brought in boxes and carried up by personal maids.

As Emerald stood near the stairs, she heard a demanding voice call to her, and she turned. The sight dazzled her. The most jewel-bedecked woman she had ever laid eyes on swept across the room with hand extended, sparkling with emeralds and gold. Her billowing skirts of brocaded blue satin shimmered in the light of the chandeliers. She wore a wig of pronounced white curls glinting with gold dust.

"Ah, m'dear Catherine, how delightsome you've joined us tonight."

"I'm sorry," said Emerald with a smile. "You've mistaken me for someone else."

"Indeed!" The older woman scrutinized her up and down. "Aren't you the earl's granddaughter visiting with him from England?" She studied Emerald's elegant gown with a direct stare.

"No." She hesitated to say who she was. "I'm Emerald," she said simply.

The name passed over the woman like water off a duck's back, and Emerald let out a silent sigh of relief.

"I am Isabeau," she said, as if Emerald should already know. The woman took Emerald's arm, and the two proceeded up the stairs.

"It's the war, of course," said Isabeau. "I suppose Felix will join his brother-in-law Avery in galvanizing the island against an onslaught from the Dutch and French?"

"I believe," said Emerald, playing her part, "that Lord Felix has been appointed sole commissioner to the governor in defense of Jamaica."

"He'll be a strong commissioner, don't you think? But I must say—" and she leaned toward Emerald and whispered "—I am horribly shocked that His Majesty gave a Royal Navy command to Felix's stepson Grayford instead of to the earl's blood grandson, Baret."

Emerald was alert now. "Why so?"

"My dear! Don't you know anything? You must admit Grayford is less qualified than his cousin. Baret did attend the Academy, you know, and graduated. More's the pity, he then suddenly disappeared from London. And of course, Baret so wanted the Royal Navy command."

Emerald digested this information in silence. Then Jette was right. There was indeed much about Baret she did not know. Evidently he had not always been what Great-aunt Sophie had called him—"a scamp."

"I admit Grayford is a dear boy, and I'm told Felix has wondrous plans for him." Again the woman leaned toward Emerald and whispered, "There he is now." She turned and gave Emerald a searching appraisal. "Are you related to Grayford by any chance?"

"Um . . . the family is so large I couldn't truthfully say."

Emerald turned her head and looked across the banister at the stepgrandson of the earl.

He was standing alone on the other side of the room, surveying the guests. Although Emerald knew next to nothing about his character, he impressed her as a man who was full of himself. Whereas Baret was earthy and dark, his cousin was urbane and fair like Lavender, and his well-fitted naval uniform presented a man who was as slim and straight as he was tall.

Geneva joined them on the stairway then. She was arrayed in satin as silver-gray as her eyes, setting off her red hair. "So you've met my cousin's daughter, have you, Isabeau?" she asked pleasantly enough.

Isabeau did not restrain her look of shock. "Karlton's daughter?" A slight look of pity shone in her haughty eyes.

"Yes, this is Emerald Harwick."

"Oh. *That* Emerald. Yes. The name suddenly springs to memory."

They had stopped on the stairs. Emerald showed nothing in her expression at hearing the woman's change in tone, but Isabeau carried on bravely.

"My dear! How charming you look. I never realized. I thought . . ." And her probing eyes studied Emerald's features as though searching for signs of African ancestry.

Emerald felt her resentment rising. It was this insidious attitude of superiority in the English that irked her the most. "You look nothing like the Buckingtons, my dear—oh, but of course you wouldn't . . . well . . . you are an eyeful, my dear. You had best watch her tonight, Geneva. She'll have every rake in Port Royal after her, including Sir Jasper."

"I'm quite able to take care of myself, thank you," breathed Emerald.

But the woman, having decided that Emerald was no one of importance after all, had already dismissed her and was proceeding up the stairs to the upstairs hall, Geneva leading the way.

Emerald was obliged to follow them down the upper hallway and across a spacious anteroom to another carpeted passage, and finally they arrived at a room so large and spacious that Emerald thought it might easily pass for a second ballroom. There were mullioned windows edged with green-and-gold satin brocade, polished walnut furniture, cupboards, tables, and chairs, as well as a large four-poster bed that dominated one wall.

Emerald took in the ornate decorations, the woven tapestries, and silver and gold plate that gave a touch of richness to the room.

Lavender was there, adding finishing touches of red tropical flowers to her hair. "Baret sent them," she told her.

"They are lovely."

"They'd go better with your hair."

"Oh, I hardly think so. Red becomes you so."

Lavender laid the flowers aside and, turning, inspected her. "How well do you know the viscount?"

Startled by the question, and that Lavender would even ask, Emerald felt uneasy. "Why, hardly at all—"

"No matter," interrupted Lavender and turned her back. "I'm surprised he asked you here today is all. I suppose you insisted."

Emerald wanted to deny the suggestion, but if she did even more innuendos would surface. She changed the subject, glancing about. "Such a grand room."

"You should see Buckington House. This is nothing."

"It may be splendid, but I should get lost in a room this size," said Emerald. "I prefer something more intimate. Notice how our voices seem to echo?"

"One gets accustomed to luxury." Lavender frowned and looked across the room at her mother, Lady Beatrice, who was adorning herself before the large mirror. "Baret should have come by now. He promised he'd attend the ball."

Lady Beatrice added a heavy jewel-encrusted brooch to the bodice of her dress. She ignored Emerald as though she were invisible.

Emerald removed her presence across the room to a blue tapestry settee and rested her feet. She was not accustomed to high-heeled shoes.

"Where did you get the brooch, Mother?" asked Lavender.

"It's made of emeralds and Margarita pearls—isn't it lovely?"

"I hear a buccaneer confiscated it from a Spanish don."

"And collected it as a government 'due' by your father," said Beatrice boldly. "It's been tastefully awarded to me as an eighteenth wedding anniversary gift." She laughed. "As for Baret—" she cast her daughter a grave look "—he's in disfavor with the earl," she warned. "The earl is furious with him."

Lavender picked up a flower and frowned. "How do you know?"

"They argued last night. Baret is likely to be disinherited if he sails with Henry Morgan." Beatrice straightened her brooch. "I've heard the wife of the lieutenant-governor has a necklace of pearls set in Peruvian gold, taken during the last buccaneering raid on the Main," she murmured.

Lavender seemed to shrug off her alarm over the news of an argument between Baret and his grandfather. "He already told me about his grandfather's displeasure. It doesn't matter. My marriage has been settled since I was a child."

And Emerald saw her cousin glance over at her with a wry smile. "Unlike my poor cousin here—whose reputation is soiled."

"That will be enough, Lavender," said Beatrice. "Emerald is a guest tonight like your other friends."

"Of course, Mother." And Lavender made an amused but playful frown at Emerald behind her mother's back.

Lavender had told her that she was destined to become a countess after the death of her invalid grandmother in London. This title from the Thaxton side of the family would make her even more of a prize for the handsome young viscount.

Several other titled ladies in England nurtured the same hope. But unlike the other daughters of London nobility, Lavender did not fear competition. She not only had the determination of her mother to aid her, but she knew that her dowry had influenced the Buckington nobility, especially the earl.

"Baret has vowed that if I would allow him the liberty to take to sea for the next few years on some purpose he cannot now explain, he will return to marry me and settle in London at Buckington House," she announced. "Even if he does join Henry Morgan, the earl will forgive him eventually. He won't disinherit him. He has too much pride in the Buckington name to see the title go to a nephew."

"I wouldn't be so certain."

Emerald wondered if she should be listening, but neither Lavender nor Lady Beatrice paid her any mind.

At the tone of her mother's voice, Lavender turned from the mirror to look at her. "What do you mean?"

Emerald thought Beatrice a woman of wintry beauty. She had the same fair hair as her daughter. Like her sister Geneva, she was accustomed to showing restraint in public, since her position made for a busy and sometimes artificial

197

social life. But even in the privacy of the chamber when she was obviously worried, Beatrice was poised.

"Why shouldn't I be certain about Baret?" asked Lavender again.

Beatrice arched a brow and stated without shame, "I discovered a letter from London in Geneva's drawer. It was written by Felix."

Emerald wondered that she would say this in her presence.

Beatrice turned to her without expression. "See you say nothing of this to anyone."

"Oh, don't worry about Emerald," said Lavender. "I've always shared our scandalous secrets with her. There's little you'll do, Mother, that will surprise her. And I too have learned many of your ways." She laughed and turned to Emerald. "Mother is convinced Geneva is working with Felix to have my father recalled to London and therefore removed as lieutenant-governor of Jamaica."

"I believe Geneva is scheming against your father's good standing with His Majesty," said Beatrice, "and I have a right to know what we're up against."

"What did Felix write Geneva? Was it about Jamaica?"

"Not this time. The scheming knave is more confident than ever of convincing the earl he should inherit instead of Baret. If Baret does show himself tonight, you best speak a word in his ear. Unless he returns to London as the earl wishes, he may end up as nothing more than one of Henry Morgan's odious buccaneers."

Lavender frowned for the first time.

Beatrice turned to her daughter as her voice became firm. "Sir Jasper has become the second most powerful planter on Jamaica. A merger of our two sugar estates would give the family an even stronger voice for the West India interests in Parliament."

"Never," said Lavender. "The man is loathsome. I suppose Father has tried to convince you I should marry him?"

Beatrice watched her daughter as the maid removed a wig from a box and held it out for display. "Not your father. It was Felix. Don't look so unhappy. You must have known that Jasper was always a possibility. The entire family agrees. And he's a close friend and sugar associate of Felix."

Emerald felt uncomfortable listening to a family squabble over whom Lavender must marry. She could see by Lavender's expression that she would not succumb easily.

Emerald turned away and busied herself by opening her own dress box and removing her fan for the ball.

Lavender went on, undisturbed it seemed by her presence. "What about the earl? What has he said to this?"

"The earl does not know yet. But he takes a great interest in what goes on in Jamaica. Sir Jasper met with him in private while in London."

Lavender's surprise must have pricked her mother's sentiment, for she said more gently, "Darling, surely you must know you cannot marry Baret if his title and inheritance are taken from him."

Lavender gazed into her mother's eyes, a look of dismay on her face. "That must not happen! I won't let it!"

For a long instant they stared at each other.

"You had best talk to Baret," said Beatrice.

Lavender turned away to allow the maid to dress her for the masquerade.

After Lady Beatrice left and shut the heavy door behind her, Emerald whispered, "I could never marry a man I did not love."

Lavender cast her a cool glance. "It doesn't matter who *you* marry, but my marriage is important since my children will be heirs to Foxemoore."

As far as the family was concerned, Lavender was right. It didn't matter. Emerald realized suddenly that she was blessed with a freedom Lavender did not have.

She watched as the maid draped her cousin with the gold-bejeweled gown and tried the matching mask over her face. Then without another glance toward Emerald, she left for the ballroom.

Emerald looked after her, refusing to allow her cousin's rejection to discourage her. She turned abruptly to the mirror and looked at her dress. There were no jewels like Lavender's, but she did have pearl combs that her father had given her when she was thirteen, and they set off her lustrous mahogany curls.

"Your mask, miss."

Emerald took the maroon satin piece with embroidered white lace and tried it on.

A stranger stared back from the gilded mirror.

The granddaughter of archpirate Captain Marcel Levasseur had at least found her way into the Great House for a ball!

Emerald went to join the important gilded guests.

Pausing on the staircase, she looked over the huge ballroom. Everyone was masked. Satin-gowned ladies wore elaborate wigs and eye masks, and lavishly attired gentlemen in black masks were arriving as a thousand candles glittered on the ceiling and walls, causing the wall hangings of gold cloth to ripple.

Emerald came down the stairs, one hand on the banister, wondering what to do next.

A voice to the side of the handrail interrupted her thoughts.

"I've been waiting for you to come down, although I shall play the game and pretend I do not know who you are."

He was dressed in uniform, and though he wore a mask she recognized him to be Grayford Thaxton, stepson of Felix.

Grayford gave a light bow and extended a hand, smiling.

"I shall be highly disappointed if you deny me this first waltz."

"I am pleased to oblige, your lordship."

"What makes you think a man in naval uniform would be titled?"

Emerald smiled. "Because I also know who you are. You were pointed out when you first arrived. You are Grayford Thaxton."

"And you are Emerald Harwick. I assume you are now a cousin since the marriage of my father and Geneva."

"Rather confusing, isn't it?"

He laughed. "I thought I was the only one to think so."

He waltzed well, and Emerald was careful to follow his lead.

"Are you pleased about the wedding?"

Emerald could not answer at once. "I'm certain I wish them well. But whether I was pleased or not wouldn't matter."

Grayford smiled, showing even white teeth. "I see you know my stepfather well."

"Actually I haven't met him yet."

"You will," he said, and something in his tone made her wonder.

"I shall be stationed at English Harbor," he said. "With any luck I shall have the privilege of sinking a ship or two. I fear another war with the Dutch is soon to break. Unlike the first war in the fifties, this one will likely include the West Indies."

"The sea appears to run in the family blood," she said. "I believe you have a cousin who is a privateer. Lord Baret Buckington."

The smile did not leave his face, but she noted that there was no humor in it.

"Ah, yes. You've broken the first rule."

"Rule? What is that?"

"Bringing up Baret," he said wryly. "I'm surprised Lavender didn't mention that he is considered an unwelcome topic in the family."

"Then I've made the first of what are likely to be numerous errors tonight. But I hardly thought that mentioning your cousin—"

"Speaking of Baret is not troublesome to me, although it is disappointing, when he has deliberately chosen to affront all he previously stood for."

She looked at him. "Because he's a buccaneer?"

"I suppose that is the polite way to put it. Though my stepfather might suggest he is far closer to following the ways of Henry Morgan, the way his father did. A pity too. Baret might have won command of His Majesty's vessel had he been more disciplined and less prone to reckless ventures."

"I did not know he had an interest in the military," she said. "I had the notion he preferred the ways of the independent privateers."

"So it seems," he said tonelessly. "I suppose what he is on the inside took time to develop."

"Then he was not always considered an unpleasant topic?" she suggested, trying to keep her curiosity masked.

"He was the earl's pride—the grandson who could do no wrong—until his father turned to piracy."

"Seems rather strange that the earl's own son would become a pirate," she said. "Indeed, he had everything in London."

His expression changed. "Another tale. One best left to the murky past. As for my cousin . . . well, Baret felt the charges against his father were false. He's done about everything he can to anger the earl—and all in the name of trying to prove his father innocent."

"So now you and he are on unfriendly terms?"

"In the beginning we went to the Academy together. He took it quite seriously. More so than I. Baret graduated at the top, but he turned against the Admiralty—and my stepfather."

Emerald tried to take all this in, wondering. Baret was more complex than she had first judged him.

"The command I now have in the West Indies would have been his, had he not been discharged," said Grayford ruefully.

She looked at him. "Discharged?"

His eyes reflected the irony he must have felt. "He entered Spanish waters near Cuba to sink a galleon," he said flatly. "While Felix and others at court were negotiating peace with Spain for His Majesty."

This news sounded very much like Captain Foxworth, she thought, and wondered that she retained a faint admiration for his boldness.

As she glanced over Grayford's shoulder, she noticed a man standing apart from the merrymakers, watching the milling dancers and a group of jugglers dressed as bears—or was he watching *her?*

She sensed that he was, though she could not be certain of his gaze beneath the dark mask embroidered with gold.

He was a commanding figure, and she was not the only woman to notice him. A few heads were beginning to turn, perhaps hoping he would favor them with a waltz.

He was exquisitely dressed and must have been a titled nobleman. Even the sedulously curled periwig and white lace ruffles at his throat and wrists—a fashion that Emerald secretly loathed on men—did not detract from this gentleman's virility.

She noted that his clothes were worth a fortune—the coat was of rich blue-green velvet, with elaborate gold embroidery. And when the jeweled pin in his cravat caught the light of the chandeliers, the colors glinted a deep blue, and she suspected they were sapphires.

Was this the earl?

"Enough hoarding of the fair damsel, Grayford," said a bold voice as the music ended and a second waltz began. A man stepped up beside them and, taking her arm, claimed her, sweeping her away before she could reply. Even disguised and wearing a mask, she knew who it was.

"No offense, sweetheart, but you owe me an apology since the occasion of our meeting was so rudely interrupted in the drawing room."

She looked up into his pale eyes and broad smile. "Sir Jasper," she breathed with exasperation, "do you ever give up?"

He threw back his head and laughed heartily. "I am a determined man."

"And fickle. I understand you wish to marry Lavender."

"The earl prefers she marry Grayford, but there is always hope. And you, my dear? Surely you're not still doting on that indentured slave Jamie? A pity! A sad heart will he bequeath you once the Harwicks hang him."

She stopped waltzing. "If you will excuse me, Sir Jasper, I've suddenly developed a headache."

She turned quickly, lifting her skirts, and in her haste collided with a large-bellied nobleman wearing a meticulously curled black wig and a heavily jeweled monocle in his left eye.

"Saints preserve me, madam!"

"Oh," she said. "Oh, your lordship! I beg your pardon—"

"My monocle! It's on the floor! Great scot, you little hussy, if it's stepped on I shall lose a thousand pounds! Henry!" he called. "Henry!"

Henry the butler, dressed in severe black, flew toward them and began to flutter about, staring at the polished floor as the big man stood pointing.

"I'll find it, sir," said Emerald and knelt to peer on the floor, hoping the diamonds would glitter in the chandelier light.

Dear God, she prayed, her face flushed, *this is the most horrid moment of my life.*

A small group of guests had come up by now, and Emerald was so embarrassed at being on her hands and knees that she couldn't bring herself to look up even when a resonant voice stated clearly, "Looking for this trinket, Lord Humphrey?"

"Trinket! Why, I'll have you know . . ." His voice trailed off as though his mood had suddenly been altered. "Why . . . er . . . yes, my lord. Thank you, indeed."

"Good," came the easy tone. "Then may the celebration continue?"

Humphrey gave an uncomfortable chuckle. "By all means, your lordship."

"Strike the music! Play His Majesty's favorite waltz."

As the guests began to move away and a soothing refrain filled the ballroom, Emerald was about to stand when a strong hand wearing a glittering sapphire ring reached for hers.

"Permit me."

That voice—Captain Baret Foxworth?

He lifted her, and Emerald, bent on immediate flight, murmured, "If you will excuse me, m'lord, I must go upstairs," but his hand did not release her, and she turned to look into a handsome face half hidden behind a dark leather, gold-trimmed mask.

The man she had seen earlier while waltzing with Grayford had been Baret.

19

BUCCANEER OR VISCOUNT?

"Not afraid of a pack of blue bloods, are you?" came Baret's smooth challenge. "Most of them could trace their ancestry back to Gin Lane if they'd admit the truth."

Gin Lane, she knew, was considered the worst district in London. She was startled that a viscount would speak so lightly of nobility, even if he did own a second identity as the captain of the *Regale*. It was clear that here, at least, he was known only as the full-blooded grandson of the earl, his birth line extending back to the Earl of Essex.

As she glanced at him, her unease only grew. He looked to be anyone but a reckless buccaneer, and she wasn't at all certain which man she felt more comfortable with. A magnificently garbed viscount was as intimidating as the sardonic pirate she had met in the ship's Great Cabin.

"I suspect our pompous Mr. Humphrey may have discovered his diamond monocle in a collection of booty confiscated from a rum-soaked pirate," he commented.

Emerald couldn't imagine the large-bellied Mr. Humphrey rummaging through pirate treasure, and she smothered a laugh. "He might call you out to defend his honor if he heard you," she said.

"I tremble at the thought."

Emerald scanned the features that were bronzed by the warm rays of the Caribbean sun, half hidden behind the masculine eye mask.

"I hardly recognized you in a periwig," she said. "What would the nobility in London do if they saw you in the role of infamous pirate?"

He mocked a wince. "Ah . . . you must not breathe a word about Captain Foxworth."

"I admit, sir, you are presently fit for royal company, but do not forget—I have seen you as you truly are."

"Then it appears we both have a dark secret to guard." His eyes glinted behind the mask, but he wore a smile.

She remembered her calico drawers.

"And I would be most disappointed to see you turn and flee like a timid mouse from a passel of snobs. Somehow your daring venture aboard my ship convinces me you have a rare spirit."

His challenge put steel in her spine. "I was not about to flee like a frightened mouse."

"Then you have the blood of a Harwick after all."

After all? She tensed a little. "I'm surprised a full-blooded Buckington would find anything in a Harwick to commend," she said defensively.

His dark brow lifted. "If my memory serves me, the Buckingtons and the Harwicks have intermarried through the years. As for good blood, I cannot imagine a seahawk like Harwick surrendering at the first shot. Nor would his daughter."

She contemplated the difference in his manner. Were his compliments sincere, or was his behavior merely suited to the moment?

He studied her. "We are standing in the midst of the ballroom while music plays, Lady Harwick. Guests swirl about us, staring. I think it best if you honor me with this dance." He offered his hand.

She looked away from the potent dark eyes that gazed back at her through the slits in his mask. She felt challenged, then gave a curtsy. "As you wish, your lordship."

She was aware of guarded glances as they waltzed, and for the moment she felt herself a countess.

"I expected Grayford to come to your rescue. I don't see him about. He must have escaped to let Felix know of my unwanted presence."

She said nothing, concentrating on her steps.

"As for my intervention," he said lightly, "I couldn't endure seeing you cast into the emperor's arena with the lions coming in—or perhaps I should liken you to an innocent lamb surrounded by English hounds?"

"I appreciate your concern for my safety among lions and hounds, but I shall not allow myself to be trapped by either. Nor by buccaneers masquerading as viscounts or lords."

He laughed quietly. "You are very much the daughter of Harwick. But you could easily pass for Morgan's brat."

She stiffened. "How dare you!"

"That was a compliment. I happen to think well of Morgan. I suppose you know why?"

She struggled to keep her poise. "No, should I?"

"I'd have expected my honorable cousin Grayford to tell you."

Under his gaze she became uncomfortable. "If you're asking if he suggested that you might soon be wanted as a pirate, yes, but with regret for your fallen ways."

"Only suggested?" he mocked. "How generous he's become. I suspect that his being awarded my inheritance has mellowed him."

"And his receiving what would have been your command of His Majesty's ship might also have helped."

He winced. "He told you that too."

"And that you graduated from the Royal Naval Academy. I must say I was impressed."

"Did you think I was raised on a pirate schooner?" he asked, amused.

"Under the present circumstances, my lord Buckington, no. And I see you also have the manners of nobility."

"But now I'm a buccaneer. As you said, I may hang at Execution Dock."

"It's your own fault."

"A lecture from you? I'd prefer anything else."

She was curious about his past and said casually, "He said you sank a Spanish galleon without authorization. Did you?"

He perused her for a moment as if deciding the seriousness of her question.

"Yes. I felt it was my duty since its captain had just opened fire on an English merchant ship whose captain was an old friend."

"And that gave you the right to attack?"

He smiled. "Quite. I believe you know the captain."

"Me?" said Emerald dubiously.

He looked satisfied. "His name is Captain Karlton Harwick."

She reacted with a startled breath.

"I thought that might alter your viewpoint," he said dryly. "Am I forgiven?"

"Did you truly—"

"Yes. And speaking of ships, I'm reminded, Lady Harwick, that you have much to explain about your clandestine purpose for coming aboard the *Regale*. Shall we begin?"

Oh, no, now it was coming.

She cast a nervous glance around the ballroom and, noticing Lavender, said too casually, "I'm afraid such explanations must still wait. Lavender has entered the ballroom and will naturally wish your attentions."

He looked at her wryly. "And I'm afraid those attentions must wait. We may not have another waltz together. What I need to know, I must learn now while I've the opportunity."

"You're leaving Port Royal?" she asked with a tinge of hope.

His mouth turned briefly. "As a matter of fact, I am. But you needn't sound so relieved, Miss Harwick. You must admit I've been more than fair with you. I might have disclosed your masquerade to your father."

A little smile touched her lips. "And have you forgotten I share your guarded secret of being Captain Foxworth?"

"Then you do think I'm a pirate?"

"I didn't say that."

Her eyes swerved to his with a hint of surprise and found them glinting with malicious humor.

"I am a pirate—if you agree with men like my uncle that attacking Spain's ships and denying Madrid treasure to supply their armies in Europe is a crime. I see it differently."

"England is not at war with Spain," she corrected. No sooner had she spoken than she saw her words provoked emotions that were anything but casual.

The laughter died in his eyes, and he said abruptly, "No? Spain is at war with the world. At this very moment Madrid's soldiers are committing atrocities against Protestants in the Netherlands who oppose their lordship over Holland. And if Spain, which serves the will of Rome, should have its way, all Europe will be subjugated to its political and religious control."

His fingers tightened about her waist. "To resist means torture. A cruel, inhumane death. And I shall fight them to the last in the Caribbean. It is here, rather than in Europe, we have opportunity to bring them to their knees in financial defeat. I'll do so with my life, even if it leads to Execution Dock."

Emerald was taken by the change in him, the rigid set of his jaw. She felt his gaze regarding her and found herself thinking, against her will, how out of place he appeared in the handsome wig and garments of a homebound aristocrat.

He was far too . . . too . . . she searched for the correct description and was surprised when she thought of the word *dangerous*. And yet she believed it true. There was something about him that reminded her of her father's secret friends in Port Royal, all of them buccaneers, and she was never certain whether she could trust them or not. They were all restless, untamed, possibly unworthy of confidence.

Presently he said slowly, a touch of surprise in his voice, "I'm sorry. I don't know why I said all that to you."

He released her. The music had ceased, and he looked away from her and across the room to the veranda.

"Would you like a breath of air?—no, don't refuse," he said, his mouth twisting lopsidedly. "I need it." And taking her arm, he steered her politely through the watching guests out onto the veranda and down the flight of steep stone steps.

Holding her skirts to keep from tripping, Emerald cast a frantic glance ahead into the fragrant shadows. "I can't disappear with you into the garden! I know what they'll say."

"You're quite safe, madam."

"From you or from gossipy tongues?"

"I'm sorry, but I need answers and intend to have them without distraction. If we stay in the ballroom, Lavender will interrupt."

"She saw us leave! What will she say?"

"I'll explain."

He steered her ahead through sickeningly sweet trumpet flowers, ducking under straggling vines as they hurried. He continued to propel her onward, keeping to the shadow of the wall, until they came to a gate.

She stopped, breathless, and looked at him with alarm. He ushered her through and down a cobbled path toward a garden slope overlooking the glittering Caribbean.

She was not acquainted with this area of the Great House. Ahead lay a small cobblestoned square, dominated by wrought-iron benches and tables, all ornately carved. English lions sat under the soft black sky, seeming ready to growl at her.

Panting from the rush, Emerald at last pulled free from his grasp and walked unsteadily to one of the lions, leaning her hand against it to rest. She was aware that she still clutched her parrot fan. Her heart thudded loudly in her ears.

Baret impatiently removed his mask and tossed it aside, along with the periwig.

Emerald turned on him, her eyes blazing in the moonlight. "Oh!" She ripped the mask from her face.

He looked at her, undisturbed by her anger.

"They're right. You *are* a blackguard!"

He folded his arms. "Is that all?"

"Is the tarnished reputation of my mother not enough, Captain Foxworth? Do you know the agony I've had to face all these years, growing up with a cloud over my head, enduring the scornful glances from the family—including Lavender!"

"Your mother's reputation means nothing to me."

"But it means a great deal to the mean-tongued ladies at the ball."

"Then I suggest you ignore them."

"That's easy for you to say!"

"Is it? My reputation is not exactly gallant, madam. But there are matters of great concern to me at the moment. You can begin by explaining your relationship to Captain Levasseur."

Emerald whirled with dismay, her hands forming fists. "My first appearance at a respectable ball," she gritted, "and now you've positively ruined it."

"Cheer up," he said indifferently. "In London you'll attend so many of these boring spectacles you'll soon wish to cancel your itinerary."

"Nay, never, and I'm not going to London, and—"

"Tell me about your relationship with Levasseur."

She held to the lion by its roaring mouth, trying to regain control of her emotions. After a moment she spoke. "I already told you. He's a cousin from Tortuga," she admitted grudgingly. She looked at him. "And I once thought him the worst knave I ever encountered until I had the misfortune of meeting you."

"What was his purpose in sending you to board my ship?"

"He did not. I went of my own accord, though mistakenly."

He stood across from her on the square, but she could still see his expression. He looked at her long and intently.

"I want the truth, madam."

"But it is the truth," she protested. "When I came aboard the *Regale,* I thought it was his ship."

"I see. And if you dislike this knave, why did you enter his cabin?"

"He . . . um . . . owed me something."

"What," he asked flatly, "did he owe you?"

She hesitated. "My dowry." She could see her answer took him by surprise.

"Your dowry?" he repeated quietly.

"Yes. A silver box from my mother's family in Paris, containing family jewels. There was a brooch, I remember, and a ring too. My mother was quite proud of them," she said wistfully, remembering. "She said her mother wore them to Court."

He was silent for so long that she thought he had either not heard her or did not intend to reply. At last he walked across the square to her and spoke. "Your grandmother attended King Henry's court in Paris?"

She stirred uneasily, for the thought was impossible to grasp. "So my mother explained when I was a child."

"What else did she tell you about France?"

"Not much—her family was imprisoned."

211

"Huguenots?"

"I think so. The cross my father wears came from my mother also. It's quite different from the Latin cross."

"What was your mother's name?"

She hesitated. "Madeleine Levasseur. She left me the silver box, and my cousin Rafael stole it. I would have forgotten about it these years, for I prefer to keep my distance from him, but—"

"Do you have any other reason for wishing to avoid him?"

She looked away. "He wishes to marry me."

"And you find that odious?"

"I find it quite impossible. There's someone—" She caught herself from disclosing Jamie, but he noticed.

"Yes? Someone else?"

She avoided an answer. "It was necessary I retrieve my dowry, and so I waited until I thought it safe. Zeddie assured me Levasseur was in a gambling house—and by the way, where *is* Zeddie?" she asked, only now remembering him. A twinge of guilt shot through her. "The man you seized."

He smiled. "He's quite safe and by now dining on a sumptuous meal with a friend of mine, Sir Cecil Chaderton. But go on. Why did you risk so much? There must be a better reason."

She smiled ruefully. "Does that mean, Captain, you no longer believe me to be a notorious thief prowling the wharves and sneaking aboard ships?"

"Let's simply say that I believe you to be in a dire situation or you wouldn't have tried it. I've been wondering if it might have something to do with your father."

"And if I said it didn't?"

"Then I would like to know what it was. Suppose you explain?"

Emerald hesitated. "I . . . needed the jewels to buy friends out of unjust imprisonment in Brideswell."

"Brideswell!"

"A slave," she said. "But he's more than that to me. His name is Ty. He . . ."

He searched her face. "Yes?"

She opened and shut her fan. "Ty is a cousin."

A moment of silence followed. "I see."

She wondered if he did, and turned away.

"You've African blood?" he asked.

She met his gaze evenly. "No. An uncle on my mother's side bore two children on Tortuga—Ty and Minette. My father brought them with me when we came to Foxemoore. I was about seven at the time."

He studied her. "You've openly accepted them as your cousins? Your courage is to be commended. The British are not known for racial generosity, you know."

"It wasn't bravery on my part," she confessed. "I've little to lose. My own social status is little better."

She looked at him, her eyes sincere. "Except for my father, who's away at sea most of the time, Minette and Ty were all I had. We've been close—sharing much the same pain from rejection."

"You also have Mathias," he said.

She smiled, thinking of the elderly saint who had taught her of Christ. "Yes, but I fear I shall lose even him. He grows old, and he's not well."

He watched her. "Tell me about Ty."

"I was given several days to come up with the means to spare him from being branded as a runaway. My father was gone at the time, and I had no one to turn to. I went to Lavender, but . . . well, there was little she could do. Or wished to do. Ty was branded on the forehead." She turned away to look out at the sea.

The trade wind began to blow in from the sea, wooing the surface of the bay into little waves, while in the distance tiny ships rested at anchor. The moon was rising, and the palm trees became shivering silhouettes. In the garden, where red and yellow hibiscus grew in profusion, a waft of aromatic scent sailed with the breeze.

"Where is Ty now?" he asked quietly.

"I don't know. That's the difficult part. He may still be held at Brideswell, or perhaps he'll be sent home with Jonah, his grandfather. My father has gone to Port Royal to see about Ty. Whatever happens, he's already been cruelly disfigured for life."

"And you expected to use the jewels to buy his freedom before the branding?"

"Yes, but I was unable to do so."

"I'm sorry. You should have told me the truth at once. Who is this scurvy rat who wanted the jewels?"

"Mr. Pitt, the overseer," she said quietly. "He came to me, demanding I go to Levasseur."

"Pitt," he repeated thoughtfully. "I don't know him. Is he the man who took your father's place running the sugar workers?"

"Yes. Lady Sophie trusts him," she said tonelessly. "Why, I cannot understand. Now he's been able to convince her there was a plot for a slave uprising. He's a vile man."

"No doubt. An overseer with a whip usually is. I'll see what I can do about getting Ty released, if Karlton hasn't already done so. But you said there were other friends in Brideswell."

She looked away. She couldn't tell him about Jamie.

"I was told he escaped. Lady Sophie has Mr. Pitt out searching for him now. I've also been told he'll be hanged." She turned toward him, her eyes pleading. "Oh, your lordship, won't you please speak to the family for leniency? I should forever be in your debt!"

He regarded her a long moment, and she could not tell what he was thinking.

"Far be it from me to see your 'friend' hanged, Miss Harwick. What is his name?"

She drew in a small breath. "He is Ty's friend too," she suggested. "Jamie Bradford is his name."

"An indentured servant?" He searched her eyes.

She turned away, hoping he hadn't guessed but somehow feeling that he had. "Yes, but he has only six more months until freedom."

"I shall speak to the family and attempt to spare his neck. Would that you please you?"

"Oh, indeed! I shall take back everything I said about you! I do humbly apologize, Lord Buckington."

His faint smile showed in the moonlight. "Then I shall try to be worthy of your confidence."

214

The moon seemed to ooze mellow light in the sky above them.

Baret's brow lifted as a meteor traced a brilliant path across the velvet sky.

The night was so still that Emerald could catch the distant murmur of the Caribbean, the sound of Baret's breathing, and the sudden pounding of her heart. She was aware of an unusual moment enclosing them, a feeling of expectancy and a strange exotic longing in the warm night.

She stared up at him, words escaping her, her warm eyes unable to tear themselves away from his.

A peacock emitted a high, shrill cry, shattering the silence.

He turned toward the Great House, frowning, then seemed to make up his mind suddenly. He looked at her, lifted her hand casually, then bowed his dark head. "I must get back. Good-bye, Emerald."

She watched him leave the square. The strange exhilaration fled on wings, leaving in its wake a dull sense of bewilderment. How could she have harbored the faintest romantic inclination toward him when she loved Jamie? She could not understand herself.

She sank to the bench and covered her face with her palms. She could not possibly go back to the ball now. She must get home. And tomorrow—what would Lavender say?

Then she heard footsteps, hesitating at first, now rushing toward her. A small cry sounded.

Emerald lifted her face, and her heart sank.

Lavender appeared, her white face harsh in the moonlight, her eyes snapping with anger.

"You!"

Emerald stood, words of denial on her tongue, but Lavender suddenly gasped and stepped back, her eyes riveted upon Baret's periwig cast carelessly aside—his mask lying nearby. In horror Emerald immediately envisioned Lavender's worst fears, and her eyes welled with tears. "It isn't true, Lavender."

Lavender gave a furious cry and drew back her palm.

Emerald's face stung from the impact.

"You wench!" hissed Lavender. "You're just like your trashy mother! I never believed it—until now." She snatched up the periwig and mask and, clutching them against her, backed away, then turned and ran toward the house.

Dazed, holding her cheek, Emerald sat back on the bench. "O God," she whispered finally.

She struggled to her feet and ran as though fiery demons in the form of jackals were at her ankles. Her cheeks were wet with tears, and she felt the wind against her face as she raced down the carriageway and beneath shadowy palms that appeared to hem her in. Her buggy was somewhere ahead, near the field . . .

A figure came running toward her.

"Oh, Minette—" She wept.

"Vapors! What is it? You look like a pack of Furies is on your trail."

Emerald nearly collapsed in her arms. "I'm shamed. They'll never believe me, not now, not ever—O God!"

Minette hugged her tightly and turned to look toward the brightly glowing Great House, scowling. Swiftly she led Emerald toward the buggy. "Come. We best get back. You can explain later. I'll believe you. You can depend on me, Emerald."

As Baret left the garden, his thoughts were unpleasant, but they did not include Sir Karlton's daughter. Returning to the Great House by a back door, he went to his room and changed into rugged clothing. It was then that he remembered leaving the periwig and mask.

He lay on his back in the candlelight, hearing the music from the hired orchestra below in the ballroom. Lavender would wonder why he had disappeared. But there was more on his mind now.

There was a possibility, though small, that his father's journal from his first voyage to the West Indies held valuable information he needed in locating him. He reasoned that if his grandfather did not have the journal, then Felix probably did. It should contain the names of certain Spaniards—political and military men, as well as landowners producing tobacco,

216

spices, cocoa, and coffee, who had done secret privateering business with his father.

These Spaniards, though serving Madrid, were not above covert trade for profit. His father had used his contacts well in order to discover the sailing times of certain Spanish ships. His hope was that his father would have recorded those names, as well as those of governors, viceroys, and Spanish commanders, that might reveal anything of his father's whereabouts—for a price. Baret stared restlessly at the ceiling, his arms behind his head. There should also be information on the friendlier Indians, who might prove willing to talk, and the Cameroons—Maroons, as they were called on Jamaica.

One of the Maroon leaders—a very old warrior named Zobi, who originally had been taken from his tribe in Sierra Leone by a slave trader—might offer information, for he looked upon Baret's father as a friend.

Did the journal also link Felix to piracy and smuggling? On the one hand, Felix was a man of breeding and clever strategy. If the journal incriminated him in any way he would have destroyed it by now. Yet Felix was also ambitious and greedy. And Baret was counting on that malady of the soul. If his uncle and the men working with him sought the treasure taken from the *Revenge*, Felix would wait to destroy the journal, believing it could contain a coded message.

Greed. It was a trap in itself.

For the first time since returning secretly to his room, he thought of Emerald Levasseur Harwick. She would be surprised to know that he had suspected all along that she possessed character—even that night aboard his ship, he thought with a reminiscent smile. Her innocence had been reflected in her eyes, her face, her every protest. Perhaps he had been too hard on her, but he had not trusted her cousin Levasseur, and for a time he believed that they were involved romantically.

His smile faded, and he frowned a little. There was a moment in the garden tonight when he sensed that he could have taken her into his arms. He had also sensed something else—an alarm warning that emotions once indulged might not offer escape. *Self-preservation*, he mused. *A necessity.*

He arose from the bed and pulled a satchel out from under the coverlet. A risk must be taken if he were to locate the journal.

He considered his situation. He must be cautious. After the attempt on his life at the Bailey, he put nothing past his enemies. If he could, his uncle would stop him from leaving Port Royal.

There was no time to waste.

He tried to recall when he had last seen his father's old sea chest, but the date was impossible to recall. He had been so taken up with the intrigue with Lucca and with his own service at the Academy that he rarely came home to Buckington House in those early days soon after his father's reported death. During that time Felix may have removed the journal and the maps.

Blowing out his candle, he collected his satchel and walked to the window to look below. There was yet time, for Felix would be attending the ball with Geneva.

He left his chamber for . . . the last time? Closing the door, he quietly walked to the end of the hall and took a small flight of stairs to the third floor—and Lord Felix Buckington's chambers.

20

FRIEND OR FOE?

In the Great House on Foxemoore, Sir Erik Farrow suppressed a cough and continued his silent vigil behind the velvet drape in the dressing chamber belonging to Baret's uncle, Lord Felix Buckington.

It was fortunate, thought Erik, that Felix was downstairs attending the ball. If Felix discovered him here, he would need to do some explaining.

Seated in a plush red velvet chair behind the drape, his strong legs in black woolen hose and boots stretched out as he listened in the darkness, he dozed between wakefulness and sleep. He drew his deep burgundy cloak about him, keeping one hand on his jeweled sword belt, an expensive gift from Lord Felix. There was also a shorter, pearl-handled blade in his left boot, a gift from Baret.

The old earl had recruited Erik to spy on Baret, who was prone to follow the steps of his father and take to a life of buccaneering against Spain. But Erik had also taken a second employment, unknown to either the earl or Baret—he was providing information for Felix.

Erik knew there was more to Baret's buccaneering life in the Caribbean than revenge against Spain for the torturous death of his mother. Baret questioned the accuracy of the information Felix brought to the trial in London concerning his father's piracy and death. Baret suspected that he yet lived, perhaps was being held as a slave in one of Spain's colonies.

Erik was privy to Baret's recent contacts with the spies who were quietly seeking information about his father. He knew about Lucca, but as yet he had not shared that crucial information with Felix or with the old earl.

It was Erik's duty in service to Lord Felix to stop Baret from leaving Port Royal and sailing with Henry Morgan and his buccaneers. Erik was to return Baret under guard to London—at sword point if necessary. Baret didn't know it yet, but Erik had been reporting his actions to Felix regularly, though he did not always explain them with as much detail as he knew.

Erik tapped his fingers against his satin vest. He casually pushed back a lock of golden hair from his forehead. He frowned. When it came to Baret, Erik was both his antagonist and his ally, if that were possible.

He smiled when he remembered first meeting Baret years earlier. Baret had been a reluctant student attending Trinity College, Cambridge. It had not taken long for Erik to discover that he was the son of the buccaneer Royce Buckington. Though Baret had excelled at Greek and Latin and theology from the viewpoint of the Puritans, he still resolved to join his father against Spain in the West Indies.

Baret had been in his teens when Erik had first met him in the armory, thinking it strange and even amusing to see a young man wearing a scholar's robe and carrying books arrive to practice the sword.

Erik's own skills with the blade had impressed Baret, and when he discovered that Erik had a reputation as a buccaneer at Tortuga, he sought to hire him as his fencing master and trainer for the tournaments. Erik accepted and soon found that Baret had already acquired some skills of his own from making friends with men at the armory, skills that Erik honed as Baret swiftly became a challenge.

Perhaps too much of a challenge, he thought wryly as he sat in Felix's chamber.

The young heir to the title of viscount was no longer a comely lad but his adult equal, and their past friendship was being tested.

Erik made no excuse to himself for his divided loyalty, though there were times when he felt uncomfortable. His primary allegiance now belonged to Felix and in some degree to the old earl. Thus he waited in the dressing chamber at Foxemoore, certain that before Baret left Port Royal to join

Henry Morgan he would seek to locate a journal that had disappeared from his father's sea chest at Buckington House.

Erik sighed. This was not a situation he liked. But if he permitted Baret to leave Port Royal, it would mean the end of his knighthood, his pay, his plush quarters in Jamaica, his sumptuous meals and wine. Perhaps more important, it would mean removing himself from a position that permitted him to associate with a certain young damsel that he cared for but could never marry, for she was nobility.

Erik silently shifted his weight in the chair as the sound of the chamber door opening convinced him that he had been right to wait.

He rose to his feet quietly and eased aside the heavy drape to look into the room.

Baret lit a candle on his uncle's desk. Opening a drawer, he searched, collecting charts and maps into a leather satchel.

As Erik watched, he was convinced that Baret would prove equal to any buccaneer sailing with Morgan. The determination was visible in the set of the jaw, in the raw glitter of restless energy that stirred too easily in the dark eyes.

In Erik's earlier days he might have rallied to that drive for adventure that now bestirred Baret. But where once Erik had been boldly belligerent and a little too ready for trouble, now he was more like a trained panther, content to remember the hunt but satisfied to have his meat brought to him. Even if the one who brought it was a man such as Lord Felix.

Smothering a slight smile, Erik parted the drape, stepped out, and said with exaggerated sobriety, "Seeking something of importance, your lordship?"

He admired Baret's measured reaction. He turned at the sound of his voice but did not look surprised and retained an almost relentless calm that bespoke cool nerves.

"I'm beginning to believe the Soothsayer's suspicions about you," Baret said.

Erik arched a fair brow. The Soothsayer—the name Baret sarcastically called the astrologer who worked for Felix.

Erik leaned his muscled shoulder into the wall, his face expressionless by choice. "What suspicions are these, your lordship?"

"The Soothsayer claims you have a druid ancestry dating back to werewolves. Since you rarely sleep, I'm beginning to wonder." And Baret deliberately turned his back and went on searching the drawer as though Erik's presence changed nothing.

Erik rubbed his chin.

"What did Felix do with my father's journal?" asked Baret.

Erik ignored the question. "I gather that striking out with Morgan is not detrimental enough to your reputation. Now you have fallen so far into apostasy, Lord Buckington, that you entertain the thoughts of werewolves."

The truth was, Baret had a solid foundation in the Scriptures, and Erik knew it. He also enjoyed a somewhat salty relationship with the scholar Sir Cecil Chaderton.

At Cambridge, Baret had brought Erik to meet with some of the Puritan scholars in the Head Master of Arts's chamber, and the two of them had spent many winter evenings sitting before a fire eating sweetmeats and debating with the Masters. Some of their theological debates had been as hot as the crackling flames that warmed their feet.

"I'm relieved to see the dagger missed its mark."

Baret made no perceptible movement. "So you know about that. I thought I saw you at Maynerd's trial. Who was the assassin? Someone hired by my uncle?"

Erik might have winced at his blatant honesty but did not. He knew Baret too well to be surprised. Erik did not know who had hired the assassin, but in order to try to throw Baret off from suspecting Felix, he continued, "An enemy of your father, no doubt. Perhaps a crewman who thinks he has located the treasure from the *Revenge* and wishes to rid himself of competition. Whether your father truly buried it or not, there is no convincing those who seek for it that it does not exist."

"Including Felix?"

Erik showed no expression at the cynical remark.

Baret turned and looked at him. "I was not meant to leave Port Royal alive. But the attempt to kill me was poorly planned. That tells me you did not order it. That leaves Felix."

"Perhaps Sir Jasper?"

"Perhaps. Doubtless they both know who the assassin is."

Under Baret's even stare, Erik showed nothing—although, like Baret, he knew that Lord Felix had men in his service beside himself who were paid not to ask questions but to perform. Any one of them was capable of having thrown the dagger.

"Take caution, your lordship, in accusing your uncle. You may be wrong about him."

Baret gave him a measured look. "Do you think I'm wrong?"

Erik played innocent. "You think he would hire an assassin to kill his nephew?"

"He seems to have had no conscience while arranging the death of my father nor in convincing the earl that Father was involved in piracy."

Erik would admit nothing that might force him to reevaluate his service to Felix. He avoided the issue by asking his own questions.

"Why would anyone wish to kill you?"

Baret's mouth curved, and he studied him. "Do you not serve my uncle? You would know best."

Erik's gray eyes flickered. Who had told him? "I hope you don't mean to imply that I had anything to do with what happened in the listening gallery?"

"No. Hiring assassins is not your way. If you wished to kill me, you would draw sword man to man."

"Then you have me in the dark. I know of no conspiracy to take your life nor your father's. While you have not gotten on well with Lord Felix, I can't believe he would hire an executioner to kill you."

"Think again. Felix knows of my plans to search for my father. I am sure it was he who betrayed him to the Spanish authorities." Baret's eyes were hard. "And I trusted you with my plans. I believed you a friend."

"A most regrettable bit of news, your lordship. But you misjudge me. Whatever information Lord Felix may have on your present plans, I have not been his source." Erik was cautious. "I work for him. And I know that you believe Viscount

Royce Buckington to be alive. But I have not told Felix your plans."

"He *is* alive. And I'm just as certain that my uncle knows it as well. The question is, does he know my father's whereabouts?"

Erik's eyes were as fathomless as deep pools. He shrugged a shoulder, hand resting near his sword hilt. "If he does, he has said nothing to me."

He felt Baret's penetrating gaze. Did Baret believe him?

"Felix knows well how I've tried to convince the earl that my father lives."

"You've succeeded in convincing him?"

"You know I have not. Now I have become a risk to Felix's ambitions. He will try to stop me from locating my father. And if he knows where my father is being held, he will seek to hire men from Port Royal to find him before I do."

Erik watched him, disturbed that he knew so much about Felix.

"Felix intends that knowledge of my father remain buried at the bottom of the sea—therefore he must remain in the hands of his captors. But I will find him."

Erik wore a mask over his emotions. "Whether your father is alive, I cannot say. One thing I do know, if you sail with Henry Morgan, your father's enemies in London will see you charged with piracy and hanged."

"I've already sunk a Spanish galleon. Do you think Felix's threats and assassination attempts will make me return meekly to London?"

Erik eyed him. "No. You are much too like your father. And yet I will stop you from leaving."

Baret's gaze was challenging. "You could always remove your sword from hire. Join me on the *Regale.*"

Erik lifted a brow. "Is his lordship that determined to turn to buccaneering? Your grandfather will hardly approve."

"You are right. But what he expects is a secondary matter. Felix has turned him against me, and one day I intend to see him answer for it."

Baret placed a chart into his satchel. "These belong to me, in case you wondered. I do not steal from my uncle, though he has stolen all that belongs to my father. It was Felix who took them from my chamber at Buckington House."

"Yes, I helped him."

"I suspected that. Let us not play games, Erik. Where is the journal?"

Erik tapped a finger against his scabbard. "I know of no journal, your lordship. If your uncle took it, then only he knows. There were your father's maps and charts, but a journal?—he must have burned it."

"Not likely. It would prove too important for discovering the possible location of the West Indies treasure."

"So you too think there is treasure yet unreported to the Admiralty?"

Baret smiled faintly. "Come, friend Erik. We both know you also search for it."

Erik sighed again. "Then if you know as much, you must also know that I cannot allow you to leave Port Royal. I will stop you by force if necessary. You will cooperate?" he said smoothly, knowing that he would not.

Baret looked up and studied him. There was a flicker in his eyes that made Erik uneasy. He knew it wouldn't be a simple task to best him as he had done at Cambridge.

"You could, of course, decide to look the other way," said Baret.

"I could, but I will not."

"I should hate to see an old friend seek to stop me. It can only end badly."

"I do not doubt your determination, your lordship, but if Royce does live, locating him on the Spanish Main will not be an easy prospect. Even if you could find and free him, he is still charged with piracy. They would hang him."

"Perhaps we shall both hang. But I shall search for him anyway."

For a moment they simply looked at each other.

"Come with me," said Baret. "If there is treasure from the Spanish plate fleet, we shall seek it together—along with my father."

Erik brushed away a lock of hair. "Leave the comforts of Port Royal? Give up my fair pay for the uncertainty of a pirate's future? The whole matter of the treasure may be a lie. It so happens the taste of sea spray has become tiring."

Baret gave a short laugh. "What a smooth deceiver you are, Erik! Behind your casual expression and velvet garb there is a pirate as cool as any who roam the Caribbean waters! Surely your new civility is a guise fit for His Majesty's masque! Or," he said with cool challenge, "was your buccaneering all a boast to impress me as a lad?"

Erik felt the hair on the back of his neck nettle. He had not only harried the Main with the worst of them, but he deemed himself the best swordsman about. He said firmly, "It was a life I did not surrender easily!"

"No?" Baret laughed smoothly and raked him with a look.

"Are you calling me a—" Erik stopped abruptly when he saw the smile on Baret's lips. Realizing he had fallen into a trap, he straightened and shook back the lock of fair hair that persistently fell across his forehead. His eyes narrowed.

"Enough of my ventures, your lordship. It is your future we must discuss. Your father is beyond your reach. The way is barbed with traps and pits. If he were alive in the Caribbean, how do you think you would find him?"

"I have no choice but to become one of the Brotherhood. You know the pirates better than I. They trust you, but still are wary of me. Eventually they will come to see me as one of them. There's bound to be men who can tell me what happened to Captain Royce Buckington that day on Providence Island."

Erik shook his head. "The buccaneers who remained to defend the island against Spain were killed after Mansfield returned to Tortuga."

"He lives! Do you think I can be content knowing this? Felix wanted him in the hands of slavers! Do you think I will forget that?" And the snap of the satchel shutting added emphasis to his statement. Their eyes met. "So what of you, Erik?" came the quiet challenge.

Erik continued to show disinterest. "My wages from Felix are very fine indeed. And if you sail with Henry Morgan, it is I who shall find myself unemployed."

A glimmer of irritation like warm coals seemed to glow in Baret's eyes. "I cannot but think that you have plans of your own. Would not your sword be put to better use with the buccaneers in the war against Spain?"

"You deliberately provoke me, my lord. I have proven my loyalty to the Protestant cause in fighting for the Huguenots as a lad." Erik's eyes were cool and hard. "My decision is made. I am no longer a buccaneer."

"As you wish. I too have made my decision. Do not try to stop me."

They looked at one another, and nothing stirred but the rain beating on the window.

"The Buckington sword, Erik—where did you hide it?" he demanded.

Erik refused to think of the sword that the old earl had given to his grandson years ago. He knew Felix had taken it from Buckington House. He changed the subject. "Has not His Majesty already hinted that he may wish you in his personal guard? War with the Dutch is inevitable. If you leave to attack Spain when the king prefers peace, you will have thrown away your opportunity to become his favorite."

"I can best serve England in the Caribbean. Every Spanish vessel the buccaneers sink will mean less gold for Madrid to use in supporting the Inquisition army in Europe. But I am loyal to His Majesty. I will fight the Dutch if I must. I've vowed that to the earl."

Erik pressed, "This time the earl will remove your name from his will altogether. It was not a light thing when you sank the *Prince Philip*."

But it was all a vain attempt. Baret seemed not to be listening. His boot kicked aside the plush rug. "Ah . . ." His narrowed gaze scanned the floor. "So that is where he hid it. It may be that both the journal and the sword are here."

Matters were not going in Erik's favor. He watched Baret stoop down to examine the floor.

Erik's gaze strayed to the bronze lion bookend sitting on the table close to his hand. Knocking out his lordship would save a good deal of trouble. He sighed, calmly reached for it, and said to distract him, "There must be just cause provoking

your uncle's decisions. Why else would he not permit the possibility of your father's being alive?"

"I could almost believe you were gullible. Neither family
affection nor justice has any place in his plans. Take my word
for it."

"Maybe. And yet, if he kept back some knowledge from
you, he must have a sound reason for doing so. Stay, my lord.
Discuss your grievances with him."

"Think as you will. Ah!" Baret removed his dagger from
his boot. "So this is its hiding place."

"For the life of me I did not know anything was there."

Baret worked with his dagger to lift a board. "I wonder
what else my noble uncle may have hidden."

Erik quipped, "If there is a morsel of your father's
Spanish booty, I beg you leave it, my lord, lest I be blamed
for coming to his chamber."

"The journal is not here, but . . ." Baret stood with a
faint smile. He held the prized Buckington sword in its scabbard boasting the family heraldic. He looked pointedly at the
bookend in Erik's hand. "A rather menacing bit of bronze.
What do you intend to do with it?"

Erik ignored him and gently set it down on the table.
"Do not be hasty in your judgment of your uncle," he said
again. "You could be wrong about everything."

Baret measured him, then casually glanced about the
chamber.

Erik watched as Baret retrieved an expensive cloak from
a high-backed velvet chair, took a key from the desk, and
walked with it to the wardrobe. He glanced back as though in
no hurry to be off.

Erik wondered about the faint smile he wore.

"Would you mind if I replace this velvet cloak? It's
jeweled," Baret told him.

Erik studied him. What did he have in mind?

"Felix owns a fortune in garments," said Baret. "As you
say, you would not wish to be blamed should one be missing."

Erik looked at the rich black cloak embroidered with
gold and sewn with gems. He shrugged. "As you wish, my
lord."

228

Baret inserted the key. "He usually keeps his wardrobe locked."

Erik watched him. Was he going to give in and stay? Would he cooperate so easily?

"Erik . . . I begin to think that you knew from the beginning how Felix betrayed my father."

Erik tensed. He straightened.

Baret looked at him. "But you sold your silence for a jeweled cloak—one like this."

Erik felt the sting. The insult, coming unexpectedly, made it more bewildering. He stared at Baret. That he would feel such discomfort over Baret's distrust surprised him, yet he managed to control his affront and said with false calm, "Strange that you would suggest so low and cowardly a motive for me. I respected your father. But you already know that."

"Do I? You have sold your allegiance. What do I know of you actually? Yes, you befriended me when I was a lad, but times have changed. It is said by some that you will do anything for a price. Anything."

Erik's eyes glittered like a cobra's. "Caution, my lord," he breathed. "My loyalty is also toward you, but it is brittle and easily broken by insults."

"Loyalty?" Baret gave a laugh. "What do you know of loyalty? You know more than you admit about my father. I insist it is so." He pointed at Erik. "And that cloak you are wearing, for example—was it payment for remaining silent about my father? It is much like this one, is it not, Erik? I challenge you!"

Erik felt his temper snap, a danger sign. The cruel goad could not be thrown off this time. In brief strides he was beside Baret.

Baret held up the black robe with green gems. "Take a careful look, pirate!"

Erik did look—and was startled by sudden darkness.

The cloak was over his head, cutting off his breath before he knew what had happened. He struggled violently like a trapped panther. Pain stabbed at the back of his neck and sent him down on his knees, dazed. Dizziness swirled through his brain and overcame him. Erik remembered the last thing he had seen—Baret's eyes glinting with malicious amusement at having won the game.

It seemed to Erik that a bolt of lightning had struck him. Stunned, he felt himself being shoved into the wardrobe where he fell into a jungle of robes, cloaks, boots, and slippers. The door shut, the key turned in the lock. Erik sucked in his breath and struggled to remove the black velvet cloak from his face. He heard Baret laughing.

"You may keep the cloak, Erik! It was mine."

Erik struggled to get to his feet, furious with himself for falling for the trick.

"You shall pay for this! I shall find you if it is the last thing I do!"

"Come then! You shall find me with Henry Morgan! Farewell!"

Erik was about to bang on the door but stopped and leaned his shoulder against it instead. No use bruising his hands. No one would hear him until Lord Felix retired after the ball—and who knew when that would be?

How clever to make him angry! He had known it would take him off guard. And it had!

21

STORM WARNING

Emerald touched her cheek, and a sickening feeling weighed heavily upon her. Lavender hadn't believed her. Her throat cramped as she swallowed back the pain of rejection. *Heavenly Father,* she prayed, *the others won't believe me either—they'll all choose to think the worst about me.*

Minette frowned. "She had no cause to slap you like that. But don't fret, Emerald. Uncle Mathias won't believe the gossip, and he knows you far better than they do in the Big House. Let her show the periwig and mask to the family. The viscount himself will deny that you did anything wrong. Don't think about it." Her face brightened. "Besides, I have better news."

Emerald glanced at her.

Minette smiled. "Jonah's back with Ty. And Ty was right when he said he'd take the branding like a man. Know what he said to me? Said, 'Christ gave me the dignity to be a man of God, and my soul is His. No brand on the forehead can change that.'"

They arrived at the buggy, shielded in the dark cane, and Emerald embraced Ty's words as an encouragement from the Lord. She glanced soberly back toward the house where golden light crowned the elite abode of the fair and favored.

"Ty's right," she said softly into the evening darkness enveloping them. "Others may falsely accuse us of evil, but if God defends His own, the charges will fall like dead seed on rocky soil." Emerald looked at Minette, who watched her hopefully, and she smiled briefly, although her heart felt lashed from the whip of cruel words. "If Ty's home safe and he's still standing tall as a child of God, then we've something to thank Him for."

Minette's amber eyes glowed. "That isn't all," she said in a secretive tone. "Jonah also brought a message from Jamie."

Emerald's breath caught. "Jamie!"

"Aye, indeed, and he isn't in the Blue Mountains with the Cameroons. Jamie's found a ship!"

Emerald caught her shoulders, and they laughed for the first time. "Oh, Minette, a ship! Surely this is the answer to our prayers. Where is he now?"

"Jonah wouldn't tell me but said for you to come right to the house."

With new energy bolting from renewed hope, Emerald dashed to the driver's side of the buggy. "Hurry, Minette, climb up. I can't wait to find out what Jamie has to say."

Minette laughed as she sprang nimbly to the worn leather seat, her long honey-brown ringlets glowing in the moonlight. "You're feeling fine again." She suddenly sobered and her expression took on a wistful look. She leaned toward her. "Oh, Emerald, will we really be able to start a new life in Massachusetts? You'll take me with you like you promised? You'll help me become a great lady?"

Emerald reached over and embraced her, and beneath the big moon their eyes shone. "I wouldn't go without you, Cousin Minette."

Minette stared at her, and at the deliberately emphasized word *cousin* her eyes glistened with moisture.

Emerald smiled. "We're already the King's daughters. What more could we want? He has provided everything we need to come into His glorious Presence fully accepted and loved in His Son Jesus. With His hand upon us, we've naught to fear, for He will surely lead our feet to the right path."

"Does He love a half-caste as much as He loves Lady Lavender, d'you think?"

The question pulsated with hope and doubt, and Emerald's heart knew a pang. "Remembered what Uncle Mathias taught us from the first chapter of Ephesians? 'Chosen' by God the Father. 'Accepted' in the Beloved One Jesus. In Christ we are one family. All of the King's daughters are robed with grace."

A short time later she turned the horse from the carriageway onto the narrow dirt lane that led a quarter mile ahead to the Manor. Her excited thoughts were on Jamie. He had a ship! She wondered how he had found it, but at the moment she pushed that question aside. It was enough that now they would set sail for New England!

Only one thought arose to float on the troubled waters of her heart. How could she bring herself to tell Uncle Mathias good-bye—and what about the Singing School? Yes, she would seek to serve the Lord in Boston, but what about the slaves and children such as Timothy and Titus?

Uncle Mathias was old and growing more frail as the days passed. Who would take his place? Yet the Lord had His ways of providing, she told herself, pushing aside the faint disturbance that stirred in her soul.

As she drove ahead, she could see the dark waves of cane on both sides of the road. The stalks and leaves rippled in the wind, and the sound grew as it rolled along until it filled her ears with sounds like the sea.

Minette sat holding the seat with both hands, staring tensely from one side of the lane to the other. "Did you hear something?" she whispered uneasily.

"The wind. Stop it—you'll spook me. We've never been out this late before is all." Changing the subject, she asked, "Does Uncle Mathias know about the message from Jamie?"

Minette shook her head, still glancing about at the fields. "He's got the fever again. I wouldn't have left him at the Singing School bungalow except Ty showed up—Emerald, look out!"

Emerald caught a glimpse of a form darting from the rows of cane, and she flapped the whip on the horse's back.

A voice called from behind her, "Emerald, stop! It's me, Ty!"

"Ty!" cried Emerald.

Minette twisted about on the seat as the horse galloped. "It's him!"

Emerald drew the reins and slowed the buggy to a stop near the side of the wagon road.

She waited with relief as he came running up, sweat glistening on his handsome face. His white cropped pants showed in the light of the moon rising above the miles of cane. He was bare-chested, and she noted with alarm that he had a machete strapped about his lean waist.

Minette must have seen it too, for she gasped. "Ty, no, you mustn't! You'll hang!"

"Hush, sister!" he scolded and turned quick, anxious eyes to Emerald. "There's no time, Emerald. You've got to listen to me good."

"Yes, Ty, what is it?" breathed Emerald, glancing behind them.

"There's to be a slave uprising."

She tensed, her eyes meeting his in alarm.

He hastened on. "I had nothing to do with it—I swear it, but you know as good as I that they won't believe me now—not after I tried to escape. And Mr. Pitt has it in for me bad. He won't let up till he sees me hang."

Emerald's heart leaped to her throat. *A slave uprising.* "Ty—"

"Listen, you and Mathias has been good to me and my sister. You've accepted us, loved us, shared Jesus with us."

"Ty—" Her throat constricted.

"You go to the Singin' School and stay with Mathias till morning. Don't come out till the sun comes up. No matter what you hear."

In a moment of confusion Emerald stared down at him. In the moonlight she saw the brand wound on his forehead, and she winced. "Ty, don't get involved. Come with Minette and me now. Jamie has a ship—you heard what your grandfather said. We can all leave Jamaica. I'll buy your freedom somehow!"

He shook his head. "It's too late for me. I must stand with the others. Please understand, Emerald. These are my people, and they are treated worse than animals. New slaves was brought into Port Royal this mornin'—I saw them. The women was naked and—"

"Ty—" Emerald groaned "—please. There's a way to end all this, you'll see! A better way than death and fighting."

"Is there?" he choked, suddenly bitter. "You say so, Emerald! Mathias says so! But God don't seem to hear our prayers! It's time to fight!"

"You can't win! They have all the weapons, the power is on their side—and the laws of Jamaica. We've got to change the laws! Remember Moses! He thought he could save his people by killing the Egyptian, but God had another way! You must be patient and wait for the moving of God."

"Good words, Emerald," he said gently, but his voice shook with restrained emotion. "I believe it. Yet there's no sign in the heavens, no moving of the winds of the Almighty. How? When?"

"Pray, Ty. That's what we must do. That's what Uncle Mathias keeps telling us, and we keep letting our impatience get in the way. I don't have all the answers, but I know the One who does. Get in the buggy, Cousin Ty, please." And Emerald stretched a hand to his dark muscled arm.

His eyes filled with a gush of frustrated tears.

"Aye, brother Ty," choked Minette. "We'll leave with Jamie, the three of us. He'll teach you to sail a ship. We'll be free indeed. The wind is at our backs now, can't you see?"

Ty gritted his teeth and shook his head. "Mr. Pitt's out for me."

"I'll stop him this time, you'll see," said Emerald. "I've a new friend now," she said boldly. "Viscount Baret Buckington is here. He's offered to intervene for you and Jamie—"

She stopped abruptly, and all three of them turned to look toward the field. At first Emerald thought it was the cane rippling in the wind. Then she heard running footsteps.

"It ain't the wind," whispered Ty. "Go, Emerald! Go! Go!"

"Ty! Get in!"

Ty gave the horse a whack, and it started with a jump. Emerald grabbed the reins as the buggy jolted down the narrow lane.

"It's the workers," wailed Minette, staring behind her, her hair flying.

In her horror Emerald expected to see angry slaves converging ahead of her, streaming in from the fields where they hid, but the narrow road remained clear.

"Ty! Come back!" Minette cried hopelessly, still looking behind as she held to the seat.

But he did not run after them, and Minette bowed her head across her arm. "Lord, help us! Please save my brother—"

Even as Emerald's soul silently joined her plea for God's mercy, she had the ominous premonition that what was now happening would not be stopped in time. The words of Uncle Mathias paraphrased from Holy Scripture burst into light across her mind: "Sow to the wind? Reap the whirlwind!"

The harvest on Foxemoore would end in blood and death as surely as reapers thrust in their sickles.

Her mind continued to race as feverishly as did the horse, whose hooves kicked up dust while the buggy tottered precariously. The words that always brought dreaded images to every white planter on the sugar islands were *slave uprising*. By morning, except by the intervention of God's grace, there wouldn't be a planter's Great House without someone with his throat cut!

I must warn the family! she thought, her heart pounding with the hoofbeats. But how? There was no turning the buggy back down that lane now! Not even her connection with Ty could save her!

In her mind's eye she could see the unsuspecting wedding guests in the Great House toasting Geneva and Lord Felix, oblivious to their danger, while docile and obedient slaves carried silver trays laden with refreshments.

She tensed. The field slaves were one thing, but were the house slaves also dangerous? How many of those slaves knew about the uprising? How many were secretly involved? How many would open the back door to allow a rebel with a machete to enter? To hide in the wardrobe of the master's bedchamber? How many loyal house slaves would decide to sound the alarm instead, knowing that if they did their fellow slaves would hang?

And who was the leader of the rebellion on Foxemoore? Not Ty! She would never believe it of him, no matter what Mr. Pitt might say tomorrow, and she no longer had any doubt but that the overseer would seek to blame him. *And perhaps Jamie as well,* she thought.

Baret—he was the only one who could help them, but how could she reach him—and her father?

She knew that the house slaves tended to be more loyal to their white owners than did the field laborers, and that was the reason for the owners' choosing them. Great-aunt Sophie believed that there was no cause to doubt those serving the family in the house, but was she right? How well did she understand the grieving anger in their hearts?

Sophie didn't understand, of course. Like the other planters, she had convinced herself that slavery and brutality were excusable, that slaves were somehow less than human or, if human, then at least destined to their lot in life.

Though her heart beat like a drum and her knees were weak, Emerald took consolation in knowing that Baret was at the Great House and would use his weapons with skill if necessary to protect the family.

A sudden dart of fear pierced her soul. Jette and the twins—where were they? Were they now safe in the house with the governess? What if Jette had gone to the Manor instead?

"Jette," she said to Minette. "Have you seen him?"

"Maybe he's with Uncle Mathias or at the Manor!"

Outside the Manor, Emerald stopped the buggy and scrambled down, catching her flounces on a nail. She jerked her skirts impatiently and ran up the porch steps with Minette just behind her.

A light burned in the lower portion of the narrow house as they entered, breathing hard, looking about with alarm.

"I'll check for Grandfather," said Minette and ran toward the cook house. "Grandfather?"

Emerald shivered as she stared up the flight of steep steps shrouded with shadows. A menacing silence wrapped about her as, alone, she picked up her full skirts and began to climb.

"Jette? Are you up there?"

She paused near the top landing. "Jette! Timothy? Titus?"

Outside in the night she could hear the faint sound of shouting voices growing louder. Too late to stop it. The rebellion had broken like a flood.

She looked down the steps as Minette came running from the back. "Jonah's not here. Maybe he took Jette and the twins to the Singing School."

"Go there and wait like Ty said. I shall follow when I can," said Emerald evasively. She was certain that Jette was not with Jonah, yet she didn't want to risk Minette's life by asking her to help search for the child. Even Minette was in danger, for the workers, especially the men, considered her white and often accused her of haughty ways.

Minette stood below, frightened and pale, but determination hardened in her eyes. "Not without you. I know what you think to do. I won't let you risk the fields, Emerald. I know what the men will do if they find you. There's a pistol in your father's room—I saw it."

Emerald already knew about the weapon, and she nodded, clenching her teeth to keep them from chattering. "I'll be all right. God is with us. We're never alone. I must try to risk the upper house to find Baret. I've got to locate Jette and the twins."

"Then I'll risk the fields," stated Minette. "They won't touch me."

"You know that's not so. They've been mad at you ever since you said you wouldn't marry a slave. Do as I say!"

Minette turned on her heel. "Not this time. *I'll* find the viscount."

"Minette!"

But before Emerald could stop her, Minette ran toward the cook room, and the hemp screen door banged behind her.

In the silence, Emerald clutched the banister, then looked toward the front door. The distant voices were growing more distinct. There was little time, yet she must make certain Jette was not hiding in one of the upstairs rooms, and she must take the extra minutes needed to change clothes before she could ever hope to run the furrowed paths!

She approached her room cautiously and opened the door wide before entering. "Jette?"

She entered, glancing about. Seeing that the room was empty, she shed her velvet garment with fingers that shook and swiftly donned a cotton frock that reached above her ankles, all the while praying aloud, "Lord, You know where Jette is. If he's not safe in the Great House, help me find him."

She raced down the hall to her father's chamber and fumbled to light the lantern. She went to his bed and stooped, pulling out the old trunk from beneath it, and searched for the pistol. "Gone!" she breathed. But her father always left it for her! Had Jonah taken it on his way to the Singing School?

A frightening shiver raced up her back. Or had one of the slaves also known about it and taken it?

A hissing sound like a snake alerted her, and her head whirled toward the wardrobe. "Psst!" came the sound again from inside, where breeches, tunics, and cloaks hung.

She stood with audible relief when a moment later Jette poked his dark head out from the clothing, his winsome eyes wide.

"Jette—"

He rushed toward her. "Emerald, I can't find Timothy and Titus. They're hiding and took the hound with them. And I can't find Baret either. And the slaves are mad at us all. Are they going to kill us?"

"Thank God you're safe. Come, we must try to reach the Singing School."

They ran down the hall toward the steps. Then, *No time!* her mind shouted, and she stopped.

There were voices below, talking in their native African tongue. She clutched Jette to her side, and he looked up at her with wide eyes. Emerald put a finger to her lips, silencing him.

He stiffened but appeared to understand their plight, and his small jaw tightened.

She might try to bring him to her room, but she had never bothered to put a lock on her door, nor was there one on her father's.

The window, she thought. The vine that grew along the wall—it was not strong enough to hold them both, but maybe she could get Jette down—

Someone was coming!

Quickly she motioned for him to enter the gallery, where she knelt, pushing him to the floor with one hand. Drawing near the rail, she peered through the lattice. Her heart wanted to stop, then began to thud.

239

Several field slaves with gleaming machetes were searching the lower floor. Ty was not among them! These men were all angry strangers.

Without You there is no hope, Lord. Help me know what to do.

One of the slaves started cautiously up the steep staircase. In moments he would find them, for there was no place to adequately hide. She shielded Jette behind her as best she could, amazed at his bravery.

Please, God, make the man change his mind. Make him go back downstairs.

A thought sprang clearly to mind. *"My soul, wait thou only upon God; for my expectation is from him."*

Could she reason with the slaves? She knew a few words in the various tribal languages but not enough to carry on a winning discourse. And the slaves all came from different tribes in West Africa, having varying dialects. Many could not converse together except in English.

Someone charged through the front door then, calling out in Swahili. Emerald looked below.

Jonah stood there with a pistol—her father's? His creased dark face, pained, glistened with sweat. "Come down," he ordered the man on the stairs.

A lump formed in her throat. Here was Jonah, ready to face death to save his white friends, for he must know she was up here. Had Minette met him on her way to the Great House to alert Baret?

Please, God, make Baret come in time to save Jonah.

Jonah said something to the other slaves, and they all turned on him with angry words. The field hand on the steps went back down, however, pointing accusingly at Jonah and shouting in a dialect she was not familiar with.

Jonah shook his head and spoke to him in English.

The man answered in broken English, a sob in his cracked voice. "You brother, you betray plot—break blood oath—warn them! They evil! See what they do to our people? Animals! Brand Ty! More women arrive today! Naked! White man Pitt, he laugh!"

Jonah's face was now wet with tears, and Emerald felt her soul ache equally with the shame the slave spoke of. If only she could tell them she understood, that she despised

240

the evil of slavery even as they did, but what could she do to stop it?

"You are right," said Jonah wearily. "What they do is evil. But for us to kill everyone? That too is evil. I warned Mathias, a friend of God—our friend too."

"Mathias a friend. Maybe! But now we die!"

While they agonized in debate, Emerald came alert to the opportunity God had given to her to escape to her room with Jette.

She clutched his hand, and they crept from the gallery into the hall, then silently sped toward her room.

Inside, she rushed to the open window and peered down into the darkness. Did anyone wait below as a guard? Or were they all in the front hall arguing?

"Jette, you must make a run for it. Can you climb down the vine?" she whispered.

He nodded, teeth chattering. "Wh-what a-about y-you, Emerald?"

"Baret is at the Great House. Minette is trying to get through the field to warn him. If she didn't make it—you tell him to hurry here to the Manor."

Jette swallowed and nodded, and tears oozed from his eyes.

Quickly she helped him through the window, judging the distance. If the vine broke . . . or if any were watching below . . . "Jesus keep you," she whispered as she entrusted the small boy to the vine.

"I'll come back, Emerald, you'll see. I'll find Baret!"

She watched until he disappeared into the darkness, and listened until the leaves on the vine ceased to rustle. All remained dark and still below.

The moments slipped by. Had he made it? Had he gotten away?

She waited, listening intently, then contemplated the risk of trying to climb down herself. She was about to try when the crack of Jonah's pistol startled the voices below into silence.

Then the sound of the shot was followed by the thud of falling furniture.

Jonah!

The door to her room was suddenly flung open.

Emerald gasped, stepping back against the window, seeing a slave looming in the doorway, his machete raised and gleaming.

She didn't know where the strength came from, but she found herself saying, "I am not an enemy to your cause. But this is not the way to bring true freedom. You cannot win. Even if you kill me, you will lose come morning. The planters have all the weapons and the laws of slavery on their side. Yet I am a friend who also believes your women and daughters should be treated with dignity! Mr. Pitt is my enemy too."

He hesitated, as though wondering why Pitt would be her enemy. The hesitation proved to be to her advantage, for she saw his weapon lower, then rise again.

Emerald thought herself mad for even hoping she might talk the man out of his rage. But she was not to know whether she had done so or not. The sound of horses beating their way up the wagon road rushed through the open window, and they both turned to look, knowing what that sound meant.

The slaves did not have horses, but Mr. Pitt and his small militia did.

For Emerald the sound of their arrival came with relief mingled with alarm, for it would mean many hangings if Pitt had his way! For the slave who stood in her room with the machete, the sound trumpeted his ultimate defeat. If Pitt had been alerted, then by now the slaves would know that their plot was uncovered. Without the element of surprise on their side, failure was certain, for the implements they used in the cane fields were no match for long guns and pistols.

From across the plantation she heard the echo of shots —and more of them, coming from different directions.

She turned swiftly to the slave. "Surrender to me, and I will see you're not hanged with the leaders! I'll protect you from Pitt."

He shuddered like some broken giant, then dropped the machete onto the floor with a clatter. He fell to his knees, weeping. Emerald stared at the weapon, knowing how close she had come to death, but then her eyes went to the man, and her heart felt compassion for his plight. She saw in him a reflection of old Jonah, of Ty, of Minette, and yes, even of herself, for at times during her young life here in the Manor she had felt a slave.

Forever stamped upon her memory would be the image of this big broken man kneeling, head in hands, his machete gleaming on the floor. She would hear his loud weeping and the anguish of his frustration.

"What is your name?" she whispered.

"Ngozi," he said. "Means 'Blessing.' But Pitt calls me Ham."

She winced. But she knew that Pitt was not the only one to rename slaves, as though they were something less than men and women.

Slowly she walked toward him. "Ngozi?"

He lifted his head, and she saw the gray in his hair for the first time, saw the hopelessness in his eyes, the scars from whippings on his flesh.

She swallowed, her throat dry. "Jesus the Son of God knows what it's like to be whipped, to be spit upon, to be mocked, to be rejected—He brings blessing to you from His Father's house. True freedom from another slavery far worse than iron chains—the slavery to sin and Satan and death. Jesus brings healing from hate, from devil worship, from confusion, from the midnight of your soul, from my soul too. In His Name I will hide you. And when you can—seek your freedom in the Blue Mountains. And when you think of Englishmen, think also of me, of my Uncle Mathias, of a white skin who also has within a heart to love because Jesus dwells there. We are not all beasts like Mr. Pitt, or like the slavers who hunt for you in West Africa, or like the selfish planters who think only of their sugar crop. If I were not running away myself, I would stay to fight for the well-being of the African women and children."

He stared at her.

Emerald turned her back to show she no longer distrusted him and went to the open window to look below at the arriving horses. Her worst fear sprang up like a snarling jackal. "Mr. Pitt!" she whispered.

Pitt was in his bare feet. His hands were clenched into fists. In the moonlight she saw that he had with him several of the indentured servants who worked under him, and a dozen planters also rode up, armed with weapons.

Baret! Where was he? Only he could save the slaves from a lynching!

She whirled from the window to see Ngozi standing there glistening with sweat, his dark eyes watching her.

"Mr. Pitt has men with him. Quick! Under the bed until he's gone!"

He obeyed, all thought of belligerence now gone. Emerald went swiftly to make certain the coverlet trailed on the floor. "Whatever happens," she whispered, "do not come out, Ngozi!"

She rushed out the door into the hall. From downstairs she heard Pitt's surly voice, followed by an explosion of musket fire. Her hand went to her throat, her face contorting with pity as the shooting continued.

If uprisings were evil, what were the forces that drove men to such desperate acts? Slavery! Brandings! Beatings!

When the shots ceased, she ran to the top of the steps and in horror looked below. Slaves lay dead or dying, and the sight of blood turned her stomach. Her anxious eyes fell upon Jonah lying on the steps, face downward, a darkened stain wetting the back of his tattered cotton shirt.

Whether one of the slaves had shot him earlier, or whether Mr. Pitt had fired, was unclear to her. She gave a cry of outrage. The gentle old man was dead.

As her eyes raced to meet Mr. Pitt, who was coming up the steps, her brain weaved, and waves of horror washed over her. *Baret! Where are you?*

Her knees were buckling as she went under a flood of darkness.

A red sunrise covered the expanse of sky above the wide empty field, its brown soil newly dug for planting. Emerald sat in her buggy with Minette beside her.

Dazed, she stared ahead. The bodies of twenty Africans swayed lightly in the early morning breeze, their necks broken. Mr. Pitt had seen to it that the ugly execution had taken place at once as a warning.

244

Emerald heard the sobbing of the women who huddled together like frightened sheep farther back in the field. A few children wailed, frightened, not knowing what was happening. A few smaller boys crouched on their haunches watching the bodies with round eyes.

Above in the pale sky, large carrion circled.

Minette sat quietly, her eyes swollen and red-rimmed from crying over her grandfather's death, her face soiled with dust.

Numb, Emerald thought again, *I promised to save Ngozi. He could have killed me but didn't. I failed him.*

She stiffened with new resolve burning in her soul. "Jonah must have a Christian burial."

Minette's eyes filled with tears as she sat staring ahead. "They won't allow it. You know that. No slave gets a Christian burial."

Emerald's fingers tightened on the reins as she turned the buggy to ride on to the Singing School to find Mathias and tell him about Jonah.

"Jonah will," she gritted. "He's no slave to me. I loved him."

Minette looked at her with pride. "They won't stop us," she agreed.

The round school building, made of palm branches and hemp, had gone untorched, although she saw other slave huts burned to the ground. The smell of smoke hung in the air as she stopped the buggy and climbed down.

The old woman Yolanda, who cared for Mathias in his illness, sat outside the Singing School on a rattan stool. Her head, covered with a yellow bandanna, was in her lap. She made a moaning sound like a prayer chant.

Emerald quickened her steps. "Yolanda?" she inquired uneasily.

The woman looked up, her dark eyes pensive.

"Is Jonah dead?" asked Yolanda.

Emerald laid a hand on her shoulder. She nodded.

Tears ran down the woman's wrinkled cheeks. "Ty escaped to the Blue Mountains," Yolanda informed her. "Two others with him. The other men are dead. Mr. Pitt, he hung 'em."

Emerald felt her anger rising again like the tide. "Yes, he killed them."

Yolanda remained seated on the stool, her voice without emotion. "Jonah and Ty did a good thing in warning you and Mr. Mathias."

"Yes—" Emerald's voice broke. "They did good."

"Jonah died for helping."

Emerald could not reply. She nodded.

"Others died too."

Again Emerald nodded, grieved. She dimly wondered why Yolanda kept stammering, until she understood what she was trying to say. Her eyes darted to Yolanda's sober gaze. "No," whispered Emerald, fear pinching her throat. "Not Mathias—"

Yolanda's eyes flooded. She pointed inside the Singing School.

With a small cry Emerald rushed past her, nearly stumbling in her haste to reach him.

The dimness blinded her, and for a moment she stood without moving, waiting for her eyes to adjust. The familiar smell of hemp and cane filled the hut. His music papers were stacked neatly on a small handmade desk next to the old out-of-tune harpsichord. Study books and papers were piled on small tables on both sides of his bunk. It had always been a comforting sight, and only now did she understand how desperately she wanted to behold him again sitting bent over those papers, trying to translate slave chants into English and then into Christian music.

I must keep him, Lord! He's all I've got, she prayed, her hands gripping the sides of her skirt and petticoats. *I can't lose him too!*

She moved softly across the room toward the figure covered with a light cotton cover, fearful she would see the gaunt face of death.

But he turned his head toward her, and a glimpse of his face reminded her of how Mathias, with his knowledge of the Scriptures, had been a shield for her, dispensing comfort and strength from the Lord.

"Mathias!" She sank to her knees beside his bunk, her skirts rustling. "Uncle Mathias? It's me, Emerald," she choked.

"Don't you die too. I can't bear it." She put her head down beside his and wept the way she had as a child.

A feeble hand reached out to try to pat her head. She looked at him through tears. His eyes were open, but she saw approaching death staring back.

Behind her, Minette wept softly.

He'd been terribly burned. Probably trying to save a family trapped in one of the huts.

He tried to speak, his hand patting her. Emerald brought herself under control in order to hear his words, bringing her ear to his cracked mouth.

"Find Karlton . . . he doesn't know . . . go to England, Emerald—"

"There's no hope anymore, Uncle Mathias. Everything has turned out badly."

"Lord . . . is not weary. Those who wait on Him . . . mount up with eagle's wings . . . wait . . ."

"I'll find Papa," she whispered. "Don't worry about me, Uncle Mathias—" Her voice cramped.

He tried to gesture to his desk. "Save . . . work."

"Yes, you worked very hard. I'll take care of the music. You can count on me, Uncle." Tears ran down her face. She wanted to hold him, but he was in too much pain. "You can count on me," she repeated.

Did he smile? His gray eyes shone with an inner peace. He tried to muster his remaining strength. He seemed to reach out to include Minette.

Emerald turned. "Minette, quickly!"

Minette rushed forward, falling to her knees. "Mathias!"

He placed a weak hand on Minette's shoulder, the other one on Emerald. "Jehovah aid thee . . . guide thee . . . keep thee both . . . till the morning break . . . and . . . shadows flee away."

"Yes," replied Emerald. "Till then."

His ragged breath heaved, and his eyelids closed. His hand grew still, reflecting emptiness, for his soul had winged its way homeward.

Gone. Her last human bulwark. There was no one left who truly understood her, who loved her at her worst, who was there to advise, to listen to her troubles, to truly care.

Grieving over her loss, she lay her head upon his chest and sobbed.

From outside Emerald heard a carriage. Voices followed, and then she became aware that someone had entered the bungalow. She lifted her head but did not turn.

"He's dead then?" The voice was quiet but stilted.

Geneva, his cousin.

Emerald pushed herself up from the bunk and turned to face her. Geneva obviously hadn't gone to bed since the ball and was still richly gowned and bedecked with pearls. She carried a basket, and as Emerald's eyes dropped to its contents she saw salve and fresh cotton strips. Geneva had come to anoint him. Emerald said nothing, and as Geneva walked to the humble bunk, she stepped aside. For the first time Emerald saw tears in the woman's eyes.

She knelt, forehead resting on her folded hands. "Mathias—what have we done?"

Emerald took in her expensive clothing, the well-set red curls, the rubies that twinkled on her earlobes. At the same time she glanced about the bungalow until her gaze fixed on the worn harpsichord.

He had wanted so little of this world's goods. Only a musical instrument. He had not been bitter toward the Harwick family for disinheriting him. He had never spoken in envy or resentment about denied wealth or lack of appreciation. Now he was gone. Geneva remained, the others in the family remained, and Geneva could become the sole inheritor of the Harwick portion of the sugar estate—except for what Karlton owned. And that too was at risk to family debt.

And yet who is the richer? Emerald wondered soberly.

She walked numbly over to his desk and, finding the satchel, filled it with his work, opening and shutting the drawers.

"He warned the house last night," said Geneva. "He came across Jette and brought him to me. I suppose when he returned here, he was caught. I begged him to stay, but he wouldn't listen."

"No," said Emerald dully. "They wouldn't have harmed him deliberately. The slaves knew he was their only friend.

They respected him, even loved him. They loved this hut . . ." Her voice cracked.

Geneva was bent over him, her shoulders shaking gently.

"This is where his work was," said Emerald. "His heart was here, with his music, his plans for the Singing School, for the slaves . . ."

"And look where it got him," said Geneva bitterly. "He's dead."

"He had friends! They tried to save him—they saved me too! Mr. Pitt is a vile man! How can you bear the sight of him?" She pointed toward the door. "How could you allow Pitt to hang those men as though they were animals! Twenty men! Now women no longer have husbands, children have no fathers. All because of Pitt."

Geneva looked up at her, white and shaking. Her lips thinned, and her eyes flashed. "I didn't know he would hang them."

Emerald's fear had long ago faded, and she faced her cousin evenly. "But you should have known. Why didn't you? Who is master of Foxemoore, Mr. Pitt or the family?"

"You dare speak to me like this?"

"Someone needs to tell you how wrong you are—all of you," wept Emerald. "Must it take the death of Mathias and the lynching of twenty men to convince the family how evil it is to own human beings as though they are oxen?"

Emerald walked toward her, her hands clenched. "Have you ever been out here before? Have you ever seen their plight?"

Geneva shook her head, still kneeling over Mathias.

"The women are naked from the waist up—"

"Stop it."

"Why? You should know! Look—and see what is happening here. Some of the children have no clothing except for the things Minette and I have managed to make. When they give birth, there is no midwife. When they are sick, they die unattended. They receive no Christian burial—"

Emerald stood beside her. "Jonah was killed for warning us. He gave his life for us. I came here to have Uncle Mathias give him the dignity of a Christian burial. Now he is dead too.

249

Mr. Pitt will try to stop me, but Jonah will be buried next to Uncle Mathias."

Geneva looked at her sharply. "You don't know what you're asking," she breathed.

Emerald looked down at her. "I do. Mathias used his life to bring spiritual freedom to the slaves," she said quietly. "We should honor his work by giving Jonah a Christian burial with him."

"Sophie will never allow such a thing. And the other planters will be upset. It's against Jamaican law."

"The laws of God are more important."

Geneva shook her head. "In all Jamaica I couldn't find a minister to conduct such a funeral. An African slave with Mathias?"

"I shall conduct the funeral," Emerald found herself saying and was nearly as taken aback by her words as was Geneva, who stared at her, stunned.

Emerald swallowed and raised her head. "I shall read Mathias's favorite words from Scripture. I-I can get some of the slaves to dig their plots."

Geneva stood up from the bunk and faced her, over-whelmed. "Do you realize what Sophie would say if I let you do this? And Felix—" She stopped and looked down at her left hand, raising it. In the shadowed bungalow the new diamond wedding ring did not shine.

"Yes, I know what they'll say. But I'm asking you for permission. Not for me, but for him," she said softly and looked toward the bunk where he lay.

Geneva turned away, head in hand as if in agony. The minutes crept by while Emerald waited.

At last Geneva's voice came so quietly that Emerald strained to catch her words.

"I must be ill. You have my permission."

Emerald drew in a breath, feeling she had won a great victory. Permission for a most common event, a burial, had been granted.

But not just any burial of the dead, she thought. *A Christian burial for Jonah.* A small but poignant acknowledgment by one of authority on Foxemoore that a slave was a man.

Emerald grasped the satchel containing her uncle's work and reached the bungalow door. There she paused and turned toward Geneva, her warm eyes glowing.

Geneva stood erect, her face pale and gaunt from lack of sleep and weariness. A long moment passed in silence as they stood looking at each other.

"You are not the only one who has lost a loved one and a friend. They managed to get into one wing of the upper house last night before Grayford shot them. Lavender saw her mother killed."

Emerald's breath caught. "Beatrice, dead?"

Geneva's shoulders sagged. "Yes." She turned away to look toward Mathias. "I've lost my sister and my cousin."

Emerald swallowed and could say nothing.

Geneva knelt again beside his bunk and began her Anglican prayers from the little book she had brought with her.

Outside, the morning sun was now blazing in a blue sky.

Emerald stood there. Now that Uncle Mathias and Jonah were gone, there was nothing left on Foxemoore she cared about except Minette. Jette would soon be gone to England. Who knew how long her father would be away with Henry Morgan? The voyages took a year and, if they went far enough on the Main, nearly two. She suspected that Morgan would go far.

There were no more tears to weep. She walked wearily to the waiting buggy. Well, she too would go far. She would take to sea with Jamie Bradford for a new life in the colony.

But her father! An ache rose in her heart. She must see him again before he sailed. She must tell him about Mathias, about Beatrice, and Jonah.

She picked up the reins and looked toward the lush Blue Mountains, her eyes glinting.

"At least Ty made it safely," she told Minette.

She turned the horse to ride away. She wouldn't look at the slaves swaying in the breeze. She must find out where Jamie was waiting for her.

As she rode back to the Manor, her emotions spent, new grief over the loss of Mathias set in. She reached to lay a hand on the satchel containing his prized translation work. "And at least I have this," she said aloud.

She sat up straighter. And just where had Baret Buck-ington been all this time?

Geneva said that Grayford defended the women in the house. Emerald was certain that if Baret had been there he would surely have done the same. By now he would know of the evil that had taken place last night, yet he hadn't shown himself. Was he with Lavender, trying to solace her?

She recalled that in the garden square he had made mention of some urgent business. Had he left Foxemoore last night before the uprising? If he had, then, like her fa-ther, Baret didn't yet know about the tragedy that left its mark on Geneva's wedding eve.

She thought of Lord Felix Buckington. What did he think of all this?

When she arrived back at the bungalow, the long-awaited message from Jamie was waiting. He had bought passage on a ship sailing to the American colonies, and she was to go to the lookout house and wait. If all went well, when the ship was ready to set sail he'd signal her and send a longboat.

Later that morning she located Minette in the cook room, seated at the table and staring at a cup of cold black coffee.

"Grandfather made it yesterday," Minette murmured.

Emerald laid a hand on her head, pushing back the mussed ringlets from her soiled face. "We're leaving Port Royal," she told her. "We're going to the American colonies."

Minette looked up, new hope born in the depths of her eyes. She stood and threw her arms around her, and amid their sorrow they laughed.

Emerald's eyes fell then upon a blue head scarf sitting on the table. She came alert and snatched it up, turning it over in her hands. On the cloth was an African lion decorated with beads and woven pieces of dyed hemp. One word was written in blue dye: "Ngozi."

Emerald looked at Minette. "Where did you get this?" she asked, clutching it.

"A slave brought it."

"Brought it here?"

"Yes. A big man. Said his name was Ngozi. Said to tell you he won't forget."

"He's alive," breathed Emerald, eyes brimming. "He wasn't one of the twenty men after all."

Understanding dawned in Minette's face. "Was he the slave you told me about?"

"Yes. Oh, Minette, this scarf means more to me than you can imagine. I shall keep it always!"

Emerald stood beside the newly dug graves with Mathias's Bible in her hands. A dozen slaves had slowly gathered, one and two at a time, keeping an eye out for Mr. Pitt.

"Dear mercy, here he comes now," whispered Minette.

Emerald looked up, her face white with the sorrow and tension of the last several days, and saw Pitt astride his gelding, riding toward her. *If only Viscount Baret Buckington would also ride up,* she thought.

She prayed for courage and stood with shoulders straight and head unbowed, feeling the hot Jamaican sun.

Mr. Pitt stopped some distance back and from beneath his panama hat watched her. She could not see his expression, but she was certain his countenance was scornful. No doubt he wondered how she had ever gotten Geneva to allow her to do this. Emerald herself wondered, when she remembered back to the moment. There had been times in the past two days when she had expected a message to arrive forbidding her to go through with the burial.

The slaves moved uneasily, casting glances in his direction, but they did not leave.

Emerald walked to the earthly remains of Jonah and read the various Scripture passages she had gathered and written out on a sheet of paper the evening before. She read clearly and reverently, and for the first time in her sixteen years she felt as though heaven itself had come to robe her with dignity and grace.

"Let not your heart be troubled.

"I will come again, and receive you unto myself; that where I am, there ye may be also.

"Precious in the sight of the Lord is the death of his saints.

"And as we have borne the image of the earthy, we shall also bear the image of the heavenly.

253

"We are willing . . . to be absent from the body, and to be present with the Lord.

"For the trumpet shall sound, and the dead shall be raised incorruptible.

"O death, where is thy sting? O grave, where is thy victory?

"I am the resurrection, and the life: he that believeth in me . . . shall never die."

Mr. Pitt turned his horse and rode away.

Emerald paused and looked after him from beneath her wide hat. She breathed a silent prayer of thanksgiving and held the Bible tighter, feeling its worn leather and pages. The Jamaican wind caressed her damp cheeks, and her eyes shone.

Beside Ngozi, another small victory had been won.

22

TREASURE AND TREACHERY

Strong wind gusts lashed rain against Emerald's face and pulled at her hood. She squinted to see ahead as her buggy hastened down High Street toward Fishers Row, its wheels rattling over the stones until coming to a shuddering halt near the lookout house.

"Maybe Jamie won't make the harbor in this weather," cried Minette nervously.

Emerald refused to consider that possibility. "He won't fail me. We've been planning for months. And now he has our passage. He won't let a rainstorm stop him. Anyway, I shall know soon enough if the ship is in. I'm going up to the crow's nest. Sound the buggy bell if anyone comes."

Minette snatched the reins, glancing about. "Do hurry. I've bad omens creeping up my spine."

Emerald climbed down and ran toward the lookout. Above, its high-paned windows gleamed with lantern light.

Rushing through the door into the small downstairs room, she threw back her hood and climbed the steep staircase that led to the topmost floor, lifting the hem of her wet skirts as she did so, her feet sinking into the woven carpet taken from some Spanish galleon years earlier. The wooden banister gleamed. The stark empty walls on either side had once displayed paintings of ships. Now these were to be sold to the Earl of Buckington.

At the top of the steps, she climbed through the small door into her father's crow's nest and tossed her cloak upon an old sea chest. Plucking his telescope from the shelf as she passed, she rushed to the glass window that faced the Caribbean.

She held the glass to her eye, searching. Her heart pounded. A ship flying His Majesty's colors was anchored out beyond the stone seawall. A dim yellow light glowed in the darkness from its upper galley.

The ship was in. She smiled with eager anticipation. Jamie had kept his word. She knew he would.

Unexpectedly, from outside on the street the buggy bell rang. Emerald tensed and whirled from the window, gripping the telescope. Could her father have come?

Her feelings tugged in opposite directions as did her conscience. She must see her beloved father again before she left, in order to inform him about Mathias, but how could she keep her plans from him until after she married Jamie? She hurried from the crow's nest to the top step and leaned over the banister, looking straight down into the narrow room below.

Minette dashed in through the front door, her eyes wide.

"Someone's here. I saw a horse! I knew trouble was on our heels!" At the sound of boot steps her head twisted toward the door.

Emerald's hand tightened about the banister. If it wasn't her father—was Jamie bold enough to come for her himself?

The door flew open with a bang. Captain Rafael Levasseur entered with a gust of wind, a tall, vigorous man in a black periwig. He was haughty, handsome, and dangerous.

He stopped in an arrogant stance, not bothering to remove his wide-brimmed hat. His restless black eyes darted about the cramped room, past Minette, and then up the stairs. His gaze confronted Emerald, and his thin lips tightened.

"So, cousin!"

Emerald straightened her shoulders and looked down at him, hoping her alarm was concealed. What had he come here for? Had he somehow learned of her previous intention to board his vessel?

She said with deliberate calmness, "A fine spectacle you make, barging into my father's house, Cousin Rafael. And what would you do if he were here to demand you knock first?"

He strode to the stairs and stopped, one boot on the bottom step, and looked up impatiently. "I will take your father as one pierces a rabbit on a spit, mademoiselle. The silver box of jewels you stole from my ship. Where is it?"

Confused, she stared down at him. Impossible! She had not boarded his ship!

She lifted her chin and folded her arms. "You are mad with rum, Levasseur. Just how would I board your pirate vessel with its malevolent crew to take anything?"

"*Mon petite,* do not goad. I am in no mood for kindness. Do you ask how it can be, when you and the half-French wench here—" he waved a hand at Minette "—and the one-eyed blackguard Zeddie are thieves of the vilest sort?"

Emerald's gaze narrowed. Had Levasseur not been her cousin on her mother's side of the family, she would have feared his ruthless nature. As it was, it had always taken both courage and patience to handle his reckless moods.

She smiled ruefully. "Silver and jewels? You surely jest. My frock is darned, my slippers are worn. You mock me, Levasseur."

His dark eyes hardened as they swept her. "I've heard how you are going to England. I know your dreams of becoming a nobleman's woman," he accused. "The men of Port Royal are not good enough for you. You've stolen to buy silks and satins—or is it to pay Karlton's debts to the English earl?"

She tensed, fearing he would threaten her father. "He has nothing to do with this. If you go to him with wild accusations, he shall turn on you."

His teeth showed beneath his narrow mustache. "He's deceived into believing his daughter is fit company for only nobility. We know better, do we not, mademoiselle? Like it or no, you have my blood and are destined to be mine, and your thievery while my crew was celebrating their victory ashore proves it, yes? In the meantime I shall look in your trunk. Where is it—in the coach?"

She hurried down the steps. "Ruin my trunk, and I will never forgive you."

He whirled on his boot heel and, ignoring the downpour, walked outside to the buggy, where two of his men waited.

Emerald was swiftly on his trail. "Rafael, no! That trunk belonged to my mother. If you break—"

"She was a thief, the vixen of Port Royal."

"How dare you insult her! *She* was your aunt!"

"Heave it down!" he ordered the two crewmen.

"If you scavengers ruin anything, I shall have you for this! I need every frock in there for my voyage!"

Emerald ran to stop them, but Levasseur grabbed her arm and pulled her back, holding her beside him.

In a rage she watched the brutes use swords to break the rope that held it to the buggy. It landed with a thud.

Lavesseur unsheathed his blade and struck savagely at the straps until the trunk was laid open to the torrential downpour. He searched through her frocks and other personal items, tossing them aside carelessly.

Infuriated, she rushed to retrieve them from damage. "You jackanapes! You will pay for this despicable treatment of Harwick's daughter!"

"Perhaps it is hidden in the house—in her room, yes?" suggested a crewman.

Levasseur looked thoroughly disgusted. "No, if my cousin had it she would take it with her. But search to make sure. And look inside the buggy—search the driver's seat." He turned toward Emerald, who clutched several of her best frocks in her arms. "It is too big to be hidden on you, mademoiselle, so I shall let you go." He glanced about for Minette. "Where is that vile urchin?"

"Gone! She has more sense than to hang around when a band of cutthroat pirates comes barging in."

"Perhaps you have told the truth after all, *mon petite*. Perhaps I have been too hasty."

"Too hasty! After you've destroyed my trunk and the only decent frocks I had to wear? You are a cad, Rafael!"

With exaggerated gallantry he swept off his hat and bowed low at the waist. Then he straightened, flung his cloak over his shoulder, and before turning to walk away reached beneath his jacket and pulled out a small cloth pouch. He carelessly tossed a dozen gold pieces atop the broken trunk. "*Au revoir*, Mademoiselle Emerald! We shall meet again." He smiled coolly. "Perhaps sooner than you think."

What did he mean?

She watched him mount his horse. "Where are you going now?"

"If you did not take the box, then your father has done this deed. I shall call him out for his treachery!"

"My father! You are mad!"

"We shall see who is mad, mademoiselle."

She closed the trunk, then watched them ride away until they disappeared. "Knaves!" she breathed.

Like everything left from her mother, including relationships, the trunk was now scarred. Emerald ran her hand over the gashes. Then she secured it the best she could with a rope while the rain soaked her. She had no time to waste. Jamie would soon be waiting for her. She picked up the coins, considering. She wished nothing from her cousin but what was rightfully her own, and yet . . . she and Jamie could use this in Boston.

"Minette!"

The girl climbed out from beneath her hiding place under the steps. "The rake," she said.

"Quick. Help me load the trunk again, then we must find Father. He's to meet Henry Morgan at the Spanish Galleon tonight. Levasseur will go there!"

"You don't think he'll call Uncle Karlton to duel?" cried Minette.

"Rafael? I put nothing past him! Come!"

Baret strode along High Street toward the Spanish Galleon. There he would join the captains of the buccaneers of English, French, and Dutch blood who were gathering to meet Morgan and sign the articles that bound them together as Brethren of the Coast. Would Maynerd's brother show himself?

He knew he must move cautiously, not only with his contact but in order to gain the confidence of the other buccaneers.

Morgan's destination on the Main was unknown, and he wasn't foolish enough to declare his daring plans until far out on the Caribbean—spies for Spain were everywhere.

Perhaps half the buildings of Port Royal were built of brick, and the rest were wood. All had red roofs and no chimneys, for most cooking was done outdoors because of the heat. Most of the houses were two stories high, and a large number were three- and even four-story buildings. The ground floor of each generally served as a shop of some sort.

Port Royal resembled the shape of a pan with an extended handle, the pan nearly surrounded by water while the narrow handle was connected to the Palisadoes sand spit by a dry moat and a bridge. Strategically situated, the seaport, once considered of little value to Spain, was now a coveted all-season port with the best harbor on the Main. Any ship attempting to enter the harbor must come from the east, and Baret knew that the overbearing winds, along with the perilous shoals and reefs lying offshore to the south, made an attack by Spain foolhardy.

It was also fortunate that Port Royal's channel was narrow and close to shore on the south side, he thought. Any ship intending to reach the harbor was forced to sail under the guns of Fort Charles and, when turning the point and entering the harbor itself, would then confront the cannon. Only a few soldiers garrisoned the fort, however, and the governor-general had to rely on the local regiment of Port Royal's militiamen, made up of sugar planters and merchants.

Arriving at the Spanish Galleon, Baret was met by glittering chandeliers smuggled from France and a rowdy din. He glanced about the throng of adventurers, his intense dark eyes centered upon a certain gaming table across the room, where Sir Karlton sat totally engrossed.

Baret was about to walk up when Karlton groaned and said, "By fire and smoke! My luck is as uncanny as a sea witch. You should know better than to gamble with me. 'Tis a good thing I'll be going with Morgan to the Main."

"You are in error, Monsieur Harwick," came the voice of a third man, reeking French arrogance.

Baret recognized the voice, and his gaze swerved to see Captain Levasseur standing a few feet from the gaming table. He wore a spotless coat of fine camlet with ruffles at wrist and throat and stood in a confident stance, one hand pointing at Sir Karlton Harwick. With catlike movements that reminded Baret of Levasseur's use of the sword, the French pirate circled the table until he faced Karlton.

This man wanted to marry Emerald. Baret could understand why, and his eyes narrowed with unexpected irritation.

He watched as Levasseur lifted a lean, tanned hand in a cloud of lace and waved the pirates in the room to attention. "Hear, one and all! I, Captain Rafael Levasseur, buccaneering arm of the king of France—"

There came an interrupting growl from the English.

A smirk played about Levasseur's thin mustache, and he looked pointedly at Karlton. "—suggest that luck has nothing to do with the success of your game, monsieur! You, who sired a daughter by my father's sister, have turned both a cheat and thief. I pronounce you an English dog!"

The men in the room were alert for excitement and danger. The French pirates under Levasseur stood watching.

Karlton glowered, showing bewilderment, then caution. "Levasseur, what is this you dare accuse me of? I've not cheated a day in my life." He looked across the table to the Frenchman he had played with. "Go ahead, Pierre. Look at the deck if you believe the words of your captain."

Levasseur stepped closer to the gaming table and pointed again. "You have also stolen jewels from my ship to pay your debts."

The room fell totally silent. Every eye turned to fix upon the two men.

Sir Karlton stood, pushing back his chair. "If it's a duel you're asking for, you shall have it."

Captain Levasseur smiled coldly, his black eyes sparkling with energy. "And in return, should I best you, monsieur, it is for the hand of Emerald."

Baret's mouth curved. "No need to prove yourself, Sir Karlton," he interrupted smoothly and turned to Levasseur. "May I suggest you reconsider your hasty challenge, Captain. Take your crew and return to your ship."

Levasseur whirled toward Baret, his surprise showing. He scanned him, and a lean smile played on his face. "Ah! Captain Foxworth!"

Baret offered a mocking bow. "At your service. It is you, Levasseur, who should explain the ways of a thief, not Sir

Karlton. You who have cowardly taken a lady's dowry and had years to repent and return it. And I do not take lightly your betrayal of one of the Brethren," he added, gesturing toward Karlton. "After all, if we cannot trust one another," he said with irony, "who can we trust? The High Admiralty Court?"

Laughter bellowed, but Levasseur grew sober.

"I do believe the Admiralty would like to see us both twisting in the wind," said Baret.

Levasseur gave him a measured look, as though Baret were forcing a fight—which he was.

Levasseur's smile was tinged with scorn as he stepped away from the gaming table to face him. "Are you now His Majesty's English agent against France, that you should seek to provoke me? If I thought it needful, I would come boldly and take you aboard your ship!"

"Then you may be bold now, Captain Levasseur."

"A duel, Foxworth! I demand it."

Baret's blade whispered from his scabbard like silk.

The sea rovers stepped back, excited as always at the possibility of a fight, and Karlton turned and faced Levasseur's crew with a warning.

"And there'll be no help from any of you, however it goes, or you'll have this sword to contend with as well."

They retreated further, cautiously, snarling like lions.

Baret remained near the door, his gaze fixed on Levasseur, who was known for unexpectedly hurling daggers. Baret's hand moved for easy access to the narrow stiletto in a wrist-sheath strapped along his left forearm. Immediately the gaming tables were deserted as men and their wenches drew back toward the walls to watch with hearty appetites.

"A thousand pieces of eight says Levasseur takes 'im!"

"Fifteen 'undred says 'e don't!"

The front door opened with a tropical gust of wind and rain, and heads swiveled impatiently at the interruption. Their expressions at once gave way to sobriety.

A robust figure in green satin stood in the doorway like a king. His heavy dark brows were lowering above eyes that were granite hard and shrewd. His wide mustache was thick and curled slightly at the tips above a full mouth. His hair was well groomed, cut straight across at chin length and paged smoothly under. He wore a wide-brimmed hat of maroon velvet, and his coat was also velvet, black with maroon trim.

"It's Morgan," came the murmur.

Henry Morgan's brows lifted as he took in the scene, a mocking expression on his deeply tanned face. "Aye, 'tis me, ye daw cocks! Put away your sword, Levasseur!" He glanced at Baret. "You too, Foxworth." He strode into the room in full command, glowering about with scorn.

"Will ye go killing yourselves instead of the Spaniards?"

"It was Levasseur," one crewman stated sullenly. "He baited Sir Karlton, insulting him. Foxworth tried to stop him."

"I can speak for myself, Sawyer," said Baret. "But he's correct. Half the Brethren will swear to it."

"He lies, and I shall have his tongue," said Levasseur.

"Enough! I'm not caring who started it, but it ends now! Or I'll flay the bones of you both. You'll make peace—now—both of you, like the Articles demand. You, Levasseur! You French peacock! Put up your sword! We've the Spanish fleet to think of—and gold!" He strode toward the buccaneers circling the room and waved his arm. "There'll be few broad pieces of eight for any of us if either Foxworth or Levasseur is killed. We'll need them both for the next campaign."

As Baret looked on, he saw how easily Henry Morgan commanded attention. He was a born leader. The Brethren no longer appeared to care about the cause for the duel. With scarcely more than a few shrugs and a lowering glance, they turned full concentration on Captain Morgan.

Baret lowered the point of his sword at the same time as Levasseur. They gestured a courtly bow toward each other. Then Levasseur strode across the room to a table and tossed down his hat. His French crew followed, gathering about the table.

Morgan walked up to Sir Karlton Harwick and threw a big arm about his shoulder. "So it's true, Karlton, you beleaguered old wolf. You've lost your cunning at last! Your merchant ship was boarded by Don Marcos Julian Enrico!"

"Aye, and I hope one day to meet him again at sea!"

Baret's attention strayed as the door opened with another gust of wind.

Emerald!

He watched her enter—though she did not see him—keeping to a shadowed corner of the room and using her deep hood to conceal her hair and face.

She glanced about as though looking for someone. Her gaze fell upon Levasseur, and he stood, offering a bow and gesturing an arm toward his table. "All is well, my cousin!"

But she jerked her head away. And when she saw her father, her boldness returned, and she swept across the floor in his direction as though a princess.

Baret smiled faintly. She handled herself well for a mere girl of sixteen. He suspected that she would do quite well in London as she grew to maturity.

"Aye, 'tis Harwick's pert brat from his French mistress," came a clear voice. "Don't be so uppity now, sweetheart! Come 'ave a smidgen of rum with Levasseur's brother."

Her seeming indifference to the roomful of buccaneers faltered, and Baret saw her hesitate, then walk on amid appreciative laughter.

"Aye, a round of cheers for Harwick's daughter!"

Baret looked on, knowing Karlton was likely to respond to the insult. He did not want Levasseur to know of his own interest, for the Frenchman would move more quickly to own her and he himself could not.

He didn't need to wait long for Karlton's wrath. Her father turned, his feet apart, one hand on his hip, the other clasping his sword.

"You'll apologize to Lady Harwick, Cutler, or I'll corpse you for daring!"

The seaman sobered and glanced from Karlton to Morgan, who this time also stood glowering. A tense silence held the room's occupants for the second time as Karlton waited.

"I'll duel any man who dares to cast a shadow on my daughter's reputation."

"Papa, no," she called bravely. "Do you think I care what these vile pirates think?"

There was laughter. "She put you in your place, Cutler," said one.

Then the strain ebbed like waves withdrawing to sea. Cutler offered a deep bow toward Emerald.

"Beg pardon, gal—I means—me lady Harwick."

A few subdued chuckles were heard. Some turned their backs and resumed their dice throwing.

Baret watched her. What was she doing here?

She brushed past the men to Sir Karlton's side and took hold of his arm. Her words were inaudible.

But Karlton glowered and said, "Is it not enough your father keeps company with the devil's men? What brought you here, lass?"

Baret wondered if she would cringe beneath her father's hot scowl, but undaunted she faced him boldly, urging him with whatever purpose had brought her.

Sir Karlton did not see Baret standing near the door. Baret allowed him to walk past, for he wished to speak alone with Morgan.

As her father led her out of the gaming room, Emerald must have sensed Baret's gaze, for her eyes turned to meet his, and a startled expression turned to a blush.

Baret smiled and swept off his wide-brimmed hat and bowed.

She tore her eyes from his and, drawing her cloak firmly about her, walked briskly across the floor beside Sir Karlton.

His resounding voice could be heard: "The fault be not mine—I've told you you're not to venture into such places. The sooner I take you from here, the better. And after this night, London cannot come too soon. I'll put you in a finishing school. You'll marry nobility if I die seein' to it!"

Baret watched them disappear through the doorway. So Karlton was indeed serious about teaching her the ways of London society and passing her on to some nobleman.

He remembered how well she had worn the velvet frock at the ball. She had been Lavender's equal. He frowned a little. Karlton could easily manage a marriage for his daughter in England, but not all the gentlemen who were likely to take up the gauntlet were trustworthy.

As they left the gaming house, the rain lashed Emerald's face. She held her hood in place and allowed her father to lead her toward the waiting buggy. She climbed onto the seat beside Minette and picked up the reins.

Karlton frowned, the rain bouncing off the brim of his hat. "So that's the cause bringing you here. It's ill news. Go to the lookout and stay until I come for you. I'll need go to Foxemoore to look into this ugly matter of the uprising. The loss of Mathias is a bitter cup. Beatrice too," he said of his cousin. "I don't know how this could have happened."

Emerald could have told him that the slaves were all against Mr. Pitt, but he already knew as much. He had previously tried to convince Geneva to get rid of him.

Her eyes saddened as she glanced at her father. This was good-bye, but she could not bring herself to tell him about Jamie, knowing he would utterly refuse to let her meet him as planned.

Yet, despite her determination, she was troubled about her silence and struggled with the dilemma, telling herself she would write him from Boston. Surely he would forgive her when he learned by letter how happy she was.

"I'll speak to Geneva and arrange your safe passage with her and Lavender to England. With the death of her mother, Lavender will be wanting to sail as soon as weather permits. Geneva can arrange to send you on to Berrymeade. And I'll come for you when I've made our fortune."

She reached a loving hand toward his strong arm. "Papa . . ."

He was obviously anxious to be off and looked at her, agitated.

Suddenly Emerald leaned down and threw her arms around his strong neck, kissing his bearded cheek, feeling the rain on his skin. "I love you, Papa."

"Now what's this, little one? One would think I was sailing away for good. It won't be long. The time is coming when my debts will be paid. I'll own my portion of Foxemoore full and free—then we'll both be returning to what's rightfully ours with heads high," he said. "And when we drive up in a fine carriage, lass, you'll have attended the finest finishing school in London, and you'll be wearing a pretty frock—not the rich satin of a Port Royal lass but the dress of a 'real' lady. And you'll have your pick of the lords. But it'll be Baret—you'll see."

Emerald smiled tenderly as she looked down at him. "Yes, Father . . . of course we will. And . . . and would you ask Lord Buckington to see Zeddie safely to Foxemoore?"

Karlton gave her a sharp look. "Zeddie? Isn't he at the lookout?"

"Well . . . not exactly."

"Did I not free him from indentured service to be your bodyguard?"

"Well . . . Zeddie is aboard the *Regale.* He's . . . um . . . a guest, waiting for the viscount to return. He insisted Zeddie stay awhile. But I would like Zeddie returned soon. You'll ask the viscount?"

Karlton squinted at her, as though trying to make sense of her explanation, but Emerald kissed his cheek again.

"Until later, Papa, good-bye." She drew away quickly, before her expression revealed her troubled spirit, and flicked the reins. The horse trotted onto the wet cobbles of High Street.

She looked back several times until the form of her father disappeared in the rain-sodden darkness.

"Good-bye," she whispered again.

Baret left Morgan and stepped from the gaming house, feeling the rain beat against his face. At the moment he did not mind, for it cooled his inflamed emotions like water sizzling on seething coals.

He stood beneath the sign "The Spanish Galleon," which was being hammered by the wind, and lowered his hat against the rain, feeling it run down his neck.

From out of the darkness a figure carrying a fishing lantern shuffled toward the gaming house from the direction of the harbor. The golden light swayed in the wind like an apparition from the churning sea. Hob, rain pouring from the rim of his battered hat while the wind whipped the frayed edge of his thigh-length coat, saw Baret and quickened his steps.

"Stormy weather be not all bad, y'r lordship. Churning of the sea be likely to cast up more'n just muck and seaweed. Sometime it cast up an odd sort of fish, if you go askin' me opinion."

Hob leaned toward him, his low voice garbled in the wind. "Trouble in the tavern tonight 'twas all a bluff on Levasseur's part to make some in the Brotherhood think there be trouble aplenty with Karlton and you."

Baret considered this surprising news, trying to decide if he believed it or not. Regardless of the dispute with Karlton, Baret was not friendly with Levasseur.

"Levasseur's sent a man askin' you to row out to his ship. Says Maynerd's brother be with him. The two of 'em has signed articles. Levasseur be wantin' you to sign too."

Baret looked at him sharply. Maynerd's brother with Levasseur?

"Levasseur vows he and Maynerd be knowin' where Lucca be now and how you can find him on the Main. It don't be sounding good, me lordship—I means Captain Foxworth. And ain't be all he knows, says he. Says your father be alive."

His father—alive!

"Says Lucca be knowin' just where your father be now."

Baret wasn't foolish enough to trust Levasseur, but the pirate's appetite for Spanish treasure could be the means of securing the information he needed. Baret had anticipated that the talk of rich treasure would bait certain men in the Brotherhood into quietly seeking information on their own about the true fate of Captain Royce Buckington and Lucca, but he had overlooked Levasseur's taking the bait.

Nevertheless the man might be able to help him. Since Levasseur was French, he could come and go freely at the French buccaneering stronghold of Tortuga, whereas the English were not welcome now that France was likely to side with the Dutch in the threat of war against England.

"Where is Maynerd's brother now? With Levasseur?"

"Aye, aboard Levasseur's ship. 'Tis a strange bit o' news, more to be told," said Hob and glanced about in the rainy darkness.

"Ah?"

"Seems Maynerd's younger brother be Jamie Bradford. And now Jamie be Levasseur's new lieutenant. Be a strange earful, seein' how Jamie ain't a sea rover like Charlie was."

Baret thought of Emerald. There couldn't be two Jamie Bradfords in all Jamaica. So this was the poor indentured servant that she had asked him to save from Mr. Pitt!

His eyes narrowed under his black lashes. She had risked boarding the *Regale* to help not only Ty but Maynerd's brother. Just how deep did her feelings run for this man Jamie? The fact that he had gone to Levasseur with the news of Lucca revealed that Jamie Bradford was not above working with a ruthless pirate.

Hob's shrewd eyes fixed on him. "You ought to be knowin' something else. Sir Karlton's pert lass be involved."

Baret felt his irritation rise. "Involved in what way?" he asked evenly.

"The lass got a message from Jamie tellin' her to meet him tonight in the longboat. Says he's bought em' both passage to the New England colony. But it be Captain Levasseur's pirate ship they be sailin' on."

"She doesn't know that?"

Hob grinned. "She be as naive as a tweety bird fallen from its mama's nest, me lordship. Only I be thinkin' . . . it be no secret about Port Royal that her cousin Levasseur be wantin' her for his own. Been all kind of trouble between Sir Karlton and Levasseur over Miss Emerald. Maybe Jamie Boy don't know this, but Levasseur, he be usin' Jamie to get himself information about Lucca and the treasure—and to get Miss Emerald aboard too. An' when Levasseur be done with needin' Jamie Boy . . . well, Cap'n Foxworth, you be followin' my mind well enough."

Baret had followed it indeed. He smiled faintly. "Well done, old friend. And just where is she to meet 'Jamie Boy'?"

"On the dock tonight."

23

SMUGGLERS

Emerald paced the darkened wharf, shielding herself as best she could from the rain. She was disguised so as not to be easily recognized should anyone be foolish enough to be walking the waterfront in the downpour. She wore a veil and readjusted the deep hood of her black cloak so that it further obscured her identity. Minette had run ahead for news of the longboat bringing Jamie.

Emerald set her mind with cool resolve, but doubts still nagged at her soul, causing unease. Why was he late? Ships could sail in worse weather, and the water did not look so rough as to hinder the longboat's arrival.

Keeping close to the overhang, she paced the wooden planks, which creaked beneath her slippers, and decided that her concerns were due to a restless conscience. Her father would be disappointed in her—and if Uncle Mathias were alive, what would he say about her deceit?

She whirled toward the sound of running footsteps. It was Minette, and Emerald breathed a sigh of relief. "Well?" she inquired anxiously.

Minette gestured down the darkened wharf. "The long-boat's down by the other landing steps. See the lanterns? They're getting ready to pull away now."

"He must have forgotten we were to meet on the north end."

"But they say there's no crewman with them named Bradford."

"Jamie's a passenger, same as we. No doubt he'll be going under the name of a gentleman. We must hurry! If they leave without us, he'll think I've changed my mind."

Minette raced back down the wharf, and Emerald hurried as swiftly as her cloak and slippers would allow.

As she neared the landing steps, several yellow lanterns were glowing in the night, and she saw men getting into the boat while others on the seawall kept guard.

"Wait," she called breathlessly. "In the name of Jamie Bradford!"

Their heads turned sharply. She rushed to the landing, and to her surprise, two men drew swords and a third crouched, holding a dagger that glinted in the yellow light. They looked past her as though to see whether she was alone. Startled, she stepped back. If she didn't know better, she would think she had come upon smugglers.

Emerald pulled her hooded cloak about her throat, glancing about. Where was Jamie?

A thickset man with a wide neck stood up in the boat. From beneath a scarf tied at the back of his head his lank hair whipped in the breeze. For a moment he appeared to study the situation.

"*Oui*, mam'zelle, an' so you're Miss Harwick?"

She felt relief. He at least knew who she was. Her gaze swept his face, searching for some sign that he was a fatherly old gentleman with white hair and ruddy cheeks. His shrewd swarthy face provoked a shiver instead.

She glanced narrowly at the men around him, wearing faded head scarves and calico shirts, some with a single gold earring. All appeared to be French.

How rough of skin they are. They've been months at sea. I know a gaggle of pirates when I see them. Could Jamie have bought passage on a pirate *ship?*

She wisely kept her distance, aware that Minette behind her was plucking nervously at her cloak. "Let's go," she kept whispering.

"Yes, I'm Miss Harwick. Where's Mr. James Bradford?" she asked the Frenchman in the boat.

"Ah, you're asking about Jamie Boy, are you?"

Jamie Boy?

"He's expecting me. He's bought us passage to the New England colony."

One of the others laughed. "So this is the lass the captain speaks of. And no wonder."

"You daw cock! Turtle your mouth!"

271

Her heartbeat quickened with caution. "I'll not get in the boat unless he shows himself."

"Ah, he is here, mademoiselle, to be sure. He'll show himself." He turned to one of the men. "Get the fair mademoiselle's trunk. Then see her safely aboard."

"But we're supposed to bring her to his ship—"

"Silence, do as I say."

Minette plucked again at Emerald's cloak, whispering, "Emerald, no—"

The man called up, "Stop your chittering, my fair songbirds, and come aboard, both of you."

Emerald sensed danger and, grabbing Minette's wrist, started running down the wharf.

"Quick, ye napes! Grab her!"

A crewman was swiftly at her heels, and before she could scream, he clamped a big hand across her mouth. She kicked and struggled, trying to bite his fingers as he carried her down the steps to the waiting longboat.

"Easy now, you stick of a wench! We're taking you to your precious Jamie Boy."

Emerald sought to jerk free, twisting and clawing at the pirate's face. Above them on the cobbled street, horses' hoofs clattered.

"The patrol!" a pirate warned.

"Gag the mam'zelle," ordered the man in charge.

She grappled to break free of his hold as a wadded scarf was pressed against her clenched teeth. *God help me, please!*

"Roll her tight in that fish net. Where's the other wench?"

"She got away."

The odorous net wrapped about Emerald like seaweed, and she was carried like baggage.

Horse hooves pounded up the street.

"Hold fast, longboat!" came a distant shout from below the fort's guns.

"Oars, pull away!" ordered the Frenchman.

"Turn back, you smugglers, or we'll blow you to pieces!"

The pirate carrying Emerald across his shoulder lost his footing in his haste to take cover. She felt a sharp pain on the side of her head as she landed hard against something in the boat. Her mind was spinning. Waves of darkness pulsated before her eyes, trying to drag her into an abyss of unconsciousness.

The boat was shoving away from the landing steps as the remaining crewmen scrambled to the oars.

"Fire!" commanded the English soldier from above.

Emerald cringed at the loud blast, and acrid smoke befouled the air. A second blast boomed, showering her with salty brine that took her breath away. The boat pitched, bringing a sickening sensation to her stomach. Emerald allowed the welcome blackness to seize her.

24

PIRATE'S BOOTY

Emerald stirred, becoming aware that the longboat was no longer tossing in the water. She reached a weak hand to her mouth—the gag had been removed. She was lying on her back on something hard and damp—her hand touched the deck of a ship!

Emerald's eyes fluttered open, and for a moment that seemed endless she looked up at blurred faces and glowing lanterns. Above the voices she heard boot steps coming down from the quarterdeck.

"Inform your captain that if he wishes to sign buccaneering articles with me, it will be done my way. Circumstances require a change of plans."

"But Monsieur Captain! You were to come with us to meet on *his* ship tonight as agreed upon! They're waiting for you now."

"We'll meet tomorrow—here. Aboard my ship. Understood?"

"What of her? He expects her aboard the *Venture*."

"She stays."

"He will not like this, monsieur!"

"Then let him come and tell me to my face."

The group of pirates surrounding Emerald stepped aside to let two men through. They looked down at her.

With a start, Emerald looked up at the viscount. No, Captain Foxworth, the buccaneer—or pirate? She stiffened as their gaze locked.

Then he scanned her and smiled, but it was not a pleasant smile. "Ah, my dear Lady Harwick. What a pleasant surprise. Welcome aboard the *Regale*."

Bewilderment held her. She struggled to make sense of what was happening. The Regale? *Baret's ship?* she thought

274

numbly. She was supposed to meet Jamie on another ship, taking them as passengers to Boston. Was Jamie here also? He couldn't be. Captain Foxworth wasn't sailing to Boston.

What had Baret just said to that odious French pirate who had brought her here? That his captain was to come to the *Regale* if he wished to sign piracy articles with him?

She attempted to sit up, but dizziness assailed her. She must have struck her head badly in the longboat.

"Jamie. Wh-where is . . . he?" she demanded weakly.

Baret's mouth curved. He folded his arms, the wind touching his dark hair. "So . . . you wish to venture upon the high seas with 'Jamie Boy,' do you? And just what, madam, may I ask, is wrong with the *Regale* or its captain?"

Speechless, she stared up at him. Had she heard him correctly?

Bending down, he swept her up into his arms.

Emerald looked into his dark warm gaze, and her breath paused.

"You're an exceedingly lucky young woman, Lady Harwick, to find yourself aboard the *Regale* instead of the *Venture*," he said in a low voice.

Was she? "Put me down."

"You are at the disposal of a gallant captain instead of a ruthless pirate. However, I suppose the latter wouldn't make much difference to you since you expected to run away with him."

"Jamie's no pirate—"

"You have me mystified. Can this be the noble young woman called of God to carry on her uncle's work on Foxemoore?"

"I have my reasons. Put me down—"

"I shall be interested in your reasons, madam. But they must wait. There is no Jamie Bradford. There is only James Maynerd, younger brother to the pirate Captain Charles Maynerd—who was hanged at Port Royal."

"I-I don't believe you—put me down—"

"Yorke!" he shouted to one of the men.

A big man with a thatch of gray hair appeared from the shadows of the deck. "Aye, Captain!"

"The thief in calico drawers has returned as a mermaid wrapped in a fish net. Deposit her in a safe place until I decide what to do with her."

Do with her! She must find Jamie! Captain Foxworth was ruining everything!

Emerald protested as he passed her to Yorke as easily as though she were a cloak. "I shall decide what to do with myself!"

Baret ignored her. "Have Hob take a look at that bump on her head," he said.

Yorke's bushy red brows glowered. "An' where do I bring her, Captain?"

Baret smiled at Emerald. "Put her in my cabin."

25

THE BUCCANEER CLAIMS EMERALD

Emerald did not know how long she had slept, but when she awoke, sunlight poured in through a stern window, and pleasant breezes smelling of the sea ruffled her hair. She could see a patch of blue sky, and the calm water told her the storm was over.

Her eyes followed the sunlight to where it fell in a stream across the captain's desk. Her gaze darted up to the lantern that hung from the dark beam, and to her relief it was not swaying, a sign surely that the *Regale* had not yet left the bay. The wick was burning low from the night before—no one had entered the cabin that morning to turn it down. And she wondered if the door was still locked from the outside. And who might have the key.

She glanced about uneasily, noting that everything was just as it had been the night before when the man named Yorke had left her.

It took considerable effort to sit up and pull herself out of the bed, holding onto a nearby chair as the blood surged in her temples.

She felt a tender bump on the side of her head, but the skin was not broken. Her hooded cloak lay on the chair, and her shoes were nearby, but she had not been strong enough to remove her elaborate dress, worn to meet Jamie. It was still wet and portions of the billowing skirt were soiled. Her imagination told her that it bore the smell of that horrid fish net. She glanced about for her trunk and saw that it was not there. Had the men left it in the longboat? It was not only her clothing she worried about but the satchel holding the prized work of Uncle Mathias.

Suddenly Emerald caught her breath. Minette! Where was she?

As dizziness overcame her she slowly lowered herself into the chair, trying to think back to the last time she had been aware of Minette's presence. She remembered a remark from a French pirate that "she got away."

She told herself to remain calm, that if Minette had escaped capture she would seek help from her father. Emerald took courage. Even now her father may be out searching for her. Yet no sooner had she taken hope than her dilemma came crashing into her mind like the ocean waves at high tide. Jamie—a pirate? Impossible! How could Baret suggest such a thing?

During Jamie's indentured service on Foxemoore he had never once mentioned that he even had a brother, let alone that his brother was the pirate Captain Charles Maynerd. She shuddered. Baret said Maynerd had been hanged.

She grimaced as she stood from the chair and made her way slowly across the floor to what appeared to be a wall cupboard. Instead, it proved to be a wardrobe holding a fine array of Baret's garments, a sea chest—locked, no doubt—and a number of other commodities and toiletries. She searched for a comb, and in the process tried to keep a distinct mood of indifference to the man whose cabin she was confined to.

"It wasn't my intention to be here," she told herself stiffly, "but his." And as she thought on this, her eye fell on—yes—she was not deceived—another smaller door. Could it be? Emerald held her breath, hoping. Yes! It proved to be the delightful discovery of a closet bathroom.

There was a ceramic basin and a jar of water, and she was able to wash her face and hands and clean her teeth. She managed to comb her disheveled hair back into an arrangement of curls and was just coming back into the cabin when there was a discreet knock on the door and it opened a crack.

"Who is it?" she demanded uneasily.

"Be only ol' Hob, miss. Be bringin' you a can o' hot water and some turtle soup."

"Come in," she said warily, and he opened the door wide, letting in morning sunlight.

Her eyes cautiously studied the familiar turtler from Chocolata Hole. Was he now serving Captain Foxworth?

The short grizzled man stood there in canvas breeches and a sea-initiated tunic. His hair was thick and peppery gray, tied to hang down his slightly hunched back. His pale eyes were shrewd, yet full of ironic good humor. In his hand was a makeshift tray, recently made, she suspected, for her convenience.

"Pert day, it is. Sea as calm as a lookin' glass. But no wind. So we sit." He set the tray down. "You took a nasty tumble, you did. If I be you, I'd rest meself a day more."

"Oh, but—" She stopped. It would do no good to vent her frustration on Hob. She must speak to the viscount at once.

"Is the captain well this morning?" she inquired with a wry note, for she had expected him to have come by now and explained her situation.

"Aye, he is." A lopsided smile came to the wrinkled face. "Alway in a fair mood, him."

"I'm pleased to hear that," she said too sweetly. "I shall appreciate it, Hob, if you would tell the viscount I wish to speak to him immediately."

He scowled innocently. "Viscount?"

"Lord Baret Buckington," said Emerald tonelessly.

"Aye, you mean Captain Foxworth, you do."

"I admit his behavior is best suited to a pirate. Among other things I wish to discuss, my trunk is missing. And I want to be brought immediately to Mr. James Bradford."

If he heard her, he evidently preferred to behave as though he had not. He set the turtle soup before her and rubbed his gnarled hands together as he feasted his eyes on the bowl. "Best soup I made in many a day, says I. Cap'n says you'll be takin' your supper at the captain's table tonight."

"Tonight! Am I to be kept a prisoner in this cabin?"

She expected Hob to hastily assure her such was not the case, but his calculating eyes gleamed as he grinned. "You best be askin' him that tonight, seein' how's he's the captain, an' he's a mite busy to spare the time now."

"Busy, indeed! I wish to be set free at once."

He grinned. "I'll tell 'im. But he be layin' plans for the expedition, he is."

At once she came alert. "Expedition?"

"'Tis a secret just where we be goin', but since there be no one to tell 'board ship who don't know an' who ain't also mighty loyal to the captain in 'is cause, I'll be letting you in on the secret, miss. No doubt be Porto Bello to rendezvous with Cap'n Henry Morgan."

"Porto Bello!" she gasped and stared at him. "But—I-I can't sail with him to Porto Bello!"

Hob assured her with grave delight that it was their prestigious destination, and he ambled out, promising to deliver her message to the captain.

Porto Bello! Henry Morgan! But she must find Jamie!

When he left, Emerald tried the turtle soup, and though it was well prepared, she could only taste it. But the coffee was perfect.

She frowned. Baret had to be in error about Jamie. Did Jamie know she was aboard? Where was he? Was he also a prisoner? But why?

She paced the cabin. Oh, what must Baret Buckington have thought when he found her unconscious on the deck wrapped in a fish net and expecting to meet a man that he believed to be the brother of a pirate?

"No," she murmured aloud. "It's even worse." Baret had said Jamie was a pirate like his brother.

She'd prove him wrong, and to salvage her stung dignity she turned her scrutiny upon his own ambiguous behavior. She was certain she had overheard him say to that dreadful Frenchman that he would sign articles with the man's captain.

Her eyes narrowed. She remembered that night in her father's office at the Manor when he had told her that Baret was searching for his father. She could understand his reason for leaving a wealthy and comfortable life in England to risk the Caribbean waters, but becoming a pirate himself . . .

Perhaps Royce *had* been a pirate as the Admiralty Court judged him to be. Perhaps Baret too had a heart for adventure and danger, and his search could simply be a ploy to let him do as he pleased.

Her eyes narrowed as she thought back to the night she had first met him, when there had been a disciplined boldness emanating from him. But she remained dubious about whether that strength was harnessed for good or ill. Her father had told her little about him, and that appeared rather strange to her now that she thought about it, in light of the fact that her father entertained the unrealistic notion that she would marry him.

Marry him! What a jest!

What was Baret truly like? she wondered and glanced about, remembering what she had discovered about him during the last unfortunate incident aboard this ship. As she stood in the silence, the cabin took on the life of its owner and seemed to rebuff the female who had intruded into its hallowed cloister. But she was quite wrong about its disclaiming all women.

Her eyes fell again on the portrait of Cousin Lavender, which remained on the carved wooden bureau. Remembering the incident at the ball when Lavender had slapped her provoked a flutter in Emerald's chest. What if she were sent back to Foxemoore? What would all the ladies say after the horrid news got out that she had been taken aboard his ship?

"Oh, I simply must keep this dreadful secret buried!"

She flushed. She had once heard of a girl who had to marry the young man who had removed her shoe after a fall from a horse—he had seen her ankle.

She paced again, trying to breathe calmly as her heart pounded. There was no cause to allow herself to be overwrought. After all, he might be an arrogant viscount, but Captain Foxworth was a reasonable man, she assured herself. Once she explained why she had been waiting on the wharf for Jamie and stood firm in her decision to marry him and voyage to New England, the viscount would allow them to depart. And Baret was also likely to be upset about Lavender's reaction. After all, he would need to do some explaining himself and would wish this horrid matter cleared up.

She took in a deep breath and solaced her distraught nerves. What did he care whom she married? Being aboard his ship this way was all a dreadful mistake.

Yes, he would cooperate. Perhaps he would even bring her and Jamie to one of the sugar islands to catch safe passage aboard an American ship returning to Boston.

There were so many questions that needed to be answered, though. What if Jamie were not aboard after all? But why had the men in the longboat known him even though they hadn't recognized the name "Bradford." "Jamie Boy" they had called him. And whose crewmen were they if not Baret's? And why had they brought her to the *Regale?*

She winced. The thought that Baret might not cooperate plagued her with uncertainty. If he returned her by boat, she would need to swallow the bitter cup of explaining everything to her father—and to Lavender. She guessed their appalling reactions, eventually resulting in a dark cloud of gossip and knowing smirks among Lavender's friends that would suggest she had deliberately sneaked aboard the viscount's ship.

This incident would bury her reputation once for all. There wouldn't be a soul at Foxemoore or Government House that wouldn't be adamant in his harsh judgment of her.

Emerald covered her face with her hands and sank into the chair. *Lord, I couldn't bear it.*

At noon Hob returned with a tray of tea.

"Did you bring my message to the captain?" she asked anxiously.

"Aye."

"Well, what did he say?"

Hob poured her tea and grinned. "He be too busy now, says he."

She cast a quick glance toward the open door. Her eyes sparked. If Captain Foxworth wouldn't come to her then—

Seeing her opportunity, Emerald dashed out of the cabin onto the deck and glanced swiftly about.

She squinted against the tropical sunlight. The wind ruffled the jade waters of the Caribbean, warmly touched her face and hair, and softly billowed the hem of her full skirt. She lifted a hand to shade her eyes. She could see Port Royal through the masts and rigging of ships at anchor. The lush greenery of the Blue Mountain range dominated the horizon.

Scanning the decks, she picked up her skirt and mounted the short wooden steps before Hob could overtake her.

When she reached the high deck she paused. Her eyes fell on Baret in black woolen trousers and a white buccaneer shirt with full sleeves. He was standing at the rail, the wind tugging at his hat as he leveled a telescope. A crewman placed a mug on the rail and, noticing Emerald, said something to his captain.

She expected Baret to turn swiftly, displeased that she had escaped Hob, but he continued to look through the telescope, undisturbed.

Emerald drew in a breath and walked swiftly toward him. She stopped beside him at the rail, but he ignored her. She said with precise dignity, "Captain Foxworth, I should like to know why I'm being held aboard your ship."

He did not reply but continued his concentration.

"Where's Mr. James Bradford, or have you put him in irons? And where is Zeddie?"

He gave no immediate reply.

Emerald's embarrassment was aroused as the protracted silence went uninterrupted. Then she heard the sound of hurried steps and saw that Hob had followed.

She turned back to Baret, who rested his elbows on the rail as he steadied the telescope.

She shaded her eyes and peered out to see the object of his focused attention. She saw nothing of importance—just a longboat rowing toward them with several men seated inside. The plumes of their wide-brimmed hats fluttered in the wind.

"M'lord—" she breathed with exasperation.

"Captain Foxworth," he corrected.

"Among the urgent matters I've already mentioned, I wish my trunk to be secured at once. There are papers inside of great value belonging to my deceased uncle, and I would be highly disappointed if anything happens to them."

"The translation of the African dialects was quite good. He wrote music?"

He kept the telescope fixed on the longboat.

Emerald scanned him cautiously, her suspicions rising. "Am I to understand, sir, that you have my trunk and that you dared to search its contents?"

"Yes to both questions. After all, Miss Harwick, you may have been running away with a pirate carrying information stolen during your first visit to my cabin. I hope you'll understand that I had to make certain. Your trunk will be returned."

His calmness maddened her, and she was offended that he'd not fully trusted what she'd told him in the garden at Foxemoore.

"But I've already explained all that, and just what information would I wish to steal from you and run away with?"

"That depends on you," came his evasive reply.

"But there is nothing in your cabin I want. Nor do I wish to stay aboard a vessel with a disrespectable captain. Will you free me or not?"

He lowered the telescope and turned his head to look at her for the first time, his dark eyes glinting. "Disrespectable?"

She refused to back down under his penetrating gaze. "I believe, sir, that you walk the thin line between questionable buccaneering and outright piracy."

"Indeed?"

She looked out at the green glare. "I was abducted from the wharf last night and brought here. What are you going to do about it?"

"I haven't decided yet."

She looked at him, startled. This was the last response she had expected. "You haven't decided—"

"No. I was going to send you and Zeddie back this morning to Sir Karlton, but I've changed my mind."

"You—you what?"

"I've changed my plans," he repeated.

"But I'm supposed to meet Mr. Bradford. Last night your odious crew implied that he was on board waiting for me."

"Fortunately for you, madam, Hob had misinformed them, and so they deposited you on my ship. They are not part of my crew but belong to the *Venture*. I believe," he said dryly, "that you are acquainted with its captain, Rafael Levasseur."

Stunned, she looked at him. "But Captain Foxworth, my French cousin is a pirate, a despicable man."

He smirked. "We agree on that much."

"And Jamie—I mean, Mr. Bradford—does not know him nor would he send men from Levasseur's pirate crew to bring me there."

"I beg to differ. Jamie Boy—I mean Mr. Bradford—" came the slightly ironic voice "—is now in league with Levasseur. And I believe, madam, that he intended you to sail with them to take a Spanish galleon." His eyes were maliciously amused.

She gasped. "How can you even suggest Jamie would do something like that? Or that I would join him?"

He folded his arms and leaned back against the rail, watching her alertly.

"Then you believed his letter?"

"Of course I believed—" She stopped, her eyes swerving to his, and a slow flush warmed her cheeks. "Sir, you are no gentleman if you read my letter."

"Madam, I assure you it was quite distasteful to my gallant nature to have done so."

"I think not. You wanted to read it. You are a rogue."

He said with feigned gravity, "But alas! My situation is such that I can leave no stone unturned when it comes to the intentions of your cousin. And," came the smooth tone, "I wanted to learn the depth to which you and he have come to these past months while secretly planning to escape Foxemoore."

She drew in an embarrassed breath, uncertain that she had heard him correctly. "I can't for the life of me guess why—"

"For reasons that will prove important."

"And are you satisfied with your discovery, Captain Foxworth?"

A slight smile touched his mouth. "Among other things, I take it that your dear Jamie Boy is rather lacking as a romantic poet."

She blushed, for the letter had spoken nothing of love— only of escaping Port Royal and their plans to start a farm.

"You can presume nothing," she said stiffly. "He's a gentleman."

"Is he? A rather cool one I would think, considering you were both emotionally attached enough to seal matrimonial doom for the rest of your years—and being no more than sixteen, you have a good many of them to invest with him in raising piglets in the Boston colony."

She saw the glint of amused challenge in his dark eyes. "I shall indeed marry him."

"Then you are, I take it, ambitious to raise piglets with Jamie Boy?"

Her face turned hot. She glared. "I don't care to discuss such personal matters with you. Jamie has nothing to do with Levasseur, and I told you at Foxemoore what I thought of Rafael."

"So he was to bring you to the Massachusetts colony?"

She smarted under the doubt in his voice. "Yes, and we shall proceed with our plans. We're to be married at Boston."

"And of course," he suggested with disbelief, "you were both going to sail on Cousin Levasseur's ship. Was he also to attend the wedding?" he asked dryly.

She had no answer, for passage aboard the *Venture* made no sense. "He—he must have been mistaken, thinking the ship was a merchant ship. What would he know about pirates?"

"Evidently a great deal. I've word from a reliable source that Jamie has joined the crew of the *Venture*. He is now Levasseur's lieutenant."

She stared, trying to judge his truthfulness. He appeared confident.

"Impossible. Jamie is no pirate. But what about you, Captain Foxworth? Did I not overhear you tell that vile Frenchman last night how you intend to sign articles with Levasseur? A known pirate, wanted in England."

She looked at him victoriously.

He merely lifted a dark brow and made no move to defend himself.

"Then you are," she said coolly, "a pirate."

"You may say that I am, madam."

"You mean you're not going to deny it?" she asked incredulously.

He smiled. "Why should I?"

She floundered, an uneasy feeling stealing over her as he watched her, the wind whipping the plume in his black hat. Her eyes faltered. "You'll hang," she whispered.

"Perhaps. Would you be sorry?"

Her eyes darted up to his, and under his gaze she blushed. "No."

"I didn't think so. You grieve me sorely, madam."

She looked stiffly out toward Port Royal.

He offered her the telescope, and she glanced at him to see a sardonic smile touching his mouth. "Perhaps you best have a look. Your darling comes. No doubt to claim you."

Emerald's eyes searched his face. Jamie was coming? Her confusion grew more acute.

"The one question remaining for me," said Baret, "is whether or not I should permit him to do so."

"Permit? . . But . . . " she floundered, taking the telescope and trying to focus it upon the approaching longboat, but her hands shook, and the ship seemed to sway gently, giving her a disoriented feeling.

He stepped beside her to steady the instrument, but she swiftly moved away. "I need no aid, m'lord."

He offered a slight bow. "Captain," he repeated. "But we'll save titles for London."

"Not London. I'm going with Mr. Bradford to Massachusetts."

"To raise piglets." He gestured an airy hand toward the longboat. "Better think twice. Levasseur has other plans, and they lie in the direction of the Spanish Main. Bradford is sailing with him. But I can't say how long Jamie will be there to protect you."

She didn't know what to think, and, turning her back toward him, she steadied her elbows on the rail as she had seen him do and focused on the longboat. This time she managed to hold steady, her heart thumping in her chest as she saw the lean swarthy face of Captain Levasseur.

His lively black eyes gazed straight ahead. He was modishly garbed in a burgundy taffeta suit with a matching dyed ostrich feather swirling from a black hat worn over his curled periwig.

Her bewilderment grew as she studied the man sitting beside him in a faded cotton shirt and leather breeches of untanned hide. Beneath his rough cap, the jaw-length chestnut hair curled slightly, matching a wide mustache on the up-

287

per lip of a masculine face weathered by the sun. Alert blue eyes were fixed on the *Regale*.

"Jamie," she whispered.

As she looked intently through the spyglass, she became aware of Hob's presence, ready to interrupt.

"She darted from the cabin like a canary, Cap'n," he explained. "I couldn't reach her before she was already up the steps."

Emerald faced them. "Am I a prisoner? If there's a decision to be made concerning my future, it's only just that I be present."

"It's all right, Hob," said Baret. "Miss Harwick will be present when we greet them. The four of us have much to discuss. And if there's unpleasantness, I'll trust that Sir Karlton's runaway daughter will refrain from fainting to the deck in a heap of flounces."

Her eyes narrowed as he offered a slightly exaggerated bow. "I must not keep the Brethren waiting."

Emerald watched as he descended to the quarterdeck with Hob behind him.

She stood there for a moment, then looked over the ship's rail as the longboat rowed up to the ship's ladder and a slave reached to tie the rope. Her anxious gaze watched Levasseur confidently mount the rope ladder.

Emerald turned to step down to the quarterdeck when she saw Hob bringing Baret his baldric, holding sword and pistols. Baret first slipped into a black velvet jacket and then passed the baldric over his head. Hob handed him a wide-brimmed hat, which he put on with style.

Emerald knew about the customs of the Brethren of the Coast. On certain occasions among the finer gentlemen who believed in chivalry, they often dressed in magnificent finery —usually before a duel.

She came down the steps with uncertainty. "M'lord! What are you going to do?" she cried, and when he didn't answer immediately, she lifted her skirt and sped toward him.

"There are certain customs," he said casually. "And your cousin sets great store by them. The French betray themselves with a fastidious love for exaggerated courtliness. Hence my dress and weapons show respect for his reputation as a buccaneer." His dark eyes were amused but sober. "Stay close to Hob until I introduce you."

"I see no need for trouble," she said nervously. "Can't you understand that I just wish to leave with Mr. Bradford?"

"You will do as I request, or will I need to have Hob escort you to the cabin?"

Her eyes searched his. "You mean that?"

His even stare was answer enough.

"I shall do as you request," she said too politely.

He turned and went down the companionway to the main deck.

Emerald trailed, wondering. She still had no idea of why he might not allow her to depart now that Jamie was coming for her.

Even if Jamie were a pirate, why should Baret care? Was he concerned for Sir Karlton? Perhaps he would insist she be brought back to Foxemoore.

I won't go back, she thought.

26

FOR TWENTY THOUSAND
PIECES OF EIGHT

Emerald stood tensely on the quarterdeck steps, the breeze moving the hem of her frock, her eyes upon her cousin, Levasseur, who came over the side.

He paused at the head of the ladder, as though considering his safety. Then, with pantherlike agility, he stepped on board and stood with his lean brown hand resting on his sword hilt. Gleaming black curls clustered about his narrow face, alert as a fox.

As yet he did not notice her.

His gaze moved from one to another on deck until colliding with Baret Buckington. He doffed his hat according to custom and replaced it, the plume dancing, then approached Baret with a glint of subdued anger in his eyes. A curled smile touched his thin lips.

"A surprise, Captain Foxworth?"

"Indeed, Captain Levasseur. A most pleasant one," he said smoothly, but it wasn't clear to Emerald who was meant to be pleased. Baret stood boldly in full buccaneer regalia, a hand on one of the pistol butts in his baldric.

"Pleasant?" said Levasseur. "But no, you have offended me! Have you not scorned my hospitality?"

"How so, my captain?" he said with a faint smile.

"I waited long into the night aboard the *Venture*—but alas, you did not keep our rendezvous as agreed."

"A mere safeguard, Captain Levasseur, I assure you. And I am most gratified that you have kept our appointment."

"But aboard your ship!"

"Of course, my captain! There is the damsel Emerald to think of."

Emerald moved uncertainly at the mention of her name, and Levasseur's black eyes became granite.

"My cousin? You have no need to concern yourself over her, Captain Foxworth."

Baret laughed. "Ah, but I have decided to become concerned."

"Must I tell you that this is a personal matter—one that has nothing to do with our business of signing articles?"

"Oh, but I must disagree," said Baret. He sat down on a cask and watched Levasseur with a smile. "I should save time by informing you that I am well aware of how she was deceived into nearly boarding the *Venture*. And that her departure is quite unacceptable."

Levasseur's eyes narrowed with mounting temper, but they studied Baret as though trying to judge his reasons. "Unacceptable, monsieur? To you?"

"Yes. I, Captain Foxworth, also a Buckington, am a man of high title—as you should well know by now from Maynerd's brother Jamie. And as such, my friend Rafael, I cannot permit a kin of mine to be lured away to marry a mere pirate's brother."

Levasseur pretended amused toleration. "Monsieur, it is no secret your titled family has dispossessed her since birth."

"True, but have I, Captain?" he asked innocently. "And my judgment was made with higher motives than even my titled family is aware of."

Levasseur's smile faded. "It is I, her French cousin, who shall have the right to make a fitting marriage for her with Jamie."

Baret smiled thinly. "Is it Jamie you wish her to marry, or do you have designs yourself?"

Levasseur smiled. "Ah, Monsieur Foxworth, you assuredly misjudge me. It is for her welfare I have come and must insist she disembark the *Regale* for the *Venture*."

"No. She stays with me. Shall we talk of the other matter for which you have come?"

"She was to be brought to the *Venture* until you abducted her."

"Alas, I confess it is so."

Levasseur appeared to be taken off guard. His shrewd eyes studied Baret, ignoring Emerald. "If you do not hand her over to me this moment, you may be challenged."

"As you have charged, I abducted her from the wharf, and I intend to maintain custody until she is mine."

"Are you willing to duel for her, Foxworth?"

Emerald's breath stopped. For a moment there was only the sound of the creaking ship.

"Yes, if I must. Are you?"

Levasseur stared at him, his inward rage barely subdued. "I, Captain? Is it not Jamie Boy who lays claim to her?"

Baret rubbed his chin as if to consider.

Emerald met his gaze, glaring, her face hot. "It is Mr. Bradford I wish to marry," she called suddenly, coming down the steps. "Levasseur, you scamp, why is he not on board?"

Levasseur smiled. "He is below in the longboat, mam'zelle. And I would bring him to you this moment but for Captain Foxworth. He wishes to duel with him."

Emerald turned to Baret, confused, mortified as his dark eyes held hers. "M'lord, how can you . . . I mean, you surely jest."

Baret strode to the rail and looked down, the breeze swirling the plume in his hat. "So this is our charming Jamie Boy, is it? Madam! It is you who jest! You would have this sniveling boy for a husband and refuse *my* advances?"

She was speechless. *Refuse his advances?*

But Levasseur was not overwhelmed. He whirled toward Baret. "You want her for yourself?"

"Why not? I exceed you in gallantry. I will make an appropriate sacrifice to obtain her or duel Jamie Boy here and now. I am also more sincere in that I readily admit to wanting her, while you hide behind a mask."

Emerald didn't move. She stared at Baret, astonished and embarrassed, but he did not seem disturbed in the slightest. How could he say such things? And in front of so many witnesses!

Levasseur stared at him as well. Behind him his officers gathered, gaping with surprise at the sudden change in Captain Foxworth.

Baret leaned against the rigging, arms folded, smiling with confidence. "What will it be, Captain Levasseur? A duel with your first lieutenant?—who I am certain is still of value to you since he has withheld certain information that you deem most urgent."

Emerald was at a loss, her heart pounding. What information did Jamie have?

Levasseur's manner became leery. "What information, Foxworth?"

"Let us not play games, Rafael. We both know why you seek me. For the same reason I have sought you—for Lucca. I, for news of my father's whereabouts; you, for the treasure of the *Prince Philip*. And Jamie holds the key to our success."

Levasseur's eyes narrowed. "How do you know that he has not already told me?"

Baret smiled. "Come! We are both pirates! Would you leave him alive to tell others if he had already told you? Alas, by now you would have run him through."

Emerald's hand went to her mouth. She looked from Baret to Levasseur.

Levasseur laughed savagely. "Ah, Monsieur Foxworth, we do understand each other then, do we not? But to make certain neither of us bedevils the other, it seems you and I must come to agreement."

"Quite so, Levasseur," said Baret quietly, unsmiling now. "And so what will it be? Shall I duel the man who holds the key? Or will you agree that I keep the girl?"

Levasseur cocked his head, measuring Baret. "It seems, Captain, that neither of us can afford the loss of Jamie Boy. As you say, monsieur, he holds the key to what we both want."

"Then perhaps you will permit me to do business with him."

His words evidently gave Levasseur pause, and while his hard gaze cursed him, his expression was fixed in a gallant smile. He suddenly bowed with elegance. "You have me, monsieur! What do you offer Jamie Boy in order to keep her?"

Emerald found her voice shaking with humiliation and rage. "You blackguards! You dare barter over me as though I were booty—"

293

"You are, madam—at my disposal," stated Baret. "I would advise you to take heart and count yourself favored that I should be willing to bid for you."

She sucked in her breath, staring at him, his dark gaze silencing her.

Baret turned to Levasseur. "And now, Captain, I shall make your lieutenant an offer."

Levasseur was keenly alert. "The price paid is for division. Jamie Boy has signed the Articles with me."

Jamie has signed articles with Levasseur? wondered Emerald.

"I quite agree," said Baret. "And since Jamie Boy is one of you, even the brother of Captain Charles Maynerd, he must agree to share the price I buy the girl for or suffer the penalty for withholding from fellow Brethren."

Emerald's mind faltered, unable to grasp all that she was hearing. But she did understand that Baret was deliberately showing her that Jamie was one of Levasseur's pirates.

"What do you offer for my comely young cousin?" asked Levasseur.

Baret calmly removed his hat as though contemplating, his eyes narrowing as they fixed upon Emerald.

She jerked away, turning her back, her face warm. The arrogant scoundrel! And to think he had her father convinced he was a gentleman!

"Jamie will never agree!" she called.

"No?" said Baret. "Shall we discover the truth, madam?"

She wanted to recoil at his challenge, her assurance faltering. But Jamie had said he loved her. She could depend on him. She turned bravely and met his challenge. "Call him!"

Baret's dark brow lifted. He looked at Levasseur. "Bring him on deck. We shall see at what price he will succumb for the woman he has vowed to marry."

"He won't be bribed," Emerald found herself saying.

"Bring him," said Baret.

Levasseur gestured to one of his French officers, who went to the rail.

Minutes later Jamie came over the ship's side garbed as one of Levasseur's crew. A scabbard with rapier was strapped about his hips. His blue eyes darted about the ship until they fell upon her, standing near the quarterdeck steps.

He grinned, his boyish face retaining all of the charm she thought she knew so well. "Emerald!"

"Jamie!" she cried. "What's happening? What are you doing with my cousin on the *Venture?*"

He scowled. "I can explain everything. I'm sorry I couldn't meet you. I was having an urgent meeting with Captain Levasseur. You are safe?"

Emerald pointed at Baret, expecting Jamie to confront him. "If being abducted and hauled aboard this pirate's ship in a fish net is safe, yes. Jamie, what do you mean—urgent business with Rafael?"

He now surged toward her, until Baret, calm to the point of appearing bored, stepped forward to block his way.

"Do restrain yourself, Maynerd. We have much to discuss, you and I."

Jamie stopped abruptly and frowned. His eyes flashed with temper, then turned to Emerald. "Who in thunder is this?"

"A man you wish to contact, I believe." Baret's lazy voice was laced with warning. "The name is Buckington, but perhaps Foxworth will suffice for what we have in mind. If you wish to partake in the treasure of my father's ship, you must also sign articles with me."

Jamie stared at him, his temper swiftly subsiding. "Aye, Captain, I do indeed. I mean—your lordship." He bowed. "My brother spoke well of you."

"Did he now? I'm honored."

"Aye, till that infamous Lord Felix had him hung! Begging your pardon, Captain, seeing how he is your uncle."

Then Jamie *was* a Maynerd. Emerald felt Baret's gaze, suspected his subdued satisfaction, and refused to look at him. She still told herself that Jamie could explain everything.

"I'll be swift to sign articles with you, Captain Foxworth."

"Good!" said Baret cheerfully. "But first there is the matter of the girl. I'm told she ran away from Foxemoore to marry you."

Jamie grinned. "Aye! We're going to Boston to buy land for farming."

"Are you indeed? Then what are you doing signing articles with Captain Levasseur and myself? Was this part of your plan?"

"No, but—it was a stroke of luck." He looked at Emerald. "A chance to make it wealthy before we set sail."

Emerald wished to hear no more in front of Baret, for it seemed obvious that Jamie had been willing to risk her on a pirate venture.

"Matters have changed," said Baret calmly.

Jamie frowned a little. "What do you mean?"

"I'll make it as short as I can—"

"Captain Foxworth wishes to buy me," snapped Emerald.

"Huh? Buy you?"

"Yes," said Baret. "My offer is twenty thousand pieces of eight. Do you accept?"

Emerald nearly gasped.

Jamie stared, eyes wide. "Twenty thousand—"

Baret's manner, cool and almost contemptuous, seemed to have an intimidating effect on him, and he halted, uncertain. "You . . . want Emerald?"

Emerald sought to restrain her humiliation.

Baret drew from an inner pocket of his doublet a small pouch. While the others gathered around greedily, he untied the mouth of the bag. "Being a viscount," he told the gaping men, "I am used to buying what I want." He shook into his left palm a huge glittering blood-red ruby. "Levasseur, what is a ruby like this worth?"

Levasseur smiled beneath his hat, his dark eyes snapping. "Perhaps a thousand pieces of eight."

"More like five," said Baret dryly. "There are three more in this bag, Jamie Boy. Think what you might do with them? Now, surely, you are willing to give me the girl."

Jamie was ogling the rubies that Baret poured like liquid fire from the bag.

"A ship of your own one day, a farm in Boston with another pretty wench—sure now, what is one pretty face more than another? With a fortune like this, you'd have your choice."

Levasseur stepped up. "A bargain, Jamie Boy. You'd be a fool not to."

Jamie licked his lips and glanced at Emerald who stood numb. His expression turned serious, and a whiteness showed about his mouth. Sweat broke out on his face, and he wiped his forehead with the back of his arm.

"A bargain, Captain," choked Jamie, then glanced at Emerald.

She turned her back, tears stinging her eyes. She had been shamed! Humiliated! She hated Baret Buckington!

"And now, Hob," said Baret, "bring my purchase to the cabin."

His *purchase!*

"Aye, m'lady," said Hob with laughing eyes, "shall I escort you to the cap'n's cabin?"

Emerald whipped about to face Baret. Her eyes searched his, and she saw nothing but a momentary flicker of warmth in their dark depths. She drew back her arm and slapped him harshly.

Laughter broke out from the buccaneers, but neither Emerald nor Baret were smiling.

"I shall never forgive you for this," she whispered. "Never."

He looked at her, then without a word, bowed lightly and walked away to where Levasseur and Jamie stood by the rail.

Emerald shook her arm free of Hob and rushed up the steps to the quarterdeck. She threw open the door to the Great Cabin and entered, trembling.

Hob appeared a moment later in the doorway. "His lordship ain't be cuckoldy, Miss Emerald, you'll see. He were doin' it for you, he was, to save you from makin' a mistake with Jamie Maynerd. Aye, but one day you'll thank him for it."

She turned away, her hands in fists at her sides. "Thank him? For treating me like a common piece of baggage before those nasty miserable pirates of his?"

Hob was grave, his clear eyes saddened. "Aye, they expected it of him, they did. Sure now, it's the way of the buccaneers. They'd think somethin' wrong if'n he didn't. But it's his father he's aiming to find, miss, and he ain't be going to let nothing stop him. But I'll let him do his own explainin."

"You can tell him I don't want to hear it."

She lowered herself into a chair, her head across her arm, trying to still the deep hurt that boiled up inside.

Hob looked at her sadly, then went out, shutting the door behind him.

Emerald's head lifted as she heard the unmistakable sound of a key locking her inside. She stood, staring at the door. *Bought for twenty thousand pieces of eight.*

Emerald awoke with a start and sat up. A glance at the open window showed a silver star gleaming in the inky sky. Her gaze shifted with dismay to the bronze lantern above the captain's desk; it swooped and swayed with a nauseating effect. She had limited knowledge of the sea, having never sailed on her father's merchant ships, but the movement of the *Regale* convinced her they had already set sail from Port Royal harbor beneath the big guns of Fort Charles and were out on the Caribbean.

The trade wind blew strongly, and she could hear the ship's canvas lifting and billowing with a glorious snapping sound.

How could he do this to her? She bemoaned her appalling situation. Captain Foxworth appeared to completely disregard her feelings. Her reputation lay in shreds!

What was it that Hob had told her earlier that morning? "'Tis a secret just where we be goin' . . . but no doubt to rendezvous with Cap'n Henry Morgan."

Morgan!

Driven by desperation, Emerald tried to open the cabin door; it was still locked from the outside, and Baret Buckington carried the key. She hammered with her fists. "Let me out! Captain Foxworth! Open this door at once!"

All to no avail. She turned and sank wearily against it, watching the swooping lantern.

"This is my own fault," groaned Emerald, dismayed. "If I hadn't deceived my father and run off in the first place, I wouldn't be caught in this situation."

Guilt turned her mind to her sins. "Oh, Lord, I'll make amends for my ways. I promise I will. I haven't forgotten the vow I made You—or the promise to Mathias about the Singing School."

But her words of commitment mocked her, and heaven above seemed deaf to her plea. Fear crept through her spirit —just how often had Uncle Mathias lamented the hypocritical repentance of wretches who found themselves in trouble?

His words rang in her ears. *No sooner does the gracious Lord come to their rescue than they're back to their whoredoms and thievery.*

"If I hadn't disregarded my conscience and sought to run away from Foxemoore with Jamie, I'd not be tasting the bitter fruits of my wilfulness. I yield my life anew to You. Have Your way in my heart, my goals, my hopes, my ambitions. Whatever You want to do with me, I am Yours. Let Your grace be my sufficiency. Strengthen me to fulfill Your eternal purposes."

Emerald watched the sun lift from the amber waves and begin to scatter the night's darkness. The wind arose and carried away the last vestige of night, and the warm tropics bloomed, caressing her face through the window.

Once again her thoughts turned to Baret. He was an enigma. How could she ever understand him? Did he even understand himself? Just what did he have in mind in holding her captive like this? What was his underlying motive? Whatever it was, he'd gone so far as to offer to duel for her, yet he couldn't have been serious.

No, he couldn't have. There was Lavender. And who was she—Emerald—but the daughter of Sir Karlton?

She turned again to the work of Mathias for consolation, going over the African slave chants that would have been turned into gospel chants instead. Instead of words of hopelessness and darkness, they would have become words of light and expectation of a great and mighty God who had heard the groaning of the prisoner and come to set the soul free.

She tried to concentrate on how she might turn those dark words to ones of a rising sun—like the Caribbean sun shooting up from the night's waters. Her thoughts raced to Psalm 19—"As a bridegroom coming out of his chamber."

Inevitably her restless mind turned to Baret. What had Hob said? That he was searching for his father and nothing would stand in his way? Not even her presence aboard the *Regale.* He would not turn back for her or for anyone else.

But what did Levasseur and Jamie have to do with it? Why had they agreed to sign articles with Baret? Perhaps more important, why did the viscount wish to associate with *them?* Previously Baret had no good to say about either her cousin or Jamie. And were they now partners in piracy?

It must have something to do with his search for his father, she thought, *but what?*

She remembered the scene aboard ship when Levasseur arrived. There had been something between him and Baret then, something shrouded with danger.

And Jamie! She shut her eyes, troubled. How could she have been so deceived about his character? Her father had been right when he insisted Jamie was a pirate.

Perhaps the humiliation she had felt when he exchanged his willingness to marry her for the rubies had been the chastening hand of her Lord revealing her waywardness. She should never have laid out her plans without seriously seeking His purpose first in prayer.

She stared at the letter Jamie had sent to her after the slave uprising. How bright their plan had shone then! It had seemed the door of escape to a new life and happiness. But even if Jamie had not flown his true colors when Baret "bought" her from him, she now doubted they would have found peace in the Boston colony. Marriage to Jamie would have been a dreadful mistake.

Both Jamie and the letter appeared a shabby counterfeit for what she was inwardly seeking.

"At least I owe Baret Buckington my gratitude for that," she murmured. "Truly the Lord has His way in the whirlwind and in the storm. The worst of situations can turn out for our good."

And in a decisive movement, she tore up a future that might have been and tossed it through the window to the trade wind.

Even here may Your hand lead me, O my Father.

A polite knock sounded, and a key turned in the lock. Expecting Hob, perhaps with tea, it was with astonishment that she greeted Zeddie, who poked his head in, his familiar white periwig well groomed and his black eyepatch in place.

"Zeddie," she cried, rushing toward him.

"Aye, m'gal, 'tis me!"

"Oh, Zeddie, I'm so happy to see you." She grabbed him, as he grinned. "I was beginning to think I'd never see you again. Your presence brings great relief."

"But your presence, lass, 'tis a sore grief to me. Yet 'tis a boon that you didn't run off with that jackanapes Maynerd after all. 'Bradford,' so he calls himself. An' all the while of the same pirate blood and disposition as old Charlie himself."

"Never mind that now. You are here safe. That is what matters. Vapors! You're wearing your baldric!" she said, pointing to his pair of dueling pistols in the leather sling. "I'm surprised the infamous Captain Foxworth has let you carry it," she said coolly. "Oh, Zeddie, you are all right? He didn't harm you during your imprisonment?"

"Harm me?" he scoffed. "Wooden idols be tossed to the flame! Why—" he grinned "—I've been treated well indeed. I've been serving the Cambridge divine himself Sir Cecil Chaderton. A grave Puritan, no less. And once a good friend of the deceased Cromwell, though he says he exiled in France with the boy viscount until King Charles was restored in '60. It seems you're not left to the rascally mouthed renegades entirely, not with Sir Cecil aboard lending his studious grace of the Scriptures."

Emerald was quite sure she didn't have the slightest notion of what Zeddie was talking about. Sir Cecil Chaderton? Who was he? A Puritan? On board the *Regale*? If there was anyone on board the *Regale* who took delight in the Scriptures, he must surely have boarded in grievous error.

"That you were treated with dignity, at least, is a consolation," she said, willing to forget her digruntled feelings toward Baret. "Yet you must be mistaken about this man Chaderton."

"No mistake, no indeed. You shall meet him soon enough. He says he knew Mathias in London before the Civil War."

Sadly she told him about Mathias's death and Jonah's.

"That odious Mr. Pitt," he said furiously. "Would fate that I'd been there! The shark ought to be hung by his thumbs! But 'tis good news that Ty escaped to the Blue Mountains. And Minette?" He looked about.

"She escaped when Captain Foxworth's nasty crew abducted me. By now she has surely notified my father."

"Sir Chaderton insists they weren't the viscount's crew, but he only used them. He says the captain is a divinity student! Fan me, ye winds! I ask you, since when does a man trained in the Holy Word at Cambridge wield a sword and attack a treasure galleon? Sink me if I can understand that one!"

"Surely this man Chaderton is exaggerating. Yet there is a minutia of truth to it," she confessed, remembering that little Jette had told her the same thing about Baret's attending Cambridge. The thought that he had spent some years studying the Scriptures was unfathomable. She felt quite certain that Baret was a pirate—and his father. But she couldn't think on that now. "What did you find out about Jamie and Levasseur?"

"They're on board. And another vile shark hath appeared—a big man with the ways of the devil himself. Sloan, he calls himself."

"On board? Levasseur and Jamie?"

"For what cause, I've not been able to find out. Perhaps we shall learn a thing or two at dinner." He frowned. "And that's why I'm here. The captain has asked you to show yourself."

"Dine with a pack of pirates? I won't go, Zeddie. I want nothing to do with him, and that now includes Jamie Maynerd. I shall have supper here in the cabin, though I'm not a bit hungry."

He frowned. "A bright and breezy decision. But I fear the captain has his mind made up, m'gal. An' I'm in no fair circumstance to refuse him. He knew you'd decline. It was his reason for sending me."

"Thinking I'll feel safer, no doubt. Perhaps, but that doesn't make up for his ill treatment and disregard of my wishes. He put me to humiliation aboard deck in view of all his nasty crew, and I'll not favor a pirate captain by eating with him."

Zeddie straightened his periwig. "Sink me! I never thought the earl's grandson would be dueling for you before witnesses!"

"The blackguard—he didn't mean it, of course, but what could he have in mind? Hob insisted it was for my protection, but I wonder."

"The viscount is a hard one to understand, m'gal. If Sir Chaderton knows him as well as he says, the earl's grandson is only behaving the scoundrel for reasons of his own. And what they are, I've no notion. 'Tis enough to try to outthink the French bloke and the lyin' tongued Jamie Maynerd."

So her cousin Rafael Levasseur was still aboard the *Regale*. What could it mean?'

27

THE YARDARM

The following day passed quietly enough, and no scoundrel came to loiter about her cabin door. As evening fell softly upon the water, and she began to accept the unpleasantness of her dilemma as from the hand of her heavenly Father, a rap sounded on the door.

Emerald approached cautiously, for Hob was never rude and always called to her first. Nor did she think the rap came from the viscount. She had not seen him since that dreadful moment on the quarterdeck when she had lost control of her emotions and slapped him. She winced as she remembered. In England, a viscount could send her to the women's prison for such behavior.

Impatient knuckles rapped again.

"Har! Open up, Cap'n's orders!"

Emerald smothered the desire to wince. "I cannot. I don't have the key. And even if I did—"

Voices outside interrupted. Zeddie was speaking in protest, but his words were drowned out as a scuffle broke out. Oh no! What was happening to poor Zeddie?

She stepped back as a key rattled in the lock, and the door was flung open. A cry died on her tongue as she stared at a huge man with a fringe of greasy black curls beneath a gaudy head scarf and lurid brows above pale eyes. Over the head scarf was a floppy black hat bearing a caricature of the devil. He wore a gaping black shirt and loose breeches of rawhide, and in the belt he bore a brace of pistols and a cutlass.

She'd never seen him before and backed away in fear.

He leered, inspecting her. "So, now. You be Jamie Boy's pretty wench, eh?"

She grasped at dignity. "Sir, you are no gentleman."

304

He threw back his head and roared. "D'you 'ear the wench, Poke," he called over his shoulder. "I be no gentleman."

"Who are you!" she demanded. "Who gave you license to break into my privacy?"

"Break into your privacy, she says! Har! Clever, isn't she?" he said to the ruffian with weapon in hand who stood like a hound at bay just outside.

"Some calls me Sloane. What you calls me don't matter, gal."

She retained her courage, praying silently that Baret would soon appear.

"Who sent you here, Mr. Sloane?"

"Har! 'Mister' Sloane, she says! I likes it. 'Mister.' Mister Sloane oughter be cap'n, says I. What say you, gal?"

"Where is the captain!"

Somehow she couldn't imagine Baret's sending this ruffian to her cabin. Her eyes darted past him and fell to where Zeddie sat rubbing his head. Once again his periwig lay disheveled on the deck.

She started toward him. "Zeddie—"

Sloane blocked her way. Aware of his awful presence and odor, again she stepped back, scanning him distastefully.

He gave her quick appraisal with bold eyes.

Emerald drew her cloak firmly about her.

"Ah, you mean Foxworth," he said with a hoarse sound that turned to ironic laughter. "He's no cap'n of mine." Then, "Well, so you was the bride of Jamie Boy Maynerd. Now I be wondering where the merry groom might'n be keeping himself? T'aint pretty manners to keep an anxious bride waitin'."

Crude laughter bubbled from the throat of the crewman watching Zeddie. The man now poked his scarfed head in through the door to stare.

A kindled gleam of hungry interest sprang up in the depths of Sloane's eyes. "Ol' Jamie Boy ain't no fool after all."

"Stay away!"

"A shrew, eh? But a rare wench! Too bad 'bout Jamie."

"What have you done with him?" she asked anxiously. "Where is he?"

"Me?" he asked innocently. "You'll see 'im all right if you have eyes in your head. He ain't goin' nowheres soon." And he gave a laugh. "Suppose I take you to him?" He leered and caught her, one arm about her waist.

Emerald struggled to free herself from an iron grip as he carried her from the cabin onto the quarterdeck. "Put me down!" She tried to turn her head from his calico shirt, reeking of rum and old sweat. *Lord, help me—*

All at once a hand latched hold of Sloane's shoulder, and a pistol muzzle rammed behind his ear.

"Put the lady down, Sloane, or they'll be swabbing up your brains—what there is of them."

The calm but cutting voice brought an end to Sloane's bawdy laughter, and as he released her, Emerald caught her balance on the rail.

"Alas, Sloane, you have no manners."

With relief, she saw Baret.

Compared to the unkempt crewmen gathered about the deck, he stood out as the image of excellence, however arrogant, and his disposition suggested that beneath his suave restraint lived a man every whit as dangerous. As though proving her measure of him justified, a quick movement of his fist landed a vicious blow to the man's belly, and when the pirate staggered like a bull, Baret struck again to the back of his neck.

Sloane thudded to one knee with a curse hissing between his teeth, his hand fumbling for his dagger. As he withdrew it, Baret stomped his hand to the deck. When his grip released the blade, Baret kicked the knife across the deck and over the side into the sea.

Sloane swore. "I'll kill you for this, Foxworth!" He struggled to get to his feet, but Baret's booted foot pushed him backward to the deck. He aimed the pistol, and Sloane grew still, his eyes narrowing into pale slits.

"Where is your captain?" demanded Baret. "You could be hanged for this, Sloane! This is not the *Venture* but *my* ship! And you'll mind my laws while you walk my decks! And if I catch you near the girl again, I'll throw you to the sharks."

Sloane said nothing, and the pirates who had congregated about him were also sullen and silent.

Baret walked closer to where Sloane was lying on his back. He looked down at him, his dark eyes cold, the wind touching his dark hair tied back with a leather thong. "Who told you to disturb the lady's cabin? Levasseur?"

"Aye, the Frenchman's our captain. We follow his orders, Foxworth!"

"On my ship you'll follow mine. Or rot in the hold with the rats. Understood?"

The pirate Sloane snarled something inaudible.

"Where're Levasseur and Maynerd?" demanded Baret.

Sloane turned his big head and leered across the deck to several of Levasseur's pirates. They grinned, eyes shrewd. They folded their arms and remained mute.

Emerald's mind swam in confusion. What were they doing still aboard the *Regale*? Surely Baret had known they were aboard before he left Port Royal harbor! But it was also clear that he had not expected the pirates serving her cousin to risk his wrath in coming to the Great Cabin.

Some of Baret's crewmen gathered, hearing the commotion. Levasseur's pirates glowered at them, but she sensed that despite the circumstance Baret Buckington was in command. Neither group of men reached toward their swords.

Emerald's nervous glance swept past Baret, took in the unsmiling faces, and saw that their attention was now riveted on the angry captain of the *Regale*, who stood, one hand on hip, the other holding a long dueling pistol, demanding answers that none of Levasseur's pirates wanted to give.

She saw their grudging respect. Knowing they were cautious restored some of her shaken confidence.

"Where is the rogue who deigns to be your captain?" asked Baret. "Call him!" he ordered a sullen black-eyed Frenchman. The pirate muttered in French and sauntered away to call Levasseur.

"Does he hide himself below like a rat in the darkness?" asked Baret.

Then from above on the high poop came a familiar voice ringing with haughty French disdain. "Monsieur, you will yet provoke me to a duel! *Oui!* But I deign to believe the two of us are destined to mingle our cause as one! And like

307

the Frenchman L'Ollonais who has sacked Porto Bello, I too shall overwhelm the Spaniards with burning arrows of pitch!"

Levasseur gave a clear laugh as he leaned his arms on the taffrail. "And you, monsieur! You are as ruthless as I!"

Emerald looked up. Levasseur stood in purple taffetas and a white ruffled shirt, his immaculate black periwig curling at his shoulders. What was he doing still aboard the *Regale?* Did he not have his own ship?

She glanced toward the sea and saw the dim outline of Jamaica far behind. Where they were headed was anyone's guess.

Levasseur left the taffrail to come down the companionway. In the silence that held them all, Emerald heard the rigging creak and groan in the wind.

"Are you looking for Maynerd?" called Levasseur. "You need not look far, my captain, and—" he bowed at the waist toward Emerald "—Mam'zelle Emerald! He is somewhere about."

Sloane and the dozen pirates serving Levasseur chuckled.

Emerald glanced at Baret and saw that, whatever he was thinking, he did not look intimidated. His confidence strengthened her own, and she took a slight step toward him.

Levasseur's gaze shifted and latched hold of her.

Baret caught her arm as though he owned her and drew her to his side.

Her first impulse was to pull away.

"I bought her for twenty thousand pieces of eight, have you forgotten? The damsel is with me. And anyone who wishes to either paw or gape will have more to contend with than her claws."

"There is no quarrel over Mam'zelle Emerald," said Levasseur shortly. "It is my stolen jewels I sent my lieutenant Sloane to find."

"From henceforth you'll send none of your crew to my cabin. Is that clear? Anything that now concerns her, concerns me. You will come to me, not to her."

Levasseur shrugged. "As you wish, monsieur. We are friends in one cause, are we not?"

"You'd betray me in an instant if you could. Let us forget pretense, Levasseur. Get on with what ails you."

Levasseur strode toward Emerald, and for the first time she took solace in Baret's closeness. She turned her head away.

"Ask mam'zelle what ails me. It is stolen jewels I concern myself with. Can it be, fair cousin, that you have taken them to run away not with Jamie Maynerd but with Baret Buckington Foxworth?"

She was taken off guard and turned to face the Frenchman.

His black eyes sparked.

The jewels! she thought. *He still believes I have them.* She also remembered with a twinge of guilt that Baret knew something Levasseur did not—that she had once intended to board the *Venture* and take treasure to buy freedom for Ty and Jamie. She glanced at Baret, but his rugged profile showed nothing, and he was watching Levasseur.

"I have none of your jewels, Cousin Levasseur," she stated. "I vowed as much in Port Royal when you barged into the lookout and ruined my trunk. You did not find them then, and I do not have them now." She gestured to his scurrilous crew. "If you are missing jewels, you should ask your own foul pirates. I suggest they had access to your booty."

Levasseur mocked a bow. "Pardon, mam'zelle, but I believe otherwise. And I suggest that if you forbid me to search your cabin—"

"It is *I* who forbid," interrupted Baret smoothly. "If there is any searching of my cabin, it is I who will do so."

"I assure you," said Emerald, "I have no jewels belonging to my cousin or to anyone else."

Levasseur smiled thinly. "Perhaps the abduction was planned. You both agreed together to deceive Maynerd but then, having stolen my jewels, also expected to find out from him where the treasure of the *Prince Philip* is kept."

"This is absurd," said Baret.

Levasseur lost his good mood. "Monsieur! You sorely try my gallantry. The stolen jewels are a family disagreement between me and my cousin."

Baret waved a hand. "As you wish. To end the matter, however, I alone reserve the right to search her trunk."

Emerald was on the verge of reminding him that he had already done so, looking for a letter he had previously accused her of taking from his cabin, but something in his gaze silenced her.

"As you wish, Captain," she said coolly. "But I do not know why you must have my blackguard cousin on board your ship when he has a pirate vessel of his own."

"An unpleasant situation, I agree," said Baret easily.

Levasseur lifted a hand to his heart, his wrist sprouting cream lace. "Monsieur, you offend my honor. If I am aboard your ship, it is because I am no fool. And do you think I will impart information without adequate guarantees? If I had not insisted on sailing on the *Regale* to our point of rendez-vous, you, Monsieur Foxworth, would have all to your advantage."

"My advantage?" Baret feigned innocence.

"*Oui!* You would have both the information on the location of Lucca *and* the fair demoiselle. And I! I would have nothing to guard me from treachery once I left your decks. Yes, yes, monsieur, I am too careful for that."

Baret regarded him, looking contemptuous. "Do you think I've willingly left my title and inheritance in England to come to the Caribbean only to cheat you? If you would altogether lose hope of gazing upon Spanish gold, talk to me again of threats and betrayal. It is true that I need you and Maynerd, but your need of me is even more dire. Lucca will talk to no one but me. Will you stand here bickering and risk losing a fortune?"

His words brought disappointment to Emerald. It seemed obvious what his plans were—piracy and treasure. "Then you *are* working with Levasseur. All your fair words of gallantry meant nothing. You *are* a pirate!"

Levasseur seized the moment with satisfaction. "I have doubted your most excellent and honest intentions to carry through on piracy, but now you may prove your true intent."

Emerald realized her error, but if Baret was placed at a disadvantage, he showed no outward concern.

Levasseur smiled. "What do you say, monsieur? Shall we talk of terms like true Brethren of the Coast? You will sign the Articles with me, here and now. Why wait until the rendezvous?"

Emerald's heart felt unexpectedly dull and heavy.

Baret appeared unintimidated. He turned to Hob. "Bring ink and paper."

Levasseur gave him a measured look, as if his willingness took him by surprise. "Very well, monsieur. On what terms?"

Baret leaned against the rail. "For myself, as captain of the *Regale,* a fifth share of the prize when we have it."

"A fifth share!" Levasseur pressed impatiently. "He says a fifth. Even the customary sixth is too much, since it will be my ship that will risk the Spanish waters."

"The treasure," Baret blandly reminded him, "is worth a million pieces of eight."

Emerald's breath caught. She looked from her cousin to Baret, and now both men appeared to be unaware of her.

Levasseur's eyes narrowed. "Before he was hanged, monsieur, Charlie Maynerd swore it was fifty thousand pieces of eight."

"Swore to whom? Jamie?" Baret smiled as though Levasseur were a child. "Did you expect him to share all the truth with his little brother? Maynerd was a smart man until he permitted my uncle to trap him on Barbados."

Levasseur grew uneasy. "Are you saying Lord Felix Buckington also knows of the treasure of the *Prince Philip* and where it is? That he made Maynerd talk?"

"Of course."

Emerald watched Baret, masking her doubt.

Baret observed the pirate crew, listening with avid interest. "I remind all of you that it was my father, Captain Royce Buckington, who took the *Prince Philip.* For its great treasure he was betrayed by my uncle and men aboard his own ship and brought to a Spanish prison! Lucca knows where he is, and I intend to find him and free him if I die doing it! As for the Spanish treasure—only Lucca remains to tell. And being the good friend he was to my father, he will die before he reveals it to anyone but me. But if you play fair with me, I shall see that you have many fat pieces of eight."

He looked at Levasseur, who was scowling, no doubt because Baret had the attention of his crew. "But if you, Levasseur, seek treachery, I shall hang before I ever breathe a word to any man."

Levasseur sprang to the center of the deck, furious. "Ah, hang, no! But you have forgotten this?"

He strode to one of his Frenchmen, who handed him what looked to Emerald to be a beaded cord. Levasseur held it up. "Surely, monsieur, you know what this is?"

There came a deadly silence as Baret's demeanor changed. Emerald saw his jaw set with anger.

"A Rosary of Pain it is called. One that has wrought many sudden incantations. It is able to squeeze a man's eyes from his head."

Baret drew his sword.

Emerald reacted with a brief cry of horror, but his blade slashed the cord from Levasseur's hand.

"And if you so much as mention such a threat to me again, it shall be your head rolling across the deck instead of the smooth rosary stones."

Levasseur stared at him, stupefied. He reached for his rapier, but Emerald found herself brave enough to step quickly between them.

"Stop it. *Stop it.* Are you both so intemperate? If it is Spanish gold you want, Levasseur, threatening the captain of the *Regale* will get you nowhere." She looked at Baret, who watched her with a brief glimmer of respect.

"And I suggest, Captain, a more sanctified use of your sword."

He bowed from the waist. "A thousand pardons, madam." He sheathed his blade and turned to Levasseur. "In the letter I received from my father when I was in London he wrote of a million pieces of eight." Baret's baiting words spread like honey among the pirates. "But in order to divvy it up, we must all work together. And since the *Regale* is my ship, I shall be in command while we are at sea."

At the mention of the treasure, the pirates grudgingly sat down.

Emerald looked on as Hob reappeared bringing pen, ink, papers, and a small table. His brows furrowed as he set them before Baret.

"Ain't be easy to explain your signature to the Admiralty, Cap'n. Be sure your uncle, Lord Felix, will see you hang all right. We all be twistin' in the salty breeze, says I."

"The terms," growled Levasseur, "are to be drawn up according to buccaneering custom."

"As I fully intended," said Baret smoothly.

Emerald watched her cousin's two chief officers walk up, their eyes shrewd.

A moment later the two top men from Baret's crew joined the signing ceremony. One of these, she noted with curiosity, was an older dignified man who looked to be more a scholar or a chaplain than a pirate. And it was during a moment when Levasseur unexpectedly took his two henchmen aside to talk in private that she overheard the scholarly man speaking in a low voice to Baret.

"If you have any decency, Baret, you will not worry the child before others so blatantly." The man he called Cecil sighed. "I am a spiritual physician who seeks to treat the ill in soul. Knowing you to be a scamp since you were eight, I cannot give up on you yet. But the sooner you get this French pirate and Maynerd off your ship, the safer your own neck will be."

"Unfortunately my hands are tied at present, but when we reach the point of rendezvous—"

He stopped when Levasseur and his crewmen returned.

"We've parleyed, monsieur, and decided you must sign your name for what it truly is—not 'Foxworth,' but the English 'Viscount Baret Buckington.'"

While Baret remained unreadable, Emerald felt the tension her cousin's demand had caused. If they were ever arrested for piracy, the English Admiralty Court might not know who Foxworth of the *Regale* was, but there would be no mistaking the name of Buckington.

She watched, expecting him to decline. Her dismay must have shown as Baret picked up the pen, dipped it, and a scratching sound broke the silence.

Baret set down the pen and met Levasseur's gaze evenly.

Levasseur snatched up the articles, checked the signature, and, satisfied, signed his name beneath. The others followed. Emerald was curious to see if the scholar named Cecil would sign.

As he picked up the pen, Baret laid a hand on his arm. "You represent the courts of heaven, Sir Cecil. You dare not play the fool for my sake."

"Yet you have done so."

"I have no choice if I would find my father. What is your reason except your loyalty to me?"

The almost affectionate glance between them alerted Emerald and helped to soothe her disappointment. Truly there was more to Baret Buckington than what he had portrayed himself to be.

But Levasseur was not moved by the sentiment. He gave a laugh. "Ah, my Captain Foxworth, you delight my heart. We are all witnesses. If one hangs, we all hang." One of his men had brought him a flagon, and he raised it in a toast with the blue Caribbean behind him and the canvas billowing.

"To the Brotherhood!" He passed the flagon to Baret with a challenge.

"To the Brotherhood," said Baret.

Levasseur's smile faded. "You did not drink, monsieur."

Suddenly Baret seemed wearied with them all. "In respect of all that is holy, have you no conscience? Sir Cecil Chaderton was head Master of Theology at Cambridge. He finds your rum-sodden debauchery offensive."

Levasseur frowned. "You offend me."

"You are too easily offended, and for the wrong reasons, my captain. You'd best get used to my intolerant ways."

A lean and swarthy-faced pirate slurred, "Let me kill him, Monsieur Captain Levasseur."

Baret turned and measured the nameless crewman. "It is to your advantage that I've a sweeter cause on my mind now than to be bothered by croaking frogs. But if you are so bloodthirsty as to wish to kill, then may I suggest that you wait until we meet the Spanish galleon of the Queen Regent, the *De La Cruz*. She is in these waters, and her wretched galley slaves are Protestant prisoners from Holland. Prove your courage with the blade by freeing them!"

Baret turned to walk away.

The French pirate cursed him and impulsively reached for a dagger.

"Baret! Look out!" cried Emerald, but a shot cracked the air bringing the pirate down, dagger still in hand.

Baret saw the seaman sprawled upon the deck. His gaze swerved to Levasseur, who held the pistol.

"Save your gratitude, monsieur. Spanish gold is the cause for my action." He walked to the crew member who had drawn the knife.

The pirate was yet alive and pushed himself up to an elbow. "Monsieur Captain!" he cried.

Levasseur drew a second pistol from his bandolier—primed and cocked for firing. He aimed the long barrel straight into the pirate's chest. "You are too much trouble, Pierre."

Emerald screamed at the earsplitting blast. A cloud of white smoke surrounded Levasseur when it was over.

She clutched the rail, pale and shaking, watching as the foul smoke blew away in a gust of wind. She heard the big man Sloane laughing.

"Heave his carcass!"

Emerald was still clutching the rail when Baret walked up, frowning a little.

"I'm sorry. You've had a trying day, haven't you?"

Pirates came to lift the dead man and carry him to the ship's rail, chanting.

> "One, for 'is wench, who'll cheer at 'is goin;
> Two, for the sea, who'll drag 'im below;
> An' three for the devil who'll claim 'is soul."

A moment later she heard the splash. She winced and turned her head away.

"I'll bring you to the cabin. From now on I'll keep the key on me. Zeddie is no match for the men we now have on board."

Sloane called out with a chuckle. "Har, what's 'anging on the topgallant yardarm?" His laughter echoed on a breath of wind.

Emerald tensed, noticing Baret's hardened expression as he turned to follow Sloane's pointing fist. Fearful of what she would find, she cautiously lifted her gaze, a whispered prayer on her tongue. "Please, God, no."

But the shocking sight sickened her. Twisting in the sunlight was a dead man, hanging by his neck. It was Jamie.

Emerald's hand clutched her bodice as Baret called out with exaggerated disdain, "Levasseur, you boast your crew of cutthroats are fighting men. These are not warriors worthy to walk the deck of a man-of-war—they are buffoons, fit to be the king's minstrels. And I risk my reputation as captain of the *Regale* in service to Morgan to have them aboard!"

Levasseur stood with his hands spread in mock helplessness. "Alas, Captain Foxworth and Mam'zelle Emerald, but what could I do? He mutinied against me, his captain." And Levasseur raised his eyes aft. "Cut him down. Send him to keep company with our unfortunate brother."

Emerald breathed deeply of the salty wind, trying to keep herself steady yet finding herself slipping slowly to the deck while staring up at the bleak, ghoulish sight.

Swiftly Baret caught her and swept her up. Her head fell back across his arm as she fainted.

Baret laid Emerald across the bunk in the Great Cabin, frowning down at her unconscious form with her hair strewn across the pillow. This was no place for a girl of her sensitivity, and he found his self-rebuke growing with each passing day she was aboard. He should never have kept her on the *Regale*—and he wouldn't have, had he the foresight to have guessed the outcome.

His frown deepened. *I should have sent her back to Sir Karlton when I had the chance,* he thought. Yet at the time he had convinced himself he had no choice. Now he wondered. Had he been irritated over her willingness to run away with Maynerd? His eyes narrowed under his lashes. Perhaps he had been too hard on her.

Well, he thought, angry at himself, *I've done more than teach her a lesson.*

With a hand on the baldric housing his long-barreled pistols, he stood quite still, looking down at her face and no longer seeing her as Karlton's amusing and feisty little brat. He saw a lovely young woman, whose predicament and safety rested in his hands. She would be surprised to learn that he thought her quite noble, and, thinking this, he became aware that the disturbing vision rushing through his mind came as a surprise to himself.

A fine quandary I'm in, he thought dryly. If the Admiralty discovers I've signed articles with Levasseur and housed these jackanapeses aboard my own ship, I too will hang. And two men had been murdered—aboard his ship.

Sloane—now here was a ruthless beast. And yet Levasseur with his calculating temper was more dangerous. Baret's hand absently touched the pistol. He knew that he would need to confront Levasseur eventually over Emerald.

Again he thought of James Maynerd. He'd been no match for a shrewd man such as Levasseur, who had played him false from the beginning. Baret had expected Levasseur to move against Maynerd, but not this soon. He had hoped trouble would wait until Lucca was found and the location of the *Prince Philip*'s treasure was made known.

Sometime last night Levasseur and Sloane must have forced information from Maynerd as to Lucca's whereabouts. Baret had been at the helm until the third watch, when he had retired exhausted, leaving charge to his trusted men. He had given orders to watch Emerald's cabin, omitting concern for Maynerd.

He turned his head as Sir Cecil entered, the lantern's glow casting his lean shadow across Emerald.

The first glimpse of the scholar's hawklike face with its sharp disapproving gaze enlightened Baret's conscience. "Don't say it. I am well aware of my grievous error in bringing her aboard."

Sir Cecil's mouth turned downward. "That you admit it is most wondrous indeed." He glanced toward the girl. "Poor child. Did she love the rascal?"

His words oddly provoked Baret. "You mean Maynerd? Of course she didn't love him. How could she?"

Sir Cecil's white brows lifted inquiringly. "That is usually the cause for running away to marry a man, is it not?"

Baret's eyes narrowed. "Or to escape from her reputation in Port Royal. Even though Maynerd had no money—until I emptied my fortune into his greedy palm. I wonder who collected the rubies after he dangled. Levasseur, no doubt. If she did love him, it was only because she was desperate. He was not worthy of her—he was a pirate."

Sir Cecil's mouth twitched with good humor. "And of course, my Right Honorable Lordship—you are not."

"No," came the flat retort. "It is a role I must carry through to the end. How else do you expect me to find my father?"

Sir Cecil sighed, and Baret knew the fine scholar did not believe that Royce lived. But Baret only knew that he must find Lucca and learn the truth. Even if he were dead, there could be no rest of purpose driving his soul, no peace or plans until he knew.

He turned away with weariness and leaned against the desk, watching Emerald. A dark brow lifted. "Now what shall I do with her?"

Sir Cecil brought his palms together, thoughtfully tapping his fingers, his wry gaze scanning Baret. "You'll need to marry her, you know. You've been so bold and reckless as to ruin the child's reputation."

Baret gave him a scrutinizing look. "Marry her, did you say?"

"I did suggest that, yes. I suppose I might perform the ceremony here aboard the *Regale*."

Baret's gaze narrowed. "Now? You're not serious?"

"Perhaps. But what do you think?" he mused. "Will she make a noble countess? You are, after all, a viscount—if," he added dryly, "you survive these dark and odious years in the pirate-infested waters of the Caribbean."

"I am to marry Lavender. You know that." And when Sir Cecil gave him a searching look, Baret added flatly, "By free choice, Cecil. And no—this girl, however charming, will not make me a suitable countess should I return to London one day."

He scowled and waved a hand impatiently, for the conversation was proving nettlesome. He turned from Emerald and began to sketch, as he usually did when deep in thought, paying scant attention to what he was doing.

"Think of a more logical and fitting future for her. Perhaps a baron . . . what of a knight? Or even a lord? Surely you know of a kind and gentle man at Cambridge. One who will keep her out of trouble, for she surely has a disposition for such."

Sir Cecil smiled wanly. "With gray hair and rheumatism in his bones?"

Baret ignored his goad. "Enough said. I shall see to the matter myself in London. A few years in school will do her wonders." He made a bold stroke with his sketching pen.

"A wise idea. But you'll need to send her to some private school. Talk will circulate in London like bees robbed of honey. And until then you'll need to guard this cabin day and night. That despicable Sloane is the devil in shoe leather."

"Until we rendezvous with the *Venture* there is little I can do about him. I've got to wait until Emerald is safe. I sent a message to Karlton the night we sailed. He'll be arriving near the place of rendezvous."

"I should hate to deal with Levasseur when he wakes on the morning of rendezvous and discovers his ship was followed by Sir Karlton."

Baret tossed aside the sketching pen and stood. He looked over at Emerald, who was stirring, moaning faintly.

"Say nothing yet about her father arriving. I want to be certain first. She's had enough disappointments for one day." And saying thus, he left Cecil and went to the companionway for his meeting with Levasseur.

28

THE ENCOUNTER

As Emerald stirred to consciousness, it all returned. Jamie was dead. She kept her eyes tightly closed, hoping to shut out the hideous sight. Despite her dismay, there were no tears to overflow from the well of her soul, so dazed was she over the dreadful situation she found herself in. Despite his having deceived her, despite all that he was, she pitied him.

She covered her face with her cold palms, feeling the grief of a smitten conscience. Never once had she taken time to discuss her Christian faith with him. She had agreed to marry him, but had she cared enough for him to first consider the eternal danger threatening his soul?

Now she could admit that she had shut the issue from her mind due to her intense desire to escape the unpleasant situation at Foxemoore. She might have even been able to help Jamie walk the right path had she brought him to Mathias. But she had made her plans without asking what the Lord wanted—Jamie was to be the instrument of her escape.

Mathias's gentle exhortation walked softly across her troubled mind. *Dear Emerald, yield yourself as clay to the potter's hand. Trust the Master Designer to shape and form a vessel of His own choosing. He knows His good plans for you.*

All of her self-reliance and conniving had done little to gain her the respect and fulfillment she longed for. *My harvest is naught but a den of pirates! And Jamie is at the bottom of the Caribbean.*

Mathias was right, she thought again. Only a trusting, loving relationship with her heavenly Father could bring the sense of self-worth she needed.

It seemed that a thousand years had passed over her soul before she wearily turned her head and opened her eyes. With a start she noticed that her trunk was open and its contents dumped in the middle of the cabin floor.

She remembered—Levasseur's jewels! Had he been here? Or that dreadful Sloane! She shuddered. What if he had returned to resume the search? She could not endure the sight of him again.

She wished for an inner bolt on the cabin door.

Not that it would aid me if any scoundrel chooses to come, she thought. Baret was her one source of protection.

She knelt beside the trunk and began tossing her frocks aside. She came across the Bible that had belonged to Mathias and lifted it out, feeling a surge of hope. At least she had been wise enough to remember to bring it. Then her hand touched something else.

She lifted her father's fine leather pistol case from the trunk and placed it on the lap of her billowing skirts. With a small key on a chain about her throat she opened the lock and lifted the lid to reveal a long-barreled pistol with a walnut handle inlaid with pearls from the Spanish island of Margarita. The gun's breech and barrel were filigreed in Peruvian silver. Yet the small coat of arms on the wood appeared to be English, and Emerald had no idea where her father had gotten it. She assumed it had been taken from a treasure galleon.

She removed the pistol from the case and drew in a small breath, staring at the weapon in her hand, remembering how her father had taught her to load. She snatched the powder flask and pulled back the trigger, holding the stop spring down hard with her thumb while she inserted powder inside the chamber. She pressed in the wadded balls and fastened the cap, then set the pistol aside.

Swiftly she withdrew her frocks and laid them in a heap on the floor. Then she stopped.

A small leather bag had lain hidden beneath a petticoat. Where had it come from?

She stared, then snatched it up. With trembling fingers she opened the drawstring and poured out the contents. She sucked in her breath, awed by the rubies, the emeralds, the gold and silver nuggets, all sparkling beneath the lantern-light.

Oh, no . . . but how! Impossible! Where had they come from?

Then with a start she realized that the frayed petticoat she had removed from the trunk was not hers, but Minette's.

"Minette," she whispered. Had she managed to take these from Levasseur on her own? She must have! How else had they gotten in her trunk wrapped in Minette's clothes?

"Levasseur would as soon throw me overboard as lose these," she breathed, sifting the jewels through her fingers.

She wrestled with the temptation to touch and adore. *God forgive me,* she prayed. *My heart can be as greedy as theirs.* And swiftly she returned the gold and silver nuggets to the pouch, keeping the jewels on her lap to hide elsewhere.

Boot steps sounded in the outer companionway. Emerald's head turned sharply toward the door. Then she glanced about wildly for a place to hide the gems. If they caught her with these, they'd never believe her. Not in a hundred years.

Her fingers moved painfully slow as she gathered the rubies and emeralds from her lap. Then she scrambled to her feet, catching up her skirt and petticoat and glancing about for a likely place to store them. *Minette—just wait till I see her again!*

She hurriedly glanced about. Inside the lantern glass? The shadow might show. The desk drawer? The first place the scoundrels might look.

The steps halted at her door.

Her anxious gaze stumbled upon her cloak, tossed carelessly on the floor. Inside the hood. No one would bother to look there! *And if I leave it carelessly abandoned on the floor as though it's ruined from the rain . . .*

She sped across the floor, snatched it, placed the jewels inside, then left the cloak where it was.

Her father's pistol was on the floor by the trunk, glinting in the lanternlight, and Emerald picked it up, surprised at her calmness. At the sound of the key in the lock and the turn of the knob she stepped behind the door, concealing herself as it opened wide, then shut.

Baret stood there. He glanced about his cabin until his gaze confronted hers, then dropped to the pistol in her hand.

She stared into his intense dark eyes, and her hand wavered.

He removed his black velvet cloak trimmed with silver, and the vesture beneath was a distinctive shade of muted green.

She saw his gaze taking in her frock, and she became aware that it was one of her best, worn for the first meeting with Jamie. Like the burgundy velvet left behind at the bungalow, this dress was also Spanish in origin and ornate, its puffed sleeves and V-shaped bodice layered with amber fringe on yards of golden-brown satin. Her hair was still in disarray because of the wind, and the gown was damp with salty spray.

She could tell nothing by his expression. He was a master at affecting calm indifference.

"A word of advice," he stated. "You best exchange the frock for those calico drawers. At least until I get you safely off my ship."

Again his gaze dropped to the long-barreled pistol in her hand. "I assume it's loaded and that Sir Karlton taught his daughter how to shoot. Would you mind pointing it elsewhere?"

She lowered the pistol to the sides of her skirt. She felt her strength coming back and said with a surprisingly calm voice, "A certain alarm is to be expected after the hideous display I was forced to behold this afternoon. You might have announced your presence, sir, instead of sneaking in and scaring me. With madmen running about shooting people, what do you expect to greet you but a weapon?"

His mouth turned. "You can expect a good deal more trouble if Levasseur discovers 'Jamie Boy's little sweetheart' totes a dueling pistol. Anyway, I wasn't sneaking into my cabin. And as for that pistol, it won't hold pirates off for long if they're determined to break in. As I said before," he suggested easily, "your best chance for protection rests in their believing I've claimed you.

"Keep the door locked," he said. "And I've convinced Levasseur you didn't come to meet Jamie Boy but the gallant Captain Foxworth."

323

"Please stop calling him that. He's dead and can't defend himself."

"He played the fool trying to deal with Levasseur. He should have come straight to me."

"His folly proves he wasn't a true pirate," she countered.

"Whatever he was, he was poor at it."

There was no sympathy in his voice, but he studied her face. "Well, your eyes aren't red from weeping."

"How can you!"

He hesitated, then must have decided to hold nothing back. "I'm not convinced you loved him."

Her gaze wavered.

His mouth turned. "I thought not."

She turned her back. "You needn't make it sound so cold and heartless. It was wrong of me, I know . . ." She weaved a little, the pistol swaying at her side.

He caught her, plucking the weapon with deft fingers.

"I'd better take that before you shoot your foot. Here, sit in the chair."

He placed the pistol on the desk, then went to a satchel and took out a small flask, offering it to her. "Medicine," he said flatly.

She turned her head away with distaste. "No."

"I won't have you fainting," he said. "Take a sip."

"I'm not going to faint, Captain."

He scrutinized her with a slight frown, replacing the flask. "I've a habit of sounding a little too abrupt." He threw his cloak impatiently across his desk. "I'm sorry I insisted you stay. Matters have turned out differently than I had anticipated."

She looked at him, somewhat mollified, but pressed, "Sorry because of that horrid pirate Sloane or for my reputation?"

"The tongues of gossips cannot be silenced. If one wishes to think evil or to malign the innocent, they will surely find a cause, real or imagined. No, it is the risk we are both in that worries me now."

"A recompense for your deed of holding me prisoner, m'lord."

"Thanks," he said flatly. "But if this is the only sour fruit I shall reap for my wayward ways, I shall have much to thank God for."

Emerald turned her face away, thinking of Jamie's death.

"Go ahead and cry," he said tonelessly, preparing to offer a handkerchief for her tears.

"I'm not going to cry," she said dully. "There are no more tears left for Jamie."

He leaned against the desk, watching her with a somewhat curious appraisal. "Your precarious circumstance will remain until we rendezvous with the *Venture*. After that I may be able to alter your situation. But I can't promise it."

"Isn't there some way you can bring me to a harbor? I shall find passage back to Port Royal to my father!"

His gaze narrowed, and a brief expression of impatience crossed his face. She could almost think it had something to do with a twinge of conscience.

"My dear, we are on the Spanish Main. Either pirates or Spaniards prowl on every island. Why did you even risk coming to meet Jamie? Did I not tell your father I'd see to your betterment in England?"

His rebuke shook her back to awareness. "On my word, sir, I didn't want to go to England. I wanted to marry Jamie!"

He cocked his dark head. "Dear Jamie was also a rogue, madam. Surely you knew that."

"I did not know. I vow it's true. I didn't know him as well as I thought," she confessed. "I know what it must appear like, but I see it was all a dreadful mistake now."

A smile touched his mouth. "Ah. If only yesterday's errors could be erased as easily as youth's burning love so quickly turns to ashes."

Her temper got the best of her, mostly because his gibe at her foolishness was true. It was too much to endure, and she lifted her chin and walked across the cabin, her back toward him.

Her foot touched something on the floor. Her eyes fell —the cloak!

But no, he would not choose this moment to show some gallantry and feel a need to pick it up.

"Allow me," came his voice.

"No! I'll get it, m'lord." She hastened to stoop, to snatch the hood, hoping against hope that the jewels . . .

But he was there beside her, lifting the cloak. There came a small clatter, and a sparkle of rainbow colors spilled across the floor. Rubies, emeralds, and a cameo brooch studded with gems lay under the lantern light, boldly smirking up at them.

Emerald's hands flew to her mouth, and her eyes raced to his.

He stood staring down.

She turned her head away, feeling the blood move from her throat into her cheeks.

There was a long moment of awkward silence.

"Ah, a tempting morsel of Levasseur's treasure after all. What luck," he said with smooth sarcasm. "What you couldn't find in my cabin, you found elsewhere. How did you sneak aboard Levasseur's ship?" came the lightly mocking question. "I hope you didn't need another midnight swim."

"Nay," she breathed, her hands clenched at her sides. "They're not mine. You must believe me. They were taken by Minette—I'm certain of it, since they were wrapped in her clothing and she expected to leave Port Royal with me. Not that I expect you to believe me."

"You are right. I don't."

He gathered the jewels, then held the brooch toward the lantern to inspect it more carefully.

"The Infanta will be disappointed. How cruel, life," he mocked. "You have her brooch." His glinting gaze, rife with amusement, met hers. "I admit you have the throat to do it justice. I hear she is squat and thick."

Emerald walked to the desk, her back rigid. "I told you, I didn't take them from Levasseur. And if he knew they were here, he'd draw sword on you to claim them." She looked at him defensively. "I see no reason to be cross-examined."

"On the contrary, madam, I am risking my head to safeguard your presence. And you must come clean with your tales about carrying aboard your lover's loot."

"I didn't take them. Yet think as you will," and she again turned her back, tears smarting her eyes. "You will anyway.

326

After all, what can one expect from a pirate's daughter," she said ruefully.

"Sir Karlton would draw sword for that remark."

"There isn't a soul in all Port Royal who doesn't believe it of me, regardless of his determination," she said wearily. "Especially Levasseur!" She looked at him accusingly. "And you, sir!"

"You underrate me. As for that daw-cock cousin of yours, it is well for us both that his greed now centers on the supposed treasure of the *Prince Philip*."

She looked at him quizzically. "Are you saying there is no treasure?"

"Did I say that?"

"You implied it. If it is but a fancy, then why did you sign articles with him? Was it not for the gold?"

She saw him musing over sober thoughts. "I suppose you've deducted the cause for Maynerd's death?"

She moved uneasily. "I suppose because of Levasseur's greed for the treasure."

"It is the way of the Brotherhood to eliminate competitors. And Jamie competed for more than treasure."

She knew what he meant, and that she was included. She rubbed her arms as if cold, searching his face for information.

"Jamie learned about Lucca and the treasure from his brother, who was hanged before he could contact me—which he fully intended to do. But Jamie went to Levasseur instead. He intended to keep silent until the point of rendezvous, but Levasseur and Sloane forced him to talk."

She swallowed, trying not to think about it. "Are you certain Lucca knows where your father is held prisoner?"

His dark eyes glinted. "If he does not, then I shall never know the truth. Felix is a master at hiding his slimy tracks of betrayal. He works with certain Spanish sympathizers in the court of King Charles. And I'm certain he has spies in Madrid as well. My worry is that Felix will find Lucca before I do and silence him. Only when I know if my father lives can I feel free to go on with my own plans."

And what are they? she wanted to ask but refrained. To marry Lavender and return to Buckington House to serve King Charles, of course.

She wondered if Lavender had accused him yet about their perceived clandestine meeting in the garden that night at Foxemoore, but decided she would not have had time to do so during the slave uprising.

She told him then about the dreadful rebellion, mentioning the death of Lavender's mother and her own Great-uncle Mathias. She was surprised when he admitted that he already knew.

"Mathias and his work will be a loss to Foxemoore," he said.

She had no time to consider his words and walked to the desk to where her father's pistol lay, thinking to replace it in her trunk.

As she picked it up, he came alert, staring intently as the light of the lantern shone down on the weapon's vein of silver. His blunt voice interrupted her thoughts.

"Who gave you that pistol?"

She tensed. Did he now think she had stolen it as well?

He strode to the desk where she stood and, ignoring her protest, snatched it from her, turning it over in his hand to inspect it with care.

"Your lordship! I object! 'Tis mine. And the jewels were not stolen by me. By the way—" her eyes narrowed "—where are they?"

His gaze held hers. "Who gave this to you? Levasseur?"

"No. It belongs to my father." She added defensively, "And he is not a thief, nor am I."

She took a feeling of satisfaction over the change in his expression, but it did not last long.

"Karlton? You are certain?"

"Quite certain, your lordship. I took it when—" She stopped short.

When she hesitated to go on, his brow lifted. "Yes? When you decided to run off with Maynerd?"

She hesitated. She must face up to her actions. "Yes. When I decided to run away with Jamie. It was soon after the slave uprising on Foxemoore, and I thought I might need it where I was going."

"You thought you might need it aboard a passenger ship with a man you knew well enough to marry?"

Why did he continue to goad her like this? she wondered crossly. "My fears were not of Jamie but for the long voyage to the New England colony. One never knows when pirates will show up on the Caribbean," she said meaningfully. "I wanted to get away and start a life of my own, as far removed from smugglers and pirates as I possibly could. Jamie offered the opportunity. We intended to settle on a farm of our own in Boston."

"Maynerd? Settle down? And honorably use a plow?" He laughed. "He'd have ended up in the local gambling den, leaving the plowing to you."

"He vowed to give up such odious ways."

"Did he now? A word of advice—never believe a man's vow until you've known him long enough to see he means it. A rogue will promise anything to get his woman. He'll even promise to be in church every Sunday."

She turned with a challenge. "Oh? And does that include rogues like you, Captain Foxworth?"

If she thought he would be taken aback, she was wrong. He smiled. "Especially rogues like me, madam."

She couldn't refrain. "Did you promise Lavender you'd mend your ways?"

He folded his arms, and the faint smile was back, but he made no comment. "So dear Jamie Boy promised you an estate in the American colony, did he? I wonder what he intended to buy land and build with?"

"I suppose you think he was willing to engage in piracy?"

"Perhaps it was Levasseur's jewels that would buy you both freedom and escape. The Infanta's brooch could buy a good many piglets."

Her eyes narrowed. "If I had stolen the jewels so we could buy a farm, then I would have told him so before he succumbed to your offer of twenty thousand pieces of eight. But enough of me, Captain 'Foxworth.' What of you?" she accused. "Your plans are quite mysterious."

"My concerns are my own, and I do not care to bandy them about or to involve others."

She gave a laugh. "But mine are open to your scrutiny."

"A prerogative of being a viscount. I would think by now you'd understand you are in enough trouble without adding to it by delving into mine."

She said deliberately, "Perhaps you only use the background of your title in London as a masquerade to hide behind. Why should I believe you? Many men of noble birth and position use their titles to cover piracy, so I've been told."

"You are very observant. As you suggest, I could be a true pirate after all. I may even keep the Jolly Roger hidden somewhere in my cabin, only too anxious to raise it when coming upon the plate fleet from Porto Bello, laden with fancy gowns," he said, cocking his head and scanning her dress again. "But I must admit, the style does not favor you. White silk, I think, would be better."

Emerald wondered that she was able to keep her poise.

"And if I am as you too boldly suggest, a pirate," he went on, "then you are unwise to remove the mask you say I hide behind. Have I not offered you my protection? But if you scorn my chivalry, what need is there to pretend further?"

She held out her hand. "My father's pistol, your lordship—and, if you'd be so kind, my cousin's jewels. I shall have them both, if you please. If you are—as you say—gallant, then you will do as I ask."

"My apologies, madam, but gallantry must often wear the three masks of Greek theater. I shall keep the pistol. However, unless I should seem totally indifferent to your concerns, I shall exchange it for another—a smaller one. But the jewels of Levasseur? They're less likely to be discovered on me. As for the smaller pistol—just be certain you don't go waving it about when I find it necessary to make use of my desk and charts. That is," he said wryly, "if you will be so gracious as to permit me to do so?" He gestured to his desk, cluttered with her belongings.

"I'm quite certain I have no cause to interfere with your duties as captain," she said stiffly and went to retrieve her things.

"Thank you." He came around the front of the desk and, using a small key, unlocked the top drawer.

Emerald stood watching curiously until his gaze came to hers. "You should remember this desk," he said smoothly.

She blushed, indeed remembering back to that dreadful night. She brought her things across the cabin and placed them on top of her trunk. When she glanced back, he had sat down to look through a drawer.

"I know about your father's journal and map that you sought from Lord Felix. Did you locate them?"

He rummaged for something. "No. Felix must keep the journal elsewhere. It is an ambition of mine to find it."

"He would have been wiser to keep it in London—hide it on one of his estates."

He leaned back in his chair looking at her. "Hm—I'd never thought of that."

She smiled.

His eyes glinted with humor. "Well, it takes a certain mind to understand the ways of pirates."

Stung, she said no more.

"Ah . . ." And he lifted a hand-drawn map from the drawer. He spread it out and pulled the swinging lantern closer. "One of my father's maps. Our point of rendezvous with the *Venture* is most likely to be about . . . here. Probably a pirate cove in Spanish waters."

"A pirate cove?" she asked uneasily, an edge to her voice.

"I wish I knew . . ." He squinted at the map and mused to himself as he appeared to trace some line along the Main.

Emerald walked to the desk and peered curiously at the drawing of the West Indies.

"I am meant to be kept in the dark," he said wryly, "until we near the location, yet I know these waters well enough. The *Venture* should be somewhere in this area. Once there, I will unfortunately need to board your cousin's ship."

"What of me?"

"If my plans do not go awry, you needn't worry. You'll be properly attended to before I board the *Venture*."

She wasn't satisfied, but since he was in no mood to explain, she turned her attention to the map. "Did Levasseur choose the cove or Sloane?"

"Levasseur. Yet I put no cunning past Sloane. I've a suspicion about his intentions where Levasseur is concerned."

She hesitated, wondering if she should say what was on her mind. "I've heard my cousin mention a cove he particularly likes. He says he could stay there for a month and never be noticed by the Spaniards."

"Could you remember the name now?"

She folded her arms. "I might."

He smiled. "Does your hesitancy mean you wish to sign articles for a share of the intended booty, or have you a reluctance to betray a Frenchman to an Englishman?"

"Neither one. The name is . . . well, rather difficult to remember offhand."

He stood and bowed her to his captain's chair.

She smiled at his lightness and sat down, bringing the map closer as he looked on, watching her with his dark head tilted, amusement in his eyes.

Emerald could not read the map and cleared her throat. "Where is Port Royal, Captain?"

He tapped his finger on the spot.

"Oh, yes, now I see. Of course."

After a minute crept by and he paced the cabin floor deep in his musings, she called anxiously, "This is it, I think."

He came to her side quickly and bent over the desk as she traced the Caribbean southward from Port Royal to Bocas del Toro near the tip of Panama.

He frowned and shook his head. "No. A dangerous spot. But here, maybe. Yes, I am sure of it now. Monkey Bay. It's near San Juan River. Ah! Sweet genius!" he said, and in a bold moment cupped her chin in his hand and planted a swift innocent kiss on her lips.

She realized the moment had meant nothing to him, and she refrained from reacting, hoping to appear as indifferent as he did. She stood quickly, smoothed her hair from her cheek, and walked to the other side of the cabin.

"Um . . . Monkey Bay?" she repeated too casually.

"Yes. Monkey Bay," came his smooth voice. "Sound familiar now? Anyway, it is so. You've been more help than you can imagine, Emerald. This is most excellent news to me, a great weight off my mind. Whatever you do, say nothing of our secret to anyone—including Zeddie."

He folded the map and picked up his cloak, meeting her gaze. He produced a small pistol. "Can you use it?"

"I think so."

"I'll have two men on guard. They can be trusted."

He now appeared in a hurry, and she followed him to the door.

"Do not under any circumstance leave the cabin unless in my company. The captain of the *Regale* is now known to be a jealous man. Let us keep it that way, for your sake."

He placed her father's pistol in his belt, and she said swiftly, "I've not given you that, sir!"

"No, you did not. I'm taking it."

"You are impossible to understand."

"Not to those who count me friend."

"But it belongs to my father," she pleaded.

"I beg to differ. It bears the coat of arms of Viscount Royce Buckington. *My* father."

She stopped, stunned. "Viscount—"

"Yes. I've seen my father carry it many times in London."

His father's pistol! But how?

"Where Karlton got it remains the mystery." His gaze hardened. "I shall find out."

"If you are insinuating my father stole—"

He opened the door and glanced into the companion-way. It must have been empty. "Bolt the door after me."

Frustrated, she whispered, "If I survive this wretched ordeal, I shall be the first to inform Lord Felix Buckington that his nephew is a blackguard! A companion of pirates! I will tell him and the Admiralty how you helped Levasseur!"

"You can still behave the little minx, can't you? Karlton is right. You could use a few years under the puckered brow of a headmistress at a finishing school." He shut the door behind him.

Emerald stood there, then abruptly slid the bolt into place. She heard the sound of his steps die away.

Her mind swam with too many questions. She looked gloomily about the cabin that was to be her confinement for weeks to come.

She thought of the pistol. He had said it belonged to his father. That would explain the coat of arms. Then why hadn't her father told her so? And what was her father doing with it?

Unless he didn't know . . .

It was difficult to believe that he wouldn't have recognized the coat of arms even if she had not. Baret had seemed troubled about the pistol. What could it mean?

Wearily, Emerald sank into the velvet chair and tried to pray, but a sense of gloom hung over her.

29

BUCCANEERS' RENDEZVOUS

A week crept by as slowly as one of Hob's turtles, which he had brought aboard and kept in a crawl for his prized soup. Emerald had not spoken to Baret alone since the night of Jamie's death.

Although she came often to the dinner table in the Round Room and obligingly sat beside him, the words exchanged between them were few. She avoided Levasseur's gaze, convinced that he was involved in Jamie's death.

Thankfully, Sloane did not eat with the captains but took his meals with the crew.

There were also evenings when she chose not to come to the table and dined in the cabin alone. Hob always brought a tray and saw to it that a precious half of an orange or lime squeezed into water and sweetened was added to her meal.

He grinned when she commented on his thoughtfulness. "His lordship's order."

During that week no member of the pirate crew lurked about her cabin. Evidently Baret had been right when he told her he had convinced the crew of his intentions toward her. One night she had awakened with a start to hear Baret's voice and Levasseur's sharp answer, then retreating boot steps. She had tensely waited in the sultry darkness, but only the sound of the sea filled her ears.

If Levasseur held to his insistence that she had stolen his jewels and brought them aboard the *Regale*, he must have decided to let the matter lie dormant for the present. Since Baret had removed them for safekeeping, she'd not heard any more about them.

It was now their first Sunday on the Caribbean, and Sir Cecil held a chapel service in the Round Room, whereupon Emerald had quietly attended with Zeddie, masking her surprise when the captain of the *Regale* and one other crewman were also in attendance, although late.

Baret remained standing unobtrusively in the back by the open door, where warm breezes filtered inside, looking out at the sea and indulging in a tin of coffee that Hob faithfully brought to him while Sir Cecil taught the Scriptures.

Emerald was unable to avoid satisfying her curiosity and glanced back over her shoulder to see what he was doing and how well he was attending to the lecture on the struggles and temptations of David while fleeing from the murderous intent of King Saul. Baret did not have a Bible, she noted, but his respect and attention to Sir Cecil awed her, and she pondered the expression on the handsomely chiseled face.

After the years of upbringing under Great-uncle Mathias, she knew enough to recognize a man's heart for God when she saw it. She stared at him, secretly pleased. Then, when he must have felt her gaze and looked at her, she turned her head and stared at the open Bible in her lap.

He does believe.

When the service was over and she stood, thinking he might come to speak to her, she saw that he had already left.

Emerald's interest grew, as much as she sought to stifle it. Baret Buckington was not the sort of man any woman could easily forget, she thought warily.

The trade wind, which had freshened since dawn, now swept the ship with early coolness. With topsails unfurled there was a list to starboard, and the *Regale* was moving through the sea on a southwest course. They were many leagues south of Jamaica now, and land was nowhere in sight.

Sir Cecil had arranged for Baret's crew to erect an awning from the cabin bulkhead extending out over the deck to provide shade for Emerald's comfort. Every afternoon when the heat in the cabin grew unbearable, she would don a light cotton frock and come out to sit beneath the shade on a cane daybed. Here she would contemplate the music that Great-uncle Mathias had gathered and was working on before he died. But she had no notion what she might do with the material if she were sent to London.

She couldn't imagine the state church in England finding any interest or value in it—though Mathias had told her there were those in the church who were heartily opposed to slavery and even preached against it before the king.

Perhaps the best part of the afternoon was when Sir Cecil came to keep her company. Inevitably he brought his King James Bible and would fall easily into a discourse on the blessings of Christianity.

"It's not merely a religion," he said one day. "It is based on the character of a Person. And all the blessed gifts bestowed freely by divine grace are wrapped up in the beloved Son of the Father. In Christ we have all that is fitting for both this life and the hereafter, when we shall look with great joy and peace upon His most benevolent face."

After his discourse they often fell into a discussion of her uncle's novel idea of a singing school for the slaves. Sir Cecil would lean back against his chair, bring palms together to tap his fingers, and ask her to be so kind as to hum a slave chant, while he considered thoughtfully.

At first she had felt self-conscious, but after several such episodes she grew bolder and even encouraged Hob and Zeddie to sound the African rhythm by beating cane sticks. Hob was especially good at this.

Then one day Emerald was remembering the aged Jonah, grandfather of Minette and Ty, and she became so totally involved in singing the chant Jonah had helped Mathias to create that she was almost unaware of the African pirate who approached. Upon hearing the chant, and Hob and Zeddie's beating the cane sticks, the pirate climbed on the rail to listen, his cutlass within easy reach.

Minutes later when her emotions had cooled and her eyes were yet moist with tears, she found him listening with an awed expression on his handsome dark face, the gold ring in his left ear glinting in the sunlight.

From below, Baret stood hands on hips, looking up, his dark eyes alert while watching the response of the pirate.

Sir Cecil, tall and rigid, saw Baret and went to the taffrail and leaned over. The gray locks beneath his Spanish hat moved in the breeze, a thoughtful half smile on his mouth.

"The dean of Saint Paul's should be so broadened in his methods as to hear and see this. What you hear, my delinquent student, is what Emerald deigns to call a 'slave hymn.'" Cecil gestured toward the African pirate. "At least Kill-Devil is impressed."

Whether Baret was or not she had no notion.

During these informal afternoon meetings, Zeddie was never far from her, usually dozing in the tropical sun. Hob would then appear, climbing the steps with a tray to bring them his private concoction of squeezed limes and sugar.

"Be the tastiest punch in all Caribbee," he'd say with a wink.

Emerald had come to look forward to these afternoon visits and discovered that Sir Cecil was indeed a renowned scholar.

"An unusual calling," he had said of her uncle's work. "Who would have thought to seek to translate the African chants into a form of Christian teaching, using their own rhythm and tone. It seems most obvious to me that they would respond best to the Savior when He speaks their native tongue."

She smiled wistfully, remembering Mathias. "So said my great-uncle. There were times when he became discouraged with the leaders of the church in England for being so blind. He used to quip that the Masters believed that God only spoke English."

Sir Cecil looked pointedly at his Bible. "There was a time, my dear, when the church insisted the Word should only be spoken in Latin. A trail of martyrs lines the way to Smithfield for insisting otherwise. I commend your great-uncle! I wish I had met him. And I commend you, Emerald. I can see your love of his work is a smoking flax ready to burst forth into holy fire one day. Let no man put it out. Saturate this cause with prayer. Seek His will and purpose. And who knows? One day you may carry that torch forward."

Her warm brown eyes faced the sea. "Mathias was the one bright spot in my life."

"And now he is gone. But there is One who will never go away nor abandon you. Christ is the true bright hope in your life."

338

She looked at the elderly gentleman almost wistfully. "A light for my path," she murmured thinking of the verse in the Psalms.

"And a lamp unto my feet," he added softly. "With such blessed light to warm and guide us, what fear need we have of all our tomorrows? Today, this moment aboard this ship, even among lost pirates and buccaneers, there is His presence."

"Yes," she murmured, her heart suddenly winging upwards, and she lifted her eyes to see the white billows of canvas snapping in the warm breeze. "He has spoken to me through you, Sir Cecil."

Thank You, heavenly Father. Thou preparest a table before me in the presence of mine enemies, she thought. Today she had feasted on heavenly food while buccaneers and cutthroats far from God manned the ship she sailed on.

She sighed and stood from the daybed, moving from the shadow of the awning to the taffrail to stand beside the godly old scholar and follow his gaze to Baret below.

The captain wore a full white cambric shirt with laced drawstrings above black breeches, and a broad dark hat that curved upward on the left-hand brim. He looked cool and, for all outward evidence, seemed oblivious to them.

Sir Cecil leaned his forearm against the rail with a musing smile. "If I didn't know him so well, I'd vow he was as dangerous a pirate as Levasseur. I suppose, in some ways, he is."

She snatched the opportunity she'd been secretly waiting for. "Tell me about him, Sir Cecil. What is he truly like? I understand his concerns to find out about his father, but how could he have turned from his life in London as the grandson of an earl?"

Sir Cecil's eyes were troubled. "That question has no simple answer. I suppose the seed was sown when as a small boy he overheard his father and grandfather discussing the hideous suffering and death of his mother."

The miniature with the golden hair woven into a cross—the pearl pendant, she thought. His mother had died a martyr's death at the hands of Spain's Inquisitors.

Emerald felt a tug at her emotions as she watched Baret below, coolly indifferent to emotional display.

"Her death not only gravely affected him but completely altered the life ambitions of his father. When the Civil War broke across England, Royce chose to avoid sides. Though he was a Royalist, he preferred to take to the Caribbean as a buccaneer against Spain.

"The day came when the earl and his family chose to leave England to follow Charles into France, joining his exile. And during that period, Baret adored hearing of his father's exploits.

"We returned with Charles the Second after Cromwell's death and entered Cambridge, and I spent long days with Baret. I taught him well."

He chuckled, remembering. "He had tried several times as a lad to run away to find his father in Port Royal, but his grandfather had him watched. He was brought back under robust guard. After a hearty disagreement with the earl, while I waited in the library assured of the outcome of their debate, Baret would return with me to school. I knew his feelings, of course—there was little he kept from me."

"His mother—she was from Holland, wasn't she? I once saw her portrait in a cameo with a cross woven from her hair. She must have been a saintly woman to arouse such strong emotions in both her husband and son."

"She was, indeed, very genuine. There was naught about her that was insincere. She loved the Lord deeply. I think she would have counted it her highest honor as His child to die rather than deny His redemption and deity. It was she who had plans for Baret to attend Cambridge to learn the Scriptures."

As Emerald considered, trying to imagine Baret bent over books of learning, Sir Cecil broke the spell with a chuckle. "I've known him since he was seven—a horrendous child, one who got the best of me on more occasions than I care to admit."

She smiled. "I suppose he was a typical son of a viscount—I mean—so wealthy, so important."

"Very customary indeed. He'd been presented to His Majesty early and attended the royal tournaments with his father before the war. Both Baret and the viscount were well thought of and deemed by the Court to be among the king's favorites."

When she inquired about his attendance at the Royal Naval Academy, Sir Cecil sighed.

"He abandoned his divinity training. I suppose the Lord never called him to the pulpit of Saint Paul's. Baret preferred battles of another kind. He wished to serve His Majesty in the Royal Navy. But when the First Dutch War broke, it provided the opening for the Peace Party in Court to move King Charles to make a treaty with despised Spain.

"Baret heartily disagreed. At the same time his uncle, Felix, brought word to the earl of the piracy charges against his father. Then came the shocking announcement that he'd been killed in a duel at Port Royal. One thing led to another. Soon he believed his father had met with treachery instigated by Felix and enemies in the Peace Party.

"He left the Academy and came to the West Indies to seek his whereabouts. You know the rest, my dear. I fear Baret too may soon be wanted for piracy. But it is a small price, says he, if he can find his father."

"But how will he free the man he calls Lucca from the Spanish dungeon? They will know he is English the moment he sets foot on any of the colonies."

"It is a great risk—one that could easily cost him his life or, far worse, Spanish imprisonment. But you have seen the manner of man he is, my dear. If there is the slightest hope of finding Lucca, he will go."

She shivered silently in the warm breeze. "He now concerns himself with Sloane. How can he trust these men when they set foot inland?"

"I believe each captain will have an equal number of men loyal to him. I would not worry about a betrayal. Levasseur and Sloane need Baret as much as he needs them. This is one time they will guard each other to the point of death."

She contemplated this odd situation. "When will we rendezvous with the *Venture?*"

He gestured to Baret, who was turning his telescope out to sea.

"Soon. We are near what the buccaneers call Monkey Bay, and Baret speaks of good fortune. It seems not only the *Venture* waits, but another ship. I think you will be pleased at what the next day may bring you."

She looked at him, surprised, and he replied with a smile, "He informed me at breakfast that I could break the good news. Sir Karlton Harwick's ship sails with the *Venture*. Within a day or so you are to be turned safely over to your beloved father."

She stared at him. "My father! This is the first I've been told of it."

"Baret did not wish to disappoint you. And Levasseur does not know about it yet, so say nothing."

Her father! Her heart sang. "But how?" she whispered. "How is it that he would know I was aboard the *Regale* and sail to meet us?"

"Baret sent a longboat back to Port Royal the night we left. News was brought to Sir Karlton to follow your cousin's ship to our rendezvous."

Emerald was quiet for a long time. She watched Baret, then turned to Sir Cecil. "I was wrong about him."

He smiled. "Yes."

She gripped the taffrail, searching his eyes. "You must love him a great deal. You too left the scholar's life to sail with him these years, risking your reputation."

His eyes softened. "Baret is the son I never had. I thought much of his father as well. It is unfortunate the earl has chosen to believe Felix instead of Baret."

Sir Cecil looked at her long and hard.

"You are a fine young lady, Emerald."

"A . . . lady . . ."

"Our Lord has woven something deep and precious into your spirit that has not yet fully come to the sunlight. But I've every confidence in Him that it will. It is for you to see that you feed and tend it with prayer and the study of His Word. Who knows? Like Esther, you may yet come to the place of authority at a dangerous time."

She looked at him, awed by the thought, yet wondering what he might mean. To have Sir Cecil Chaderton speak so well of her brought moisture to her eyes.

"Your compliment means more than you could ever know."

He smiled gently and took both of her hands into his. He grew sober. "Let us pray together, my dear, to seek heaven's benediction on your path."

As she heard him praying, speaking her name before God, she remembered Mathias. It seemed the two men had become one in cause. Emerald felt her heart warmed, and a sweet reassuring peace of the Lord's direction flooded her soul. She prayed silently, *All that I am and hope to be in this short life by Your grace, I trust to Your nail-pierced hand. Take me. Use me to glorify You. Amen.*

Emerald knelt before the teakwood chest. It smelled of old things. Books. Lots of them! Books by the Puritan fathers in England, Reformers Martin Luther and John Calvin, and a Bible. She picked it up gently and opened it, finding the pages worn, underlined, and with handwritten notes. "In a different language at that!" she breathed aloud.

"Greek. A difficult language, I assure you. Sir Cecil was a hard taskmaster. Depending on how I look at my past, I either suffered unbearably or was blessed to be so nurtured in soul and intellect."

At the sound of Baret's voice coming from the cabin doorway, Emerald might have jumped to her feet and whirled about as though a child caught with hand in the cookie jar, but she took a deep breath and counted to five.

"You have found what you're looking for?" he asked a moment later.

Fingering his Bible, she knew the answer was yes, but she dare not be so bold as to admit it. Since yesterday afternoon when Sir Cecil had informed her of Baret's background, she had been motivated by growing curiosity.

She returned the Bible to the chest and silently shut the lid. Rising to her feet, she turned, knowing there was color in her cheeks.

Baret watched her. His garments of finery had been replaced by a leather jerkin, calf-length boots, a loose-fitting navy blue tunic open at the front, and a belted scabbard. One thing remained—the wide-brimmed hat. This one was less fashionable, a dark blue, absent its cocky plume. Unlike the "viscount," he did not remove it and bow.

She could never tell his mood by his smile or what thoughts might be churning about in his tough mind. It was the eyes that disturbed her. For they did give him away this time. They were brilliantly dark beneath narrowed lashes. Emerald knew that despite his casual manner at catching her in his things again, he was not pleased.

He stood, arms folded, and if she now searched for the divinity student who had risen before dawn to study Greek and recite long passages in both Greek and Latin, he did not emerge.

His gaze fell on his chest of books. "I don't know why I brought them with me," he said too casually. "To appease Cecil maybe."

"I think it was more than that."

He seemed surprised.

Emerald quickly walked over to the door and looked out, seeing Levasseur below with the telescope. Baret had previously given orders to heave to, and they were stopped. She glimpsed a distant shoreline rippling with fringed green palms.

"We are near the rendezvous?"

"As near as it is safe to bring you. Cecil told me he informed you of the news of Sir Karlton's ship. You'll be transferred tonight."

She turned happily and smiled at him. "Yes, he told me. I'm deeply grateful."

"Well—that's the first time I've seen you smile."

"Perhaps it's my first cause in weeks. I feel I've much to be thankful for. Not only my father's ship, but I've a friendship with Sir Cecil which has brought me new wisdom."

He studied her. "It does you well." He then turned away, whistling, and unlocked another chest that he hauled from beneath the bunk.

She smiled. "I promise not to break into any more of your drawers and trunks," she stated lightly.

"So you've been reformed at last," he said. "Does this mean I shall miss seeing you in pirate drawers and head scarf again? Rather disappointing."

Her smile turned rueful. She watched him remove a black-and-silver costume that would have passed for one belonging to a Spanish *cavalero*. Remembering the dangerous trek inland to locate Lucca, her smile left.

"A clever disguise," she said. "But dangerous."

"Let us hope it remains clever under Spanish vigilance."

She tensed. "Have you any notion yet where Lucca is held?"

"It remains secret until I board the *Venture*. I've my guess, however. Since they chose Monkey Bay for the point of rendezvous, it can only mean somewhere near Porto Bello."

"Porto Bello! It will be heavily under guard! The viceroy is stationed there."

"So he is." He stood and tried on the Spanish hat, squinting at his reflection in the glass, and touched his pencil mustache. "At least my Spanish is fluent. Another gratitude to Cecil. After my mother's martyrdom I despised the language and refused to try to master it until Cecil baited me. 'You'll need it when you attack Madrid's galleons,' he used to say." Baret smiled, remembering. "I wonder what he would have done at the time had he realized he would live to board a galleon with me."

"You were privileged to have a friend like him."

"Yes," he said quietly. "Very honored." He looked at her. "You like him."

She smiled. "He prayed with me about my future. I'm at peace now."

He said nothing and, turning away, lifted a tight-fitting black jacket with silver, scrutinizing it. "Peace of heart, of purpose—it does not come easily. One must surrender to Another's lordship first. I take it you've done so." His gaze came to hers. "I'm glad for you, Emerald. I want you to believe in yourself. You can, if you know He has planned a fair future. All His children have equal acceptance. There's no room to think less of yourself, no matter your earthly parentage."

Her heart warmed. "You've never spoken that way to me before."

"No, I suppose I haven't."

He seemed to wish to dismiss the personal seriousness as quickly as he had permitted it to surface. He scowled a little and changed the subject. "I've planned and waited for this moment of finding Lucca for several years. Risk is a part of life, no matter how you live it. To find him will be worth the danger. I'll know the truth then. No more wondering whether my father lives in suffering or is peacefully buried somewhere. Lucca holds the key."

"And God holds Lucca in His hand."

"A pleasant thought." He turned and faced her fully. "I shall come to see you in London."

She colored. "I would like that very much. I shall be at Berrymeade."

"Ah, yes . . . the Clark farm, poor relations of your father, I understand. I think not."

"What?"

"I think London will be better suited for what I have in mind." He tried on the Spanish jacket.

Her heart paused. *"You . . .* have in mind?"

"Yes. School."

"Oh."

"Several long tedious years of it."

"Oh . . . yes, of course. Very generous of you to see to it, your lordship."

His dark eyes glinted with malicious amusement as the came back to hers. "Do you think so? After twenty thousan(pieces of eight, I've good cause to see to the betterment of m investment."

She turned away and looked back out the cabin door Levasseur was still at the rail with the telescope. "What make: you think my cousin and that awful Sloane will allow me to board my father's ship?"

"They won't like it, of course. Neither man yet knows your father is coming. I'll insist on your departure."

His indifference troubled her. "How can you be so casual?"

He looked over at her somewhat surprised, and his eyes held hers. "My feelings are not at all as you suggest."

For a moment she could almost vow he had meant more than what was on the surface of those words.

From behind them Hob said, "Cap'n, that barracuda

346

Levasseur be calling for you urgentlike. Spotted more in that glass than one ship, says I."

"Ah . . . the second ship." He smiled, satisfied. "That should make him sweat. Where's Sloane? Have you seen him?"

"Throwing dice with the sharks. Sopping up on rum."

Baret left the Spanish uniform on the bunk. He took hold of her arm. "Wait here. There may be trouble."

Levasseur lowered the telescope and spun around to glare at Baret, who walked up with a smile. "A bright and comely morning, my captain."

Levasseur abruptly handed him the telescope, his eyes narrowing. "It seems, monsieur, we have unwanted company."

Baret feigned innocence. "Indeed? Well, well! A fat Spanish galleon perhaps? What luck," he said softly, "to find it here ripe for picking."

Levasseur's black eyes were malevolent. "Such jests I can well do without. It is English," came his menacing tone. "And I would swear to it that you, monsieur, knew all along it would be here waiting for us when we arrived."

"You give me uncanny powers, Levasseur. I am not certain I wish to claim them. How would I arrange such a feat? Have you and Captain Sloane not kept from me the point of rendezvous with your ship?"

"Ah, yes, yes, but I now suggest you knew all along it was Monkey Bay where my crew would be waiting."

"A convenient guess perhaps, made so by my experience in this area of the Caribbee and by the direction of our sail these weeks. But alas! I could not have known of our rendezvous while in Port Royal."

Levasseur was furious. "That night! When the half-caste slipped away in a cockboat, I should have killed him then. You sent word to Sir Karlton of the demoiselle's presence aboard the *Regale*. You must have given him orders to follow my ship when it sailed!"

"An interesting deduction, but there is not time to quibble. We have much to do. And you had best keep Sloane sober if he is to go with us to find Lucca. I've no intention of risking my years to a Spanish dungeon because he bungled the job."

"Ah, then you admit the second ship belongs to Sir Karlton Harwick."

"You have just said it is. Why bicker?"

"Because, monsieur, there is a third ship not far behind!"

A third ship! Baret snatched the telescope and turned it to sea. His jaw tensed.

Levasseur sneered. "Ah, so now you see, monsieur. And like me, you know whose ship it is. No fat Spanish treasure galleon as you make jest of, but the *Warspite!*"

Baret fixed the telescope on the sleek brigantine with its guns, its flag flying. He would recognize that ship anywhere.

Levasseur paced. "Harwick! He brings another. A man neither I nor you, monsieur, wish to see at this time. We must stop him!"

Sir Erik Farrow, thought Baret. He must have followed Karlton, or else Karlton had informed him of his intentions to keep Levasseur's ship in view.

Levasseur said something beneath his breath. "That fox. Farrow knows what we are about, monsieur, and he will insist on his share. Harwick must have told him!"

Baret was grave. "You have your quarrel with Farrow, and I have mine for quite another reason, but we can neither fight nor run, since Harwick is with him."

"You must sink his ship, monsieur! Or at least run with the wind. The *Regale* is the match of the *Warspite.*"

Baret knew as much, yet he had no desire to fire on Erik Farrow, even though he believed he could outposition his ship. Had he come on his own, or was he out to stop him from reaching Lucca? Had Felix sent him?

Baret lowered the telescope, his gaze thoughtful and troubled. Determination set his jaw. If Erik was out to stop him, there would be no choice but to fire on the *Warspite.*

Some of the crewmen stood aloft, shading their eyes to study the oncoming ships, by now knowing what was happening.

Baret looked again through the telescope. "They've spotted us."

Now sharply authoritative, he stood by the ornately carved rail of the quarterdeck at the head of the companionway and shouted for his master gunner to ready the gun crew, to clean the gun tackles, to load and run out the guns.

Levasseur, unlike Baret in coolness, paced with great excitement. "If only I were on the *Venture!* I should surely blow him from the waters!"

The buccaneers came tumbling from the forecastle and stood about the hatch in the waist, anxious for a fight.

Baret shouted aloft to unfurl the topsails and topgallants. Even as the buccaneers sprang to the ratlines in obedience, the *Warspite* was seen to alter her course and swing in pursuit.

Baret's eyes narrowed with grim calm. So Farrow wished a fight, did he? *Then he'll have it.*

"We're committed to our present course," he ordered. "But we will fight as well." He looked aft toward Emerald's cabin. Zeddie stood gaping. "See to your ward!"

"Aye, Captain!"

Then he looked ahead at the *Warspite*'s sails. The broad target offered him the better chance of crippling her. He shouted orders down to the quartermaster at the whipstaff.

Then came the bustle on deck, the rush of feet, the dragging of tackle, the noisier movements from the wardroom beneath them where cannon and culverins were being run out. Down in the sweltering room, the gun crew would be moving about, their backs bent over for lack of headroom.

But Levasseur was furious. "Board and board!" he shouted. "Monsieur! Your men and mine, we shall take both ships! I shall signal to the *Venture*—"

"No. We shall do as little as necessary to cripple him."

"You are mad, Captain! And share the booty of the *Prince Philip* with Erik Farrow and his crew?"

"Captain!" shouted the bosum, swinging from a ratline. "She's signaling! She's askin' for a show of colors!"

"Prepare to signal. We'll see what Farrow has to say for himself."

Levasseur turned on him, whipping his rapier from his baldric. "A mistake, monsieur!"

Immediately his Frenchmen backed him, spreading across the deck.

The quartermaster scowled but remained steady. "Holding steady for orders, Captain," he called up from the whipstaff.

"Don't be a fool, Levasseur," gritted Baret, glancing toward the *Warspite*. She was coming on strong. Baret stood his ground, showing no intimidation, for he knew that Levasseur, like a shark once smelling blood, would move in for the kill.

"What will it be, Levasseur? A free-for-all here and now? We need every man for Porto Bello! You shall have blood and death for your folly here. There will be no Spanish gold for any of you," he called to the French pirates. "And you, Levasseur, will die first. I shall see to it! I am captain of this ship, and you are a mutineer!"

The threat of lost treasure rippled through the French seamen like a groan, as Baret had hoped. At the same moment the buccaneers of the *Regale* showed themselves with cutlasses drawn.

Levasseur's temper waned. The red eased from his swarthy face. "Easy now, monsieur. Pardon! But if you think to double-cross me by siding with Farrow or Harwick, I shall have you."

He sauntered to the other side of the deck with the French pirates gathering to his side. They cast sullen glances toward Baret and his armed crew, who looked on in serene but deadly silence.

Baret looked toward the sea. The *Warspite* drew closer, but Sir Karlton Harwick's vessel had already slowed, probably uncertain over what would happen. He would wish no fight, knowing Emerald was on board.

Again the *Warspite* was lowering and raising its Union Jack—the signal for the *Regale* to heave to while a longboat was sent for a parley.

Baret showed no emotion, but he was relieved that Erik Farrow had not yet opted to show the face of an enemy.

He recalled locking Farrow into Felix's wardrobe, and he laughed to himself. "Strike colors," he ordered. "Heave to across her bow."

"Aye, Cap'n!"

"Prepare to receive visitors," he shouted.

30

BRETHREN OF THE COAST

Baret stood at the rail looking across the darkening blue waters toward the two ships, their lanterns glowing golden and their sails ghostly white against the deepening twilight.

He affected indifference as tall, gaunt Sir Cecil came to stand beside him, but he felt the penetrating gaze of the old man. Yet Baret was determined not to let the dignified scholar goad him into compliance, despite Baret's strong affection for him. He knew of the daily meetings Cecil was having with Emerald around the Scriptures, and while Baret was impressed with the girl's apparent dedication, and he hoped to do well by her future in London, he wished for no further emotional involvement.

There was and always would be Lavender, he told himself.

Nor would he return to London to fulfill his family responsibility until the matter of his father was known. And then there was the looming war.

He thought he knew what was on Cecil's mind, for it was apparent that he had come to a fondness for Emerald. Baret said nothing as he gazed out on the two vessels now at anchor in the calm Caribbean.

"Karlton's daughter prepares to be rowed out to her father's ship. Is it not wise that you accompany her to explain matters?"

There was more in the question than what first appeared, Baret knew. Remaining indifferently composed, he turned his dark head to look at Cecil, the plume in his hat moving gently in the warm breeze. The handsome eyes were remote, deliberately so. "I see no cause to do so. She'll be returning with him to London as soon as this matter with Morgan is put away."

"He'll not take lightly to her reputation being bandied about these weeks. She was aboard your ship. In your cabin."

Baret's eyes narrowed beneath his lashes. "Are you suggesting I marry the child?"

Sir Cecil arched a silver brow. "A bit more blunt and to the point than I would have stated it, but Harwick is also a blunt man, I am told, and one with ambitious plans where his daughter is concerned."

Baret showed no alarm. "I know all about Karlton's ambitions." He picked up the telescope and fixed it upon Erik Farrow's ship. "And they do not intimidate me. I rescued the girl from the mistake of marrying and running off with Maynerd to the American colony. Karlton has much to thank me for. We shall leave it at that."

Sir Cecil's thin mouth turned with irony, and he leaned his elbow against the rail, watching him. "Harwick is likely to wonder why you would risk so much to stop her. There are witnesses aplenty to the twenty thousand pieces of eight for which you bought her," he said wryly. "As well as the challenge to duel Levasseur."

"A necessary action to prove to her what Maynerd was. Nothing more."

"Harwick is certain to ponder. His ambitions are known."

"And so are mine. I intend to marry Lavender. As for the rubies—I am a generous man. I am permitting her to go free to her father," he said smoothly.

Sir Cecil stroked his pointed beard. "Yes . . . well . . . Harwick is likely to cry foul when it comes to his daughter's reputation."

Baret looked at the sea. "If I am correct, her reputation is already the topic of scandal where her mother is concerned. Come, my good Cecil! I've no time to mourn reputations, including my own. She's spirited and brave of heart— she'll manage to hold her head high."

"Is that all you wish to say about her to Harwick?" Cecil inquired dubiously.

"What more am I to say? Prepare the pinnace to bring her to his ship." He reached into his vesture and handed Cecil a letter. "All is explained in here. Including my offer to see to her upbringing at the best finishing school and her introduction to society in London. I'll take full responsibility for her wardrobe and jewels. Surely Karlton will be satisfied. After all," he said dryly, "she might be aboard the *Venture* right now instead of the *Regale* if I hadn't intervened. She'd be married to 'Jamie Boy'—or should I say to Levasseur? Tell Karlton that!"

Sir Cecil took the letter. "As you wish."

They stood for a moment in silence looking out to sea and ships, feeling the wind, smelling the salt air.

The wind caught Cecil's ankle-length dark cloak, worn over rough tunic and hose, and gave it a jaunty snap. Beneath the grim exterior, the old Puritan scholar might rejoice at a Protestant blow to Spain. Yet Baret knew him well enough to know that Cecil was not thinking of battle for battle's sake but about Baret's risky venture into Porto Bello.

"Morgan will have at least a dozen ships," Baret breathed with pleasure. "All dedicated to teach the Spanish viceroy a grievous lesson. It's my guess he will wish to strike Porto Bello at this time, rather than Panama."

"Or Maracaibo. They say twenty vessels, if you wish to count the barks of the smaller pirates coming in from Tortuga."

"You are right. And never underestimate the bloodthirsty scoundrels aboard the small barks. They've been known to take many a Spanish galleon and leave her bones to sink to the bottom of the Caribbean. They are relatives of the men and women who knew the Inquisition in Holland and France. They do not forget easily," said Baret.

"There are none who wish the demise of Spain more than I. But eventually, Baret, you must bury your hatred for Madrid with your baldric and return to London a free man in heart and soul. The grace of God, like the wide expanse of the sea, may yet wash the heart and soul clean of its bitterness. Only when that root of bitterness is dug up and buried with the dead will you truly be free."

Baret said nothing. He had heard it before, many times, in different ways. He knew this as well as did Cecil but had up to now not come to grips with the necessity. And he would not think of it yet. There was too much to be done.

And like the deathblow to his fair mother and the injustice done his father, Spain was responsible for holding Lucca, a crippled old man, a prisoner.

Baret's palms sweated as he held the telescope. His jawline tightened. He changed the subject, as he always did. "The Dutch buccaneers are hungry to land a volley of cannon in the side of a few Spanish ships."

"The Dutch may soon get their opportunity to land a few into the side of English vessels if it comes to war. The matter between England and Holland grows more serious as the weeks pass. If you stay in the West Indies, you will need to grapple with the difficult decision of taking sides."

"I've vowed to the earl it will be England."

Sir Cecil looked rather surprised. "Have you the heart to attack a Dutch ship?"

Baret wondered. If it hadn't been for his grandfather's threat to give Lavender to his cousin Grayford in marriage, he would never have promised to fight for England.

"Let us not discuss Holland yet. It is Spain who poses the threat."

Whether war with Holland loomed or not, Baret had no intention of giving up his plans to locate Lucca. He couldn't simply turn and sail away from everything that tried and tested his heart.

He looked at Cecil, who wore a thoughtful frown as he gazed across to Karlton Harwick's ship.

"I have always said, my lord Viscount, that you should have been born the son of Karlton, for the Harwick side of the family has the liberty to enjoy the ways of sea adventure, whereas you have responsibilities in London to His Majesty."

"By now I'd have thought you would have given up on your lectures," said Baret with a lean smile. "Have you voyaged with me these three years for naught?"

"I am a man of enduring patience," jested Cecil. "One can always hope you would give up. You might as well know that I've made arrangements with the earl to leave for London with your brother once this raid with Morgan is successfully completed. I shall be Jette's tutor, even as I was yours."

"He told me," said Baret.

Cecil looked surprised. "I should be anxious to know your thoughts on the matter."

Baret smiled. "I think Jette could not have a better scholar, and I am fully in agreement. I would also see Karlton's daughter to your training in London," he said easily.

"You think Harwick will agree to it?" asked Cecil with lifted brow. "I dare say he has much more on his mind for Emerald than three or four years of academic and social learning. He has certain plans in which you are included. What a victory over the Buckingtons it would be to have won the allegiance of the viscount! And what more could he have but you as his son-in-law."

Baret looked at him, amused. "Son-in-law! Am I also to be bought, not with pieces of eight but with a comely daughter? I am not so dense as all that, Cecil! She's a sprightly girl to be sure—but there is Lavender."

"Is it nonsense that Harwick's share in Foxemoore is in desperate need of funds lest he lose it?"

Baret knew of Karlton's financial penury because of his debts and lost shipping. That was the reason he hoped to gain bounty through the attack on Spain. But he had never been so blatantly bold as to hint that he wished Baret and the Buckington wealth and title to be gained by marriage. And although there were times when Baret had suspected so, he would not admit that to Cecil.

Baret's dark brow lifted. He laughed quietly. "The last thing I shall do is marry anytime soon. I'm here to pursue my own plans as I see them. It is neither to goad my grandfather nor to oblige Harwick, though I admit to a high regard for the man's prowess at sea."

It was then Sir Cecil who arched a brow, a thin smile on his mouth.

Baret turned away. "Of course Karlton has dreams for his daughter," he admitted impatiently. "What father would not? She has spent a pretty time enduring the scorn and rejection of both Harwicks and Buckingtons since a child."

"Indeed. And Harwick, if he can make something of your claiming Emerald, is likely to do it."

Baret frowned. "I know him too well to think he would demand that which I am unable to give at this time—or in the future. He knows about Lavender. We've been promised to each other since I was twelve."

"Some would say that while it is the way of nobility to match future countess with future earl, it is not always the way of the human heart to cooperate."

Baret turned to him with a dry smile. "Rest assured my heart is my own to do with as I choose. Is that why you came here? To warn me against some intrigue by Harwick in a match with his daughter?"

"It was only a small part of the reason why I came. And I do not see it as a warning, for the girl will one day be a worthy enough prize for any man. She has a heart for God, I am certain of it."

Baret chose not to think about it. "Until I return to London ready to don the garments of my responsibility as Viscount and future Earl of Buckington, I shall take my chances with Morgan—and my friendship with Harwick. Before I settle down to the life of the court, I shall see my father vindicated and Felix brought to justice. There is no more I wish to discuss."

"It may not be entirely left up to you to decide at your leisure."

Baret ignored the smooth warning. He frowned and looked again at Karlton's ship. The man was a stalwart scoundrel at times, to be sure. Then he grinned. But he liked Karlton's buccaneering ways. And as for himself, he would not be browbeaten by Karlton into anything he did not want. He believed Karlton knew that as well. "I shall not personally escort Emerald aboard his ship," said Baret and sobered, his eyes turning hard. "And now I have a rendezvous with Erik Farrow."

The pinnace was about to be lowered to bring Baret to the *Warspite* when Levasseur came striding across the deck, followed by two of his crew.

"Monsieur!"

Baret turned, and the buccaneers, wearing full regalia, measured each other.

Levasseur's black eyes were cynical. "Sure now, Captain Foxworth, you don't expect me to stay aboard while you discuss with Erik Farrow the *Prince Philip*? I am in the meeting.

Why should I trust the two of you alone together? Would you not eagerly hope to betray my interests?"

Baret was under no delusion as to his intention—Levasseur heartily disliked Erik. Baret displayed no resentment at the accusation, however.

"If you wish—just as long as you understand there is to be no trouble. We talk. Nothing more."

Levasseur eyed him with a faint sneer but offered no objection. Within ten minutes the pinnace was lowered, the rowers chosen from men loyal to Baret and Levasseur by lot, and the oars were slicing through the soft glimmering sea toward the *Warspite*, its lanterns lit and waiting for their arrival.

31
ABOARD THE *WARSPITE*

Seated in a plush red velvet chair with white and gold design, Captain Erik Farrow lounged on the deck of his ship beneath the full golden moon, showing no outward sign of hurry as his fellow Brethren arrived. He watched the viscount board, looking every inch a pirate, followed by the lean swarthy Frenchman Captain Levasseur and a score of men loyal to each, wearing their deadly rapiers and pistols.

Erik waited for Baret to cross the freshly sluiced deck to join him at a table spread with refreshments.

The table and chairs, the wine from Madrid, along with the rest of the ship's elaborate furniture had all been taken at one time or another by Erik, who enjoyed a taste for splendor.

Farrow's legs, in black woolen hose and boots with shiny silver buckles (buckles taken eight years ago from the boots of a Spaniard), were stretched out and crossed at his ankles. He waited, feeling no pleasure at the upcoming confrontation with his lordship. Nor, for that matter, with Levasseur. But it was chiefly Baret who disturbed him.

The night was tropical with the sigh of the Caribbean wind, and he felt a stirring in his blood for the old ways, ways that he had told himself would never again rise like baying hounds to entice him to lead his ship and crew. And yet . . .

Several matters had changed since he had last confronted the viscount in the chamber of Lord Felix on Foxemoore.

He laid aside his embroidered burgundy satin jacket, revealing a frilled white silk shirt. Out of habit, he kept one hand on his jeweled sword belt, hearing the siren song of the wind and feeling her fingers in his fair hair.

Baret Buckington walked up to the table, Levasseur behind him.

Erik stood then, arms folded, the breeze whipping his hair. He said nothing, giving the viscount a measured look. He noticed the dangerous energy visible in the forceful line of his jaw and the raw restless strength that stirred in the dark, compelling eyes.

Baret retained an almost relentless calm even as a hint of a smile touched his mouth. His voice was wry. "Somehow your being knighted by my uncle does not lend itself to the same mystique as the days of King Arthur. You might at least have waited until I became earl. I would have performed the service before His Majesty."

Erik lifted a fair brow at the gibe. "It is your uncle who expects to win the title of viscount from the earl, your lordship. And you must admit, you look more the offspring of Henry Morgan than an English nobleman of the blood."

Levasseur chuckled. "Perhaps he is, Captain Farrow. And, monsieur, do you dare seek the Brethren after walking out on us at Gran Granada?"

Baret glanced over his shoulder at Levasseur. "I am in command, Rafael. You will be silent."

Levasseur smirked, pulled out a chair, and turned it around to rest his arms against its back as he sat down. With his hat still in place, he reached for the ornate bottle of wine, sniffing it with pleasure. "One thing about you, Captain Farrow, you have always shared the exquisite manner and tastes of France."

Erik felt Baret's keen gaze. Baret was measuring him, perhaps wondering why he had come. He remembered having been locked into Lord Felix's wardrobe. Seeing Baret's suspicion, Erik gestured for him to sit. "What reason would I have for coming except your invitation? Did you not bid me to join with you on Morgan's expedition?"

As Baret continued to weigh his words, Erik added, "I believe, your lordship, it was the last challenge you offered before leaving me in the . . . dark. 'Come,' was your invitation." And Erik stretched out in the chair and reached for his glass.

Baret scanned him thoughtfully.

"We want no more partners," stated Levasseur, watching Erik evenly.

Baret sat down. "What did Felix offer you to find and try to stop me? I cannot believe you'd set aside your new favor to take to sea again, even though a few hours left to contemplate fate in the dark has done wonders to change your loyalties," came Baret's dry voice. "I know how much a title means to you."

He did know. Erik was an illegitimate son, and a sense of inferiority had long plagued him. He knew not who had fathered him nor yet the woman who had given him birth. He grew up on the sooty streets of Bristol as an errand boy for bloodthirsty pirates. He had sailed as a lad with a number of cutthroats who had met their end on Execution Dock. He now knew Morgan and a host of other pirates, some evil to the core and others—perhaps like himself—who had been swept along with the relentless tide until so far out to sea there seemed no hope of recovery.

Yes, a title meant a good deal to him, even if it had come by the hand of Felix as a bribe.

Baret pushed the glass away and opted instead for a ripe papaya. Erik watched him carve it with his dagger.

"My decision is made," said Erik. "I am no longer under the employ of Lord Felix."

A moment of silence dragged on, in which Levasseur watched him with barely concealed malevolence. Baret said nothing and contemplated the slice of fruit as if having never seen such before.

"You expect me to believe that, Erik?"

"It is the truth."

"He jests," mocked Levasseur. "Do not trust him, *mon ami.*"

Erik watched Baret, wondering if he believed him or not.

"What did he offer you this time to betray me?"

Erik's gray eyes turned brittle. His hand tightened on his scabbard.

Levasseur, too, tensed, his black eyes darting from one man to the other. Only Baret showed no difference in his manner. He took a bite of papaya.

"I have not informed Lord Felix of your plans to search for Lucca in Porto Bello."

At the mention of Porto Bello, both Baret and Levasseur looked at him sharply.

Erik masked a smile. "Of course I knew. Charlie Maynerd's brother came to me with the information before he went to you, Levasseur."

Levasseur tensed. "Do you lie to me, monsieur? Do I not know that you and Foxworth may well work together to my disadvantage?" He stood indignantly. "You'll sign no articles with me, Farrow!"

"Then I'll sign them with Captain Foxworth, considering it is I who know the true whereabouts of Lucca, not you or Sloane."

If Levasseur was stunned, Baret only watched Erik with something like irony. "Sit down, Levasseur," he ordered. "We'll hear what Erik has to say."

"You dare cross me, Foxworth? You dare order me about like crew?"

"When your tantrums put to risk our getting the treasure of the *Prince Philip*, I shall do so and more, my captain. If your crew learns you have spoiled their opportunity for sweet Spanish gold, what will you tell them?"

Erik, outwardly unperturbed, smiled to himself over Baret's disarming the Frenchman.

Levasseur stood peering down at the viscount, who sat calmly considering him from across the table. Slowly Levasseur's expression changed and he sat, but he was not happy.

Erik took the advantage that Baret had provided him and reached beneath the sleeve of his billowing shirt to draw out a letter. "If you would know where Lucca is being held a prisoner, it is in this letter taken from Charles Maynerd before he was hanged by the wishes of Lord Felix."

Baret stared at the letter.

Levasseur was angry and suspicious. "Do not trust him, my captain," he said to Baret. "How do you know he speaks truth? It is a trick, one agreed upon by him and your uncle."

"It is no lie," said Erik. "And if you were as clever as you think yourself, Rafael, you would not have so easily believed everything Jamie Maynerd fed you like fish bait. The letter speaks for itself." He handed it to Baret.

Baret opened it and by the light of the lantern, with Levasseur at close attendance, read the words.

Erik watched. The letter was from Charlie Maynerd to his brother, confiscated by Lord Felix when he arrested him at Barbados and brought him to Port Royal. The letter stated that Lucca was being held not in Porto Bello but in Maracaibo.

Moments later, Levasseur cursed Jamie. "Dangling from the yardarm was not good enough for him. The lying, thieving swine! He knew all along that Porto Bello would lead us to a trap!"

While Baret was pondering the letter, Erik disagreed.

"He did not know. It was I who convinced him of Porto Bello. The ruse was mine alone."

Both Baret and Levasseur looked at him. Levasseur stood and reached for his rapier. "I shall have your innards for this, monsieur!"

Baret stood and turned on him. "Put that away, you French dog! Can you not see he is on our side?"

"On our side? On our side, he says! How so! It is the foulest of treacheries! We might have fallen into your uncle's trap!"

"Yes," said Baret wryly. "And would have, had Erik not come to reveal the truth to us in time. Does that not say anything of his trustworthiness?"

Levasseur hesitated. His dark mood, however, was unwilling to admit the obvious. "May it be wise, monsieur, to ask Captain Farrow what he may wish for this act of generosity?"

"A share in the treasure of the *Prince Philip*. What else?" He turned to Erik.

Erik saw through the simplicity of his suggestion. He and Baret both knew that he had come for more reasons than that, yet neither wished Levasseur to know.

"What else would I come for, Levasseur? A portion of the *Prince Philip*'s great treasure. And only Lucca can tell us where it is. Would I wish my fair viscount to be taken in Lord Felix's trap, thus killing the one man whom Lucca will trust enough to share his coveted secret? I had to warn you both. And have done so."

"And done well, my honorable colleague," Baret told him. "You shall indeed sign articles with me and Levasseur."

There was something in Baret's smile that put Erik on alert. Why did he wish him to sign articles with Levasseur?

"And I have taken the liberty to have the Articles brought here to the *Warspite*," said Baret.

"You brought them here? To his ship?" demanded Levasseur.

Baret lifted the paper from beneath his jacket. "We share and share alike. What is the Brotherhood for?"

Levasseur grudgingly relented, watching as Erik, minutes later, dipped pen to ink and prepared to sign his name below the others.

Erik hesitated, seeing the reason Baret had insisted he sign. Baret had signed as Viscount Baret Buckington, not Foxworth. It could mean his arrest on piracy charges. And Baret was forcing him into the same fire.

Erik's gray eyes narrowed frostily as Baret smiled, lifting a brow. "If all you speak is true, Captain Farrow, and, of course, I have no doubt but that it is—you may sign as 'Sir' Erik Farrow."

Erik's jaw turned rigid. Then he scratched his new title across the bottom of the paper.

"Ah," was all Levasseur said.

"To the Brotherhood," said Baret, lifting a glass.

"To Maracaibo," said Erik.

Levasseur smiled coolly. "And the Spanish gold."

Baret did not go back to the *Regale* until the moon was setting and stars dotted the velvet sky. Levasseur, convinced at last that there was no more to be said of the matter, had departed with members of his crew and Sloane for his own ship, the *Venture*.

Baret, alone with Erik in the Great Cabin of the *Warspite*, faced him across the captain's table.

He was satisfied that Erik's friendship had won out in the end, yet he wondered at the trigger that had set him on a different course from what he had charted that night in his uncle's chamber.

"Then if Felix knows where Lucca is being held, he will have already sent spies to see to his death. We have no time to lose. We must set sail for Maracaibo at once," Baret said.

He watched Erik, comfortable with his loyalty yet a little uneasy now that they were alone and Erik sat frowning to himself. "Why did you choose the risk of aiding me to find Lucca? Friendship is one thing, but you made it clear you were content with the wage and promise of Felix. He gave you the title—was that not enough, or did he hold back?"

He saw the remoteness return to Erik's gray eyes. Emotion had fled his somber features, but Baret knew him too well to believe he was at peace. "Whatever he failed to give you, I shall see you have it."

Erik sighed, as though distressed to speak his next words.

"Nay, my lord . . . you cannot offer me what he has failed to deliver, for you wish it as well as I. It was a certain woman."

Baret felt the blow, surprised at this confession. He remained unreadable, yet something in Erik's voice set him on edge. A certain woman . . .

Erik stood and walked over to the desk, his back toward him.

The reality of what Erik was about to say dawned on Baret, and his eyes hardened.

"Your uncle offered me the hand of Lavender in marriage. Not all the treasure of the *Prince Philip* nor His Majesty's blessing could have meant more to me. I confess, your lordship, that I was at times hard pressed into a willingness to betray you for her hand." He turned his head and looked calmly at him. "I never meant to fall in love with the same woman as you—it simply happened. When your uncle vowed her to me for my services to betray you, I was on the edge of doing so."

Erik turned and leaned against the desk, his golden brows furrowed and his gray eyes narrowing upon Baret. "But alas, I could not. But do not think your friendship means more than hers—I am no saint. For her I would have done nearly anything. It was the earl who sealed my doom. I confess it so."

Baret stared at him across the cabin. The news stunned him, yet he made no comment. His anger began to boil.

Erik sighed and threw up his hands.

Baret stood, looking deadly cold. But if Erik expected

trouble, his hand refused to move to his scabbard. For a disquieting moment they stared at each other.

"A duel would be folly, my lord. Is it not enough that neither of us shall have her? Shall we add to the mockery we find ourselves in by also killing each other?" Erik's expression turned sympathetic.

It was the first time that Baret had seen emotional display.

"You yet have Lucca—you yet have the possibility of finding your father alive. I vow to work with you in any way I can to find and free them both!"

Baret was moved, yet his mind had picked up on something unusual that Erik had said.

"Speak plainly. What do you mean—'neither of us shall have her'?"

Erik said nothing for a moment. "She will marry your cousin Lord Grayford Thaxton tomorrow at Foxemoore."

Baret did not move. He would not accept this. He knew Lavender cared for him more than for any man. She would never marry his cousin.

"Tomorrow?" His voice was calm to the point of being studious.

Erik nodded. "I have spoken to her for myself . . . and for you. She has given me a message to give you."

He picked up a letter from his desk. He brought it to Baret, then walked out of the cabin, his boots ringing.

Alone, Baret tore open the letter, and his eyes fell on the terse, cruel lines written in Lavender's hand:

> *You have scorned and belittled me before family and friends by running off with that despicable little wench of Karlton's. I never wish to lay eyes on you again. And to prove it, I have agreed with your grandfather the Earl of Buckington to marry Lord Grayford. Should an unfortunate occurrence take place in London by which I am forced to look upon you, you shall see Countess Lavender Thaxton, the wife of Lord Grayford Thaxton."*
>
> *Know that I shall forever heartily despise you for your betrayal.*
>
> *Lavender*

Baret's lip twitched with subdued anger. He left Erik's cabin and came onto the quarterdeck. He gripped the rail and looked into the dark Caribbean waters. It seemed Lavender's fair face and golden hair gazed up at him with mockery. He crumpled the letter and threw it over the rail, then turned and, with a brisk command, called his men to board the pinnace.

As the boat slid across the swells toward his ship, looking ghostly against the starlight, he thought of Lavender. Tomorrow at this time she would be in the arms of his cousin Grayford.

Aboard the *Warspite*, Sir Erik Farrow stood at the rail and watched the pinnace make for the *Regale*. *And so*, he thought wryly, *we have both lost the woman we wanted.*

He turned slowly at the hesitant sound of footsteps.

The girl Minette stood there, looking like a sea urchin with tousled amber curls and eyes as luminous as the Caribbean moon.

He frowned. She had come aboard his ship in Port Royal as he was ready to set sail, a girl wild with terror, telling him that Emerald had been abducted by smugglers and that she could not locate Sir Karlton to warn him. But through one of his own spies who worked the wharf and taverns, Erik had already learned what had transpired between Baret and Levasseur over Emerald.

Baret had sent a message to Karlton informing him that he had his daughter aboard the *Regale*. Karlton was to rendezvous with Baret at the appropriate time by secretly following Levasseur's ship.

Erik, who had made his own plans to follow, reluctantly agreed to let the girl sail aboard his ship to join Emerald at the point of rendezvous.

"Sir Farrow, when will I be brought to my cousin Emerald?"

He was anxious to be rid of her. The half-caste girl had some silly notion of thinking herself a lady.

"She is likely to be aboard her father's ship by now. Sam!" he called his serving man, and the big Carib approached, bare from the waist up and wearing a blue scarf about his head.

"Bring the girl to Harwick's ship."

"Aren't *you* going to bring me?" came Minette's disappointed voice.

He turned, almost sharply, wondering that a girl with half-African blood would dare speak to him thus. As he looked at her in the moonlight, she appeared to gather her robes of dignity about her. It angered him, for he did not wish to notice.

"No. Can you not see I am a busy man?" He gave a dismissing wave of his hand. "Go, then," he said and strode up the quarterdeck steps.

Minette watched him go, once again stung by his indifferent rebuff. *I'm not a lady. I'll never be one. I'm not even worthy of his respect,* she thought again. *I'll always be a slave in the white man's eyes.* Tears welled, but she squared her jaw and blinked them back.

Minette turned at the Carib's voice. "Is you wantin' to board Sir Karlton's ship now?"

"Yes," she breathed, "as soon as possible, Mr. Sam."

"Come along, gal. I has the boat ready soon."

She followed him across the deck to where a rope ladder waited. She noted the broad smile on the serving man's face. He looked to be of Indian and African blood.

"Ain't a female known to turn the head of the great Sir Erik Farrow 'cept one. An' she done upped and married an English lord."

"If I wanted your opinion, I'd have asked for it."

He chuckled, and Minette looked at him, unable to keep her curiosity down. "Who was she, d'you know?"

"Lavender Harwick. She got mad at Cap'n Foxworth and married his cousin instead."

32

HEART'S
UNSPOKEN DESIRE

The sun had long since set behind a silver-edged cloud as Emerald's footsteps echoed hollowly on the planking of the *Regale,* lolling gently in the water. With eager anticipation she watched the motley crew lower the pinnace into the twilight waters, purple in hue beneath a shadowed sky. Soon now she would be swept into the strong arms of her stalwart father!

Above, stars flared and glittered like diamonds. She turned at the sound of boot steps, as surprised to see Baret Buckington as he apparently was to see her.

He paused, as though contemplating, before momentarily joining her on the wind-washed deck. "I thought Cecil and Zeddie had brought you to Karlton by now," he said, nothing in his voice.

She did not know why, but the lack of warmth in his tone was disappointing. "There was a delay in getting my trunk aboard the longboat," she explained in an equally toneless voice and turned away to look out at the sea, feeling the wind in her hair. "Naturally, I'm anxious to leave."

"Naturally, you would be."

She gave him a side glance as he stood there, the wind touching the billowing sleeves of his white shirt, his dark hair blowing.

He was watching her, but she could not see his expression. Then he walked to the rail of the ship and glanced below. "I wonder what's keeping Cecil?"

She too glanced about. "He was here a moment ago."

They lapsed into silence. He looked out across the sea. "A beautiful evening."

"Yes," she said, gripping the rail. "It is." She looked up at the stars, then at him.

Baret's expression was suddenly enigmatic, and he lifted his head to stare up at the masts barely visible against the darkening sky.

The moon rose above the water, a glorious white orb sagging in the purple twilight, strewing pearl-like glimmers across the sea. The wind that came on its heels carried the scent of the Caribbean and lifted the hems of Emerald's skirts.

She turned toward him, feeling his gaze, and grew still as their eyes held.

Baret turned away. "Your father is waiting." And he left her to hear his boots ringing as he went up the steps.

Good-*bye,* she thought and turned away too, stung by his disinterest.

Sir Cecil came walking up, accompanied by Zeddie, and she was brought without further delay to the rope ladder where a pinnace waited below, moving gently in the water.

Minutes later she was seated comfortably in the boat and looking out with expectancy toward her father's ship. Zeddie too seemed pleased—and relieved—as the oarsmen began rowing their way across the water.

"Well m'girl, we made it after all, thanks to his lord-ship."

Yes, she thought, and grew more tense as she pondered meeting her father.

What would he have to say about this adventure?

369

33

MARACAIBO

Sunset's flaming streaks scribbled across the sky of the Spanish port of Maracaibo. Along a narrow cobbled street, still retaining heat from the day's sun, a tall-storied house with its high windows screened in alabaster stared down on a sun-baked courtyard, ancient with tales of old Spain. Amid gnarled olive trees, Baret Buckington stood concealed in the shadows, waiting.

Tonight he wore a wide-brimmed Spanish hat and the exquisite uniform of a Madrid *cavalero,* its black collar embroidered with silver thread. A Latin cross hung from a silver chain around his neck, and beneath the tight-fitting black jacket he wore fine chain mesh from Toledo.

Having "borrowed" horses, he, Erik, and Levasseur had ridden into Maracaibo disguised as soldiers. Thus they had accomplished the first stage of their dangerous journey and had sheltered in a shadowy coffee house until dusk approached, behaving as men wishing for nothing more than to gamble among themselves. As dusk settled over Maracaibo, they casually found their way here to the courtyard of the villa where Lucca was held under guard.

Meanwhile, the pirate crew, consisting of men from the three captains, had left a small sloop in Lake Maracaibo and were now concealed on shore among the trees waiting with a pinnace for them to return with Lucca.

Erik was somewhere about, as was Levasseur. But just where, Baret was no longer certain, and that was what bothered him. He felt confident about Erik, now that he had made his break with Felix, but Levasseur was as treacherous and wily as any serpent coiled on a rock.

Except for the fact that Levasseur and his crewmen believed that they needed him to extract from Lucca the information about the *Prince Philip's* treasure, Baret would fully expect a dagger in his back the moment he brought Lucca to the waiting ship.

He frowned. There was trouble and danger ahead. The expanding tale of Lucca's knowing where treasure was hidden was only a pirate's wishful dream that grew with the size of the spoken tale. Lucca was an old scholar, nothing more, a man who had changed his cowl for a heretic's Bible and who had sailed with Viscount Royce Buckington aboard the *Revenge* as friend and confidant.

Baret doubted if Lucca knew anything of the remains of the *Prince Philip* beyond the fact that it had been sunk off the coast of Panama. Baret had not yet planned his response to Levasseur and his pirates once the truth was known. Of course he now had Erik to back him up. Levasseur would be a fool to come against them both.

His intense gaze was riveted upon a high window in the upper chamber where Lucca was being held by the Spanish viceroy, Petros de Guzman. The official was elsewhere in Maracaibo tonight, attending an official banquet to greet the admiral sent from the queen regent.

As darkness settled thickly over the courtyard, Baret listened, alert, his senses trained to recognize danger before it struck. Someone was following him? The chirping crickets ceased. A tense silence began to close in about him. A breath of sea-laden wind whispered. He did not like it. The rustling leaves could cover the approach of someone moving closer.

His head turned away from the window to the seasoned brick wall that bordered the flagstone courtyard. Trotting hoofbeats from several horses belonging to Spanish soldiers echoed with a hollow sound across the cobbles, followed by the rise and fall of lazy voices.

The wind cooled dots of perspiration on his handsomely defined features as the horses drew nearer to the courtyard wall. The point of his sword lifted slightly, and he waited.

The horses moved on, the sound of their hooves fading with the twilight. Overhead, the olive leaves brushed against each other, rustling. There was little time.

A rising wind coming from the Gulf hinted of a sudden storm. The crew keeping the pinnace would be growing uneasy about the sloop secretly anchored in the shallows of Lake Maracaibo—a sheltered extension of the Gulf of Venezuela. The lake, as Baret knew, was no secure place to be anchored when a hurricane was brewing.

Again, he well knew that were it not for Levasseur's greedy ambition to locate the plunder, the treacherous pirate would think nothing of taking the pinnace back to the sloop and leaving both him and Erik trapped in Maracaibo.

He was unable to see in the darkness settling over the courtyard, but his instincts told him he was not alone. And he sensed this was more than either Erik or Levasseur, who were also concealed somewhere among the trees. The presence he felt in the courtyard belonged to someone else—or was it his imagination? He tensed. Did that presence, perhaps of a fourth man, belong to one of the other pirates, sent to follow him here from the shallows where the pinnace waited? Sloane, perhaps. Was Levasseur leery, thinking that Baret might fail to keep his side of their bargain? Or did he have something more devious in mind?

Baret had written a one-line message to Lucca in Greek —a language certain to not be known by the Spanish soldiers—informing him that he waited below. Then he had rolled the paper about a smooth stone and carefully tossed it through the scholar's window.

Once certain the prisoner had retrieved it, Baret waited among the olive trees for the reply.

Perhaps an hour had passed while Baret waited. When the old one did not appear at the window, concern gnawed at his insides. What was detaining him?

Behind the alabaster window, a small and arthritically twisted man, a scholar of Greek letters who had served as Cromwell's appointed secretary to Viscount Royce Buckington on board the *Revenge*, sat hunched over his desk, his quill scratching busily.

Lucca was aware that the whereabouts of a certain treasure chest that Viscount Royce Buckington was reported to have stashed away containing jewels and gold from the prized *Prince Philip* had elicited profound interest within the English government—and without. He was not so certain that all in the Admiralty Court who held interest in the chest did so for the good of the Crown, as was suggested.

Scholar Lucca was convinced that certain men from Parliament who were working silently for his release from the Spanish viceroy were doing so not for King Charles, nor for his own sake, but with the treasure in mind and, more important, to silence his knowledge of the fate of the viscount.

Lucca found this to be a strange matter, considering that the Admiralty Court had already declared the viscount to be dead.

Evidently not all who speak of his reckless death in a duel at Port Royal believe their own words. Does the Admiralty believe in ghosts? he thought with a cynical smile.

Obviously those men who spoke the loudest of the man's death were the most certain he yet lived.

Lucca would gladly return to London in order to testify before the Admiralty Court of Captain Royce Buckington's innocence of piracy. For Lucca, London was not a terror. Execution Dock posed no threat to a man such as himself. He would set sail for England at once except for the misfortune of being held in Maracaibo on charges of heresy.

He frowned as his quill underlined carefully chosen words in the forbidden black book authorized by James I of England in 1611, a book that had belonged to the viscount. When his own Bible had been confiscated and burned as heretical, he'd managed to conceal the viscount's, and this he intended to turn over to Baret.

Lucca smiled wearily. The Bible would be the least likely book that pirates would open to read, thus missing the information they sought on the whereabouts of the viscount. He had chosen the section in the Acts of the Apostles where Paul was in a storm on the Adriatic.

A faint sound caught his attention. He held his quill poised in silence.

Did it come from below in the courtyard? Perhaps Baret grew impatient. He must hurry. He hesitated a moment longer, his ear tuned to the slightest sound. He glanced toward the closed door. All remained silent in the villa.

Swiftly now he wrapped the Bible in a piece of cloth and tied it with a leather strap. He set it aside to write a letter—

one that would only be a decoy to plant false information for the enemies of the viscount and Baret. He wrote:

> *And so, your lordship, how the infamous scoundrel named Levasseur came to discover my whereabouts here in Maracaibo, when I was certain my situation was such that I could never again contact you, is a mystery to me.*
>
> *Yet I shall not divulge the information they so strenuously seek to anyone except you, the viscount's fair son. The words you wish to hear are best left to a face-to-face meeting, whereupon I shall tell you all the known truth of where the treasure of the Prince Philip is located.*
>
> *But it is my sad duty to report to you that your beloved father, the Viscount Royce Buckington, is dead—*

Lucca's quill dropped from his fingers. His head jerked toward the door. Rushing footsteps sounded in the outer corridor!

He struggled to his feet, tipping the chair in his haste. His jaw clamped, and he gritted his teeth against the stabbing pain in his crippled body as he sought to hurry.

He snatched the Bible and stuffed it inside his tunic, then attempted to reach the window to drop the half-finished letter into the courtyard.

The wooden door crashed open. He caught a glimpse of a Spanish uniform as he reached for the window.

"Stop, heretic! The letter in his hand, Marcos! Take it! Bring it to the viceroy and the English lord, Felix Buckington!"

Below in the courtyard, waiting in the shadow of the olive trees, Baret came alert. Shouts sounded within the villa— from Lucca's chamber.

Lucca! Then was the letter too, with its precious information, in the hands of the soldiers? Was it possible to rescue him? He must!

He stopped. Another sound, this one from behind him.

Baret whirled, and with a whisper his blade lifted from its scabbard, the point coming up and reflecting in the moonlight.

A Spanish captain stood illuminated, his sword sheathed. For a moment Baret forgot that he was donned in Spanish uniform.

Evidently the captain suspected nothing and spoke to him in rapid Spanish.

Captain de Francisca thought him to be a guard by the name of Marcos, who had been on duty all evening.

If that were true, then where *was* this guard named Marcos?

Perhaps he was with the soldiers in Lucca's room. How many soldiers were there? Could he find out without arousing suspicion? Somewhere in the garden Erik also waited, and Levasseur . . .

Baret's own Spanish rolled from his tongue smoothly like oil. *"Capitan!* Why do I stand here doing nothing to assist in the battle? Should I not strengthen the hands of my comrades inside the heretic's chamber?"

The captain looked at him with contempt. "Battle? The old one is bent with disease. The order to put him to death is nothing. It has come from the English ambassador."

The English ambassador! Why would any Englishman wish the viceroy to have Lucca put to death?

"Kill him? Is he not to be brought to Cadiz for the Inquisitors?"

"You ask too many questions, Marcos."

"The English heretic is wily. And so are his friends. Who can trust them?"

"The Englishman Lord Felix Buckington has sent word from Jamaica. Lucca is to be put to death."

Felix. Naturally he would have read the letter from Charlie Maynerd before Erik had been able to retrieve it.

"Capitan, the soldiers may need my help."

"Three soldiers are enough."

He pretended shame. "You are right, *Capitan.* Three soldiers of our illustrious queen could thwart a dozen heretics. I will go guard the horses. There are many thieves loose this night."

The captain gave him an impatient look. "What is ailing you, Marcos? Pedro is on watch. What thief would steal the viceroy's horses on the lighted street?"

Four men . . . plus this captain . . . if he could continue the masquerade a little longer, perhaps . . .

He sensed the Spaniard's measured look.

"You, Marcos," came the proud voice. "How long have you waited in the courtyard?"

Was he growing suspicious?

"Only a short while, *Capitan*."

"Step forward into the moonlight."

So . . .

"As you wish, *Capitan*."

When Captain de Francisca saw Baret's slight smile and the point of his blade lifted, his swarthy face hardened, and he shouted a warning.

But before he could draw his sword, Baret landed a heavy blow to his jaw and another to his belly. The man doubled. A quick jab to the back of his neck sent the prison captain facedown onto the courtyard.

Baret stooped, unsheathed the captain's sword, and threw it into the darkened trees.

The captain's shout had alerted the soldiers inside the villa. Baret heard the clatter of their boots rushing over the flagstones. *Where are Erik and Levasseur?*

Two soldiers appeared. One ran ahead with sword drawn, while the other impatiently struggled with Lucca, dragging him along. The scholar tripped on his black robe, and the guard struck him.

That injustice fired the anger in Baret's heart. He deliberately stepped into the clearing with the moonlight falling on his Spanish uniform, the silver of his blade reflecting.

A third guard came running, not from the house but from the direction of the horses near the street. For a moment, the Spanish soldiers did nothing as they saw his uniform. *Where are the others?*

Then one man noticed their captain lying on the court and shouted, pointing at Baret, "An impostor! Take him!"

"Lucca! Quick! Away!" commanded Baret, but Lucca could do nothing more than raise himself to an elbow on the stones, a shaft of moonlight falling on his silver hair beneath the cowl.

"The Bible," he rasped. "Important . . . message . . ."

His urgent cry alerted Baret. He wondered what he meant, but there was no time to ask.

"Thy Word . . . a light . . . for your path . . ."

The soldier who had kept the horses rushed at Baret, seemingly anxious to make a name for himself.

With a swift blow and the ring of metal, Baret sent the Spaniard's sword flying from his hand to the courtyard.

Stunned, the young man gaped at his empty hand, then at Baret. There was bright fear in his eyes as he saw nothing between him and Baret's blade.

For a moment their eyes held. When Baret did not thrust him through, his look of fear turned to confusion. He stared, then backed away, stumbling over a loose cobble.

The other two soldiers were more cautious. They came at him together, their expressions grim. They would kill him if they could. It was impossible for him to take them both.

Baret could feel the heat of the night. He blinked back the sweat.

The soldier on his right lunged, but Baret coolly, deliberately, halted his thrust and fought off his rush, their Toledo steel smashing, ringing in the sultry darkness beneath the white moon. The soldier proved an excellent swordsman, no doubt taught in Seville. He shifted his feet, feinting, and came again.

Baret pressed him harder, using the fencing patterns that he had learned from Erik. *Erik! Levasseur! Where are they?*

Baret's sword point darted past his opponent's and made deadly contact. The soldier drew back, wounded, was about to lunge but was now out of position. The opening was there. Baret took it, quickly thrust, and withdrew his blade. The man slumped to his knees, holding his chest.

Baret stood grimly. Only then did he realize that death should also have claimed him this night. Why had the other soldier not run him through?

He turned and understood. The Spaniard lay sprawled on the court, unconscious—as far as Baret knew, dead. But how . . .

He looked across the courtyard and saw the young soldier that he had spared. The boy was holding a rock, which he dropped with a small thud. "We are even, *Señor*," he whispered breathlessly.

"You are a gentleman and a soldier," said Baret.

The youth was grim as he stared down at his unconscious comrade. "Perhaps I am a fool. He will waken and wonder who struck him."

"Perhaps tell him another heretic came from the trees to my aid. We took the prisoner and left."

The soldier swallowed nervously, glancing toward the street. "Please, *Señor*, be quick."

In a few strides, Baret was beside Lucca, but he was too late. Lucca was dead—the last witness to bear proof of his father's innocence. The one man who could have told him if his father yet lived and where to find him.

Baret clenched his fist and muttered his anger.

"*Señor!* I beg! Be swift to fly!" hissed the young soldier from the dark olive trees.

Baret gently touched the old man's silver hair and brought the cowl up over his head. As he did, he noticed his hand clutched against his chest. And hope sprang to life. He reached beneath Lucca's tunic and retrieved a Bible.

But where was the letter?

Desperate now, he searched Lucca but found nothing.

He wiped the sweat on his forehead across his arm and glanced about the plaza. Could the two soldiers have discovered it?

He tensed. Two? Or that Marcos! Where was he? Baret stood, gazing intently toward the villa. Was the man yet in Lucca's chamber? Why had he not come with the others? Or had he escaped to warn other guards?

"The soldier named Marcos," he asked the young soldier. "Where is he?"

"He went to report to the viceroy's captain. The old one is dead—you best leave at once, *Señor!*"

"Did Marcos carry a letter belonging to the prisoner?"

"I do not know. Perhaps he carried something—yes, a letter, I think. It will be brought to the English ambassador."

His head jerked in the direction of the street. "Horses, *Señor*, quick!"

Baret too heard them. His jaw clamped. Marcos had escaped with the letter! And the letter would end up in the hands of Felix!

A groan sounded from beneath the olive trees, and he remembered the unconscious captain.

Horses' hooves thundered over the cobbled street outside the courtyard.

Baret darted in the direction of the back wall, where olive branches overhung the street. A quick glance over his shoulder caught a glimpse of the young soldier who had aided him also making a speedy departure. At last—a Spaniard he liked. A Spaniard that did not wear the face of the despised Inquisitors.

Another groan from beneath the olive tree, and Baret disappeared over the brick wall into the dark night of Maracaibo.

He had not gone far when he saw a soldier sprawled prone in the shadows. Someone had run him through without giving him opportunity to draw his blade. Was this Marcos, who escaped with the letter from Lucca?

Heart thundering in his chest, Baret swiftly turned him over. The soldier was sorely wounded, yet still gasping for breath.

"Marcos?" he demanded.

A hoarse whisper gurgled in his throat. "*Sí*."

Baret searched thoroughly but found nothing on the man. He clutched his shoulders, whispering in Castilian. "The letter! Where is it!"

"Stolen."

Baret's dark eyes hardened. While he had been busy fighting for his life, either Erik or Levasseur had been lying in wait for Marcos. Or had there been a third man?

Had it been Erik's plan all along to make off with the letter? Then did he yet serve Felix?

He glanced down upon the dying Spaniard. *He has reaped the death planned for me*, he thought.

And the pinnace hidden in the shallows to return him to

the sloop—was it yet there now that the desired information was in hand?

What a fool I was to trust him.

There was little time! He must get to the shallows!

Once away from the courtyard, Baret melted into the dark night. Appearing in no hurry, he walked through the loiterers in the plaza to where the horses had been kept.

He had already noted several escape routes through the back alleys of the town. Soldiers were everywhere. It was crucial that the horses he had hidden behind the wall of the secluded coffee house be there. But was he not a fool to think they would be?

He quickened his pace as much as he dared.

It began to rain—big splashes wet the adobe and filled the warm moist air with the smell of thirsty dust. He lowered his Spanish hat and drew his cloak around him. As he did, his hand brushed against the Bible he had taken from Lucca. The feel of leather brought to memory the quiet, innocent years he had spent at Cambridge and the many times he had heard Sir Cecil expound the New Testament in Greek.

And thinking of those hard, disciplined years of training in Calvinistic theology caused Baret to think again of his father. With Lucca dead, the last hope of locating his father's whereabouts had also died. Before he could confront his uncle, Felix would send an assassin to kill Royce Buckington.

The warm rain drenched him without mercy.

The shops were usually open until midnight in the tropical locale but now began to close early, the stalls being boarded up against the coming storm.

He turned a corner into a narrow cobbled street with a high wall. There was a little-used postern gate, and he quickly took it to where he had tied the horses.

They were gone!

So. He was trapped in Maracaibo.

He must find a horse and make it swiftly to the shallows.

Carefully he considered his position as the wind blew strongly against him. He quickened his pace down the wet street, keeping his hat low. He approached the entrance of the Spanish coffee house. Here soldiers and merchants did their business, lingering over thick coffee and wine. He might be able to obtain a horse for the right price before news of what had happened at the villa began to circulate. But he must act at once.

The coffee house was yet open and beckoned with golden lanternlight and the sound of guitars. He entered to be greeted by the pleasant smell of hot olive oil, onions, and garlic. A rosy glow from the torches fixed in bronze wall sconces wavered on the flagstone walls. Rows of small wooden tables and chairs faced a simple platform with a single balcony, shadowed and sequestered. The tables were crowded. Amid the din came music from a group of guitar players.

Baret stayed in the outer shadows, distancing himself from the others. The doors swung open, and a group of Spanish guards burst through with hard eyes scanning the patrons. One shouted, "An enemy to the viceroy has escaped. A stranger in uniform, an Englishman. Has anyone seen him?"

Standing next to the shouting officer was the young soldier who had aided him in the courtyard. How long till he noticed Baret? Would his past friendliness continue?

Baret glanced to the side wall where the red drapes were drawn, partly concealing a flight of steps.

He felt no lack in his skills with the sword—and some would see his confidence as arrogance. But he was aware of his weaknesses too, and he knew the overwhelming odds against him, a lone man traveling through enemy territory even if on horseback—a nearly impossible journey.

In a moment the young soldier would see him. There was no choice but to make his move.

Swiftly he was gone, passing through the thick drape to where short, squat steps led upward. No one was in view. With hand on sword, he was mounting the stairs when the door at the landing flew open and a thickset woman stood there with tangled dark hair and bold eyes.

He raced up the steps and pushed past her into her room, shutting the door. He looked about for an exit. There was none.

He spoke in rapid Spanish. "The window—is there a ledge?"

She eyed him sullenly.

His mouth curved. *"Señora,* for your pristine silence, my heart—and this." He lifted his left hand, where a sapphire gleamed, and then presented it to her.

Her eyes widened with delight. She rushed to the small window and threw it open.

Baret was beside her, feeling the wind-driven rain.

She glanced toward the door. "Hurry, *Señor."*

He stepped out onto the small ledge, and the woman closed the window, snatching the drapes shut again.

The rain lashed against him as he inched his way along the narrow shelf, feeling the vines brush his face and snag his clothing, until he could climb down the wall into the alleyway. He was darting toward an adobe patio when a man appeared in the shadows with drawn sword.

Swiftly Baret unsheathed his blade.

Sir Erik Farrow stepped out. "You took long enough. I was beginning to think I must rescue you. This way."

Surprised, yet cautious, Baret looked at him.

But Erik turned and ran ahead.

Baret cast a glance backward. Soldiers had entered the narrow street. He was swiftly behind Erik.

They darted this way and that, climbing low adobe walls and rushing through yards where chickens ran squawking for cover and mangy dogs barked and snarled at their heels.

At last Erik slowed and ducked beneath a low archway into a dark street, now abandoned because of the pouring rain and increasing wind.

Two horses were concealed behind flowering shrubs. Erik grabbed the reins of one and had started to mount when Baret took firm hold of his shoulder.

"Where were you in the garden?"

Erik's fair brow arched. "Are you accusing me of treachery?"

"Only you would know. Lucca is dead. The letter stolen."

Erik's mouth hardened, and his cool gray eyes measured him. "When the skirmish broke out I was attacked by Sloane outside the wall. He was a poor swordsman but owned the strength of a bull. It took all my time and expertise with the blade to hold him off. By the time it was over, Spanish soldiers were swarming everywhere. I trailed you to the coffee house."

Could Baret believe him?

In the moonlight peeping from behind the dark clouds, Erik wore a dour smile. "Come, your lordship, I could have attacked you in the alley if I were working against you. The letter is stolen, the treasure remains a secret. Yet I have brought your horse. For what reason would I do so except friendship?"

Baret believed him. His hand dropped from Erik's shoulder, and he mounted, turning the reins to ride.

"Levasseur has the letter," said Erik.

"Maybe not."

"Who then?"

"Someone serving Felix is my guess."

Erik mounted, frowning.

"You said Sloane was a poor swordsman."

"He is dead."

A moment later they were riding swiftly toward the shallows.

The great freshwater Lake Maracaibo, nourished by a score of rivers from the snowcapped ranges that surround it on both sides, was 120 miles in length and almost the same distance across at its widest point. It was in the shape of a great bottle, having its neck toward the sea.

Baret and Erik dismounted, walking cautiously forward, swords in hand. They hesitated, listening for any human movement but hearing only the sounds of nature. Baret stepped out, walking to the edge of the small cove, unusable by any vessel except the shallowest craft.

The rough wind-tossed water curled its foaming lips upon the shore where he stood in the darkness, gazing out toward the shadowy hulk of the sloop. It was still there.

Then from the concealing trees and vines, footsteps crushed across the leaves, and a moment later Levasseur appeared, his lean face in a rage. The two French pirates with him looked sullen and suspicious.

"Lucca is dead! The letter stolen! Where have *you* been?" demanded Levasseur.

Baret exchanged glances with Erik, and he could see that Erik was thinking the same thing he was. Levasseur's fury gave him away. He did not have the letter.

"Where were you when the Spanish soldiers attacked in the courtyard?" demanded Baret.

Levasseur threw up a hand in exasperation. "You take me for a fool? When I saw Lucca was dead and you fought the soldiers, I searched him for the letter, of course!"

"You were there when two soldiers fought me and did not come to my aid?"

"Monsieur!" He winced as though Baret's charge were of no account. "The letter was not on Lucca—only a Bible. I then climbed the lattice to Lucca's room to search. Soldiers came, and I barely escaped with my life! I have waited here until nearly trapped! A storm comes!"

"And if you wish to live, my captain," gritted Baret, "you will be wise enough to silence your tongue. The Spanish garrison is alerted to our presence and not far behind."

Levasseur looked back over his shoulder, then scrambled after the crewmen who had already boarded the small boat and were putting muscle to the oars.

Baret's eyes hardened as he looked out toward the strait between the islands of Viglias and Palomas, opening to the sea. The sloop waited in darkness to slip away unseen and bring them to the *Venture*.

He thought of Lucca. Now that the respected scholar was gone, he had no witnesses to prove his father's innocence. And unless he recovered the information from the missing letter, he too would be wanted by the Admiralty.

Felix, he thought. There was no choice now but to confront Felix. Lucca's letter would have been brought to the English ambassador and sent on to his uncle. But by the time he returned to Port Royal, Felix would have already learned the news of Lucca's death.

There was nothing more to do now but rendezvous with Morgan at Tortuga.

34

THE PIRATE
STRONGHOLD OF TORTUGA

Tortuga! So this was my place of birth! thought Emerald, overwhelmed with dismay as she looked about her.

Arriving at the island that headquartered the Brethren of the Coast aboard her father's ship, the *Madeleine,* so named after her mother, Emerald came to shore with him and trusted members of his crew in a cockboat. Then she had been ushered by him into a palanquin and carried by four stout members of his crew into the island stronghold, her father walking beside her, wearing scabbard and pistols.

She had never see him in this role before and frowned a little, for he exuded much of the same reckless manner as Captain Baret Foxworth. She was surprised that so many of the pirates knew and hailed him from where they congregated on the sandy beach or on the boardwalks of the wooden taverns.

Emerald scanned the pirates and buccaneers that milled about, drinking or gambling or snoozing in hammocks slung between palm trees, fanned by mainly female African slaves, although she saw many half-castes as well and some full-blooded whites, either French or English.

The pirates were not greatly different from those she had seen in Port Royal, perhaps only more ruthless, if such a thing were possible. There were French and Dutch and, of course, English. All looked to her to be a rowdy lot, an untrustworthy band, wearing head scarves or wide-brimmed hats. All were decked with gold or silver, some with the largest pearls she had ever laid eyes on. Their clothing as usual had been confiscated from Spanish galleons or was French in gaudy style.

She saw lace, bright satins and velvets, feathers, and cuffed boots—yet there was no doubt in her mind that these were rugged men. However, if she believed them to be untrustworthy, her father seemed to have no alarm at bringing her, and this in itself caused her to wonder.

"They have their laws," he said. "The Orders and Articles of the Brethren of the Coast are a strict code that we can count on. There's not a one of them who'd break them lightly. And if he did, he'd answer to the hierarchy—same as any civilized country," he said with a twinkle in his eye that made her laugh.

"I'm not so certain I believe you," she told him.

"I'm counting on the Articles," he said. "Ah, yes, little one, I'd not have brought you here if I didn't know what I was doing. Only a short time and you'll be on your way to London—and yes, you can take Minette with you. Now that Jonah be dead, God bless him, and Mathias too, all you have is each other. After I've seen to your bright future, it will be up to you to see to Minette's. And don't think you won't have much say-so in the matter, for you will."

Bright future? She nearly laughed and would have, except for a despairing glance that told her that he was convinced of his plan, whatever it might be.

With Minette seated beside her in the palanquin, Emerald looked about as they neared what looked to be an abandoned ship built on a high foundation and surrounded by trees and shrubs.

"And to think we was both born here," whispered Minette, her eyes curious as she gazed out from beneath her hooded cloak, leaning closely against Emerald.

"We won't be here long," Emerald encouraged her. "We'll be sent to England, he says. With me not daring to show my face at Foxemoore after what's happened, I shall be glad enough to go to Berrymeade."

But Minette looked sorrowful, even frightened. "That's all good for you, Emerald, but what will your Uncle John Clark have to say about me being there on his farm?"

Emerald pushed the troubling thought aside. "They'll accept you too. They'll have to," she said firmly. "If they don't, I won't stay either. You're my cousin just as much as Lavender is, and I'll see to it you're treated so."

Minette glanced at her doubtfully. "First thing they'll do is stare at me. 'Her mother was from Africa,' they'll say. 'How come she's not dark—'"

"Hush." And Emerald laid a comforting hand on her arm. "Remember, my reputation is also in shreds. We'll need to face the future together and with our Lord as our Shepherd—surely He has good plans for us. His Word is a light for our feet, a balm for our spirits. Try to look at our future as an . . . an adventure," she said bravely. "One that God has planned for our good."

Minette sighed. "Maybe. But I know what those English folk will say about me . . . about us—"

"Look! We're stopping. This must be the gathering place for all the buccaneers."

"They look like plain pirates to me—mean—and they'd as soon run away with us as sweep off their hats!"

Emerald agreed, but hoping to give Minette courage, she put on a brave facade.

A hand-carved sign read "Sweet Turtle" in French, English, and another language she could not read. The meeting place was two-story and looked to be made of pieces of ships, mainly Spanish galleons, with ornate wainscoting and tapestries hung on its high walls.

As she entered with Minette, following after Sir Karlton, Emerald saw a huge room having many long wooden tables that glowed with wide candles in oval bowls. A motley group of seafarers and wenches loitered about, some gambling and drinking, others eating. All looked dangerous and shrewd of eye.

A heavy-link chain was looped across the ceiling, holding French chandeliers better fit for the Louvre in Paris. Fat candles gleamed from within and shone down upon pirated urns and vessels.

Someone had hung a gilt-edged portrait of the king of France on one wall, and, not to be outdone, another had gotten hold of a haughty portrait of King Charles dressed in velvet and pearls, a faintly sardonic smile on his mouth. There was also a portrait of some admiral who looked to be from Holland, sword in hand.

As rum flowed into mugs, cards and dice were shuffled and clicked. Merry music filled her ears as a group of men played instruments and a wench donned in calico drawers and tunic did an Irish jig. Bright plumed parrots sat bored in gold perches on the walls. Swords, pistols, and ammunition were everywhere. A fire burned in an open hearth where several men were roasting some manner of meat. There were stacked barrels along one side of the wide room. On the other side, a double flight of wooden steps went up to the next floor.

It was to these steps that Sir Karlton brought Emerald and Minette, as a few friendly shouts of greeting were called to him and curious eyes followed her.

Later, in the room she shared with her cousin, she learned that the pirates already knew who she was and that the word was out that she was to become a "high-born wench," a lass already claimed.

Why would they think this? There must be some news about her that she did not know. And she had been puzzled since first arriving on her father's ship, because she had expected him to be very upset with her. To her amazement he had been in a pleasant mood.

When she started to go into her long, prepared discourse on what had happened and why she had thought to marry Jamie and leave Port Royal, he had hushed her to silence with a benign smile and a fatherly kiss of acceptance on her forehead.

"Now, now, little one, your father is knowing all about your poor judgment. He's already forgiven you. And the Almighty has looked well over your mistakes by His grace. Matters have turned out for the best."

Then he had smiled cheerfully, setting her down in his cabin to sip "good hot English tea, because you'll be soon sipping it in style at Buckington House. Nae fear of that. Ah, yes, matters could not have turned out better, so I'm thinking."

She had wondered then and still did so now as she loitered at the open window in their small room above the meeting hall. They had been in Tortuga going on three weeks, and when Emerald asked her father about the delay, he dismissed her questions with no concern.

"No matter. Your father knows what he's doing. You've not been accosted or treated with insult, have you?"

"No, Papa, but we're bored with the room and—"

"Whisk, now, there'll be none of that. You'll both behave yourselves until the time comes. What did you do with the fine cloth and sewing things I brought you?"

"We're putting them to use, and the satin is so lovely, Papa. And Minette is delighted with the prospect of some new frocks, only—"

"Only what? You're impatient to be on your way to London, are you? Well, that's to be expected. Patience, little one. The negotiations of your father need a careful and wise hand indeed. But things be going well." And he had chuckled over some musing of his that he would not share.

As Emerald drew a chair to the open window and sat resting her elbows on the sill, the sun was setting on Tortuga, and the music and raucous noisemaking were still underway below. Her father had gone down to the beach to see to some "business," and as usual she and Minette were under strict guard by Zeddie and a member of her father's crew.

"I don't understand him," she murmured, looking out at the blue-green waters. "I would have expected him to be outraged over what happened. And he wasn't even angry with me about planning to marry Jamie."

She stared thoughtfully at the sun dipping into the Caribbean and the sky above turning a bright pink-orange. The palms were dark swaying silhouettes, and the breeze was pleasant as it came against her.

She had donned a simple white muslin frock with Holland lace at cuffs and throat, and her dark hair was drawn back into lustrous curls that sloped down her neck and back.

Minette sat in the midst of the bed, sewing the blue satin frock, yards of Holland lace strewn out beside her. Her waist-length amber hair tumbled in a mass of wafflelike ringlets about her shoulders.

"He treated me like a slave," she murmured to herself.

Emerald scowled, for the remark was no answer to her own musings about her father's reaction to her situation.

"My father?" she asked in disbelief.

Minette looked up, her eyes wide. "Oh, no, Emerald, not Uncle Karlton. Him," she said coolly. "That conceited friend of the viscount. Remember him? The man we met on the road?"

"Oh," said Emerald, realizing that Minette was still talking about Erik, Baret's buccaneer friend. "Well, I wouldn't let his boorish manners hurt you. What do you expect? They're both rogues!"

Emerald wearily leaned her elbows on the windowsill and looked out to sea, a strange, unknowable ache in her heart. She watched the dozens of sloops and brigantines all anchored, their masts gleaming in the twilight.

"I wonder what England will be like," she mused. "My father's right about one thing. I do desperately want an education. And to learn all the right behavior and customs. But more than that, Minette, do you know what I want for the future?"

"To be a great lady?"

"Well, yes, that too, I suppose—but I want to attend the Christian meetings in London where men of profound understanding are able to teach the Scriptures like Mathias. And someday I want to put that knowledge to use—maybe doing what Mathias did."

"They'll never accept you at Foxemoore now. You can be certain Lavender has spread vile tales about you to everyone. If you're going to have a singing school, you better open one up in London."

Suddenly Emerald straightened and drew in a breath.

Minette looked at her, alert. "What is it?"

When Emerald didn't answer, Minette scampered from the bed and sped across the room to stand beside her at the open window.

"What's wrong? What is it? Oh! Why—isn't that Lord Buckington?"

"Yes," murmured Emerald, staring below. "It is. What's *he* doing here?"

"I don't know. Do you suppose he knows Uncle Karlton's here—and us too?"

Emerald's hand tightened on the drape as she watched several buccaneers walk up from the beach, garbed in royal finery and fancy hats with plumes. She recognized the dark good looks of Baret immediately and the contrasting fair appearance of Erik Farrow.

"Why—it's *him*," said Minette, a strange note in her voice.

"Yes," murmured Emerald a bit coolly. "And they fit the manner of the reckless men below with the worst of them!"

As though he felt her narrowing gaze, Baret looked up at the open window where she remained, leaning on her elbows. The men were just below the window now, and he stopped. With a smile that could be no less than a smirk, he doffed his hat with a deep bow.

Emerald drew back from the window, angry at herself because her heart pounded. She had hoped she would never see him again, least of all on Tortuga!

"He didn't bow to me," said Minette a bit crossly. "That Sir Farrow is a rude man, Emerald. He's no gentleman at all—but I s'pect he would be to a real lady," she added more quietly.

"What are they doing here?" murmured Emerald. "Oh, I wish we had set sail yesterday!"

"Vapors! Uncle Karlton is coming—and he looks angry. Oh, Emerald, something is dreadfully wrong! He's carrying his weapons!"

Emerald's heart pulsated in her throat. Her father strode toward the Sweet Turtle wearing a dark scowl, his baldric slung over a shoulder. It was then she saw that Baret had stopped and turned to face him.

"You blackguard!" shouted Karlton. "So you've shown yourself, have you? 'Tis about time! I've been waiting for you to dare!"

"Well, Karlton," came Baret's pleasant greeting. "So you've rendezvoused on Tortuga with the rest of us. When's Morgan due?"

Emerald was puzzled and frightened all at once. Evidently Baret had taken her father's gruff greeting as a jest, but Emerald knew him better. He was angry.

Her father stood feet apart, scowling, his brows lowered. "You'll answer for shaming my daughter, Buckington! I'll have your head for this, or you'll have mine. But we'll not leave Tortuga till it's over. I vow it."

Emerald's heart seemed to stop.

"Perhaps we best talk inside, Karlton. I am sure I can explain everything to your satisfaction."

"Satisfaction? I'll split your innards and leave them for the gulls to peck! Inside, he says!" her father shouted at the gathering Brotherhood. "After the man has sullied my fair lass? It's a duel, Buckington! Fair and square. And we'll be letting the Brotherhood decide when and how."

"Now wait a minute, Karlton—"

"We'll meet inside all right. I demand it." He turned to the pirates. "The sea lawyer, where is he? Where's old Tobias?"

"Inside," said a black-haired pirate wearing a bright red coat and black hat. "He's digging up the Orders and Articles of the Brethren of the Coast this minute." He leered at Baret. "You heard 'im, Foxworth. Harwick say we best 'ave a meetin'."

As they walked into the Sweet Turtle, Emerald whipped about to face the astounded Minette.

"I knew it," whispered Emerald. "Papa's good mood was a ruse. That's why he's been keeping us here. He knew Captain Buckington would be at Tortuga until Henry Morgan arrived."

"What will you do?" breathed Minette. "Uncle Karlton was madder than a wet parrot!"

"I've got to stop them, of course. If there's trouble, what chance does Papa have?"

She rushed to the door and opened it, looking out onto the narrow walkway that overlooked the wide room below. She could already see the men entering.

Zeddie, who had been snoozing by the wooden steps leading down, saw her and, straightening his periwig, stood up. The crewman at the bottom of the steps also stood and looked up at her.

"You can't go down, m'gal," said Zeddie. "Sir Karlton's orders."

"I must! Don't try to stop me, Zeddie!" She brushed past him, hurrying down the stairs, holding up her skirts to keep from tripping, but midway down she was stopped by the burly crewman.

Blocked from her descent, Emerald faced the room, her hands gripping the rail.

At a large table the buccaneers had gathered, some seated, others standing about the outer walls, looking on. A grizzled old man, who looked more of a pirate than a scholar, was seated at the head of the table with several parchments in front of him. He put on a brown hat with a bright ostrich plume.

Her father had entered, and so had Baret, who appeared bewildered and impatient all at once. He looked up to the steps, and his gaze swept her.

She lifted her head with an attempt at dignity, but she blushed. Her father was making more of a spectacle of her than anything she might have faced at Foxemoore!

"I demand a duel." Her father's clear, robust voice bounced off the plank walls.

Baret looked away from Emerald to confront Sir Karlton on the other side of the room.

Emerald found her voice. "Papa, no! Please! This is absurd!"

"Absurd, is it? Is that what you call it?" And Sir Karlton strode toward the steps to look up at her. "Will you have this scoundrel abduct you from the wharf and make off with you like a common wench?"

"Papa—" Emerald felt her face turn hot. Her hands formed into fists at the sides of her pristine white skirts. Her eyes swerved to Baret, who now appeared calm and cool, and a sardonic smile played on his mouth as he watched her, then Karlton.

How can he be amused? she thought, horrified.

Karlton turned back to Baret, hand on his sword hilt. "Well, you black-hearted scamp, what have you to say for yourself?"

Baret's voice came smooth and hinting of cynicism. "What would you have me say for myself, Captain Harwick? I am most certain you have this all planned out."

"Planned out? Before the Brotherhood, I demand you

answer me! Did you not abduct my fair and comely lass from Port Royal against her wishes?"

Baret folded his arms across his chest. He glanced up at Emerald. "Aye, I did. Honor forces me to confess."

"And did you not bring her aboard the *Regale* for nigh unto three weeks, keeping her in your cabin?"

Emerald jerked her head away, gripping the railing.

"I did."

"And did you not buy her from the scamp she had intended to marry, James Maynerd, brother of poor Charlie hung at Port Royal by your uncle, Felix Buckington?"

There was silence. Slowly Emerald looked at Baret.

"I bought her for twenty thousand pieces of eight."

"Ah . . ." came Sir Karlton's voice, reeking of accusation. "I demand a duel, Buckington. For the honor of my daughter. And I'll have your heart cut from you and tossed to the sharks for this!"

Baret stood staring at him, his smile gone now. He measured Karlton, who stood unrelenting. "Karlton, there is no need. I return your daughter fairly and with not so much as a strand of hair touched by me or any of my crew. If you'd simply calm down and let us speak alone in private I can explain—"

"No, Buckington. It will be settled here and now in public before the Brotherhood." He turned toward the head buccaneering official, who still sat at the table with the parchments spread before him.

"How does it read, Tobias?"

Tobias drummed his fingers on the table. "As a sea lawyer I pledge you there's nothing in the Articles against you dueling Captain Foxworth for the honor of your daughter."

"What's the law on it?" demanded Sir Karlton.

"Wait a minute," said Baret. "According to the Articles of the Brotherhood a captain is privileged to do with his prize as he pleases. And I please to return Captain Harwick's daughter to him."

"On the other hand," said Tobias, picking up the parchment, "prisoners taken at sea are usually sent home in good condition and worth their weight in ransom."

"I relinquish the ransom," said Baret with a scowl. "And I relinquish the twenty thousand pieces of eight—already divided up between Maynerd and the crew of the *Venture*."

Sir Karlton took a step toward Baret. "And you're forgetting something, Buckington. According to the Orders and Articles of the Brotherhood, I've a right at duel for my grievance without interference from others."

Emerald stood horrified as her father took off his wide-brimmed hat and smashed it down on the table. He unsheathed his sword.

"Papa!" she cried. "No! He didn't hurt me! I vow it! He's telling the truth!"

"Nae," he growled. "A duel, Captain Buckington."

"You heard him," said Tobias to the buccaneers. "Give room! Move the tables back!"

Emerald struggled to get past the crewman who continued to block her way, but he wouldn't budge.

"Then a duel you will have," Baret said. "But to draw blood only."

"Nae, indeed, but to the death it shall be."

Emerald ceased her struggle, her wide eyes swerving to look first at her pale father, then to Baret, who stood gravely. He seemed to judge her father's seriousness and, as if now believing it to be genuine, folded his arms again.

"You are not a fool, Karlton. I could kill you. You know that."

"I do."

"And yet you will go through with this?"

"Aye. To the bitter end. Naught too much a price to pay for the pristine honor of my daughter, Emerald."

She saw Baret's eyes narrow under his lashes. His jaw tensed. The silence grew in the room as all eyes were on the two men. Emerald's knees were weak. Surely, oh, surely! All this must be some hideous nightmare. An ironic joke?

Yet her father was deadly serious. She could see as much. And from Baret's expression she now knew that he realized it as well.

"And if I refuse?" said Baret.

Sir Karlton met his gaze evenly, refusing to give an inch.

"Then you'll be stripped of all buccaneering honor. You'll be banned from Tortuga."

Emerald's gaze went past Baret to the doorway where a handful of pirates had entered, tall lean Frenchmen with a challenging way about them. She stiffened as one of them approached. *Levasseur!*

Her cousin's face was sullen, and his gaze angrily took in the scene, then fixed upon Emerald on the steps. His shrewd black eyes flicked then to Baret.

"And what is my alternative to an honorable duel?" came Baret's voice.

Emerald noticed that Baret was now smiling slightly, as if he understood something that she completely overlooked. But the next words spoken by her father brought her clear understanding.

"You will marry my daughter, Captain Buckington."

"No!" Emerald found her voice saying loudly and with dignity. "I will not marry him, Papa!"

"Silence, lass, 'tis your father who will arrange your future."

"And if I marry her," said Baret smoothly, "will you end this duel to the death?"

Sir Karlton smiled for the first time. "If you marry her, you'll be my son-in-law now, won't you? Now, how could a father be going to duel his own son, I ask?"

Laughter began, quietly at first, and then, as it began to dawn on the pirates what Karlton had intended all along, the laughter turned uproarious.

Baret turned and looked up at her, a dark brow lifting.

Emerald glared down at him. "No," she said, but her voice sounded feeble in the laugher.

Baret walked toward the steps, and a smile formed on his mouth, a sardonic lazy smile, she thought, blushing furiously at this despicable scene.

He swept off his hat and bowed. "I accept your terms, Karlton. I will, on my honor, marry your daughter."

A roar went up.

She caught her breath.

"On one condition, however." He turned toward Karlton, who was having a difficult time masking a triumphant smile.

"What condition?" asked her father.

Baret looked up at Emerald and gestured easily. "That my betrothed go to London first to attend to schooling and social customs, which she lacks. After all, gentlemen," he said to the room full of buccaneers. "I am a viscount."

Again there was laughter.

"And a foul and wicked pirate too," came a good-natured gibe.

"Granted," said Baret indifferently. "But I shall not marry her in Tortuga. After all, the lady deserves more than a haggle of pirates apt to swing at Execution Dock for her wedding audience. Surely you agree, Karlton?"

"Aye, indeed, your lordship! Most heartily agree! To London it is! To school and fair social graces, and then to your side."

"I accept," said Baret. He looked at Emerald, and as she stared at him, aghast, his dark eyes challenged her. "Well, madam? Do you accept your destiny fairly enough?"

Emerald's throat was dry, and no words would come. Surely he didn't mean it—he couldn't—what of Lavender?— what of her lowly position and all the horrid gossip?

"She accepts, your lordship," came Sir Karlton's firm voice. "It is settled. I give you Emerald my daughter to be your betrothed, to be married at the fitting time." He smiled and rubbed his palms together.

Suddenly someone was pushing through the throng. Levasseur, wearing a lean smile on his swarthy face, confronted Baret.

"It is not settled yet, Monsieur Foxworth."

The laughter subsided into a deadly hush, and the buccaneers moved away, leaving Baret and Levasseur alone in the middle of the room.

Levasseur stood arrogantly, one hand on his hip, the other sweeping back his cloak. "You have betrayed me once too often, monsieur. First with Lucca, now with my cousin Emerald. I will yet find the treasure of the *Prince Philip,* for I call you a liar and thief! And added to this effrontery you would also take the girl from me. Not so!" He whipped out his rapier and stepped back. "Harwick will not duel to the death, monsieur, but I will."

"No, Rafael," called Emerald. *"No!"*

Levasseur smiled. "Did you not offer to duel for her aboard the *Regale* before you offered twenty thousand pieces of eight?"

Baret angrily ripped off rings and jewels and tossed them on a table. "For thirty thousand pieces of eight!"

"To the death," said Levasseur.

"As you wish." Baret drew his sword.

And Emerald gave a cry.

"Zeddie! Take her to her room," Baret called up.

Emerald struggled to free herself from Zeddie's grasp as both he and the crewman guarding her came to whisk her back up the steps to her room.

Minette loitered at the open doorway, pale and shaking. "God help them," she breathed.

Emerald tried to break free, but Zeddie held her.

"Now, m'gal, be the lady you are and sit tight. There's naught a thing you can do now. None of us can. It's been movin' to this moment since they set eyes on each other aboard ship. There's no stopping it."

Dazed and shaken, Emerald sank into the chair, head in hands, as Minette hurried to solace her.

The door locked behind Zeddie and the crewman.

"Oh, Minette! A duel! Oh, this is truly the most horrid moment of my life!"

"Least his lordship agreed to it. That says plenty to me. I'm thinking now that he wants you more'n Lavender. Think of it," she breathed. "Why, Emerald! If he marries you one day—why, you'll be a countess."

Emerald groaned. "Do you think I care about that? What if he's killed? Levasseur is an excellent swordsman!"

"And so's the viscount, so they say."

Emerald fell to her knees to begin urgent prayers, tears welling in her eyes.

35

THE DUEL

The buccaneers withdrew from the tables to line the walls, and silence filled the gaming room.

Baret removed his hat and outer jacket—as did the pirate—and Erik came to take them. He was poised, but there was tension in his face. "Caution, your lordship. He is quick and deadly. Permit me to cause an argument with him that I may take your place."

"I fight my own quarrels, Erik. You should know that by now. But your friendship is worthy of remembrance. This quarrel is over Emerald, and it must be settled between myself and Levasseur."

Erik was grave but said no more. Taking Baret's hat and jacket, he stepped back.

Baret unsheathed his blade. He had no desire to kill Levasseur, but the man was leaving him no choice. It was kill or be killed. And there was no mistaking that the pirate was an excellent swordsman.

And now he faced Levasseur.

"To the death," Levasseur repeated.

Levasseur came toward him with confidence, an arrogant smile on his thin mouth. "I was always the better swordsman, monsieur. You play the fool."

"A man's boast often leaves him in an embarrassing situation, Levasseur," said Baret and began with care, for he knew the Frenchman's reputation.

Levasseur turned Baret's blade, but he parried the blow, and for an instant he was out of position. Baret might have killed him then, but he stepped back.

The pirate, briefly humiliated, turned color.

"So soon?" Baret taunted. "Is your reputation all boast, Captain Levasseur?"

Levasseur came at him with French fury, and Baret was then fighting for his life. Desperately at times, almost wildly, he fought off the pirate's rushes.

"Ah!" cried Levasseur jubilantly, nicking Baret's wrist, then narrowly missing his throat. "Come, then, Englishman!" And wearing a scornful smile, he moved in steadily.

Suddenly Baret shifted his feet, feinting as Erik had taught him.

Levasseur reacted quickly according to pattern, and Baret's sword point made contact.

Levasseur drew back, and Baret moved in. His slashed wrist was bleeding, and he worried that it would make his grip slippery.

Around them the buccaneers could no longer keep silent at the fever pitch of the swordplay. Up and down the room they fought, and the buccaneers were upping their ante and throwing pieces of eight on the table as they gambled over who would win.

Levasseur was a wiry man, apparently full of boundless energy. But Baret had trained long and hard, and he could see signs of exhaustion beginning to show in the Frenchman's face. He saw as well that Levasseur was unfamiliar with the tactics he had learned from Erik. Baret wanted the man to taste defeat, to savor humiliation, and he pressed him harder. Coolly, deliberately, he began to teach Levasseur what he did not know.

"You bore me, Levasseur."

Sweat beaded the Frenchman's brow, and his face paled, but his black eyes flashed with hatred. He lunged, but Baret turned the blade and wounded his arm.

Enough, thought Baret.

Levasseur's sword arm was weak now, and as Baret feinted, the pirate was too slow to parry. Baret could have run him through but with a ringing blow struck the sword from his hand. It clattered across the floor out of reach as Levasseur lost his footing.

A cheer went up from the buccaneers.

"Kill him," someone shouted.

"Run the Frenchman through," another challenged.

Baret walked over to Levasseur, who stared up at him, exhausted and beaten.

"So run me through, monsieur!"

Baret was grave as he wiped the sweat from his forehead. "It is enough, Levasseur. Do you admit I have won the right to speak for Emerald?"

Levasseur gritted. "You have won. But may your way be cursed!"

Baret's mouth turned grimly.

Then unexpectedly someone rushed through the door, shouting.

"*War!* England and Holland are at war—and France has sided with the Dutch! *To arms! To arms!*"

Baret's eyes met Levasseur's, whose gaze narrowed. "So, then, monsieur! What will *you* do!"

Baret stepped back, and Hob rushed forward with a cloth to clean his blade. Then Baret sheathed the weapon.

"Go," he said to Levasseur.

Levasseur stared up at him, clearly surprised yet refusing to show gratitude. He managed to get to his feet as members of his sullen French crew came to his aid, bringing his sword. Levasseur turned arrogantly and walked out the door followed by his crewmen.

War . . .

The duel was already forgotten. The roomful of buccaneers drifted away, soberly discussing the conflict and whose side they would fight on. Among the buccaneers there was little anger toward Holland, but rather staunch loyalty among the Protestants, be they English, Dutch, or French. And the thought of attacking Dutch ships was met with reticence.

Left to himself now, Baret sat down. His wrist continued to bleed.

Sir Karlton smiled grimly and joined him. "Well done, Baret, my son. I am grieved that I had to place it upon you. 'Twas not my first thought to do so."

"I would never have fought you, Karlton. But Levasseur —he would not have been content otherwise."

His men moved aside, and someone pushed through the throng. He masked his surprise as he saw Emerald, her anxious gaze scanning him, centering upon the blood. Baret took satisfaction in the look of anguish that came to her eyes.

"You are wounded, m'lord!" she breathed.

Erik Farrow, Sir Karlton, and Hob exchanged subdued glances. Then, as though on cue, they drifted away, followed by the rest of Baret's crew, leaving them alone.

Emerald had brought clean white cloth and wine to pour on the wound, and she knelt before him. He extended his wrist and saw her wince. He watched her, drinking from the flask as she attended him.

It was quiet in the large room, except for the voices outside discussing the war.

Her eyes lifted to his, and he saw faint embarrassment mingled with something else. There was a glow in her warm eyes, a lovely flush to her cheeks. He took in her hair, the lovely contour of her face.

"You—you need not keep your bargain," she whispered. "I understand it was a task of honor—that you fought my cousin to spare me from his claim. And my father!" Her blush deepened into one of exasperation. "It was a sorely evil trick he played upon you. Demanding you duel him to death or marry me! He did so knowing you would not harm him, forcing you into obliging his unreasonable request. And I . . . well . . . I want you to know that I am not so bold as to think you meant it, seeing how you are a viscount and I am only—" She stopped.

He watched her, wondering at his own boldness to have made such a commitment, wondering over the mixture of odd feelings that stirred like the restless sea in his heart.

"The commitment was unjustly forced from you," she repeated.

His mouth turned wryly. "You underestimate me, Emerald. I am not a man who allows himself to vow lightly."

He unwillingly thought of Lavender. Irritation set in. He knew it was wrong to take advantage of the girl before him.

"I have every intention of making good. A bargain is a bargain."

Shaken, Emerald grew more confused by the glint of warmth in his dark eyes. She swallowed. "I—I would not

402

marry a man because of a bargain, sir, even if he did risk his life to spare me marriage to a pirate."

She thought she noticed a spark of irritation.

"Nevertheless," he said, standing, "I have not only bought you from a pirate but fought another for you. Your father and I have made a bargain. It is now a matter of honor. And you have very little to say about it."

Startled, she caught her breath and stood to her feet. The challengelike statement left her not only bewildered but strangely hurt.

"Have you forgotten your vow to Lavender, m'lord?"

She saw his jaw tense.

"I have not forgotten," he stated. "We'll not discuss that now. You'll be sent to England as I agreed upon with your father. I have a war to fight." He added, "A few years of growing up will benefit you." He picked up his jacket and placed his hat on his head. "I shall be in touch with you in London."

Emerald thought herself already quite mature. She watched him, offended, smarting beneath the businesslike attitude. And yet there had been that earlier moment when he had seemed vulnerable to her. Had she only imagined that? Or *did* he care? Was it possible?

But what of Lavender? Was he choosing of his own accord to break his engagement and marry her instead? She wondered, but she dare not consider for long.

His distant attitude remained, and she found herself matching it.

"Is there anything else, m'lord Buckington, before I leave for England?"

A slight smile showed. The change in his eyes caused her breath to pause.

Sir Erik Farrow appeared at the doorway. "Pardon my interruption, Lord Buckington, but Henry Morgan has arrived."

Baret turned to face him, and she could see his alertness. "Yes?"

"The governor of Jamaica has issued letters of marque to attack the Dutch settlements in the West Indies. Morgan's own uncle will be leading a force against the Dutch-held island of Statia. He bids you come to the gathering of captains aboard his ship. Will you be joining him?"

Emerald could see that the thought of war with Holland troubled Baret. She thought of his mother's ancestry.

"Give me a minute longer," he called to Erik, who went out, and Baret turned back toward her.

"You will fight against Holland?" she asked dubiously.

He frowned. "I vowed to my grandfather. I am, after all, obligated to King Charles."

She said nothing, distressed by the thought of war. She tried not to look at him, thinking that it would be perhaps three years before she would see him again if he did carry through on his bargain.

He seemed to read her thoughts. "You will have much to keep you busy in London. I've spoken to Sir Cecil. He will see you have the best schooling and training. And there is Jette." His eyes searched her face. "I understand he attended the singing school your uncle began."

She nodded. "Mathias taught him well."

"And you helped?"

She felt a small surge of pride at having been involved in the honorable work during her years on Foxemoore.

"It was a cause Mathias lived for, died for. I have his unfinished work with me and will bring it to England."

"A noble beginning. Jette will be going to England also. Since you think highly of him, I've left word with Geneva that you are to help Cecil with his care."

She felt honored that he had already seen to the matter. She also knew that her heart was beating much too fast, and she struggled against the feelings sweeping over her.

"You won't mind?" he asked quietly. "About Jette, I mean?"

She shook her head no and smiled. "I've deep affection for him."

His eyes held hers.

She looked away. Then, not trusting her own confusion, she said, "Good-bye. May God care for you in the war."

As she went past him, he caught her and drew her back and into his arms.

"Please don't," she said quietly. "You won't come to England. We both know that."

"I *don't* know that. Neither do you. I will come," he promised. "If I live, I will make good my vow to your father."

Her eyes went to his. It was not Baret's vow to her father she wished for, but his vow to her.

He won't come, she thought again. *Once I'm gone, he will forget all about me. It is Lavender he loves.*

And yet he reached a hand behind the back of her head and drew her face up toward his. "Until England." He bent, his lips on hers.

Her heart pounded and weakness assailed her. She swiftly pushed away from him.

She saw him looking at her with faint surprise, though whether at himself or her was not clear.

Emerald turned quickly and rushed for the steps, not stopping until she climbed to their room. The door was open and Minette was already packing their trunk for boarding her father's ship.

She paused, holding to the rough banister to look down at him.

Baret stood looking up at her. There was no smile on his face. He turned and walked from the buccaneers' meeting hall and out into the sunshine where Erik Farrow waited for him.

Emerald looked after him. It seemed her world had exploded. Had he felt the same? She didn't think so.

What would the future hold for her in London? What would it hold for Baret in the war? Would he truly come to Buckington House?

Why had he said yes? She could understand why he would have vowed in order to keep from killing her father, but he could have simply yielded to Levasseur and relinquished his commitment to her.

But he had not. Did that mean Baret Buckington actually did have feelings for her? And how deep were they?

Karlton's ship sailed from Tortuga the next morning. Emerald stood at the rail of the *Madeleine,* enjoying the breeze as they made for deep water. She was watching the *Regale* also set sail.

Somehow she had thought he would come on deck, for he knew her father was departing as well. She watched the *Regale*'s white canvas billow and snap as it caught the wind.

I'll make good my opportunity to seek education in London, she thought. Surely this much of her new life was a gift from the Lord.

She looked back across the blue-green Caribbean toward Port Royal. A tiny smile formed on her lips.

"And if he does come to England in the future, Baret will see a far different Emerald Harwick. But what of you, Baret Buckington? Will you come at peace with your Lord and your father's past? Or as a buccaneer disguised as a viscount?"

Her smile faded. Her eyes had found him on the deck of the *Regale*, a handsome figure in white Holland shirt and black breeches. Her heart caught. He *had* come, knowing she would be at the rail.

He lifted his wide-brimmed hat and smiled, and Emerald smiled too and lifted a hand in farewell.

"Until London," she whispered, and her eyes were moist.

Aboard the *Regale*, Baret watched her dark tresses blowing in the breeze, saw the hem of her skirts billow as she stood on the quarterdeck steps.

An image to remember, he thought wistfully.

But now there was the war.

And the dream remained that he would locate his father. He thought of Lucca's Bible.

When the image of Emerald had melted into the warm Caribbean morning, he left the deck and went to the Great Cabin. He pulled open the drawer of his desk and removed the Bible. Perhaps within these holy pages he would find the answer to all his dilemmas.

As he sat looking at the leather cover, he became aware that the Bible was familiar not because it had belonged to Lucca but to his father, Royce Buckington.

He tensed, quickly opening the book and leafing through it, a sudden unexplainable expectation in his heart.

The last words of Lucca in the courtyard at Maracaibo—
what had he said? "The Bible . . . important message . . ."

Baret had wondered at the time what he meant. "Thy
Word . . . a light . . . for your path . . ."

Dare he hope? What if the stolen letter brought to Felix
had not contained the true message? What if Lucca, knowing
the importance that Baret placed on the Scriptures and his
past training at Cambridge, had written the truth in his father's
Bible?

Baret leafed through the pages but found nothing written in Lucca's hand. He had nearly given up when he came
across a portion in the Acts of the Apostles where certain
words were boldly underlined. At the bottom of the page was
written "Lucca."

His heart was pounding as he read the underlined words:

> *where two seas met . . . ran the ship aground . . .
> soldiers' counsel was to kill the prisoners . . . kept
> from their purpose . . . delivered the prisoners to the
> captain . . . a soldier kept him . . . two years . . . pris-
> oner . . . P . . . B . . .*

Baret stared at the words, going over them again carefully. Then he set the Bible aside and took out his chart of
the West Indies. He traced a line from Port Royal down
to . . . P . . . B.

"Porto Bello," he breathed.

His father was yet alive and held a prisoner at Porto
Bello!

Hob came into the cabin, bringing a mug of black coffee
and sporting a new parrot of blue and yellow.

"His name's 'King Charlie,'" he said with a gleam in his
wily old eyes, as he deposited the bird on Baret's desk. "He's
yours, says I. Meant to give it to that pert lass you upped and
claimed."

"He's alive, Hob! My father is a prisoner at Porto Bello.
And I shall find him when we attack with Henry Morgan!"

Hob looked at him cautiously. "How now be you knowin'
all that, seein' as how poor Lucca were killed?"

Baret smiled and picked up his father's Bible. "Where
else would the truth be found? Lucca left a message for me in

407

the one way he knew it would be safe. Neither Levasseur nor Felix Buckington would ever think to pick up a Bible and read."

Hob's eyes twinkled. "Heard say old Morgan has his eye on Porto Bello. Heard say more'n two hundred thousand pieces of eight just be waitin' for the pickin's." He chuckled. "And Lord Felix ain't be knowing the truth since he has that trick letter. Pert smart of old Lucca to leave a false trail, says I. And I be thinkin' 'bout that assassin threw the dagger at you. Ten pieces of eight says it be Sir Jasper or one of his smugglin' cronies."

Baret remembered that day at the Bailey. He'd long suspected that his uncle had something to do with the attempt on his life, using Sir Jasper who, as Hob pointed out, had deadly contacts among the smugglers.

King Charlie squawked and stretched his bright blue wings. He cocked a black shiny eye toward Baret, who offered him a piece of plantain fruit. Just then, Baret's eyes fell upon the portrait of Lavender sitting on the bureau.

Hob handed him the mug of coffee. "Then your mind's made up? We'll be sailing with Morgan?"

Baret accepted the coffee. He took the portrait down and placed it in a drawer of his desk. "The best is yet to come, Hob."

Hob scratched his chin and cocked his head as he looked down at Baret's half-finished sketch of a girl.

The dark windblown tresses and sweetly innocent face could not be mistaken.

Hob grinned. "Aye, Captain Foxworth, you be makin' the right decision, says I. First, Morgan—then Sir Karlton's pert lass be waitin' in London."

Baret lifted the sketch to study his work with a critical eye. He crumpled it into a wad.

When Hob looked at him, Baret said with a faint smile, "You're looking at the wrong portrait, Hob."

He opened his drawer and produced a second sketch. Emerald wore purest white silk, carried a lace parasol and a Bible, and several African children were gathered about her skirt as though for protection. There was a noble expression

408

on her face, and she wore a wistful smile—one that he remembered well.

Hob sighed. "A noble woman, your lordship. Always did think so of her anyhow. Too bad you didn't show it to her, I mean. She'd have set a big store by it, knowing how you saw her in your mind's eye."

Baret placed it in his drawer and shut it quietly.

"Is the pinnace ready?" he asked, finishing his coffee and trying to shut Emerald's face from his mind.

"Aye, it is. All set to bring you to join the other captains on Morgan's ship."

"War does not wait," said Baret. "Nor will Porto Bello."

He wondered just how long it would be until he went to England to see her and, when he did, what he would find the more mature and educated Miss Emerald Harwick to be like.

Baret slipped his leather baldric of weapons over his head and put on his hat. As he walked out into the Caribbean sunshine to board the pinnace that would be rowed to Morgan's ship, he paused. One thing he was quite certain about. He didn't think he would be disappointed in what he found her to be.

He frowned a little, his dark eyes narrowing as he looked at Morgan's vessel lying at anchor. Perhaps it would be Emerald who would eventually be disappointed.

Before his task was complete in the Caribbean, his Uncle Felix might yet arrange with King Charles to have a warrant out for his arrest for piracy. There were no living witnesses left to swear to his father's innocence. Royce Buckington must live in order to have audience with King Charles. And a dangerous path lay between his ultimate freedom and any future in England.

Baret felt the wind tugging at his hat. He thought of Emerald.

May the Lord be the Guardian of our paths.

Moody Press, a ministry of the Moody Bible Institute,
is designed for education, evangelization, and edification.
If we may assist you in knowing more about Christ
and the Christian life, please write us without obligation:
Moody Press, c/o MLM, Chicago, Illinois 60610.